TWO
SISTERS

ALSO BY KERRY WILKINSON

TWO
SISTERS

KERRY WILKINSON

bookouture

Published by Bookouture
An imprint of StoryFire Ltd.
23 Sussex Road, Ickenham, UB10 8PN
United Kingdom
www.bookouture.com

ISBN: 978-1-78681-209-4
eBook ISBN: 978-1-78681-208-7

THEN

'I'm sorry to inform you that your parents have been involved in a car crash,' the police officer says. There's momentary pause, an audible blink and then: 'They're both dead.'

He is holding his hat in front of him as if using it as a shield. There's been no messing around. First he confirmed that I am, indeed, Megan Smart – and then, *bam!*, dead parents.

There's another pause in which I find myself staring at his shoes. They've been shined to the point that they're almost mirrors. The white of the hallway lights are reflecting back at me like stars in the night sky.

He shuffles and glances to his colleague during the silence, then turns back to me. I'm avoiding his stare, worried that my eyes might betray me. It's awkward – but then I doubt death knocks are ever fun and games.

'Oh,' I say.

'They were both in your father's car,' he adds. 'Our colleagues are investigating the cause of the crash. We don't know any more at this time.'

Another silence.

'Has someone told Chloe?' I ask.

'Officers are with your sister now.'

'Right.'

I take a small step backwards into my flat, one hand on the front door, as the other officer – a woman – moves forward. She puts a hand on my shoulder but quickly removes it when I wince away.

'We can wait with you if you want?' she says. She has a slight Scouse accent. No doubt she drew the short straw in having to come out and make this type of visit.

'It's fine,' I say. 'I'm going to call Chloe.'

'We can arrange to get you down to London if that's—'

'No!' I answer too quickly and the air sizzles. Like the moment after a glass is dropped and everyone turns to see who smashed it. Both officers step backwards from the doorframe and I finally look up to their faces. Match their stares.

I've screwed up because instinct is hard to fake. I should be breaking down, throwing my hands into the air. I should have questions. The *who*, *what*, *where*, *why* and *how*. That's what normal people would ask.

I'm trying to think of a question that sounds right but all I can manage is a weak, 'Are you sure it's them?'

'We're sure,' the man replies.

'Oh,' I say. 'I guess that's that, then.'

CHAPTER ONE

I have barely opened the front door when Chloe dashes past me. She heads across the kitchen and down the hallway, pushing doors open on either side as she goes.

'Bagsy the big bedroom,' she calls, poking her head into each room before ducking out and trying the next.

The front door doesn't seem to fit in the frame: probably the years of rain and heat causing it to swell and shrink over and over. It sticks as I try to close it, leaving me to shoulder and boot it into place as it squeaks in annoyance. There's nothing like a quick bit of violence after five hours in a car. Three hours on the motorway was bad enough, but the subsequent two hours on twisty-turny country roads would bring out the worst in anyone. Gandhi might have banged on about peace and forgiveness – but he never had to drive from London to Cornwall in a battered VW.

'I don't think there is a big bedroom,' I call after my sister.

Chloe is already at the back of the cottage, almost hidden in the murk of the hall, pointing to an open door. 'Shotgun this room.'

'Fine.'

She disappears inside and there's a thump as her bag hits the ground. She'll be unpacking already. Everything in its place and all that. In some ways – this one in particular – she's unquestionably our mother's daughter.

I dump my own backpack on the crusty welcome mat and head towards the fridge. Chloe was six, possibly just seven, when she was last in the family cottage. I was ten and, a decade on, it was literally half a lifetime ago for me. I *do* remember this cottage, this kitchen. I see it in flashes, like scenes from a forgotten television show I've not watched in years. One that wasn't very good and that I'd rather forget.

There's a thick wooden dining table in the corner, the type of thing that's so big people remove window frames to get it inside. It ain't IKEA, that's for sure. There's a coating of dust on its surface, but this is the sort of furniture that could survive ice ages and meteor strikes. Long after the human race has gone and the mosquitoes have taken over, this hunk of varnished wood will still be here.

I was sitting at that table when Mother told me I couldn't have a cheese sandwich because I was already pudgy enough.

Chloe drifts back into the kitchen, her phone aloft. 'No reception,' she says.

'Try upstairs.'

She moves back towards the hall before stopping and turning, half a grin on her face. 'You almost had me then.'

As well as the organisational skills and desire for things to be in their rightful place, Chloe also got Mother's looks. Naturally blonde, with those big round eyes. There was a time when I called her 'the Aryan child'. Never to her face, obviously. That was a different me. I was meaner then. Sometimes I miss that girl who spoke first and thought second.

Chloe edges into the kitchen again, straining across the sink and reaching her phone towards the window.

'Nothing,' she says, turning in a circle. 'Not even a single bar.'

'Try the WiFi.'

She taps the screen once and then looks up. 'Be nice to me.'

I grin. 'We'll figure it out. There's probably a phone mast on a hill somewhere. There'll be Internet in the village. We'll live.'

It's sacrilege but Chloe lets it go. She runs a hand along the draining board, taking a layer of dust into her palm. 'When was the last time anyone was here?'

'I think Mum was down a bit before Christmas. I don't know.'

'She could've sorted out the WiFi. It's like… I dunno, Victorian times.'

'I don't think there's ever been a phone line.'

I look around blankly, as if expecting to see the type of ancient technology that involved a phone connected to the wall with a cable. All that's there is a musty layer of dust on everything.

It's only when I find myself searching through the drawers for a duster or a tea towel that I realise how mumsy *I'm* becoming. Chloe's watching, saying nothing and I wonder if she's thinking it as well. I'm twenty going on fifty sometimes. Ancient.

'Why's it so hot?' Chloe asks.

'There's no air-con *or* central heating. I bet it's freezing in winter and boiling in summer.'

She huffs in annoyance. 'I'm going to unpack.'

Chloe hangs around for a second, probably subconsciously waiting for permission. It's taken us both time to realise we don't need to wait for our parents' approval any longer. I don't say anything, so she disappears off to the back room and I give up on finding a cloth. Half the drawers are stuck closed and it's not like the dust is going anywhere. I take a tiny amount of pleasure from knowing that, if Mother *were* here, she'd be on the brink of a panic attack at all the cleaning that needs doing. A decade ago, she'd have done it herself. In recent years, she'd have been clicking her fingers and calling for Gabriela. The memory is so clear, so close, that I can even hear the intonation in her voice. *'Gabby,'* she'd call, *'Gabriela. Will you look at this?'*

I sometimes wonder what might have happened if poor Ga-briela had simply *looked* at the mess and left it there. When it came to our Polish help, Mother had somehow turned clean-ing a single five-bedroom house into a fifty-hour-a-week job. No working time directive on our road. That didn't stop my parents from voting to 'send them all back', of course. Mother actually said that to me when she asked how I'd voted.

Cookbooks sit in a row on the counter, spines faded by the sun. All the celebrity chefs have their names on show and I won-der whose benefit these books are for. Even in the old days, I don't remember either of my parents cooking. It was sort yourself out, or find somewhere that delivers. Mother didn't eat, so why should any of the rest of us have to bother with such a pesky thing?

This is where *I'm* unquestionably my mother's daughter.

I run my fingers along the spines, sending a clump of dust onto the floor. It'll be good to toss the lot into a skip one day soon. Leave a nice trample mark on Jamie Oliver's face. That's what I think of your Italian Kitchen, *mate.*

The living room is a similar story to the kitchen. It's a smaller room, perhaps more of a study. It's dusty and the air is clogged and thick. There are bookcases filled with hardback crime and ro-mance novels, yet I doubt either of my parents ever read a fiction book. A cricket bat is resting inexplicably in the corner. Neither of them much cared for playing or watching sport, so who knows where it came from. The rocking chair stirs another memory. I think I sat in here, reading quietly. Children should neither be seen nor heard and all that. I set the chair bobbing back and forth, sending a flurry of dust to the floor. There's nothing else in here that feels familiar.

The second study is cosier than the first: all throws and cush-ions. Like a bomb went off in the home section of John Lew-is. The soft furnishings are more likely to be from Harrods, of course, or imported from who knows where. Somewhere expensive. The rest of the house might have once been like a show home but this room is all Mother. There's even a soothing purple lightbulb. I bet there's a CD of whale music somewhere nearby.

I have no recollection of this part of the cottage. I remember the thick kitchen table, the cheese sandwich denial... and that's about it. I had wondered if being here might jog some memories – but there's nothing there to be jogged. My ten-year-old brain was obviously concerned with other things.

It doesn't surprise me that the food memory has stuck. I sometimes wonder if absorbing so many random facts about food – if not the food itself – has pushed everything else away. Like, there's only room for so much knowledge in a person's head at any given time. That cheese sandwich would've been 500 calories minimum. Forty per cent fat, twenty per cent carbs. If we had an Internet connection, I'd Google it to make sure.

I'm busy thinking of melting Cheddar with speckled dots of grated onion when a gentle series of clunks echo through the house. I emerge into the hall at the same time as Chloe.

'Was that you?' I ask.

'I think someone's at the door.'

She nods behind me, towards the kitchen, and I realise that she's right. The silhouette of someone's head is distorted by the rippled glass in the front door. Mother's voice is at the back of my mind again.

Gabby, there's someone at the door. Gabriela...?

I have to push my foot into the frame and pull to make the front door open. It scrapes and grinds, then flies open, almost making me topple backwards. Not quite the elegance and poise those private school fees paid for.

Daylight beams into the sullen kitchen and the woman on the other side jumps back a little. She squeaks like a trodden-on puppy.

'Oh,' she says. 'I, um...'

She's wearing the type of oversized sunglasses that scream an airy lack of interest in anything other than herself, yet she removes them to examine first me and then Chloe. Her eyes narrow, which is quite the miracle given the smoothness of her forehead. I hadn't realised Botox was available this far out in the sticks.

'Is it really you?' she asks.

'Well, I'm me, so...'

Her face stretches tighter, momentarily confused, straining against the facelift. Six months old, I reckon. There's the merest hint of a scar skimming her hairline. It's only showing because of her tan: a narrow cream line against the browned skin. She's in a smart skirt suit. There was a time when I would have known the brand simply by looking. Either way, it's expensive – and completely out of place, considering this cottage is surrounded by forest.

'Megan?' she says, before turning to my sister. 'And is that little Chloe...?'

She'd raise an eyebrow if she could.

'Do we know you?' I ask.

The woman turns back to me and stretches out her hand. Her fingers are long and slender, her nails baby pink. 'Alison,' she says, as if this should mean something. 'Alison Wood.'

We shake hands, if it can be called that. Her grip is so limp that's more an incidental brushing of palms.

'I was friends with your parents,' she adds. 'We've known each other for years. We did a charity gala thing and Anne was on the Burning Boat committee a while back. That was—'

'She was on the *what* committee?'

Alison blinks, not used to being interrupted. There's a flicker of annoyance that is gone so quickly that I half-wonder if it was there at all. I learned at school that people who come from money aren't accustomed to being spoken over. They talk, you listen.

Alison bats a dismissive hand. 'You poor things. What happened to your parents is such a tragedy. They were so young, so kind, so talented. And to be taken by a car crash…'

She tails off, but neither Chloe nor I add anything. What is there to say?

'Did you get my card?' she adds.

I glance at Chloe, who is leaning on the doorframe, arms hugged across her front. She's nowhere near over what happened yet. It's been a long three months for her; a blink for me.

'We got a lot of cards,' I reply. 'We didn't know most of our parents' friends. That's what happens when you're hidden away at boarding school.'

Chloe tenses but Alison seems not to notice the bitterness in my tone. I don't think she was listening.

'I remember you both as little girls,' she replies airily. Her eyes become glassy as she glances upwards. She bats her hand in front of her face, warding off invisible tears. 'I suppose the last time I saw you was the summer that everything happened…'

Alison tails off, takes a breath and then continues: 'It was so brave of your parents to come back and check in with the place every few months. It must have brought back such terrible memories. I've been keeping half an eye on the cottage ever since I heard what happened to them. That's why I noticed your car.' She turns to look at my scuffed Volkswagen. When I turned eighteen, Mother offered to buy me a 'proper car', but I wanted to pay for something with my own money. I was craving disapproval at the time.

Alison has paused, waiting for me to fill in some details. I know that expectant, docile look. I used to wear it myself. When I was at school, there was a time when I used to feed on gossip. A succubus for controversy and titillation. Takes one to know one. It was an age thing with me: I grew out of it.

'Are you staying for long?' she asks eventually, when she realises I am not going to say anything further.'

'We're not sure,' I reply.

'I suppose you have things to sort out. You must have had it so hard. I can't begin to understand.' She licks her lips and takes a small step backwards. She glances between us, but I can't read her this time. She seems confused more than anything.

'We're here for a break,' Chloe says. It's the first words she's spoken since the knock on the door. 'We figured we'd get away from London for a while.'

Alison takes us both in, nodding along. 'That sounds nice. Does this mean you'll be staying around? They say it's going to be a hot summer.'

I jump in before Chloe can reply: 'We're gonna wing it. See how things go.'

Alison winces momentarily at my filthy slang.

'Well… If you need some help, or want to ask about the area – anything like that – we're right by the "Welcome to Whitecliff" sign.'

She points towards the main road. There's only one route to the village. We must have passed her house when we drove in.

'It's called The Gables,' she adds. 'On the right as you enter. You can't miss it.'

'I think I saw it on the way in,' Chloe replies.

Alison smiles in reply – or as much as she can. Her lips twitch upwards. 'There's a buzzer on the gatepost,' she says. 'Come by any time. My husband's called Dan. Either of us will be happy to help if you need something.'

She takes another step away, crunching awkwardly across the gravel and onto a crumbling set of paving slabs that serve as a pathway.

'Your husband's name is Dan?'

Alison stops and stares back at me. 'Right…'

'I think I *do* remember you,' I say. 'Didn't you have a son? My age?'

It's more of a dream than a memory. The vaguest inkling that I once played on the beach with a boy named Somebody Wood. My father was chatting to his father, who was called Dan. I don't remember Alison at all.

'Eli?' I ask. 'Something like that. Edward…? Evan…? Something with an "E"?'

It takes her a few seconds, but Alison slowly starts to nod. 'Cambridge,' she says breezily. 'He stays there during the summers. Loves the place.' She doesn't confirm his name.

We all pause for a moment more, no one quite sure what to say.

Alison finishes with, 'Well, you know where we are…' and then turns, heading back along the track towards the road.

When she's out of sight, I wrestle the front door back into place and then turn to see Chloe with her hands on her hips.

'That was rude,' she says.

'Me?'

'She was only trying to help.'

I want to tell Chloe that she's young, that she's naïve. That women like Alison Wood don't *only* help. There's always something else going on, even if it's just gathering gossip for the rest of the village's Official Nosy Bastard Society.

'We're fine on our own,' I reply.

'I never said we're not – but she was only making sure we're good. She was friends with Mum.'

I start to reply but then stop myself. It's not worth arguing. Mother and Father mean something different to Chloe than they do to me.

Chloe makes a move towards her room, then turns back. 'How long do you think we'll be here?'

We had to visit the cottage at some point – or at least one of us did. Inheriting an estate is ludicrously complicated. This place is equally ours now, even if Chloe's share is being held until she's eighteen.

That's not why we're here, though.

'I should have told you earlier,' I say. 'I thought it'd be better if I waited until we were here.'

I cross to my bag and struggle with the spaghetti tangle of ties and zips before removing the postcard.

'This arrived on the day of the funeral,' I say, passing it across.

Chloe stares at the front, which is a photo of a steep cliff towering over a beach. 'Whitecliff' is printed in the corner. I've spent hours looking at the picture, wondering what it means.

She flips it over and glances at the back. There's not a lot to see. On the right, our London address is written in green capital letters. It's addressed to me. On the left, in the space for the message, is a single letter.

Z.

Chloe turns the card around, checking she hasn't missed anything, then she holds it up for me to see.

'Z? What does that mean?'

'I'm not sure.'

There's a moment where Chloe's body tenses and I think she might screw up the card. In the three months since I received it, I've thought about doing precisely that several times.

'Zac...?' Chloe speaks with wide-eyed disbelief. I can't remember the last time we talked about our brother. About what happened to him.

'I don't know.'

'Why didn't you say something before?'

I look away, not quite able to tell her the truth: that I wanted this to be *my* secret. That there's a part of me that's enjoyed having something for me and only me.

'There wasn't a right moment,' I reply. 'What with the funeral and everything. You were upset and...' I tail off, hoping she'll let it go.

Chloe's eyes narrow slightly and, for a moment, I think she might push me harder. I could have told her at several points between the funeral and now but I hadn't wanted to. Once I'd opted not to tell her first time around, it would have been difficult to explain why I'd continued to keep it a secret. At least now we're here, I've got a reason to tell her. I can pin it on being back in the cottage after so long.

She nods slightly and I know my sister well enough to see I'm off the hook. If things were reversed, I wouldn't have let it go so easily.

'You can't think it's from him...?' she says, before adding quickly: 'It must be a coincidence? A mistake?'

I take the card back, smoothing the front and returning it to the safety of my bag. Mine.

'I honestly don't know.'

CHAPTER TWO

Chloe's gentle hums drift through the cottage like the dawn song of a pain-in-the-arse bird. There was a big bedroom, after all: the one our parents shared when they stayed here. I don't remember the room itself, which makes me wonder if I was ever allowed in. Probably not. Our parents enjoyed their secrets.

Chloe is busy unpacking, cheerful about being here. It's somewhere different, a break from the endless video conferences with solicitors and the lengthy list of things to do. Her exams were barely a month ago. Her school offered to let her defer them for a year, but she took them anyway. She's on holiday now and I don't blame her for being cheerful, for wanting to forget everything that's happened. She's happy to be here – and, I hope, happy to be *with me*.

We've been at different private boarding schools for most of our lives and not just because of the age gap. We would have had a year or two overlap at the same school, but Mother sent Chloe somewhere different, saying I would be a bad influence. Because of this, we haven't spent a lot of time together. We've only seen each other for part of each summer and at various family occasions. We've kept in touch with WhatsApp messages. Emails, in the old days. It's not the same as living together, though. Sometimes I forget how little we know each other. Especially because, at times, it's like she's a younger me. Nicer, of course. Kinder.

She's already brushed off the postcard from 'Z', figuring it was a mistake. I'd have never done that, even at sixteen going on seventeen.

I listen to her humming and singing, which is an accompaniment to the opening and closing of drawers and wardrobes. My bag rests untouched against the too-soft bed in my room.

It's not long before I feel like the walls are closing in. I stare at the spiral swirls of mould in the corners where the walls meet the ceiling. It's so humid in here that it feels like I'm breathing in bubbles.

I call for Chloe and meet her in the hallway. She's taken off her trainers and is walking around in bare feet.

'Let's go out,' I say.

'I'm still unpacking.'

'You can do that any time. The sun's out – let's explore.'

Chloe bobs from one foot to the other, wavering. She'd clearly rather stay here but says, 'One minute,' anyway and disappears back into her room. A moment later and she's ready, wearing sandals, shorts and a strappy top.

It takes me a minute or so to fight the front door and lock up. There's a patch of crumbling paving slabs and then a gravelly track that leads from our cottage to the main road. A separate darkened trail disappears into the woods. We opt for the route to the road but it's still dim and moody under the shadow of the swaying trees. The temperature is a degree or two lower outside the cottage – and it's another couple of degrees cooler again in the shade.

After a minute or so, we reach the road. Glancing back, I realise that there's no way Alison Wood could have seen my car unless she came down the track. And the track only leads to the cottage, so I wonder what she was doing. Perhaps it is as simple as that she was 'keeping half an eye' on the cottage, as she said. Suspicion comes easily.

We walk along the edge of the road for a short while and then the trees open up, unveiling the wonder of what's below. The cottage is at the top of a hill – the type of brutal, unrelenting steep road that Britain does so well. Switchbacks are for softies.

The blue of the ocean stretches far into the distance below, only ending when it reaches the sapphire sky. The cliffs from the postcard are off to the right: craggy walls of rock topped with grass and trees that tower over a smooth stretch of beach. Dark dots of ant-like people are scattered across the sand, baking in the afternoon heat.

Then there's Whitecliff itself.

From the top of the hill, it's a sprinkling of roofs atop cosy cottages and weathered houses. As we head down, the blend of cobbled and tarmacked streets becomes more apparent. Half a dozen boats are docked at a jetty on the edge of the village, close to a pub. There are photocopied black and white posters advertising an upcoming festival, plus some others about water safety. The streets aren't exactly heaving with people, but the village feels lived in. There are flower baskets hanging beside various front doors, a sign pointing the way to the beach and telegraph poles with cables looping down to the buildings.

It's a far cry from the people and noise of the cities I'm used to – but undoubtedly a step up from the isolation of the cottage.

Chloe stops to check the menu on the side of the pub and I stand with her, staring out towards the boats. There's a topless, tanned man hunched over the front of a vessel marked 'Chandler Fishing'. He's mid-twenties or so. Sweat is pouring along his arms and back, dripping on the wooden dock at his feet. He's big, with only a bristle of dark hair across his head. There's far more on his back, upper arms and, well… everywhere.

Almost as if he can sense me, he stops, turning and wiping his brow with one hand as he clutches a spanner in the other. He squints, trying to figure out who I am.

'The only vegan option is chips,' Chloe says.

I turn away from the man to Chloe, who's pointing at the board. 'Huh?'

'Everything's got meat in it, except the chips,' Chloe says. 'We'd have to ask if they use sunflower or vegetable oil.'

Assuming they're deep fried, that's a good 400 calories per portion. Possibly more. It's hard to tell without a set of scales and knowledge of the oil they use. I blink the thought away.

'We'll figure something out,' I reply. 'There's probably a shop somewhere. We can get food there.'

Chloe frowns and I feel like our mother again. I'm not a vegan, but that doesn't mean I shouldn't care that Chloe is. She checks the board once more and then turns, finally realising that we're being watched. The man by the boat hasn't moved, his stare fixed directly on me.

'Making friends...?' Chloe says quietly.

'I have this effect on people.'

We continue past the pub, leaving the tarmac road and venturing onto the cobbles. It's like moving back in time as we pass a row of thatched houses built with thick wooden beams.

There are more festival posters here and more about safety on the beach and in the water. Others shout that fishing licences are needed and then there are the standard warnings about locking up valuables.

There is nothing about Zac.

It's been ten years since he was here, of course. There's no particular reason for him to be mentioned anywhere and I'm not sure what I expected. Something, I suppose. A plaque or a sign. I don't know.

I'm lost in my thoughts when Chloe calls me over to a small building with a sign in the shape of a sun.

'Let's go in here,' she says, heading up the creaky wooden steps and inside without waiting for a reply.

I follow, taking in the 'Sunshine Gallery' sign, and emerge into a bright room filled with paintings. It's not quite the white-washed walls of the Tate; this is far homelier. It's like walking into someone's living room. There's a sofa and a couple of armchairs facing the walls, allowing people to take in the paintings in maximum comfort.

Chloe is already at the counter, talking to an old man with a grey beard, no hair and tiny rimless spectacles. He's in a rocking chair, calmly bobbing forward and back.

'This is my sister,' Chloe says, turning to introduce me.

'Arthur,' the man says, not motioning to stand, or to shake hands. That's fine with me.

Chloe turns back to Arthur. 'Is this all your work?'

He scoffs. 'I wish! Some of it is. The weaker pieces.'

Chloe and I both turn to take in some of the paintings. Most of them seem to be of the local area. There are the cliffs and beach, boats at sea, cobbled lanes and battered houses.

'Many come from visitors,' Arthur says. 'They get the bug for this place and return to paint new scenes year after year. I display on their behalf. Are you an artist?'

Chloe shrinks under the question, mumbling a reply. Arthur doesn't catch what she says, leaning in, eyes narrowing. He nods in the way people do when they don't hear something but are too polite to say so.

'She's good,' I reply.

He twists towards me as Chloe continues to wilt.

'Is that right?'

I turn to Chloe, asking if she brought her things, meaning her paints, pencils and pads.

Chloe nods, suddenly dumb and shy.

'You can bring your work in if you want,' Arthur says. 'Many do. I always like to see new interpretations of Whitecliff. If it's good enough, I'd be happy to display. If it's *really* good, someone might want to buy it.'

Chloe continues to nod, blinking away embarrassment. She's never been one for praise. I guess neither of us are.

'I'll do that,' she says.

We say our goodbyes and head back out into the sun. The village has a high street of sorts, with perhaps a dozen shops and stalls stretching from the pub along the beachfront. Chloe and I reach a dead end and then turn back to retrace our steps. The closeness of the higgledy-piggledy properties and narrow lanes have turned even this small village into a maze.

The general store is called Arkwright's and Chloe waits outside as I head in. Her concern about a lack of vegan food is quickly confirmed as I browse the fridges. There is fresh meat and fish, plus milk, butter and cream – but little in the way of anything non-traditional. There are boxes of cereal, but no sign of almond or coconut milk. The only vegetables in stock are tinned.

'Can I help?'

The woman from the counter has been eyeing me over her glasses ever since I entered the shop.

I put down the tin of corn and head towards the front. 'Do you sell tofu? Or veggie burgers?'

Her features crinkle into one big frown. It's hard to guess her age. The craggy wrinkles say seventies, but her bird-of-prey eyes say fifties at most. She's wearing a cardigan, despite the heat. It's a curious old person's thing – jumpers and coats even in the middle of summer.

'To*fu*?' She emphasises the last part of the word as if it's something she's never heard of. Foreign muck.

'Vegetarians eat it instead of meat,' I explain. 'It's all protein.'

She shakes her head while pouting out a bottom lip. 'Not here.'

'Do you know anywhere that might sell it?'

'Not in the village.'

I offer a weak 'thank you' that I don't mean and am about to turn and go when I notice the spinning rack of postcards on the counter. I don't need to twist it because a very familiar image is front and centre. There's the steep cliff towering over a beach, with 'Whitecliff' stamped in the corner. I pick up the card and hold it up.

'Do you sell many of these?' I ask.

The shopkeeper eyes me as if looking at a particularly stupid toddler. 'It's summer. What do you think?'

'Right.'

'It's thirty pence or four for a pound.'

I dig into my pocket, even though I know I have no cash. I never do. Whenever beggars ask for change, I want to ask if they take cards. Change is a curious throwback; heavy and not even worth much.

All that's in my pocket is my debit card – but I've not even offered it before the shopkeeper makes a strange clicking sound.

'Minimum of a tenner if you want to use a card,' she says.

I put the postcard back onto the rack, offering the thinnest of smiles. 'Another time,' I say.

Her only reply is a tut, which I guess is what passes for customer service around here.

CHAPTER THREE

Chloe is sitting on the step outside the shop, holding her phone in the air.

'Any luck?' I ask.

'Nothing.'

'I'm sure there'll be a spot somewhere that phones work.'

Chloe stands and puts her hands in her shorts pockets, angling towards the road. 'Shall we go back...?'

She takes a step away, wanting to return to the cottage.

'Let's go to the beach,' I say. 'We're practically there already and I don't fancy that hill quite yet.'

Chloe turns and stares up towards the woods that arch steeply towards our cottage. The hill looks far sharper from the bottom than it did from the top. She says nothing, but nods slightly and latches onto my side as I head back to the pub and then loop around the front of the gallery onto the sand.

After the serenity of the village, the beach is another story. Twenty or thirty teenagers have massed against a sandbank. Their towels are spread on the ground and around half of them are soaking up the sun, with the rest in the ocean or playing volleyball.

As we get closer, it dawns on me that there's not an adult in sight. Even more worryingly, it occurs to me that, at twenty, I might be the oldest person here.

Chloe has tucked in half a step behind me. I've noticed this sort of shyness with her before. She's comfortable enough with adults but seems to want to avoid contact with those her own age.

I'm thinking about turning to go, when one of the lads waves us across with an enthusiastic, 'Hi!' He's in red swimming trunks: all bronzed muscles and hairless chest. Pure *Baywatch*. At best, he's eighteen – but I can tell from the way he has his hands on his hips that he's one of those cocky types who can get by with a lopsided grin and forgive-me eyes.

'How are you doing?' he calls – and there's no way out now.

'We're good,' I reply. We're close enough to talk at a proper volume and I notice some of the others peering over their sunglasses to look at the newcomers.

'I'm Brad,' he says.

'Megan and Chloe,' I reply.

Brad is ridiculously good-looking. He's got the whole cheekbones and straggly blond hair thing going on. Good genes. Mother would like him.

'You down for the summer?' he asks.

'Maybe.'

'Where are you staying?'

'Where are *you* staying?'

He laughs, running a hand through his damp hair as if he's in a bloody shampoo commercial.

'We're all in the caravans up by the lightning tree. It's better than it sounds. You?'

'Our parents have a cottage.'

Brad nods approvingly.

'Is there anywhere to get mobile signal around here?'

Before Brad can answer, the girl lying on the towel at his feet sits up. She lowers her sunglasses and shields her eyes. 'Lightning tree,' she says.

The girl has perfectly smooth black skin and is in a two-piece silver bikini. Her dark hair is in a tight ponytail. It's hard not to wonder whether we've accidentally stumbled across some sort of breeding factory for models.

'What's the lightning tree?' I ask.

The girl waves a hand up towards the hill and the main road. 'Follow the road up; it's before you get to the Whitecliff sign. There's a tree in the middle of a field that was struck by lightning. You'll know it when you see it.' She pauses, then offers her hand to me. 'Ebony,' she adds.

Every syllable is perfectly pronounced. Pure Queen's English stuff. I suspect she went to private school as well, and the smoothness of her skin indicates that she's rarely got her hands dirty in her eighteen or so years.

Still, I'm hardly one to talk. It's not like I've been grafting in the steelworks.

Ebony and Chloe shake too and then we go through the whole thing again with Brad. It's all very formal; no sign of the fist-bumps or flappy-handedness that often passes for greeting among others our age.

Brad turns and introduces more people, but the names largely go in one ear and out the other. It's all too much for one go.

Someone called George has a guitar – because there's *always* a wanker with a guitar in a group like this. He's strumming away quietly to himself, but if he starts up with a twenty-minute rendition of '*Live Forever*' or '*Hey Jude*', then I might have to garrotte him with his own guitar string.

There's a Will and a Sophie – nice, safe middle-class names. We're only missing a Toby or a *Tobias* to get the full set.

The only other name I remember for sure is Mia. She has long, straight dark hair and matching brown eyes, with olive skin. The type of girl whose parents would be questioned by mine about where they 'really' come from. The reason I take note of her name is that she has a little black French Bulldog named Popcorn, who introduces himself by sniffing my ankles and then sitting on Chloe's feet.

My sister might be shy around others her age, but she has no such issues with animals. She crouches and scratches the dog behind his ears. He responds by licking her legs and, before I know it, Chloe and Mia are happily chatting to each other.

That leaves me standing awkwardly, not quite sure what to do. I'm only a year or two older than everyone else but it feels like more than that. The others are here to lounge and play but that's not why I've come to Whitecliff.

I smile an apology and drift away from the group, towards the one person on the beach who might be older than me. It's the lifeguard, who may or may not be asleep on his high chair. He's wearing sunglasses and a set of tell-tale earphone cables are dangling from his ears to his back.

I call out, 'Hey,' and he jumps, sitting up straighter in the wooden chair and twisting to face me.

'Okay?' he asks, quickly shielding his eyes and scanning the water in case he's missed someone drowning. That sort of thing tends to put a black mark on the CV of a lifeguard.

'I'm Megan,' I say.

When he realises I'm simply saying hello, he breathes a sigh of relief and peers down at me.

'You new in town?' he asks.

'Got in this morning.'

He climbs down the ladder, throws a glance towards the beach kids and then lowers his sunglasses slightly. 'Luke,' he says.

At close quarters, he's even older than I thought: probably twenty-four or twenty-five. He has long, floppy hair and the can't-be-arsed bristle of someone who hasn't shaved in a couple of days. The faint smell of weed clings to him like sand to wet feet.

'Welcome to Whitecliff,' he says.

'Thank you.'

'There's not much to see, but you can surf…'

'Not my thing.'

'What *is* your thing?'

'This and that. I have been making friends with the Ark-wright's shopkeeper.'

There's a pause of a second or so, as if we're in slightly different dimensions. I suspect whatever he's been smoking is responsible, but he does laugh in the end. 'Gwen,' he says. 'Gwen Arkwright. She's harmless enough. She's been running that place since the dawn of time.'

Gwen. This is one name I will make sure I remember. Who-ever sent me the postcard with 'Z' written on the back likely bought it from that shop. And Gwen probably sold it to them.

'What's the deal with the beach kids?' I ask.

Luke shrugs and scratches his head. 'What deal?'

'Seems like a lot of people for one small village.'

He shrugs again. 'They come in every summer. Stay up in the caravans and spend the days surfing, sunbathing, or whatever.'

We take a few seconds to watch the beach kids doing their thing. I wonder if this would have been my life if things hadn't happened the way they did with Zac. These teenagers are here because it puts them out of their parents' way. Their mums and dads are free to lounge in Saint-Tropez, or off on a yacht in Mo-naco, without their annoying children to get in the way.

I shiver when Luke speaks next. It's like he's read my mind. 'Where are your parents this summer?' he asks.

'Not around any longer.'

'Oh…'

'My last name is Smart,' I say. 'Megan Smart. My parents were Anne and Ian. They owned the cottage up on the hill.'

I can feel Luke watching me, though I don't turn to face him.

'What?' I ask, although I know what he's thinking.

'I know that name.'

'Ten years ago, my brother, Zac, went missing somewhere around here.'

We stand in relative silence, listening to the lapping of the waves and the gentle babble of the beach kids.

'Were you here then?' I ask. 'When Zac went missing?'

'I've never lived anywhere else.'

'So do you remember him?'

A pause. 'Not really. I know the name.'

I'm not sure what to say and if there's one thing I've learned from my expensive education, it is to shut the hell up unless I am asked something.

I do precisely that.

'Why are you back here?' Luke asks eventually. Someone else will always break a silence if the wait is long enough. It's a compulsion.

I think of the postcard in my bag and the single letter on the back. What can I say? I think that my missing brother invited me here? My *dead* brother wanted me to come?

I take a breath of the warm air, tasting the dusting of sand.

There's only one way to reply.

'I don't know,' I say. 'I really don't know.'

CHAPTER FOUR

I don't have much to talk to Luke about. It only takes me a couple of minutes to realise that almost his entire experience of life comes from the few square miles that encompass Whitecliff. I bring up Zac once more, but Luke ends up talking about the weather. If he did know my brother, then he seemingly has nothing to say.

Back with the beach kids, Chloe is still playing with an ever-excitable Popcorn. Brad and George-the-guitar-player are now sitting close to her and Mia in a circle of four. I catch Chloe's eye, offering the merest of nods towards the hill and she stands, brushing the sand from her shorts. There's a glimmer of a moment in which she glances at Brad, but then she steps away with a small wave.

'You could've stayed,' I say, when Chloe is at my side. 'I was only telling you that I was heading up.'

'I'd rather go.'

'You seemed to be making friends…?'

'I guess.'

I'm not sure if her lack of enthusiasm is because she's unconvinced by her own ability to make friends, or if she's not that bothered by them. We make the slow trudge up the hill towards the cottage. Neither of us speak, though in my case at least, it's because I'm struggling to breathe. A combination of the heat, the gradient and the fact I've not eaten all day.

We're outside the cottage when Chloe says she's going to head out to the cliffs to draw. I tell her I'll bring a book and follow, mainly because I'd like to figure out how each part of the village connects to the rest. She is clearly excited by Arthur's offer to look at her work, but I wonder if she knows he was probably just being nice.

I wait in the kitchen, allowing myself two glasses of water (zero calories, no carbs) as Chloe heads to her room and gathers her sketchbook. She offers to share a protein bar with me, frowning when I check the label. Half the bar is 130 calories, which isn't too bad. There are dates and prunes in it, too, which helps.

Chloe says nothing as I measure the bar with a tape from the drawer under the sink and then slice it exactly in half. She takes her section and then we head back outside.

It's easier than I thought to find the lookout point. We walk to the top of the hill and then follow the line of the cliffs into the woods. The trail isn't marked but the thinness of the grass and moss makes it easy to follow in the footsteps of others. It takes around ten minutes to make our way through the trees and then we emerge onto a patch of uneven rocks. There are tufts of fern and I would imagine it's like a skating rink when wet. In the baked summer heat, it's simple enough for Chloe and me to giggle our way across in flip-flops.

We've travelled far enough around the coast to be past the beach and the ocean is raging into the rocks far below. It feels a lot noisier up here than it did when we were down on the beach. A colony of seagulls is circling overhead, chirping and probably plotting to drop an unwanted gift onto one of our heads.

Chloe leads the way, wobbling across the rocks until we find ourselves on an errant plot of lush green. Daisies and dandelions are smattered among the grass and my nose twitches from the pollen. I used to tell our old PE teacher I had hay-fever in order to get out of cross-country. It's amazing what a few eye drops and some forced sniffles can do. I wonder now if all the faking actually brought it on for real.

Chloe plops herself down on the grass, a couple of metres away from the edge of the cliff. The ocean continues to roar, but there's a contradictory peace to it, too. The village is far below, snug between a pair of cliffs, with the beach stretching away towards the rocks. Brad, Luke and everyone else have been reduced to hyperactive black dots against the cream backdrop.

I follow the line of the road up the hill, looking for our cottage – but it's well-hidden by the trees.

Chloe has her sketchbook in her lap and a pencil in hand. I watch her for a moment as she swishes the lead across the paper. I didn't bring a book after all, more through forgetfulness than anything else. I move carefully towards the edge of the cliff, taking small quarter-steps until it feels as if the world is at my feet.

In some ways, it is.

I risk a peep downwards, watching as the white surf crests and hammers into the exposed rocks. The waves quickly follow each other, one after the next, with barely a moment of respite between strikes.

It's hard not to wonder whether Zac once stood on this spot. To consider whether, perhaps, he tumbled from here.

That's the problem when someone goes missing. If a person dies, it's final. There might be questions to answer, but their ultimate fate is known. With Zac – with anyone who disappears – there are only questions.

I blink and there's a moment of dizziness. I know this feeling only too well. Keeping my eyes closed and not daring to breathe, I can feel the world spinning on the other side of my eyelids. The ground rushing towards me. The ocean, the roar.

There's no need to count, because this is natural now. I breathe in slowly through my nose and then out through my mouth. The half protein bar is burning a hole in my pocket and I know I should eat it. Only 130 calories. That's all. I've earned that simply by walking down the hill and up it again, and then out here.

When I turn away from the edge and open my eyes, I'm relieved to see that Chloe hasn't noticed anything wrong. She glances up from her drawing and smiles at me with her lips closed, silently letting me know she's fine.

I check my phone, but there's no reception here. I suppose one of the next jobs will be to find Ebony's lightning tree.

I'm wondering what I should do now, when I spot a shadow marching across the rocks. It's a man, his arms swinging rigidly back and forth as if he's on morning drills. He's in the full get-up: hiking boots, cargo shorts, linen shirt, utility vest, backpack and a wide-brimmed hat. It's all a bit Bear Grylls having a midlife crisis.

He spots me at the same time as I see him and he waves and calls out a cheery, 'Hi!'

As he gets nearer, I do wonder if there's anyone in this village who isn't good-looking. He might have bought one of everything in the North Face sale, but he has the sort of salt-and-pepper stubble that only men of a certain age can pull off. His eyebrows are thick and striking, his calves bulging from the hike. He's the sort of rugged-looking bloke they get to advertise 'Just For Men': playing Frisbee in the park while some girl half his age saunters over and runs a hand through his hair for no reason.

'Hi there,' he says, as he gets within a metre or so of me.

'Hey.'

'Fancy seeing you out here.'

There's a moment in which I stare at him, bemused. He's made it sound like we know each other.

'Dan,' he says, stretching out a hand. 'Dan Wood. Alison said she'd seen you at the cottage and here you are.'

I wonder how he knows what I look like, but decide it's not worth mentioning. He has the type of handshake that's firm and reassuring without being overbearing. I can't stand the alpha-types who grip as if they're desperately trying to get some blood to the limp vestiges of their long-gone erections. Those ones who yank you towards them because it'll somehow make up for the lack of their parental love they were shown as a child.

Dan turns to Chloe as he releases my hand, adding: 'It's great to see you both again. It's been so many years.'

There is a weird cheeriness to his tone that turns the atmosphere into something that, from nowhere, infuriates me. Mother often said I had anger issues. It was her way of trying to shut me up, but there are times when it feels like I'm desperate to prove her right.

Before I can react, his face falls and then he adds: 'Wish it could be in better circumstances, of course.'

There's a pause, in which it takes me a second or two to figure out that he means our parents dying. That does tend to put a damper on a reunion.

'Did Alison say to come over if you need anything?' he asks.

'She did.'

'Great!' He spins and points in the vague direction of their house. 'It's by the "Welcome to Whitecliff" sign,' he says. 'You can't miss it.'

Given I've already driven past it once and not noticed, I'm not sure that's true.

He turns back and stands with his legs apart, hand on hip. *I'm a little teapot.* 'So…' he says. 'How have things been?'

'Busy.'

He nods. 'I was really good friends with your father at one point. We used to go golfing together. I bought a few antiques from him over the years. Just bits and bobs. He was a great guy.'

His chumminess annoys me. It's been like this for months: total strangers telling me what fantastic people my parents were. How it's a 'tragedy' or a 'crying shame'. That they were 'taken too young'. That it 'always happens to the good guys'. And so on.

It's easy to be great, fun people when your kids have been packed off to boarding school. Easier still over a couple of glasses of red and some discounted antiques – which isn't a euphemism.

'He never mentioned you,' I say. The words are out before I can stop them. I can feel Chloe staring at me disapprovingly.

Dan takes a half-step back, almost as if I've pushed him.

'Sorry,' I add, quickly. 'A lot's been going on. He probably did mention you. I don't know many of his friends.'

Dan eases the tension with a laugh – and he's back to being that bloke in the park with a Frisbee again. Mother's voice is at the back of my mind once more:

Y'know, Megan, you can be a real bitch sometimes. I don't know where you get it from.

The irony of it all. The obliviousness.

Dan's being a teapot again. His outdoorsy gear is spotless, looking suspiciously like it's only been used indoorsy.

'What brings you to town?' he asks.

'Affairs to put in order,' I reply, shortly. I've been saying things like this a lot recently.

'Well, this is a beautiful place,' Dan replies. 'I hope you can enjoy it while you're here.'

'Last time I was here,' I say, 'my brother went missing.'

Dan's grin vanishes. 'Yes. Um…'

'Do you remember him?'

'Yes. I mean, I…' He interrupts himself, rotating his hand in a circle as if trying to make the words come. 'I was part of the search campaign,' he says. 'We spent days combing the coastline. Up here, down in the caves, everywhere. It was such a tragedy.'

That word again. *Tragedy.*

'I suppose I lost a bit of contact with your mum and dad after that,' he adds. 'We were so close at one time and then…'

'What happened?'

He blinks. 'I suppose they weren't so keen to return after what happened with Zachariah. Can't blame them, of course. I gather they spent odd days and weekends here – but nothing substantial. They used to be here for entire summers. We never had time to catch up.'

Dan shuffles from foot to foot and glances from me to Chloe. She's stopped working on her pad, but says nothing. It's odd that he uses the name 'Zachariah'. Only my mother used to call him that. My brother was Zac.

'What do *you* remember about it all?' Dan's gaze has suddenly zeroed in on me, steely and strong. It's a question I haven't expected – mainly because the past three months have taught me so much about the way people talk following trauma. After the car crash involving my parents, it's been a litany of 'tragedy' remarks. People have been lining up to tell me how *they* feel about it. Rarely do they ask how *I* feel. How Chloe feels. Instead, they speak of business deals they had with my father, of garden parties, weddings and holidays together. They talk of what lovely people my parents were. Of how they'll be missed. Over and over and over.

It takes me a second or two to process what Dan's asked.

'What do I remember about Zac?' I reply.

'I know it was a long time ago.'

I shake my head. 'I don't remember much. I barely even remember the cottage. I know that I woke up one morning and it was really light. I went into the kitchen and there was nobody there. Then my mother came in and said that Zac wasn't coming home with us.'

The memory is fuzzy, grey around the edges, as if it's not quite whole. I'm not completely sure it *was* Mother who told me Zac wasn't coming home. It might have been my father. I don't remember Chloe being there at all.

'What do you remember?' I ask.

Dan blinks again and looks between us. He puffs out a long breath and scratches his head, willing the memory out. 'Your parents came up to the house,' he says. 'Both of them. They asked if we'd seen Zachariah… Zac. They asked us because you have to pass our house if you're leaving the village but we hadn't seen him. We assumed he'd turn up soon enough, but before long everyone was looking for him. Someone sent the fishing boats out in case he'd been washed away from shore. I took a couple of people to the caves; others went through the woods. One day became the next…'

I look to Chloe. Her eyes are wide, fascinated by details we've never heard in person. For years, bringing up the subject of Zac with our parents was met by either silence or anger, depending on which of them we asked. It became The Thing Of Which We Do Not Speak.

Dan angles a thumb over his shoulder. 'There's an envelope of cuttings about his disappearance at the house. If you ever want to check through them, come on over. Some of it's probably online anyway but I kept all the local stuff at the time.'

'I might do that,' I say.

'I'll dig them out and leave them on the side in case I'm out. Alison should know where to find them.'

'Thank you.'

Dan turns between us once more and then hefts his bag higher on his back. It doesn't take him much effort and I wonder if the bag actually contains anything. 'Anyway,' he says, 'I want to get out and back before dinner. Nice to meet you both.'

He smiles and nods, then marches away, tracing the line of the cliff until he disappears over a ridge.

Chloe is staring into the distance, in the vague direction of the village, her pencil hanging in mid-air.

'It's weird,' she says.

'What is?'

'No one – literally not one person – saw him, did they? I know Mum and Dad would never talk about it, but I've Googled it. You must've Googled it, too?'

It's not really a question. Of course I have.

Chloe turns to me. 'What do you think happened?'

'I don't know. They stopped searching because everyone assumed he was dead.'

We both look out to the endless expanse of water. It does seem like the obvious conclusion. Of course people assumed Zac had died. Why wouldn't they? Cliffs, caves, the ocean. So many hazards in such a small area. I'd bet it's the same in any place that borders the sea. Someone disappears and there's an assumption the body will wash up in a day or two.

Only, Zac's never did.

Chloe says nothing, turning back to her sketchpad. I sit on the grass, twisting and trying to get comfortable when a flicker of movement catches my eye. Something dark is clinging to the edge of the treeline. At first, I think it's a shadow of a tree, perhaps the scurry of a small animal, but gradually, I realise it's larger than that. The size of a person. I squint into the distance but whatever it is has stopped moving and is hiding behind a bush.

Or, I think it is.

I wait, wondering if whoever it is will move again. Wondering if the person is watching us specifically. Wondering if I'm imagining it.

'Meg?'

Chloe's voice makes me jump and I spin to face her. 'Huh?'

'You all right? You're all zoned out.'

I wonder how long I was watching the trees. When I turn back, the shadow has gone. If it was ever there.

'Meg?'

'I'm fine.'

Chloe goes quiet as I continue scanning the trees, watching for the merest flicker of movement. If there was something there, some*one*, then they're gone. The feeling of being watched remains, however. Anonymous eyes in the woods.

Except there's the postcard in my bag and a voice at the back of my mind telling me that those eyes might not be anonymous at all. That they might belong to my brother.

CHAPTER FIVE

When we get back to the cottage, I still can't face unpacking. It'd be too final, an admission that we're staying here for a while. This cottage might be half mine in a legal sense but it'll always belong to my parents.

Chloe disappears off to her room and closes the door. She's often quiet and private but I wonder if she's been upset by all the talk about Zac. Or by the fact that we've not yet gone to look for the lightning tree and the holy grail of phone reception. Or that there's still nothing to eat in the cottage.

I take the half protein bar from my pocket and lay it on the kitchen table, then find the tape measure once more. A quarter of this – an eighth of the original bar – is only thirty-two-and-a-half calories, which I can definitely justify. I eat the eighth, then have two more glasses of water and stop to stare at myself in the full-length mirror that hangs on the hallway wall.

The strange thing is that I know exactly what I'm doing to myself. I know better than most people. I've read so much about nutrition and exercise that I could probably teach a class on it. I bet I know more than my GP back in the city. That doesn't change anything, though. The remaining three-eighths of a protein bar is burning such a hole in my pocket that I tear it out in a flash of anger. I scrape the kitchen window open and throw the rest of the bar out onto the edge of the woods. It lands satisfyingly on a patch of moss. The rabbits can have it.

I feel much better after another glass of water.

It's easy to walk past the mirror this time. I find myself back in my mother's study, the room that's filled with expensive throws and cushions: the sort of meaningless crap she so loved.

I'll have to clear this out one day, even if that means picking everything up and dumping it in a skip.

I can't wait. I'd burn it to the ground if I could.

The first thing I do is rip the woven blanket from the back of the wicker chair and hurl it into the corner. It feels good, so I send a pair of empty pearl-decorated photo frames the same way. A lamp crashes into the wall after them, splintering but not breaking. A shame.

I pull out one of the drawers and empty the glass tea-light holders inside onto the floor, then stamp on them until I feel a satisfying splintering under my shoe. It's wonderfully therapeutic. Crash, stamp; crash, stamp.

The next drawer is full of papers and they join the pile, then it's on to drawer three. I'm on a roll, ready to tear the whole room apart, but when I yank open the third drawer, I find my brother's face staring back at me. It stops me on the spot.

'Have You Seen' screams across the top of the page and then 'Zachariah Smart?' is in smaller letters at the bottom. There's a phone number for the police under his photograph and that's about it. I empty the drawer. There are at least a hundred pristine posters in there. Zac stares out from each of them, eyes unwavering. The worst flickbook ever made.

I return the posters to the drawer, lining the corners up so they're straight and then slide the whole thing back into the chest. My momentum has been lost. My heart rate is slowing; I can't even remember what I was angry about. The glee of destruction has gone.

There's another photo frame on the windowsill and when I pick it up, I don't have the urge to throw it into the corner with the others. As I wipe the dust away, I smear finger marks onto the glass accidentally.

Gabby! Gabriela. Will you look at this?

It's a photo I've never seen before; one I didn't even know existed. A photo of all five of us. Mother is sitting on a bench, knees crossed, back straight, sunglasses covering most of her face. Father is standing behind her, hands on her shoulders. Neither of them are smiling – but us three children are. Chloe has bows in her hair and is wearing a pretty pink dress with matching shoes. This is when she was full-on Aryan child. I'm wearing pink, too. When I peer closer, I realise the dresses are a pair. We look like bridesmaids on either side of our parents. I'm taller and thinner than Chloe, standing rigidly with my chin high, looking so damned happy with myself.

And then there's Zac. He's at my side, the same height as our father. He's the odd one out, in shorts and a vest, with golden tanned skin and flip-flops. A thick chain with a star hangs around his neck. It looks like a rogue surfer has accidentally stumbled into our family portrait.

There were no photos of Zac at our house in London – or at least, none in the open. Not that I spent much time there. With no reminders, I can go months without thinking of him – and then, from nowhere, he'll be in my mind. It's not *him* that I think of, though. Not really. My memory of him has faded. This is the first time I've seen a photo of him in years.

He has floppy light hair, bleached from the sun. The rest of us are posed but he's leaning to the side. Relaxed. He's the normal one; we're the aliens.

It's only when I look past him that I realise the photo was taken in front of the cottage. The stone brickwork is part of the faded background and there's a hint of the thick beams that surround the windows.

I knock lightly on Chloe's door and she calls for me to come in. She's lying on her bed, playing some game on her phone. I pass her the photo and ask if she remembers it being taken. Chloe's eyes widen as she realises what it is. She takes it in for a few seconds and then hands it back.

'I don't remember it,' she says.

Intrigued, we go outside and, together, find the precise spot where the photo was taken. There's no bench there now, not even a hint that there was once one on the spot, but it's undoubtedly the right place. Almost exactly where my car is now parked.

'When do you think it was taken?' Chloe asks. She has the photo in her hands and looks down at it.

'I look about ten and you look about six. Zac's all tanned, so… I guess it's from the summer he went missing. I don't remember being here all together apart from that.'

She nods, as if I've confirmed what she was thinking. She continues to look at the photo for a moment, then she takes a breath and offers it back to me. 'Do you remember him?' she asks.

I shrug. 'Not really. We were at different schools and then, in the summer, he was out with his friends or off at camp. Or *I* was at camp. There wasn't much crossover.'

There's a silence between us. I know that Chloe is thinking what I am thinking: that this could have been our story, too. If it weren't for mobile phones and technology, we'd likely not know much of each other.

'Where'd you find it?' Chloe asks.

'The study with all the throws and pillows.'

She nods but doesn't ask anything more. There's no way she missed the sounds of various things crashing into the wall.

'Let's go to the supermarket,' I say, wanting to change the subject. Wanting to be away from Mother's things. 'There's one a few miles out of town. It's the only place we'll find food for you.'

'Can I finish my game first? I'm on a really hard part.'

'Sure.'

Chloe scampers back inside and I lean on the bonnet of my car, staring towards the house. It's so strange seeing a picture of myself of which I have no memory. It's not like I was a baby when it was taken: I was ten years old. People remember most things at that age – or I think they do. And yet it's as if I've blocked out most of the family memories from that time.

'All right, stranger?'

I spin to see lifeguard Luke emerging from the trail that runs into the woods. He's wearing the same swim shorts as earlier, with a crusty vest on top. His hair is long and straggly and it suddenly strikes me that he looks a lot like Zac might have done by now. It's hard to tell. The difference between a sixteen-year-old – the age Zac was when he disappeared – and someone ten years on is literally boy to man.

'What are you doing up here?' I ask.

Luke nods towards the woods across from where we're standing. 'I live down there.'

'Do you?' I don't mean to make it sound so disbelieving, but Luke laughs, waving me across to where there's a second trail into the woods. The trees are denser here and I'd not noticed it before.

'Two minutes down there,' he says. 'Pop over if you want a chat or a smoke, or whatever. You can't miss it.'

'People keep saying that about things around here.'

He laughs. 'It's that kinda place. Not big enough to miss things. If you want to borrow sugar or whatever, you know where I am.'

'Do people borrow sugar?'

Luke screws up his lips. 'I dunno. Just something people say, innit?' He shrugs, nodding to the route he just took. 'Anyway, see ya around. I have to cut through your bit of garden to get to my trail. Hope you don't mind.' He doesn't wait for a reply, turning and disappearing back into the trees with a cheery wave. The smell of weed wafts behind him.

I begin to wonder how many other cottages might be hidden around the woods, but am distracted when Chloe calls me back to the car, saying she's ready to go. I lock up the cottage – which is proving to be quite the feat of strength – and then drive us along the track to join the road.

This time, we do notice Alison and Dan Wood's house as we pass it. They were right – it *is* hard to miss. There's a large sign reading 'The Gables' that tops a pair of large metal gates. If the 'Welcome to Whitecliff' sign is in the right place then, technically, they live outside the village. It's not far from our parents' cottage, but their eagerness for us to 'come by anytime' makes me want to avoid the place more than I do white bread.

The fact that there's only one road in and out of the village makes it relatively easy to find a supermarket. At the first crossroads, I follow the sign to the nearest town and ten minutes later, I'm pulling into a Tesco car park.

Chloe and I grab the regular things – tins of beans, wholemeal bread, brown rice – and then I leave her to fill the trolley with whatever else she wants. She skips away to hunt for vegan cheese and fake chicken burgers.

I head back the way we've come, making my way to the chilled counter next to the bakery. It's my favourite place in the supermarket. I'm drawn instantly to something called a bucket of chocolate. It's so big that I need both hands to pick it up. There's some sort of brown custardy ganache at the bottom, which takes up a good two-thirds of the tub. On top of that is a thick layer of whipped cream, then it's topped off with chocolate shavings, chocolate buttons, half a dozen profiteroles and a bunch of glittery silver things.

All the good stuff.

I'm actually shaking when I twist it around to stare at the label. One portion is almost 650 hundred calories – but that's only a sixth of the bucket.

One sixth!

That's nearly four thousand calories in my hands!

It's almost entirely fat and carbs.

I'm still trembling when I return the dessert to the rack. I have to swallow to stop myself from drooling. It's like getting the sugar rush without actually having to eat it. I think about taking a photo of the label on my phone to look at later, but then someone in a blue uniform rounds the corner and I change my mind. I pick up the packet of four chocolate eclairs, but they're only 280 calories apiece. It's hard to be excited about that after the thrill of the bucket. I quickly check the label once more and then drag myself away.

I find Chloe in the biscuit aisle with a packet of peanut butter cookies in her hand.

'Vegan!' she says.

I check the label, ostensibly to make sure she's correct. It's right there, of course: 'vegan-friendly'. What's more important is that they're 200 calories apiece. There has to be at least twenty in the packet and the thought of these sitting in the kitchen cupboard, torturing me, is so delicious that I have to force myself not to grin. Back in the day, I'd hide family-sized bags of M&Ms under my bed. I'd never open them but would stare at the packet and crunch the sweets through the wrapping.

I place the cookies carefully in the trolley.

'Aren't you getting anything?' Chloe asks.

'I'll be fine with everything in here.'

I know she's watching me but she never asks the question out loud. Nobody does.

We use the self-checkout, which is the usual mess of unexpected items in the bagging area. The poor woman on duty has to help us three times until we've convinced the machine that we're not trying to steal the bag of frozen beefless bites.

I've been driving for about five minutes when Chloe cranes her head, noticing the orange light that's been present on my dashboard for the past three weeks.

'What's that?' she asks, a gentle tinge of concern to her voice. 'Dunno.'

She pauses for a moment and then adds: 'Is there something wrong with the car?'

'Don't think so. It feels fine. It got us all the way down here.'

'It probably means something.'

I let it hang because she's right. The light will be telling me to check the engine or the oil. Something like that. I haven't looked up exactly what it means and I won't, of course. If the light remains on and I manage to get from one destination to the next without breaking down, then I win. I enjoy the small victories.

'I'll drop in a garage sometime,' I say – and she lets it go, probably because she finally has phone reception. She says little else, spending much of the journey tapping away until we reach the outskirts of Whitecliff. It's like crossing into a black hole. She drops the phone into her lap, cut off from the outside world once more.

Back at the cottage, Chloe heads to the boot as I fight the front door. It's surprisingly satisfying to slam my bony shoulder into the wood. Each thud moves the door by a millimetre or two, until it flies open with a welcoming whoosh.

Chloe takes a couple of bags inside and starts loading things into the freezer. I'm about to retrieve more from the boot when I stop, staring through the dusky light at the footprints scuffed into the dried earth outside the door. I try to tell myself they're mine – but the shoe size is too big. Probably a man's ten or eleven. There is a series of marks around the door and then more heading towards the trail that leads to the village.

I feel cold as I stare out towards the woods, remembering the shadow from up on the cliffs. The trees mask the lowering sun, leaving everything drenched in a murky grey, like wearing sunglasses at night.

'You okay?'

Chloe is behind me, about to head back to the car.

I blink back to the present. 'I'm fine,' I say.

I don't want to scare her with the truth: that I've felt watched since the moment we got here.

CHAPTER SIX

I'm drifting and dreaming when a knock on the door rattles through the house. There's a moment in which I'm not sure where reality starts and my own little world ends. As if I can choose between the two versions, with the echoing wood inhabiting both.

It's only when Chloe calls that she'll get it that I roll myself out of bed. My stomach throbs with pain but that's nothing new. I'm in a pair of pyjamas – shorts and a spaghetti-strapped top – that I don't remember putting on.

The kitchen floor is cold as I 'ooh' and 'ah' my way across it barefooted, joining Chloe. She is leaning backwards as she yanks on the door handle. It jumps open with a satisfying pop to reveal Alison Wood.

It's hard for her to smile with all that nipping, tucking and injecting but she tries her best anyway, giving us a cheery, 'Morning!'

I watch her register what I'm wearing. 'I hope I didn't wake you,' she adds.

'I've been up for hours,' Chloe says – and I realise she's already dressed. A quick glance to the kitchen clock tells me it's almost ten.

Alison has the full-on domestic goddess look about her today. She's wearing a headband-handkerchief thing on her head, a knee-length tea dress and an apron. Her hair is shiny and tied up into the tightest of buns, stretching her plastic skin even tauter.

She holds aloft a picnic basket that's covered with a tea towel. 'I've brought you some goodies,' she says. 'There's all sorts of fresh stuff in there. Dan went to the farm shop earlier, so there are eggs, as well as some jam and bread. There's fresh fish, a pheasant, a couple of steaks and some thick-cut bacon. I didn't know if you preferred smoked or not – so I got both. I couldn't stand the thought of you going hungry.'

Chloe takes the basket and leans awkwardly against the doorframe.

'Is something wrong?' Alison asks, noticing the look on Chloe's face.

'Chloe's vegan,' I say.

Alison's neck cranes back like a confused ostrich. She's had a lot of work done, but the surgeon hasn't done much about the skin at the base of her neck, which has bunched and creased.

'Oh… I didn't even think.'

She reaches for the basket and Chloe allows her to take it.

'I'll take out all the meats. There's still cake—'

'Vegans don't eat eggs or butter.'

'Oh.'

Mother once told me that a therapist would really 'do a number' on me – a direct quote – and she was unquestionably onto something. The awkwardness of this situation is almost overpowering and yet I'm thriving on it. I was asleep a few minutes ago but now I feel alive.

Alison tugs the tea towel from the basket and reaches inside. 'Here's some bread,' she says. 'That's vegan, isn't it?'

Chloe takes it. 'Yes, sorry,' she says.

Alison bats away the needless apology. 'No, it's my fault. I should've asked.' She continues to fish in the basket, handing over the jam and a jar of pickles.

'I think that's it,' she says, deflated.

'Thank you,' Chloe replies.

They apologise to each other once more and then Alison rocks back on her heels. 'Dan says he saw you on the cliffs,' she says. 'Have you settled in okay?'

'It gets cold at night,' Chloe replies, 'but it's fine other than that.'

Alison nods and bites her bottom lip, glancing towards me nervously, clearly wanting to ask something. I realise that the only reason she came over was for information. The grapevine is alive and well in Whitecliff and it needs feeding. The picnic basket was a kind gesture but a smokescreen nonetheless.

Alison waves a hand, gesturing to the cottage. 'I guess I was wondering what's going to happen to the old place…?'

Chloe looks to me, her arms laden with food. One slice of white toast with raspberry jam has to be a good 140 calories. The voice I rarely listen to wants me to ask Alison for the cake as well, regardless of the fact that it's been made with eggs and butter. That just means that Chloe won't want to eat any. More for me to not eat.

'We've not decided yet,' I reply. 'That's largely why we're here.'

'Did you, um…' Alison looks both ways – even though there is nobody around but us – and lowers her voice. 'Did you inherit *everything*?'

It's the way she says 'everything' that leaves me momentarily confused. There's an implication that our parents owned something she had her eye on.

'Sort of,' I say. 'Chloe gets her half when she's eighteen. Everything is split between us, but we won't be able to sell any property or anything until she's the right age.'

Alison nods along, making mental notes. She'll have a lunch date with her girlfriends in the country club later on. Manicure; Caesar salad; couple of glasses of Prosecco; you'll never guess who so-and-so's daughter is getting married to; those Smart girls have inherited all their parents' money. That sort of thing. It's like spending a day with Mother again.

Y'know, Megan, you can be a real bitch sometimes. I don't know where you get it from.

'What happened to your father's antiques?'

Alison's question takes me by surprise. She takes my moment of confusion to continue speaking. 'He was such a talented dealer,' she adds. 'Such an amazing eye. What a loss…'

I can't go through all this 'tragedy' stuff again.

'The business was sold,' I say.

'Oh.'

'The assets couldn't sit stagnant until Chloe turns eighteen. We worked it out with the solicitor, who found some loophole. We sold everything to one of dad's rivals.'

There's a lengthy pause before she replies: 'How *awful* for you.'

'It wasn't much use to us,' I say.

'Did you get everything valued?'

I smile sweetly – I can when I want – but don't give a specific answer. Alison can read between the lines if she wants. The one thing she really wants to know is so obvious that she might as well have tattooed it on her forehead. The artist would have a smooth enough surface on which to work.

She wants to know how much it went for. What is everything worth – the business, the house, the cars, this cottage? How much money is in my bank account? How much will Chloe get in a little over a year?

I'll never tell her. It's none of her business anyway but I'll never tell her because she's so desperate to know. Sometimes rich people think they're owed information simply because of their wealth. There's this chummy quid pro quo: another thing I learnt at boarding school.

Alison waits but it's only a couple of seconds before the awkwardness becomes too much even for her.

'Well,' she says, 'I suppose I should be getting back.' She lifts the basket an inch or two, her bicep flexing to show off the gentle bulge that downward dogs and aggressive portion control gives a person. 'Don't forget to drop round if you need something,' she adds. 'It was nice to see you again.'

With that, she gives a weak-wristed wave and then crunches her way back towards the road.

Chloe waits until she's out of sight before she rests her head on my shoulder. 'I feel bad for her,' she whispers.

'Me, too,' I reply, not meaning a word of it.

CHAPTER SEVEN

The sun is already high, the sky a cloudless, brilliant blue. The exhilaration of an early morning bit of discomfiture leaves me feeling energised.

I used to run in the mornings but gradually got out of the habit. It was leaving school that did it. Everything was about competition there. Everyone was trying to prove they were better than the next person. *My father has a newer car than yours. My mother flew out to Milan for a stylist appointment.*

Naturally, we moved on to competing with each other. I was never going to be the prettiest girl, or the smartest – but I could sure as hell run faster and further than almost all the others. Even when I couldn't, I'd get up at four and wait on the side of the track until someone else came down. Then I'd douse myself in water, mention something about hammering out a quick 10k and head back to bed.

'I think I'm going to go down to the beach,' I say now.

Chloe looks at me with crooked, curious smile. 'To relax? *You?*'

'Yes.' A pause. 'Well, no. I think Zac spent most of his time on that beach, so I want to see if anyone actually remembers him. There must be someone.'

Chloe looks at me with suspicion, for which I don't blame her. She doesn't question me, though.

'I'll come too,' she says.

I remember the way she looked at Brad and wonder if there's hope for one of us yet.

We get our things together and opt for the trail through the woods, instead of heading for the road. The path is marked with a series of white dots painted on the tree trunks. The track is littered with loose stones and tree roots and with the way it dips down sharply, it has a bit of a neck-breaker feel to it. I find myself clinging onto a couple of tree trunks to stop myself from going too quickly.

'It's like a rollercoaster,' Chloe says as she races past me. She's semi-crouching and her legs are doing the Scrappy Doo thing: seemingly moving too quickly for the rest of her body. She's giggling and I allow myself to laugh as well, mainly at her. Nothing pleases me more than when my sister is happy.

She gets to the bottom before me, skidding on her backside and holding up her hand for me to pull her up.

'Let's go again,' she says.

'I don't think it's as much fun going up as it is down.'

'True.'

Chloe wipes herself down and we head past the docks and pub, moving towards the beach.

There are already a couple of dozen young people in place: towels laid out, volleyball net standing tall.

Something feels different. It's only as we get closer that I realise some of the faces are new. The volleyball game has Brad, George and some other beach kids from yesterday on one side – but the lads on the opposite side of the net are all faces I've not seen before.

Chloe takes a spot on the sand next to Ebony, Mia and Popcorn the dog. I don't want to cramp her style, so drift away, finding a space next to the sand bank at the back and laying down a towel. I've barely sat down when one of the lads starts shouting at Brad. Fingers are wagging, voices are raised. They'll be measuring dick size next. It's all a bit testosteroney for my liking.

'It's like this every year.'

I turn to look at the girl who's spoken. She's sitting nearby in a fold-up canvas chair. She's wearing a long-sleeved dress, despite the heat. Her gingery hair is tied into a loose ponytail and a paperback lies closed in her lap.

'Hi,' she says, with a roll of her eyes.

I think it's that which makes me instantly like her.

'Megan,' I say.

'Vanessa. Call me Vee. Everyone else does. That's what happens when your parents put three syllables in your name.'

I shuffle closer to her.

'What's going on?' I ask.

'This happens at least once a summer. Our lot play your lot at volleyball, football, cricket or whatever. Before you know it, they're rolling around in the sand arguing over who's got the biggest dad.'

The shouting calms down. The boys settle back to patting each other's backsides whenever a point goes their way.

'Who's your lot?' I ask.

Vee nods backwards towards the village. 'The locals. We *actually* live here.' There's delicious spite there.

'Who's my lot?'

'The beach kids.'

I suppose it's not that strange but I have a momentary tug of recognition: that's what I've been calling them, too.

Vee turns sideways and stares at me properly. 'You *are* one, aren't you? A beach kid?'

'I suppose. My mum and dad owned the cottage up on the hill. I'm down here with my sister.' I point towards Chloe.

A pause. '*Owned?*'

'They died.'

'Oh.'

She stops stone-cold, in the way people do when they hear my story. I've encountered this type of thing so many times in the past few months. An 'oh', followed by silence. Most people talk with the same stock phrases and sentences. There's a rhythm to it. When they're told something unexpected, the response isn't there. It takes a few seconds for the brain to kick in.

'I'm sorry,' she adds.

'Does that make me a beach kid?' I reply breezily, not wanting to dwell.

She takes a couple more seconds, weighing up whether she should show more concern. She's twirling a lock of her hair absent-mindedly. 'You're an in-betweener,' she replies with a slim smile. 'I'll let it go.'

We sit and watch the game for a minute or two. Chloe is closer to the action but seemingly oblivious as she tickles Popcorn's belly and then tosses a ball for him to fetch.

'Why do they fight?' I ask.

Vee sighs. She reaches for a bottle under her seat and swallows a mouthful of water. 'Do you really want to know?'

'I really want to know.'

She twists and waits for eye contact. Hers are blue and surrounded by soft freckles. 'Nobody around here has any money,' she says. 'We get the odd caver or rock climbing group through the year – but they don't stay for long and don't spend much. Then the beach kids come in every summer. They've all got rich parents who are off in France, Italy or wherever. They dump their kids here and leave us to babysit.' A pause. 'They don't like *us* and we don't like *them*.'

I suck on my cheeks, weighing it up. I'm not really the enemy in all this. I'm Switzerland.

'They can't *all* be bad,' I say. A calculated risk.

Vee holds my stare for a second and then looks away. 'I guess not. It's still *our* village, though. They treat it like they own the place.'

I give it a moment, let her metaphorically cool off.

'How do you mean?'

'Ever walked outside your front door and found a used condom on the doorstep?'

'Well, no...'

Vee folds her arms. '*That's* what I mean.'

'Is it the same faces every year?' I ask.

'Not always. Sometimes you get these generation things – someone's brother or sister will appear a year or two after you think the family's gone for good. Other times, you get the same people back for a couple of summers in a row – then they head off to university, abroad or to some bank in the city. I don't know.'

Vee waves a dismissive hand towards the volleyball court, which has been marked with white rope. 'We used to have a village police officer who would stop them getting out of hand,' she says.

'How long ago?'

'When I was five or six. There's no one now. The nearest police are twenty-odd miles away. People get away with doing whatever they want.'

Vee looks close to my age, meaning the village officer must have gone AWOL a few years before Zac. That fact alone gives me a tiny jolt of interest. If someone unfamiliar with the area had to trek twenty miles along the country roads and traverse the drop into this village, then it's reasonable to assume the investigation might not have been full and thorough.

'Surely if the beach kids get out of line,' I say, 'the local adults step in?'

Vee scoffs. 'You'd think!'

The volleyball game once again descends into a shouting match. One lad is claiming the ball was in, while another insists it was out. In-out-in-out, shake it all about.

Children.

The lads look across to Ebony, Mia and Chloe, demanding to know what they saw. I feel my shoulders tense, fists ball. No one takes that tone with my sister. The three girls shrug, so the lads go back to arguing among themselves. One of them kicks sand towards the others.

'That's Kev,' Vee says.

'The sand-kicker?'

'He lives two doors down from me. We were in the same class at school for eleven years.'

We say nothing for a minute or two, watching the squabble play itself out. Kev and Brad sum up the two factions. Brad is tall and lean with perfect teeth: the product of good breeding and a lifelong avoidance of real work. Kev is rough around the edges: short, dark hair, dirt under his fingernails, bushy eyebrows, a bit of puppy fat around his belly. Not unattractive as such; the type of boy that would have been worth taking home to Mother, if only for the hysterical overreaction.

'We need their money.'

Vee speaks so quietly that I almost miss it.

'From the beach kids?'

'Right. Look how small this place is. How do you think the pub, the board shop and everything else keeps going? It's not us. Everyone makes enough in the summer to get through to the next year.'

She makes it sound obvious – and it is.

'How long have you lived here?' I ask.

'Forever. Parents, grandparents. It's a family thing. Came over from Ireland, landed here and never left. We're not the only ones.'

'What do you do?'

Vee nods backwards towards the village. 'My dad owns the board shop. My older brother manages it and I work there.' She pauses for a drink. 'I've got the day off.'

The dynamic is interesting. Neither Chloe nor I fit into either of these apparent warring factions. Zac wouldn't have done, either.

The powder keg finally explodes in front of us. F-words and c-words are thrown around liberally and then, predictably, Kev tackles Brad to the ground. I lean forward, thrilled by the spectacle. Kev throws a couple of a wayward punches, then one of the beach kids pulls him off and hurls him to the floor. Brad's up off his feet and throws himself at Kev – but his punches are even lamer. It's like he's treading water and flapping around to keep himself afloat.

George the guitar player has backed away, probably wondering whether he should launch into a rendition of 'Kumbaya' to calm the whole thing down.

Despite my initial twinge of excitement, I've seen better riots at the Boxing Day sales. They'll be pulling each other's hair next.

That is until Hairy Back from yesterday comes storming across the beach. Last time I saw him, he was busy banging a spanner onto a boat. Now he stomps across from the direction of the pub and it's as if the world has paused. Brad and Kev have stopped fighting and are frozen in place as Hairy Back gets closer.

'You!'

The beach kids and the locals are largely similar sizes, with teenager levels of muscle and fitness. Hairy Back is bigger than all of them.

Luke the lifeguard is off his seat and starts to say something but Hairy Back ignores him and continues past. He doesn't bother waiting for explanations or reason, gunning directly for Brad and picking him up by the throat.

Despite the heat, it's as if everyone breathes in at the same time. A collective gasp of shock.

Hairy Back tosses Brad to the floor effortlessly and then stands over him, muscles tensed. 'What have I told you?'

Brad's eyes are wide and he mutters something I don't catch. Just when it feels as if things are really going to get fun, Luke the lifeguard slips underneath Hairy Back's arms and stands between him and Brad.

'C'mon, man…' he says.

Hairy Back stands a little taller. 'This is nothing to do with you.'

'Or you.'

The two are surprisingly close in height. It's only the width of Hairy Back's shoulders that make him seem so imposing. One second passes. Two. Then Hairy Back slumps slightly and it's all over. A shame.

He angles around Luke, jabbing a pudgy finger at Brad and snarls, 'Got my eye on you,' before turning and stomping back along the beach. All a bit of an anticlimax.

Brad picks himself up and dusts away the sand from his shorts. He mutters something to George, clearly wanting to pretend none of this ever happened. Kev mumbles something that might be an apology. Moments later, the two teams have reassembled and Luke has returned to his lifeguard lookout.

'Who was that?' I ask.

'Scott,' Vee replies. 'The local dickhead. His dad runs the pub. Scott goes out on the fishing boats most days.'

'He seems to have anger issues.'

Vee laughs. 'You could say that. In fairness, he's not the only one. Someone pulled a knife on him a couple of years ago.'

'One of the beach kids?'

'Right. Nobody ever learns. It's like this every year. Someone will end up dead one of these days.'

I have to force away the chill, wondering if, perhaps, somebody already has.

'We had a brother,' I say. 'He was older than me. I'm twenty; he'd have been twenty-six now. He disappeared ten years ago.'

I can feel Vee looking at me, but I don't turn to face her this time. I'm watching the volleyball, which is boring now that the boys are tiptoeing around each other. One of them even concedes a point.

'Disappeared…?' Vee says.

'Zac Smart,' I reply. 'We were staying in the village when he went missing.'

From the corner of my eye, I see Vee turn away. 'I remember the name,' she says.

'Do you remember him?'

'I don't think so; I'd have been too young.'

'Do you know someone his age who might remember him?'

'Scott…' Vee pauses. 'Maybe Luke. Sorry, I don't know who else to suggest.'

'Scott doesn't seem the talkative, sharing type.'

'No.'

We sit quietly for a couple of minutes and then make small-talk about more normal things. Vee points me along the beach in the direction of Whitecliff Caves, which she says can only be accessed at low tide. She tells me how all the village kids go to school on the same bus, which takes them to the nearest town. They're in classes with children local to that area, meaning they're outsiders in almost everything they do. I find myself fascinated and do far more listening than talking. Vee seems genuinely pleased to have found someone who wants to hear what life is like in the village.

The volleyball game soon disbands, though I couldn't say who won. Some of the village kids head back to work, while the beach lot cool off in the sea, or return to lounging. It's a hard life.

Brad takes a spot close to Chloe and I spend a good fifteen minutes half-watching the pair of them. Mother would definitely approve of Brad; I wonder who his parents are. Lawyers or city-types are the easy guesses but his athleticism must come from somewhere. One of them might have rowed for Oxford or Cambridge, something like that.

Perhaps sensing my silent interest, Brad turns and nods towards me. 'Meg, is it?'

'Megan.'

Yeah, mate. Two syllables and you can use them both. Only Chloe gets away with calling me Meg.

'Right.' He angles towards Chloe. 'We're having a barbecue tonight,' he says. 'You should both come on down.'

'Where?'

'Here.'

I feel Vee tense at my side. The whole do-what-they-want-thing.

'I don't eat meat,' I say.

It's a lie. I do eat meat – but I don't want Chloe to have to shout up that she doesn't. Not in front of Brad.

'That's fine,' he replies. 'Neither does Ebs.' Brad waves a hand at a prone, sunbathing Ebony. 'We've got veggie stuff. Whatever you want.'

'Sounds good,' I say, not completely committing. The thought of all that melting cheese, dribbling fat and white bread is exciting, even if I won't eat any of it.

'What are you doing for the rest of the day?' I ask.

He seems surprised by the question, shrugging and pouting a lip. 'Not much. You?'

'Fancy a wander down to the caves?'

He glances to Chloe and then back at me. 'Yeah, why not.'

'Chlo?'

I'd assumed she would come too – especially now Brad is on board – but she shakes her head.

'Vee?'

I turn to face her and see her expression of shock, as if the idea of mixing village, beach and in-betweener is beyond the realms of possibility. It's oil and water stuff. I'm a proper Martin Luther King.

'You sure?' she asks.

'We're all people, aren't we?'

It's such a worthy thing to say, so ridiculously lame, that I struggle not to laugh at myself. It works, though. Vee snaps her book closed. I don't think she was reading it anyway.

'Thank you,' she says. Then she reaches out and squeezes my hand.

CHAPTER EIGHT

Turns out I timed the cave trek to perfection because just as I'm getting to my feet, George finds his guitar. He asks for requests and it's all I can do to bite my tongue.

Perhaps because of the impending karaoke storm, Ebony gets to her feet too and ties a sarong around her waist, saying that she's coming with us to the caves. She's so damned statuesque that it actually makes me a little sick with envy. Mother would call her a 'good little princess from the colonies'. She said that to one of my schoolmates once. Not a school *friend*, obviously.

Vee leads Brad, Ebony and me along the beach, tracing the base of the cliffs. None of us have much to say, with the increasing heat of the day sapping our enthusiasm. Vee is the only one wearing shoes sensible enough to get over the slippery rocks. She tiptoes across comfortably, while Brad hops around barefooted, arms out wide for balance. I'm in sandals and manage the first part of the journey with a couple of wobbles. Ebony's elegance goes out the window as she bumbles from side to side like a kangaroo that's smacked off its tits on Jack Daniel's.

The three of us stand on a large, flat rock, watching as Ebony slips and lands hard on her backside.

'Get a move on, Ebs,' Brad calls.

'I'm trying.'

'The tide's going to be in by the time you get here.'

'Piss off.'

She scowls up at him with the type of venomous fury that is usually only reserved for couples who've been married for twenty years. Brad shuts up and I don't blame him.

It takes a while but Vee leads us over some more rocks, out of sight from the beach and the village. We continue, further along the base of the cliffs, until we reach a small sandy outcrop. Towering over us is a huge gaping mouth carved into the rock. There's a large white sign blathering on about 'DANGER' and 'DO NOT PASS THIS SIGN' – but those are for amateurs. None of us even blink at it. Beyond the opening is only darkness.

'This is the entrance to Whitecliff Caves,' Vee says.

'How far back does it go?' Brad asks.

'No one's quite sure. Much of the cave network is uncharted. Divers have gone through a bunch of times and found maybe a dozen new caverns beyond the regularly accessible ones. They reckon it could stretch on for miles underneath the moors – but you can only get past a certain point if you have diving gear.'

Brad glances back at the tide, which is far into the distance. There's no way he's going to admit he has even the remotest concern about being stranded, so he turns on the torch from his phone and strides ahead. Ebony slots in a little behind him, leaving me and Vee at the back.

'People think my brother might have drowned in these caves,' I tell her.

'Really?'

'It's on the Internet, so it must be true. I found a news story on his disappearance and there were a load of theories at the bottom.'

'Like what?'

I pause for a moment as we step beyond the opening of the cave and darkness consumes us. The flash of light from Brad zips around ahead and, following his lead, Vee and I both switch on the torches on our phones to light the way. I still don't have any reception. I'm not even sure why I'm carrying the phone around; it's just a reflex, I suppose.

'Most people think he drowned,' I say. 'I think that's what the police decided.'

'People *do* drown out here,' Vee replies.

'In the caves?'

'Not recently, but yes. Before I was born.'

'Zac's body has never been found. There were comments on-line saying he probably just ran away. Someone else reckoned he was sold to some Eastern European paedo network…'

I only really say that for shock value, although there was a commenter who wrote precisely that. Below-the-line-arseholes.

Vee barely reacts.

'No body?' she repeats.

'Right.'

My phone's torch skims across a circle of mashed-up cigarette ends left on top of some rocks. At least a couple of people have been here recently. I move the beam around a wider area. It's all a bit sombre and unspectacular. Wet walls and stunted, dome-shaped stalagmites. It vaguely reminds me of a school trip to some caves when I would've been seven or eight. Everything feels so vague from that age.

The first giant cavern leads into a second, where Brad and Ebony are waiting at the entrance. The ceiling here is a good ten metres high, offering a steady percussion of drips.

The four of us remain close now, using our collective lights to follow the path.

'I should've worn shoes,' Brad says, to no response. People with the most expensive educations really can be the most stupid.

'Why are you here?' he adds. It takes me a moment to realise he's addressing me. I can see his face turned towards me in the half-light.

'In the caves?' I reply.

'In Whitecliff. You and Chloe.'

'Oh.' I take a breath. May as well get everything out in the open. 'Our parents own the cottage on the hill. They came here in the summer for years but Chloe and I haven't been since our brother disappeared here ten years ago. Our parents died three months back, so we're here to tie a few things up.'

It sounds a bit more real when it's all strung together. I don't mention the postcard with the 'Z' on the back.

He pauses: the same pause everyone gives as they wonder what to say. Brad doesn't know me and wouldn't have met my parents.

'I'm sorry,' he says, in a predictable tone of concern. Is the to-ken, 'I'm sorry,' meant to make *me* feel better, or is it for himself? I don't know. I'm past caring whether or not people mean it.

'It's fine,' I reply, probably too harshly. 'As well as sorting out the cottage, we're largely on holiday. It's been a long few months. Chloe's just finished her exams.'

It's near enough to the truth.

Brad doesn't say much to that and we continue on through the second cavern. Our footsteps echo, mingling with the endless dripping to create a perfect metronome of annoyance.

We soon reach a fork in the path. The opening on the left is low enough that we'd all have to duck to get through, while the one of the right is almost door-shaped.

Brad turns to Vee, careful to keep the glare of his torch light below her eye-line. 'Which way?'

'Either,' she replies. 'They both loop round to the next cave. There's only one after that which can be reached on foot.'

We go for the lower entrance, crouching under and emerging into a smaller cave. The ceiling is barely above head height, the drips plopping more readily onto our hair.

We've barely taken a couple of steps when Ebony speaks up. 'I don't like this,' she says. 'It's too close.' She grabs onto my arm, presumably because I'm the nearest.

She's right: it is close. It's more of a tunnel than a cave. Brad is at the front, his light darting neurotically around the ceiling, which doesn't help the sense of being closed in.

We have to duck again to get into the final cave, which, to Ebony's clear relief, is more like the second. She lets go of my arm again. The ceiling is higher but there's no real path. The stalagmites are tighter together and Brad, because he's a boy, decides he's going to try to climb one to the top of the cave.

Ebony, Vee and I wait at the bottom, shining our lights towards him as he shimmies and grunts his way up the cylinder of rock.

'It looks like he's shagging it,' I say, which gets a laugh.

There's a moment of relative silence, broken only by the drips of water and Brad's dry-humping… And by something else. It's only when Ebony asks if we should be worried about the sound of running water that I realise there is an undercurrent of rushing noise. It sounds like a river is babbling somewhere nearby.

'It's under us,' Vee says. 'There are vents in the far corners of this cave. There are grilles covering them now – but it wasn't always like that. You have to drop down into the water flow to get into the next set of caves. There's a YouTube video of it somewhere.'

'How long have you been coming here?' I ask.

'Forever,' Vee replies. 'One of my earliest memories is of having a picnic in here with my brother and his friends. Those danger signs didn't used to be outside. We used to come here most days when I was little. That was before someone fell and cracked his head open. They couldn't get an ambulance this far out and the tide was coming in. It was a big deal at the time.'

'Was he okay?'

'He was fine. His friends carried him back over the rocks.'

'How long ago was that?'

'Twelve years? Thirteen? Ages ago. It was one of the beach kids. Afterwards, his dad went on about suing the council, so all the signs went up. My dad stopped us coming here for a year or two.'

I think of Zac. Dan Wood told me he'd spent time searching these caves. I can only imagine how dangerous they are when the tide's in.

From nowhere, Ebony shrieks, saying she felt something on her foot. Vee remains calm, not even looking down.

'It's probably a rat or a bat,' she says.

This only freaks Ebony out further. She shouts up to Brad, saying she wants to go. He's almost at the top of the cave, his muscled legs clamped tightly around the curved stalagmite as he shimmies upwards.

I angle my light up for him as he shuffles the final few centimetres until he can strain and touch the sodden roof. After an echoing, 'Woo!' he slips down, landing with a squelchy thud.

'You're such a show-off,' Ebony says.

'Takes one to know one.'

It's light-hearted enough but I wonder whether it comes from a place of genuine dislike for one other, or whether it's flirty banter. They'll be up half the night playing hide the sausage. I might have to mention it to Chloe, just in case.

Although she said she wanted to go, Ebony has seemingly calmed down now that Brad's back on the ground. She tiptoes away to a shallow pool, removing her flip-flops and striking a star-shaped pose, her arms wide.

'Can you take my picture?' she asks, handing her phone to Brad.

'I don't think there's enough light.'

'Can you try?'

Vee and I watch. We say nothing but I can feel Vee tense at my side. There were good-looking girls at school but Ebony is something else. She's that perfect mix of toned and slim. Her skin is seemingly flawless. I wonder if her look is genuinely effortless, or if there are hours of prep that go into it. I'd love to think it is the latter.

The suppressed voice at the back of my mind hopes that our return trip over the rocks will be even more perilous. That Ebony might slip and crack open that perfect head of hers.

One can only dream.

Brad takes a few pictures and Ebony checks them over before deciding she's satisfied. If we had phone reception, one of them would be on Snapchat or Instagram within seconds. I'm sure her hormone-fuelled friends can wait an hour or so before stuffing their hands down their pants to celebrate Ebony's latest offering.

Vee tells Brad and Ebony we'll meet them outside. We head back towards the cave we missed on the way in. It's not as claustrophobic as the tunnel through which we came, though the ceiling is still unnervingly low. The passage is wider, speckled by a series of curved alcoves on either side. It's almost as if someone has sliced two- or three-person pods into the rock. The most natural of love seats.

I stop for a moment by one of the alcoves, running a hand across the damp, smooth rock that has worn into something close to a bench. For some reason, I feel drawn here. My fingers slip into a set of grooves. I pause: run my hand over them again.

Vee has moved a few steps ahead, but when she realises I'm no longer beside her, she stops and turns, her torch swinging back towards me.

'What?' she asks.

I settle my own light on the bench, illuminating the shapes that have been etched into the rock. It's as clear as could be, chiselled away into the stone:

ZS 4 CA

'What have you found?' Vee asks.

It takes me a couple of seconds to reply.

'Zac,' I reply. 'Zac Smart.'

CHAPTER NINE

As Chloe and I emerge from the wooded trail across from our cottage, it takes me a little while to catch my breath. The steepness of the slope and the warmth of the evening is a killer and my top is clinging to my back. The sweat is pooling, running down towards the gap at the back of my shorts.

It's me who sees it first. The message couldn't be much clearer. In the space between my car and the front door, a little away from the gravel, someone has chalked 'Go Home' onto the paving slabs.

Chloe stops at my side and I can feel her deflating. 'Oh,' she says.

'Nice warm welcome,' I reply.

I take her hand, squeezing her fingers, and we move slowly towards the writing. The letters are thin but have been reinforced by the sign-writer scraping the chalk back and forth on the ground.

'Who d'you reckon?' Chloe asks softly.

'One of the local kids,' I say. 'I wouldn't worry. Vee says there's conflict every year. To the villagers who live here, we're outsiders.'

We're still for a moment, not quite sure what to do. I think it affects Chloe more than it does me. As she hugs her arms across her front, I sense her twinge of fear. I wouldn't say I expected having to deal with something like this but there is a part of me that relishes it. It's a challenge. Go home and it'll all be fine; remain and anything could happen.

'I'll clean it up,' I say. 'Then I'm going to head up to find the lightning tree, see what all the fuss is about. Want to come?'

I watch Chloe's expression as she tries to make up her mind. She seemed happy enough on the way back up the trail, largely because she's fallen in love... with Popcorn. We've never had pets, mainly because we haven't spent that much time in any place other than school. Popcorn is a revelation to her: a seemingly endless bundle of energy, happy to chase balls all day long and faithfully track back to Mia or Chloe for a belly rub. I can understand why Chloe finds that unconditional affection so appealing.

That joy of discovery has left her now, though. Her shoulders have sagged. 'I might go back down to the gallery instead,' she says. 'I want to take my sketchbook for Arthur to see.'

'Do you have a key for the cottage, in case I'm not here when you get back?'

She pats her shorts pocket and says she does. We fight the front door to get in and then I fill a bucket with water while Chloe gets changed. Before she goes, she helps herself to a couple of peanut butter cookies from the cupboard. It's hard to watch.

'They're yours, too, remember,' she says cheerily.

'Thank you.'

'I'll see you later.'

'Deffo.'

Chloe tucks her sketchbook under her arm and hoists a small bag onto her back before heading out into the summer warmth once more.

I watch her go, count to twenty and then retrieve the cookies from the cupboard. I rip back the packaging, pull out the plastic tray and inhale the sweetness of its contents. I pick up one of the cookies, hold it directly under my nose and breathe it in.

That's as much as I allow myself. Chloe's cookies are dispatched back to the cupboard and I quickly down a glass of water. I pour myself a second, which goes down more slowly. Chloe bought a multipack of crisps at the supermarket, so I take the packet on top – salt and vinegar – and crunch it up tightly in my hand. The brittle shards crack and splinter within the packet. I keep squeezing until it feels like there is only dust remaining, then I empty the contents into the sink. Everything is washed away and I place the crumpled packet in the bin where Chloe can't miss it.

There's celery in the fridge, which I ration into small bitesize segments. My stomach strains and heaves with each swallow – and then the double punishment kicks in afterwards, as it craves more. I allow myself the tiniest crumble of Chloe's cheese. The vegan Cheddar melts on my tongue and it's so tremendously wicked that it's all I can do to not eat the entire block.

I chew on a fingernail instead.

I'm never going to be one of those women with perfect manicures: rainbow nails, with those stupid microscopic jewels that people glue on. I don't know how they do it. I sometimes dream of gnawing my own fingers down to the bone. The rest of my body can pull off feminine but my nails will always look like I've been doing double shifts at a builders' merchant.

Another glass of water and I'm as settled as I'm going to be.

The chalk washes away quickly enough but as I'm turning back to the cottage I catch a flicker of movement in the corner of my eye. I stop and stare towards the trees, where I'm sure there's the shape of something… *someone*… a few metres into the undergrowth. The trees are compact and tight, their shadows stretching far in the afternoon sun.

'Hello?'

I take half a step towards the woods, angling my head from side to side for a better view. It's hard to tell if I'm seeing things because the plants and trees are so encompassed by the shadows. It could be nothing – except I'm sure I saw someone in the trees up on the cliffs yesterday.

I take another step. And another… And then there's a frantic scuffle from a spot a couple of metres from where I was looking.

I turn but it's already too late. All I catch is the flutter of leaves, the rustle of branches. I rush towards the trees in the direction of the movement but, by the time I get to the spot where I saw something, tree limbs are already swaying twenty or thirty metres further on. I race further into the woods but can't get close enough to see what I'm chasing. After just twenty or thirty seconds, I realise that everything in front of me is still.

I stop, turning in a circle. Aside from the forest, the foliage, there's nothing to see.

'Hello…? Hello…?'

I call louder and my voice echoes around the trees, bouncing back until it seems like I'm shouting at myself.

Nothing.

I retrace my steps, telling myself it must have been a squirrel – but knowing it was more than that. It was a person, someone watching from the woods, in the exact way someone watched me on the clifftops.

It suddenly feels very lonely back at the cottage without Chloe. I grab my phone, lock the front door and then hurry down to the road.

Ebony was right when she said the lightning tree couldn't be missed. It's in the middle of a field, high on a ridge, standing alone like a telegraph pole. Its defining feature is the scarred, shattered top half, which has literally been sliced in two. Even from a distance, the blackened trunk is vivid against the green of the surrounding grass.

At the bottom of the field are the box-like rows of metal caravans, where Brad and the rest of the beach kids are presumably staying.

The whole setup is surprisingly close to the cottage – only a ten-minute walk or so. It's on the same side of the road as us, so probably accessible through the woods beyond our bedrooms. If someone were to walk from the beach to the caravans through the trees, instead of on the road, it would be difficult to miss our cottage.

I cut back in from the road, hopping over a small gully and crossing the treeline. It's a few degrees cooler under the towering branches and there is a scuffed track of tiny animal paw prints in the dirt.

I walk along for a while, busy longing for that bucket of chocolate from the supermarket. I'm lost in my own cravings when I realise I can hear voices up ahead. I'm not sure if it's human instinct or my own conniving nature that makes me duck and creep from tree to tree until I can see where the sounds are coming from.

The sight is so surprising that I struggle not to gasp.

It was only a few hours ago that Scott had Brad by the throat down on the beach – but now they're chatting and smiling away as if they're long-lost best friends.

CHAPTER TEN

Brad and Scott are standing close to the border where the trees open out onto the rows of caravans. They're speaking quietly and the breeze only lets me hear the sound of their voices – the words are too hard to make out.

Scott is the taller and bigger of the two but the way they're talking makes it look like they're on an equal footing. After a few seconds, Scott taps Brad on the shoulder, Brad laughs at something and then they seem to shake hands. It's hard to tell from the angle – and it happens so quickly – but it looks as if they have exchanged something. Brad instantly tucks a hand into his pocket and then withdraws it. He says something more to Scott and then they go their separate ways. Brad strolls towards the caravans; Scott strides into the woods, heading towards the village – and me.

At first, I press against the tree behind which I'm hiding. I hold my breath – but then change my mind, stepping out and deliberately stamping on a crumbling dry twig. It has the effect I wanted, with Scott turning to stare through the trees until he focuses on me. We lock eyes and there's no way I'm going to crack first. I say nothing, simply returning the stare he's giving me. It feels dangerous, even if I'm not quite sure what it all means.

I'm not sure how long we stay like that. It could be a couple of seconds but it could be far longer.

Scott turns first, his features creased into a confused frown. He bounds away into the woods, not bothering to look back. I continue to watch until he's out of view, then turn towards the caravans.

Brad is nowhere in sight but, as I cross the border, I spot a gravel track that runs along the hedge surrounding the field. I don't bother stopping at the caravans, instead following the path up to the tree.

The lightning tree is even eerier close up. There's a circle of grass surrounding it that's stained darker than the rest of the lawn. The bark higher up the tree is blackened and dead, the bottom crispy and dry. I have no idea how long ago lightning struck, but there seems to be a charcoal, smoky smell about the place – although this could, admittedly, be my imagination.

Ebony was right that there's reception up here. My phone blinks from nothing to three full, glorious bars. I can't help but think of some of the girls with whom I used to go to school. The idea of not being in constant social media contact with people they hate with every morsel of their beings would drive them to despair.

I give it a couple of minutes, but it quickly becomes apparent that I have no texts, no direct messages and nothing on WhatsApp. There are two missed calls from the solicitor dealing with my parents' affairs but the last thing I want to do is get into another twenty-minute probate conversation. I delete the voice-mails without listening to them and repocket my phone.

This time, I head back to the cottage through the woods. Despite there being no marked path, it's easy enough to follow the gentle slope downhill until I emerge in the clearing at the back of my bedroom. If the beach kids use this route as the quickest way to the beach, it would perhaps explain the footprints Chloe and I found after returning from the supermarket.

I'm about to head inside when a different idea occurs to me. I cross to the second, smaller path which Luke told me he lives two minutes along. He was wrong about that – it takes more like five minutes to get to his place. The trail is well marked with more white spots on trees and I emerge into a second clearing with a cottage at the centre. It's strikingly similar to ours, with its thick beams and low roof. So much so that I turn to double-check that I've not somehow walked in a giant circle. It's only when I realise my car isn't outside that I convince myself it's *not* our cottage. This one is more remote, only accessible on foot.

I knock hard on the door and wait, initially assuming Luke's still on the beach, but then the door creaks open.

Luke is standing there, wearing only a pair of boxer shorts. A red plastic bowl is in his hand and he's eating cereal from it with a matching red plastic spoon. He has the spaced-out, crooked-eyed gaze of someone who's only recently finished a joint.

'Meg!' he says.

'It's Megan.'

He waves his free hand. 'Yeah, Megan. Come in.'

Luke gulps down a mouthful of Weetabix and I'm silently disappointed that it's not something unhealthier. One of the girls in my school dorm used to hoard those mini boxes of cereal in her dresser. The type of thing only bought by hotel chains or people who can't make up their mind about what they like. She'd have them as late-night snacks and, after lights out, I'd creep across to the bin. I kept the flattened empty boxes of Coco Pops between the pages of my textbooks.

I follow Luke into the cottage. As with ours, the front door leads directly into the kitchen. There's no massive table in here; not much of anything, really. Luke flops into a foldable deck chair next to the sink and puts his feet up on a milk crate. He nods to another, identical chair and I press back into it, not feeling entirely at ease with the sparse setup. This cottage is deeper into the woods. The shadows are longer and darker and there's little natural light creeping through the kitchen window.

Luke seems unaffected by the gloom of our surrounding. He continues to munch on his cereal.

'Want some?' he asks.

'I'm good.'

''Lectric only works in here,' he says, indicating the kitchen, as if answering my unasked question about the gloom.

'Good job it's light until ten o'clock.'

'I know, right?'

I look around the room and notice a red plastic plate on the side, covered in crumbs. 'Are all your plates and bowls made of plastic?' I ask.

Luke gobbles down his final mouthful and then tosses the plastic bowl into the sink, where it lands with an echoing thunk. 'Yep. Easier to clean,' he replies. 'Plus, they don't break when you drop them.' He yawns, leans back until he's almost upside-down and puts his feet up on the counter.

'Is the cottage yours?' I ask.

'Mum left it to me,' he says. 'She wanted me to have it.'

'How long ago?'

'Five years.'

I almost say, 'sorry' and then catch myself. I've spent months hearing half-arsed apologies.

Luke doesn't seem to expect anything. His neck muscles twitch and I see a touch of something close to embarrassment in his expression. He knows what I'm thinking: there's little chance this cottage would've been such a mess when his mother was alive. A few minutes down the path and the comparison is stark. No one has spent more than a few days at a time in our cottage for the past decade – but I assume my parents paid cleaners or caretakers to keep it in good stead. Luke's cottage has an ingrained, faint smell of marijuana. The type of undertone that can't be removed with mere cleaning. It's as much a part of the cottage as the walls or the chimney.

Luke gulps – an involuntary sound that makes me look sharply at him. He is avoiding my eyes and I'm suddenly struck by an unusual sense of melancholy. He's spent the five years since his mother died smoking cannabis and letting his home go to ruin. There *is* something sad about that.

It's probably because of that but I decide not to ask about his father or any other family. I won't even ask about the message on our path – and that was the whole reason for me coming: to find out if he'd seen anything.

'How'd you come to be a lifeguard?' I ask.

He shuffles his boxer shorts around, scratching at his inner thigh. 'Not qualified to do anything else, am I? Why would I want to? Summers in the village, days on the beach… Don't get better than that, does it?'

Luke says this without even the merest hint of irony.

Perhaps it's because of the crinkling, squeezing tug of my empty stomach, perhaps it's because of the sincerity in his voice, but I suddenly feel trapped. I'm in a dark cottage in the dark woods at the arse-end of nowhere. I'm with a man who has picnic chairs as furniture and who eats from plastic bowls with a plastic spoon.

Something inside me wonders if things *won't* get better than this.

I think of Chloe – of the fact that, for now, for this summer, it's me and her together. But she'll be back at school in a couple of months – and who knows what the future holds for her after that. University? Jobs? Travel? Without her, there's only me. And it's me that's the problem. It's me *on my own* that's the problem.

'So you used to come here as a kid?'

Luke's voice brings me blinking back into the room. I'm confused for a second, forgetting where I am. I can live with the hunger and the stomach pains. The headaches are manageable. The dizzy spells come and go. It is these moments of bewilderment that really scare me.

'Years ago?' Luke prompts.

'Once,' I reply. 'I only came here once before. Or I only re-member once. It might have been a couple of times. I think Chloe and I were here together during the summer that Zac went missing. He'd been here the whole summer, largely by himself. He came down after doing his exams. The rest of us came down later.'

'Why didn't you come down with your brother?'

'Too young: I was only ten; Chloe was six. We always went off to separate summer camps straight after school was done. We'd have only come down here for a short holiday towards the end of the summer.'

'Do you remember much…?'

'Flashes,' I say. 'I'll see a rock, or a sign and it seems sort of familiar. I don't remember much.'

Luke eyes me for a moment but then takes the hint that I don't want to talk about it. He drops his feet back to the floor. It's be-come darker in the few minutes we've been talking and I can only see half his face. I feel cold – but I wonder if that's just me. Luke's wearing only a pair of boxers and seems comfortable enough. The knots in my stomach keep tying and untying themselves. The tugs are so intense that it's as if my entire body is being com-pressed into my middle. I can usually control this feeling through sheer force of will, but right now, my body is betraying me.

'What about your parents?' Luke asks, apparently changing his mind about backing off – either that or he *didn't* take the hint.

'Huh?'

'If your brother was here and you and your sister were off at camps, where were they? What were they doing?'

'Working,' I reply. 'Socialising. Schmoozing. Sometimes I'd call from school and find out they'd gone to France for a week-end. I was never quite sure what they were up to.'

'What did they do for a living?'

'My mother didn't *do* anything.' I snap the reply and the fe-rocity surprises even me. I don't usually let my guard down this much. I hug my knees to my chest, trying to calm my stomach. The pain is throwing me off.

Luke doesn't seem to notice the intensity of my response. 'What about your dad?' he asks.

'My dad bought and sold antiques,' I say, more calmly.

This has been one of my get-out-of-conversations-free cards over the years. It's such a boring profession, so inaccessible to all but the dullest of the dull, that practically nobody has a follow-up question about it. The girls at school would witter on about their parents who were lawyers, bankers, CEOs, Members of Parliament, or whatever else – but thankfully, nobody was interested in hearing about my own mother and father. The only question they had – which was always asked silently and which I never answered – was: how could antiques pay my tuition fees?

I always thought of him as the man with the magic beans.

It's about faith. A magic bean is worth nothing unless the buyer believes it is. A wooden chair is just a wooden chair unless someone like my dad says it's worth a hundred grand. My father's greatest skill was in moving in circles with men – for it was always men – who believed what he said to be true. That doesn't mean I think he was a con artist – though I wouldn't rule it out. It simply means that I don't believe any old bit of tat is worth what certain people choose to pay for it.

Not that I complained about that when my allowance came through every month. Not that I'm complaining now.

Predictably, the insipidness of my father's job kills off the conversation with Luke about my family. He sighs, kicks his legs, stretches high and changes the subject. 'Winters aren't so fun here,' he says.

'In what way?'

'It gets cold. Sometimes the power goes off completely. I have to go down to the pub, where it's warmer.'

'I can think of worse places to spend a winter than in the pub.'

He laughs humourlessly and then opens the drawer under the sink, pulling out a pre-rolled cigarette.

'Want one?' he asks.

'What's in it?'

He winks with the eye that's in the light. 'What do you think?'

If it was tobacco, I'd go with it, it might calm my stomach, but marijuana has never been for me. It's supposed to relax a person but, for me, it does the opposite. The food cravings are too much. I need to be on the precipice of hunger, where I can manage things. I need to stand on the edge of the cliff, enjoy the sensation and control of not going over. Of not giving in.

It's power.

But, with marijuana, the hunger becomes too much and I always, without fail, give in and gorge myself with food. That loss of control creates such a burning anxiety that it can take me hours or days to regain jurisdiction over my own body.

'I should probably go,' I say, pushing myself up from the chair.

Luke stands too. He hasn't lit the joint. 'Oh… You don't have to.'

'I need to check on Chloe.'

'You'll come back, though? Bring your sister. I'll cook for us all.'

I look around his meagre kitchen, eye the pile of plastic plates in the sink.

'It'll be good,' he adds. 'Honestly. I can cook. Promise. I'll show you a bit of Whitecliff hospitality.'

I picture the 'Go Home' message and wonder if I've already experienced that 'hospitality'.

I want to say no to his offer – and not only because eating in front of people who aren't Chloe is something I never do. The truth is that I simply don't want to come here again. This dank and dirty cottage depresses me.

But I can't quite bring myself to refuse him. There's something about Luke that's so damned pathetic. I'm many things to many people: the catty put-downs, the dark thoughts and vicious remarks. The outright meanness of some of the things I've done.

Y'know, Megan, you can be a real bitch sometimes. I don't know where you get it from.

But I've never quite been able to go the whole way. Knocking people off perches drives me but kicking someone who's already on their knees does nothing.

'My sister's a vegan,' I reply. This is a convenient get-out for me when trying to avoid social situations. I always feel bad for using it, mainly because Chloe is so earnest about it. She's passionate about animal welfare and saving the world.

Luke breezes right past the hurdle anyway. 'That's fine,' he says. 'I can cook something she'll like. Honest.'

I cross to the front door and open it. This one doesn't stick.

'I'll let you know,' I say.

It's better than an outright 'no' – and it's still not a 'yes'.

'See you around,' I add.

'Be safe,' he replies.

It's not until I'm back at our own cottage until I realise what a weird thing that was for him to say.

CHAPTER ELEVEN

Chloe isn't at the cottage, so I head down the trail to the village, where I find her outside the gallery. She's happy, telling me that Arthur has given her some good tips to help with her art. I go with it, allowing myself to be a little bit mumsy with lines like, 'that's good' and 'how kind of him'.

'I'm hungry,' she says, then. 'I don't want to wait for the barbecue.'

The thought of climbing the hill back to the cottage appeals to neither of us, so Chloe decides that chips from the pub will do for now. My stomach growls dangerously. I wonder if the stench of Luke's cottage has tricked my body into somehow feeling as though I've been smoking the same stuff he has.

Walking into the pub feels like an old-fashioned saloon scene from a Western. The heavy door bangs shut behind us and it's as if everything stops momentarily. Heads turn; mouths hang open. We're a pair of outsiders in a foreign land. If there were a piano playing, the music would have paused mid-tune.

Chloe feels it, too. Her bouncy enthusiasm from spending time at the gallery dissipates; her shoulders drop. My sister wears who she is like a transparent dress. Anyone can see what's going on under the surface: there's little filter or mask.

'I'll find us somewhere to sit,' she tells me, even though the place is largely empty and no seat-saving is needed. It's no surprise when she scuffs her way across to a darkened booth near the back of the pub. She wants to be liked and those staring eyes are providing anything but that.

The barman is a big bloke, the type of figure that would be expected to run a pub in the middle of nowhere. He's got the pockmarks of someone who's seen the odd rumble in his time and the meaty, hairy fingers of a man who's no stranger to hard work.

I have not spoken a word before he slaps a hand down on the bar in front of me.

'You must be the Smart girl,' he says. 'I knew your parents. Heard all about what happened to 'em. Poor sods. You have my condolences.'

He bows his head, showing off a bald spot that's in danger of engulfing the rest of his hair. Something about him seems familiar – but it's hard to put my finger on exactly what. The twinges of déjà vu I've had from the village and beach are becoming one with the ache in my stomach. I'm not sure what's what any longer.

'Megan,' I say.

'Pete,' he replies. 'Pete Chandler.'

This rings a bell. 'I've seen that name somewhere.'

He throws his head back and laughs, showing off a pair of missing teeth. The rest are yellow. 'Aye – prob'ly on one of the fishing boats. You might've met my son.'

He nods to the corner of the room, where I now notice that Hairy Back is sitting with a woman.

'That's Scott and his wife, Chrissie.'

I'd not noticed him when we entered the pub – but Scott has certainly spotted me. It's only now that I remember Vee has already told me that Hairy Back was the pub owner's son. Scott is still in his vest from earlier but his hairy shoulders and arms make it look like he's wearing long sleeves. Chrissie is like a child's doll next to him. She's slender and petite, with mousy dark-blonde hair. Scott's staring across the bar at me but Chrissie's almost hiding behind his arm, her eyes fixed on the floor. They couldn't be more different.

'He's a grumpy sod,' Pete adds. 'Always has been.'

Father and son look at one another and Scott cracks first, twisting away from the bar and muttering something to Chrissie.

Pete has apparently not noticed any tension and turns back to me. 'Your mum and dad used to come in here a fair bit back in the day,' he says.

'Did they?'

'Aye. Good customers. Your dad liked a bit of the strong stuff.' Pete taps one of the bar pumps. 'What can I do yer for?'

'What oil do you cook your chips in?'

He stares at me as if I've thrown a physics equation in his direction. '*Oil?*'

'My sister's vegan. She'll only eat them if it's sunflower or vegetable oil.'

He scratches his chin, utterly bewildered. Evidently, veganism has not hit this part of the country. 'Vegetable oil,' he says.

'Great. Can I have a Coke, a fizzy water and a bowl of chips, please?'

His eyebrow twitches slightly. 'Sure you don't want anything stronger?'

'Chloe's only sixteen.'

Pete glances past me towards the booth at the back. He doesn't say anything specifically, but there's the slightest of shrugs to suggest that such a thing wouldn't necessarily stop her from getting served.

'We're fine with just that,' I say.

He gives a '*suit yourself*' raise of the eyebrows and then disappears through a door, where I hear him shouting, 'Chips!' to someone. He returns and pours our drinks into old-fashioned thick bar glasses with handles and dimples.

'How much?' I ask.

'On me,' he replies. 'Respec' for yer parents, like.'

'Are you sure?'

'Aye. I heard what happened to 'em. Tragedy.'

So I keep being told…

I pick the first glass up, underestimating how much it will weigh. It's like lifting something made from real gold. Not necessarily heavy as such, more surprising for its size.

'How long are you staying in Whitecliff?' he asks.

I put the glass back down and lean on one of the bar stools. 'People keep asking us that,' I reply.

Pete acts like he hasn't heard, flicking away a speck of dust from the bar and offering a grunted, 'Huh?'

'I'm not sure. I've got a few things to sort out at the cottage, plus this is a bit of a break for Chloe and me. It's been a hectic few months.'

Pete nods acceptingly and I decide that if he can ask a nosy question, then so can I. 'What's the deal with the fishing boats?'

'How'd yer mean?'

'Running a pub and running a fishing business doesn't seem to go naturally together?'

Pete leans back slightly, as if this has never occurred to him before.

'Fishing's a family thing,' he replies. 'From my dad. From his dad. Was never my thing, truth be told. My lad's more into it than me. He likes the sea.' He pauses, glancing across to Scott and lowering his voice slightly. 'Business is on its arse.'

'Fishing?'

'Everything.'

A pair of men take up stools nearby and Pete looks across to them. They mutter something I don't catch. It's only when Pete replies that I realise they're talking a different language. One of the men glances over the other's shoulders to me and the three of them laugh, then Pete starts to pump glasses of ale. The veins in his beefy forearms pop as he wrenches the handle down, sending spurts of light, frothy liquid into each glass.

'Cornish,' he says, turning to me, answering my unspoken question.

'Oh.'

I'm not quite sure what to make of it. My mother would glare at anyone who dared to speak anything other than English in her presence. On the rare occasions that I was invited to France with my parents, I'd spend large parts of the afternoons listening to my mother complaining about the attitude of the local villagers.

I know they can speak English, she'd say, *but they choose not to. It's so rude. Such a rude people. Can you believe it, Megan? Can you? So rude.*

Unlike my mother, I'm not usually the type of Little Englander who is consumed by paranoid delusions that anyone speaking anything other than English must be talking about me. But as Pete slips from English back to Cornish and continues talking to the men, I'm filled by an overwhelming sense that they *are* discussing Chloe and myself.

They laugh again and I feel really small.

Perhaps Pete senses this, because he turns back to me and smiles. 'If you need anything, feel free to drop in,' he says. 'Even after-hours. I'll only be upstairs. Knock and come in; the doors are rarely locked. Shout on up. You might need a hand at some point – sometimes the power goes out up on the hill. That sort of thing.'

'Thank you.'

'You're welcome, young lady.'

I turn to head to the booth and then I turn back, spilling the words out before I can stop myself: 'Someone wrote "GO HOME" on our path,' I say.

Pete squints at me, curves his lips into a pouty 'O'. 'When?'

'Sometime today, while we were at the beach.'

His unkempt eyebrows meet in the middle of his creased forehead. 'They can be an awkward lot round here. Want yer money; don't want you.' He glances around the bar, as if indicating the exact kind of people he means. 'Wouldn't read too much into it if I were you. You get any trouble, you come straight to me. I'll put 'em right.'

Something within me tingles at the idea of that. I've seen Pete's son trying to put Brad 'right' on the beach with his hand around the smaller lad's throat. Pete is even bigger than Scott. He could definitely do some damage.

'How long have you been in the village?' I ask.

'Forever. My dad. His dad. His dad, too. There've been Chandlers in the books around here as long as records go back.' He stands tall with pride, chest puffed out.

'Do you remember my brother?' I ask. 'He went missing ten years ago?'

Pete glances to the pair of men at the bar, who are silently eavesdropping.

'Aye, I remember,' he says. 'Ten years already, eh?' He snaps his fingers. 'Like that.'

'What do you think happened to him?'

Pete takes his time in answering. He sucks on his teeth, looking directly at me in the way so few people do. It's rare that people actually listen to what's being said. They want to turn conversations around to their own interests or suggestions. In this moment, it actually feels as if Pete's trying to come up with the best answer he can.

'Don't know,' he says. 'I'd tell yer if I did. I didn't really know him.'

I nod in thanks and am about to turn away before I remember something.

'Do you know who the initials "CA" might belong to?' I ask.

'C-A?'

'Right.'

He pouts out his lip and shakes his head. 'No idea. Should I?'

'I guess not.'

I pick up both drinks and cross the pub, slotting into the booth next to Chloe. It amazes me that she can drink the full-sugar Coke. If I did, I'd be tripping for the rest of the night. Chloe asks what we were talking about at the bar and I tell her in a not-telling-her kind of way. I mention that Pete was friends with our parents and more or less leave it at that.

It's only a minute or two until someone emerges from the kitchen with our chips. He puts the bowl on the table between us and points us towards the knives and forks over by the bar.

Chloe's quiet and I'm not in the mood to make small-talk, so we sit in relative silence. She starts to play a game on her phone. I relax into the soft backing of the chair and take in the rest of the pub. There are a dozen or so local faces dotted around in twos and threes. The interior is basic. No pool table or television, no posters on the wall. It's a surprise Pete's made a concession to serve food.

'You not eating?' Chloe slides the bowl of chips closer to me. They're thick-cut and covered with so much salt that I can see the speckles at arm's length. I hesitate but then grab one with my fingers and blow to cool it down.

'I had a packet of crisps earlier,' I say.

'Good.'

It's only one chip. There's nothing to it, really. Potato, salt and oil. Nothing complicated. Perhaps thirty calories. A gram or two of carbs.

I nibble the end and then devour the rest in one, chewing and chewing until there's nothing left. The salt leaves a bitter aftertaste that I try – and fail – to wash away with the fizzy water. My stomach lurches angrily, but I breathe in through my nose, forcing the faint sense of sickness away.

I eat carbs for Chloe. That's how much I love her.

'Be right back,' I say, standing and moving away from the food. I'm still in control. I have the power here and that gives me confidence as I cross the pub, heading for Scott and his wife in the corner.

'Hi,' I say.

He looks up to me, eyes darting side to side with surprise.

'I'm Megan Smart,' I add. 'I'm living in my parents' cottage up on the hill. I wanted to introduce myself.'

I offer him my hand and perhaps because he's in shock, or perhaps because his dad is only a short distance away, Scott takes it and shakes. I also swap a handshake with Chrissie, although she never quite lifts her gaze from the floor.

'My brother went missing ten years ago,' I say. 'His name was Zac. I think you were about the same age. I was wondering if you knew him?'

Power is a strange thing that can come from so many places. I know I'm never going to hold physical power over anyone but that's not necessarily a problem.

There's wealth, I suppose – but money is only power if people allow it to be. A person can buy an expensive car but the best weapon against that is indifference. If they've bought it for themselves, then it's not a problem. If they've bought it show off and are met with a 'so what?' shrug, or a 'who cares' eye-roll, then it's worthless.

Confidence can be power and I feel it now. Scott picks up his half-filled pint glass, holding it between us like a shield. He fidgets in the chair, speaking too quickly:

'I don't know nuffink.'

'I'm not saying you do, it's just—'

'I didn't know 'im.'

'It's just that there was a big search and so on. If you were fifteen or sixteen at the time, around his age, then I thought you might—'

'You deaf?'

Scott's reply is a conversation-ender. A verbal punch to the face.

I glance at Chrissie but she's still staring at her feet.

'Sorry,' I say. 'My mistake. No offence meant.'

I turn and amble back to my table, feeling the stares of both Pete and Scott on me. I'm not entirely sure what just happened.

'Still making friends?' Chloe asks sarcastically.

'Something like that,' I reply.

CHAPTER TWELVE

The bonfire is already burning as Chloe and I head along the beach from the pub. The sun is starting to set but it's a long process at this time of the year. An ageing singer going through the third encore, not realising it's time to leave.

The purple-orange glow of the sky casts everything in a vibrant haze. A hum of music and voices drifts on the gentle evening breeze. The tide is in but there's still a vast patch of sand where the water is yet to touch.

We're within shouting distance of the beach kids when I clamp a hand on Chloe's wrist and we stop. This evening feels importantly inconsequential.

'You can be whoever you want to be tonight,' I tell her.

Chloe looks up to me and in that moment, she seems so young. 'Huh?' she says.

'None of these people know you or me,' I explain. 'They don't know what you are like at school, who you are as a person. If you act confidently, they'll think you're confident. It doesn't matter if you're scared or nervous inside. Nobody will know that. You can be a new person.'

She looks back at me, her eyes narrow. I can see that she gets it – but we don't usually have these sorts of conversations. It's not what our family does. We don't do earnest; we do mopey silences.

There's the old saying – 'it's what's inside that counts' – but that's nonsense. What's inside is irrelevant: it's what you show others on the outside that matters. You might be quiet, nervous and timid on the inside but if you march on up to a bunch of snooty-nosed cows and tell them what you think of them, that's all that gets remembered.

'I'm fine,' Chloe says.

'I'm just saying. We're here to get away from our normal lives. From London, from boarding school, from university, from whatever. From all the people who know us. No one's going to judge you here. Definitely not me. If things don't work out, we can go home and no one will ever care. It's not like we have to come back.'

Chloe bites her lip and looks past me towards the beach kids. 'I know,' she says quietly.

It's then that Brad notices us. He's in long linen trousers and a loose shirt. Hippy chic. He waves us over to the fire and I leave Chloe to her own devices. She gets little choice as to where she sits anyway, because Popcorn shoots out from the circle of people and launches himself at her feet. Chloe crouches and picks him up. The little dog's tail is flashing back and forth like a windscreen wiper on full pelt. He licks her face as she carries him back towards Mia, Brad, Ebony and George.

There are a little more than a dozen beach kids here in all, with no sign of Vee or any of the other locals. The fire is small but the flames are dancing high. Everyone is dotted in small groups around the burning wood and it feels like a cosy gathering of friends rather than anything sinister, as Vee seemed to suggest.

I find my own spot on the sand. The gurgles from my stomach have largely sorted themselves out. It might have been the single salty chip that quieted them but I prefer to think it was my willpower.

George is busy playing his damned guitar, though I can't pick the tune. If he starts singing I might actually throw the thing in the fire. I catch the eye of one of the girls – Sophie or Sonia, something with an 'S' – and she raises her eyebrows. We're sisters-in-arms for a moment and she holds up a large bottle of vodka, waggling it back and forth.

Usually I'd resist but tonight I have a strange desire to be accepted. The girl rolls the bottle across the sand to me and I wipe it down before unscrewing the lid. The alcohol is going to be hell for my nearly empty stomach but there are times when I crave precisely that.

I hold the first gulp in my mouth, waiting and waiting, letting it burn the back of my tongue as if it's stripping paint from a wall. When I swallow, I can feel the fire as it swills its way down to my stomach.

The second gulp is stronger than the first, as if I'm swallowing razor blades.

When I hold the bottle up in the air, Sophie or Sonia shakes her head, indicating another by her feet. Around the circle, everyone is suitably lubricated. There are four-packs of lager and cider, plus large bottles of vodka, gin and rum. The beach kids are all roughly clumped in small groups, but I'm by myself and, for now, I'm fine with that.

The sun is even lower now, dipping over the corner of the cliff as the orange blaze spreads wider across the sky. The moon is out and so are the stars. It's like staring up at the cover of a sci-fi novel.

I wonder if this is how Zac spent his last summer here. Friends, music and laughter. A bit of harmless underage drinking. With Chloe and myself at school and our parents off doing who knows what, did he spend his days on the beach? Did he sit around night-time campfires and pass around bottles of spirits? Flirting with 'CA'? Was it one of those intense holiday romances in which it feels like the world might end when the summer does? He was sixteen – was CA his first girlfriend?

I'm assuming *girl*friend. It's not like I'd know for sure.

Without warning, someone plops down next to me and I turn to see Luke. He's got a T-shirt on now – thankfully – though he's only wearing swim shorts and flip-flops with it.

''Ello, stranger,' he says.

I pass him the vodka bottle but he shakes his head, stretching for a carrier bag and tugging out a can of Strongbow. He digs into one of his swim short pockets and passes me a cigarette. I start to wave it away.

'It's a regular one,' he says. 'No funny stuff. I rolled it just for you.'

I take it, partly out of politeness. He lights it for me, watching as I suck hard on the tobacco, holding the smoke in my mouth. When I breathe it out, I'm starting to feel light-headed.

'I thought you might turn it down,' he says. 'Tell me that they'll kill you.'

'Everything kills you in the end,' I reply.

We sit quietly for a minute or two. George has thankfully put the guitar down and someone's playing music from their phone via a Bluetooth speaker instead. I still don't recognise the tune. It's poppy and bouncy. Two of the girls are dancing with each other. Their dark silhouettes are illuminated by the flickering flames, their slender bodies pressed closely together. They're each wearing skimpy bikinis and they know they're putting on a show. They have their arms high, hips swaying.

Luke is staring at the girls – although, in fairness, so am I. 'Enjoying yourself?' I ask.

'Not my type,' he says.

'What *is* your type?'

'Whatever's available.'

I glance sideways and his teeth flash brightly in the fading light.

'Just joking,' he adds, even though I don't think he is.

The song ends and the two girls return to their blanket, picking up some gin and taking it in turns to drink from the bottle.

'Your sister's enjoying herself.'

I'd forgotten to watch her but, at Luke's prompting, I peer around the fire to Chloe's group. Popcorn is sleeping on her feet and Chloe is busy giggling at something either Brad or George have said. Ebony and Mia are laughing, too. The five of them look like lifelong friends. There's a can of Carlsberg in Chloe's hand and the image of my laughing, happy, tipsy sister is so unfamiliar that I almost can't believe it's her.

'How old is she?' Luke asks.

'Does it matter?'

'Not to me.'

I wait for a beat. 'Seventeen tomorrow,' I say. 'In two hours or so, I guess. She didn't want me to tell everyone it's her birthday.'

'Why not?'

'She's usually really shy.'

As I say that, Chloe's head rocks back with amusement. Brad pats her knee, holding it there for a second too long.

Perhaps I'm seeing things.

The combination of the vodka and the cigarette is making me giddy and I'm not sure if that's a good thing. I have another swallow of vodka anyway, holding it my mouth once more. Waiting for it to burn. To hurt. I finish the rest of the cigarette and flick the butt into the fire. It spins and fizzes, disappearing among the rest of the flames.

I realise I've closed my eyes. When I open them again, Luke has shuffled nearer. He's close enough that I can feel the heat from his body creeping across the gap between us.

'You cold?' he asks.

'No.'

His knee touches mine anyway and then he stretches out an arm, pressing it down onto the sand behind me to support himself as he leans closer. I turn to face him and the orange of the fire flashes across the face, making it look as if he's ablaze. His eyes spark red like a demon ascending from the depths.

'Has anyone ever told you how pretty you are?' he asks.

I turn away and bite back a laugh. 'Don't…'

'What?'

'I don't do chat-up lines.'

He leans a little closer and I can feel his breath on my neck. I stop anything more from happening by grabbing the vodka and gulping another mouthful. I don't hold it this time, simply swallowing it down. It doesn't burn but, when I drop the bottle onto the sand, my head spins.

My eyes have closed again and, when I open them, Luke's face is right in front of me. There's barely a couple of centimetres between us. He leans in, our noses rubbing together as he presses his lips to mine.

It's my decision and I decide to let it happen. His tongue slips into my mouth and I don't object. When his hand cups underneath my ear, I nuzzle into him.

The kiss doesn't last for long before he pulls away. I have another swallow of vodka and when he tries to kiss me a second time, I shake my head. He frowns in confusion.

'Did I do something wrong?' he asks.

'Not you,' I reply.

I can feel him wanting more of an explanation but I'm not sure I have an answer.

There's a moment in which I forget everything that happened to my parents and instead picture the outraged fury of my mother if she found out I was roughing it with some village yokel – as opposed to getting myself felt up by some nephew of a cabinet minister. If she was still around – *especially* if she was here in Whitecliff – I'd have definitely let Luke do a lot more than just kiss me. I'd have sneaked off to the sand dunes with him, ensuring as many people as possible saw us go. He could have done literally anything he wanted to me and it would have been fine – as long as news of it got back to Mother.

'Why are you here?' I ask.

I only realise after I've said it how aggressive this sounds. 'I mean, because it's all beach kids,' I add quickly.

'I can get away with it,' he replies. 'Being a lifeguard. The locals think I'm an embedded spy; the beach kids think I'm one of them.'

'Which are you?'

'Bit of both. Neither. What about you?'

'Bit of both,' I say. 'Neither.'

Luke reaches forward and rests his hand on mine. I don't stop him.

'I've been doing some adding up,' he says.

'Two plus two?'

A laugh. 'You must be a millionaire,' he says. 'Whatever you've inherited, even between the two of you, it must make each of you millionaires?'

I take my hand back and scratch my chin, trying to make it look as if that's what I was going to do all the time. Trying to pretend he hasn't rattled me. I wonder if he's Googled me or my parents on some illicit Internet connection. I glance across to Chloe, who is drinking from her can of Carlsberg. I don't know if it's the same one as before, or if she's moved onto a second. Or third. She's stroking Popcorn's sleeping back and talking to Mia.

It's almost dark; the orange and purple of the sky are being replaced by the darkest of blues. Beyond my sister, out at sea, the shape of a fishing boat sails away from the port, its motor offering the gentlest of undercurrents to the noise from around the fire.

'Is that a Chandler boat?' I ask.

Luke turns from side to side, seemingly not seeing what I can see. 'Where?'

I point out to the ocean. 'There. You can see the lights.'

He angles forward. 'I guess so.'

'Why's it going out at night? Is that when they fish?'

Luke leans back, lying flat on the sand and staring up at the star-filled sky. 'No idea,' he says.

Thursday

CHAPTER THIRTEEN

When I wake up, I have the kind of headache that I know could incapacitate me for a day. The easy assumption is that it's down to the alcohol but I've awoken in this state too many times before: I know that it's not. This sort of thumping, searing pain can occur regardless of what I've had to drink the previous night. It's so intense, every movement makes the world swirl. Every thought feels like I'm wearing a swimming cap with drawing pins on the inside.

Perhaps the greatest thing my mother left behind – her enduring legacy in many ways – was the collection of prescription medicines in her bedroom dresser. I sent most of my parents' possessions to charity but squirrelled away every single bottle and tube from that drawer long before anyone else got to look there. I have no idea how she accumulated so much but the sheer range of painkillers, antidepressants, anti-inflammatories, anticonvulsants, slimming drugs and various creams she had would keep an entire pharmacy going for a couple of months. It'll keep me going for years.

I slip a tramadol from the side pocket of my bag, washing it down with an extra-strength paracetamol and an ibuprofen for good measure. The first time I did this, I Googled to make sure I wasn't going to accidentally overdose. I could kill myself a hundred times over with my stolen medication – but if I'm going to do that, I'd at least want to make sure it was on purpose.

It takes fifteen or twenty minutes before the fog starts to clear. The drums between my ears dim, leaving a faint euphoria from the drugs. The cocktail of pills used to make me woozier and I know enough to realise that I'm probably becoming accustomed to them. There's no time to think about that now, though. When I'm finally able to get up from the bed properly, I hunt for a Seroxat and swallow it just because I can. I'd never taken antidepressants before finding Mother's hidden treasure; now I can't imagine life without them.

It's not long after seven but the sun beams into the kitchen through the window and my bare feet can already feel the warmth on the tiled floor.

The oven isn't like the one at home, which can be started with a simple switch. With this, I have to open the door and practically climb inside to light the flame at the back. It takes almost ten minutes before I manage to get the fire to catch, by which time my face and palms are covered with a sooty shower of dark dust. I look like I've blacked up, which reminds me of a few Christmases ago, when my parents held the only fancy dress party they ever had. It was around the time that *12 Years A Slave* came out at the cinema and two separate couples thought it was hilarious to turn up at the party dressed as an owner with slave. One of them even had a leash around his neck.

After setting the hob going, I wash myself in the sink, fingering the bones in my cheeks and chin, pressing hard and scrubbing until my skin *feels* clean. It's not enough to simply *look* it.

I pop three veggie sausages in a pan, then cut the bread into thick slices and put them under the grill. After that, I empty half a tin of beans into a saucepan and set it to boil.

Perhaps it's the smell of the food cooking, or the sound of me clanking around, but Chloe emerges from her room, stretching and yawning. She looks across the kitchen through barely open eyes.

'Happy birthday,' I say, watching and grinning as she slumps onto a chair at the table.

'Ugh,' she groans, holding her head in her hands.

'Cans of European lager will do that to you,' I say.

'I'm never drinking again.'

'Everyone says that. I'm making you a birthday breakfast.'

She looks at me through her fingers. 'What is it?'

'Veggie sausages and Heinz beans on toast.'

Chloe sits up straighter. 'That sounds like the greatest meal ever invented.'

I laugh and then pull out the bread, flipping it over before returning it beneath the grill.

'Are you eating?' Chloe asks.

'Already did. Had some Marmite on toast before you got up.'

Maybe it's the hangover but Chloe doesn't question me further. I pour her some water and continue cooking while she rests her head against the wall and closes her eyes. She groans at intermittent intervals and I allow myself a little grin at her expense. We've all been there.

When everything's ready, I assemble Chloe's breakfast on the plate and then place it in front of her with a, 'Ta-da!'

'Do you want me to sing "Happy Birthday"?' I ask.

'I'll pay you not to.'

'How much?'

'Half of whatever Mum's car was worth.'

'Deal. I'll get onto the lawyer to sort out the paperwork.'

Chloe opens her eyes properly and picks up a fork. She grins wearily at me. 'Last night was fun,' she says.

'I thought you weren't ever going to drink again?'

'Changed my mind.'

'That was quick. The first time I gave up alcohol, I held out for almost forty-eight hours.'

'How old were you?'

'Never you mind.'

Each forkful is delivered achingly slowly to Chloe's lips but I don't miss a single one. It's as if I'm devouring the food with her.

I can't handle other people watching *me* eat but there's a delicious fascination in watching others. I love it when they shovel it all in with a furious blur of cutlery. Kids are the best at this – especially those with mothers who couldn't care less about manners. I've seen those piled-high plates at hotel breakfast buffets, where sweet and savoury are lumped together like forbidden lovers. Evening dos at weddings can be beautiful for this kind of thing, too, where the combination of free alcohol and food sends everyone a bit loopy, to the point that it's only a matter of time before someone's puking up in the toilets.

Other times, like now, I love it most when there's time enough for me to take a rough guess at how many calories are in every bite a person consumes.

I watch Chloe until she's finished, at which point she thanks me for cooking. I tell her she can thank me better by doing the washing-up. She plays the, 'it's my birthday' trump card, so I do it anyway – as I was always going to.

When everything's cleaned up, I join Chloe on the sofa, which is against the back wall of the kitchen. She's hugging her knees tight to her chest, her eyes closed.

'I got you presents,' I say.

'What are they?'

'That's the whole point of opening them. You get to find out.'

I reach under the sofa and pull out four separate boxes. Chloe's eyes sparkle as she reaches for the first. She tries to dig her fingers into the corner but fails. She flips it around and tries again from a different angle.

'How much tape did you use?'

'It's no fun if you can just open it.'

Chloe keeps spinning the present, thrusting her nails into the folds but never quite able to pick one apart – even though she has proper nails, not like my bitten husks. I get the scissors from the kitchen drawer and then watch as she cuts free a vegan baking book, some paints, coloured pencils and a new set of wireless headphones.

'I've never baked anything in my life,' she says as she flips through the colourful pages of cakes and cookies.

'I'm training you up to be a proper little housewife,' I say.

'Good luck.'

She sits and continues flicking through the pages. I do sometimes wonder – perhaps *hope* – that Chloe turned vegan simply to annoy our mother. If I'd thought of it first, I'd have definitely done it. Good on her, if that's the real reason.

Chloe came out as vegan to the family a couple of summers ago. It was a weekend when we'd both been trotted out for someone's wedding. Mother had ordered in her own stylist to sort out our hair and make-up and had bribed us with the promise of a double allowance if we did everything she said. It was the usual scene: big church, then a massive golf club in the middle of nowhere. Loads of people wearing expensive clothes and jewellery. I had to be all curtseys, cheek kisses and remaining quiet as my parents' grubby male friends eyed my meagre cleavage. Chloe's wasn't off-limits, either – and she was fourteen at the time.

When it came to the wedding breakfast, Chloe refused to eat the starter – or any of the other courses – announcing to the entire table that she had turned vegan. Mother looked at her as if she'd told everyone she was pregnant, gay, or dating an Indian guy. It could only have been worse if she'd said she was pregnant *by* a gay Indian guy.

Afterwards, Mother packed Chloe back off to summer camp, saying she'd spoiled the entire weekend for everyone. That night, I texted my sister emojis of every single vegetable. She became my hero.

Chloe lifts herself off the sofa now and crosses to a painting on the wall of the kitchen. It's a print of a hayfield – definitely not an original. It's hanging at a slight angle. Chloe straightens it and then takes a step back, tilting her head to make sure it's right.

'Don't go all OCD on me,' I say.

Chloe grins but then the painting slips to one side again. She tucks her fingers underneath the frame and lifts it off the wall, then gasps.

'Ohmygod,' she says, all one word.

I blink, wondering for a second if the drugs have hit me too hard. I stand and move to Chloe's side. It's only as I run my hand across the smooth metal that I convince myself it's actually there.

There's a safe set back in the wall. A safe with a ten-digit button-panel on the front, along with a digital screen.

'What do you think's inside?' Chloe asks. She's wide awake now. Excited.

'A severed human head,' I reply.

She slaps me with the back of her hand. 'Don't be silly.'

She stretches forward and types 1-2-3-4 into the panel. Nothing happens, so she adds 5-6 to the end. There's a low beep, a red flashing dot and then nothing. She tries 6-5-4-3-2-1 next but gets a similarly disapproving red dot.

'Well, I'm out of ideas,' she says.

'Try your birthday.'

Chloe tries it. Two-digit day, two-digit month, two-digit year. Nothing. She tries my birthday next, but if that had worked, I'd have *known* the drugs were making me hallucinate.

Mother's birthday doesn't work, nor does Father's. I have a momentary buzz of excitement when I think it could be Zac's birthday – but keying in those digits gets an identical beep and dot of denial.

'It probably contains receipts and stuff,' Chloe says, losing interest. She heads back to the sofa and rubs her head. 'You know what they were like.'

I *do* know what our parents were like. I know what their friends were like. I was at some of the lavish parties they threw and attended. I know how much it costs to spend a month in a villa in the south of France at peak season. I've seen photos of them on yachts in Monaco. I know what the house and cars were worth. I know how much money was in their various investment portfolios when they died. I know that the solicitor has questions about money that can never be resolved, because the people with the answers died at the side of the road somewhere north of Sevenoaks.

And it's precisely that which makes me curious to know what's inside the safe that's hidden away in the cottage that they owned in the middle of nowhere. The cottage they only visited once or twice a year and in which they hadn't spent any significant time for a decade.

I try a few more safe combinations while Chloe neatly folds the wrapping paper and puts it into the kitchen bin. I try something relating to our house number, then our parents' wedding anniversary – but nothing works.

'I'm going up to the cliffs again,' Chloe says. 'I'll use my new paints. Thank you.' She pauses. 'What are you going to do today?'

'I've not decided yet,' I say, keying in another combination. 'Perhaps start to put some things in boxes. I'm not sure there's anything here that's worth keeping.'

Chloe glances towards the safe. 'Don't spend all day on that.'

'I wasn't going to,' I reply. Too quickly. Too defensively. Sometimes it scares me when she says things like this. I don't like the idea that someone, *anyone*, knows me in such a way.

'I know,' Chloe says. 'I was just saying…'

I return the painting to the wall as if to emphasise my point. It slips instantly to the side and I stare at it, wondering if there's some sort of clue hidden in plain sight. If there is, then I can't see it.

It takes her twenty minutes but Chloe gets her things together and heads out of the cottage with a cheery, 'See ya!' After she's gone, it takes some serious levels of self-control not to pull the painting from the wall again and spend the entire day typing in codes. It's only when I realise there are a million possible combinations that I limit myself to a few hundred guesses, starting with 0-0-0-0-0-1 and moving upwards. Before I know it, more than an hour has gone by.

I tear myself away from the safe, get dressed, lock up and scuff my way down the path to the village. The pub is closed and the beach is nearly empty. The ashes and smouldering wood from our bonfire have been cleared; there's no sign we were there the previous night. Either Brad and his friends are exceptionally good at picking up after themselves, or people from the village have done it on their behalf.

The cobbled streets are deserted and there's an eerie hush that's punctuated only by the faint wash of the waves.

The door to Arkwright's creaks as I head inside. Gwen watches me like a starving hawk in the middle of winter. She's in the same cardigan as the other day, bundled up toasty warm ahead of what's forecast to be one of the hottest days of the year. The spinning rack of postcards is next to her on the counter. I glance at the one I received from 'Z' as I walk past.

'May I ask you something?' I say, courteously.

My polite voice is something that I learned through Mother's outright hostility towards me. Before I was old enough to go to school, she would say things like, 'Don't take that tone with me', if I spoke in any way other than with perfectly prim politeness. If I dared to use anything she considered slang in the house, she'd give me the silent treatment. I cared in those days. I did whatever she wanted in an attempt to please her.

Gwen the shopkeeper boggles at my question as if I've asked whether she sells crack pipes. She doesn't quite say 'yes' but she does mumble a bemused, 'Uh-huh.'

I tell her my name and explain who my parents were. I've got this down now: name, sister, parents, cottage, decade, missing brother.

None of it seems like news to Gwen. If mobile phones worked anywhere near as well in Whitecliff as its grapevine does, then I'd have full reception.

'I was wondering if you remember my brother?' I ask.

Gwen's stony features remain unmoved, regardless of my politeness. 'Not really,' she says.

'Did you know my parents?'

'A bit.' Her eyes narrow nastily. 'They'd be *disgusted* by all this.'

I stare at her for a couple of seconds, wondering if I've heard correctly. 'All what?'

'You. Your sister.'

The hairs on the back of my neck stand up.

'I heard you all last night,' she adds. '*Saw* what was going on.'

'Saw what?'

'The drinking. The smoking. Everything else. This is *our* village. It's not Sodom or Gomorrah for you and your tawdry little friends.'

There's a second in which I wonder if she's joking. Then I see her hand trembling and I realise that she isn't. She actually thinks a few teenagers having some drinks on a beach might bring about divine retribution.

'I hardly drank anything,' I say. It's a pitiful response but I'm trying not to let the volcano erupt. I need to try to remain civil if I'm going to get her to help.

'I should report you to the authorities,' she hisses. I thought I was a good hisser, but this is something else. This is coiled cobra levels of righteous fury.

'For what?'

'That sister of yours. How old is she? Your parents would *never* have let this happen.'

And with that, the briefcase has been delivered and she's entered the nuclear codes.

I lean closer to her, baring my teeth. 'You don't know anything about my parents,' I say.

'Oh, don't I?'

'My *parents* wouldn't even notice how we spent our time. They were vacuous nobodies and we were trophy kids. My *parents* sent us to boarding school and camps to get us out of their way. Anything that meant we weren't around.'

Gwen grins, eyeing me up and down. 'I wonder why they did that?'

I swear, if it wasn't for my slightly doped-up senses, I'd throttle her with her own glasses chain. I'd watch her eyes bulge, the veins pop.

And I'd enjoy it.

'You're a nasty little girl, aren't you?' she taunts.

'I'm my mother's daughter.'

'I'll tell you something, young lady. You're not special. That Luke's had a different girl every summer for years.'

This leaves me temporarily speechless. How does she know about Luke? It's not as if he and I did anything other than share a single, short kiss. Was she spying from the shadows of the sand dunes? Or has word gone around the village so fast that last night's happenings are already common knowledge?

Then: 'Good for him,' I snarl. 'Why should men have all the fun? How many boys do you think *I've* had this summer? How many *girls*?'

I haven't been with anyone else but she's hardly to know that. The stunned look on her face almost makes the exchange worth it. She seems unsure whether to be angry, upset, confused, or a bit of everything. She steps back and lowers her eyes to the floor, turning slightly to the side.

'I think you should leave,' she says.

It's only now, with her face angled down, that I see the resemblance.

'Chrissie's your daughter,' I say, surprised. 'Scott's wife.'

'*Leave*,' she says, more forcefully this time.

I set the postcard rack spinning and do as she wants. I'm trembling now, the adrenalin rushing, blood pumping. It's not often I lose control like this, but my fury has at least gleaned one thing: Chrissie Chandler was once Chrissie Arkwright.

And ten years ago, it was ZS 4 CA.

CHAPTER FOURTEEN

After leaving the shop, I sit on the step of the gallery for a couple of minutes, waiting for the fire inside me to dim. I chew on my already short fingernails, wishing they'd grow faster. I tug so hard with my teeth that the some of the skin of my index finger detaches itself. A slim trickle of blood coils around the joint and I suck hungrily on it until the red has gone.

The village is still quiet, the beach empty except for a dog walker at the far end underneath the cliffs. The pub doors are closed. It's only the steepness of the hill that stops me returning to the cottage. Instead, I loop around the pub towards the docks, taking in the empty space where Scott's fishing boat was stationed when we first arrived. There is a second Chandler Fishing boat moored there now, older and rustier, plus an old-fashioned wooden boat bobbing up and down on the waves.

I'm not sure what I'm looking for – but then it's almost as if worlds have aligned when there's a creak of a door from the back of the pub. A fence surrounds the beer garden but the gate is low enough that I can see a yawning Chrissie emerge with a clothes basket. She places the basket on the path and then heads back into the pub, returning a moment later carrying a baby's car seat, which she places on the lawn. She crouches in front of the car seat, unclips the straps and then places a child on a blanket underneath the washing line.

Her hair is wet and she's wearing a dressing gown with fluffy slippers. She's humming softly, the delicate notes carrying across the garden to where I'm standing at the gate.

I call out, 'Hi!' and she shivers slightly, looking up from her washing to me and quickly turning away.

'Can I come in?' I ask.

She doesn't say yes, but she doesn't say no, either, so I open the gate and move across the garden.

'Do you want a hand?' I ask, indicating the washing basket.

'Um...'

'It's no bother.'

I pluck a pair of pegs from the holder next to the basket and then pick out a pair of jeans. After shaking them straight, I clip them onto the line.

'I'm Megan,' I say, ready to launch into the usual spiel. 'We met in the pub yesterday.'

Chrissie cuts me off with a quiet, 'I know.'

She picks up a pair of tights from the basket and starts pegging them to the line.

'Were your initials CA?' I ask. 'Chrissie Arkwright?'

It takes her a while to reply but then she whispers, 'It's Chandler now.'

'But your initials were CA ten years ago, weren't they?' I press. 'You knew my brother, Zac...?'

I wait but Chrissie doesn't answer, so I continue: 'I saw your initials in the caves. "ZS 4 CA"...'

Chrissie stops picking up clothes and stares down at the child, before glancing off towards the village, then the beach and the caves beyond. 'Zac did that,' she says. Her voice is barely distinguishable over the quiet lapping of the ocean.

'The carving in the caves?'

'In a few places.'

'Are they from the summer he disappeared?'

A nod. She opens her mouth but then closes it. She crouches and picks up the baby, cradling it into her shoulder.

'What's her name?' I ask, hoping the pink bonnet has given the gender away.

'Eden.'

'She's beautiful.'

That gets a smile. Praising other people's kids always does that. Or *almost* always. I'm not sure my mother would've been too bothered by it.

'Can you tell me about Zac?' I ask. 'I don't remember much. I was too young and didn't see him a lot.'

Chrissie glances nervously towards the back door of the pub and then the gate. I pin a vest to the line, as if it's perfectly normal for me to be putting up someone else's washing.

'I didn't know him that well, either,' she replies. 'Only that summer. A few weeks.'

'But he carved both of your initials into rock. He must have liked you a lot…?'

It takes her a few seconds to reply, as if one of us is in space and the signal is taking time to reach its destination.

'I suppose,' she says. 'It was a long time ago. We were the same age. It felt really… intense.'

'Intense, as in good?'

She smiles again. 'He was very sweet, but…'

Chrissie bites her lip and I let her comment sink in for a moment. It's hard to think of my brother as sweet. I guess I never knew him well enough. 'But what?' I ask.

'My mum didn't like him.'

'Why?'

She shrugs, staring past me towards the docks.

'Because he was a beach kid?' I prompt.

Chrissie nods ever so slightly.

'Was that the only reason?' I ask.

'She thought locals should stick to locals.'

Eden starts to fidget and Chrissie pats her back.

'How did you and Zac meet?' I ask quickly, fearing she might turn and head for the house.

'On the beach. The village kids didn't fight with the beach kids so much back then. Zac and I went for a walk along the sand one night. The moon was out… It was like in the movies. Special. I saw the village in a new way.'

A shiver whispers its way along my spine. It's haunting. Chrissie is still absent-mindedly patting Eden on the back, as if she's lost in the memory.

'What happened on the day he went missing?' I ask. 'What do you remember?'

Chrissie takes a breath, kisses Eden on the head and then returns her to the blanket.

'He'd been working on the boats during the day. Then—'

'Zac worked on the boats?'

Chrissie shrugs, as if this is information everyone knows. 'He'd been doing it all summer,' she says.

This is news to me. I've read the archived news reports from the time and there's no mention of Zac working on the boats. My parents never mentioned it to me either and it isn't something I remember – if I ever even knew about it.

'What did he do on the boats?' I ask.

'Fish. He would be up early, like five-ish. He'd go out on the boats all morning and then be back at lunch. We'd spend the afternoons and evenings together. We must've done that every day for five or six weeks. I stayed at the cottage some nights – not the weekends when your parents were down.' A grin creeps across her face: a real one, where the eyes crinkle and a person's entire features soften.

'I remember you,' she adds. 'From that summer.'

This takes me by surprise. 'Really?'

'Zac never said he had sisters and then, suddenly, you were both there. Your sister was all blonde and bright. The politest little girl I'd ever met. You were, um…'

I laugh. 'You can say it.'

Chrissie bites away the smile. 'You *weren't* the politest little girl.'

My laughter at this infects her and she chortles to herself as well. She clamps her teeth together quickly, shaking her head, making the laughter go away.

'Zac had been out fishing that morning,' she says. 'We spent the afternoon at Fisherman's Cave.'

'Where I saw your initials?'

'No, those are Whitecliff Caves. The famous ones that everyone knows.' She nods behind me, past the docks, in the opposite direction. 'Fisherman's Cave is that way. It's not on the maps. It's more of a local thing. Anyway, we'd come back from there and said goodbye at maybe five or six in the evening. We didn't go back to the cottage because you were staying there that night and he had to work anyway.'

'On the boats?'

'I guess.'

'I thought that was a morning thing?'

A shrug. 'I don't know. I didn't ask.'

'Do they fish at night?' I ask.

'I don't know.'

There's an edge to her voice this time, so I don't push it. I think of the Chandler boat I saw heading out under darkness last night. Luke didn't seem that bothered by it.

'Did he work for Scott?' I ask, forgetting for a moment that Scott is her husband – and that he would have been too young at the time to have been in charge of a fishing boat. The three of them – Zac, Chrissie and Scott – would have all been about the same age.

'He worked for Pete,' she says.

'Scott's dad? Who owns the pub?'

'Pete used to go out on the boats each morning,' Chrissie says. 'His own dad – Pete Senior – had not long bought the pub at that time.'

There's Pete, Pete and Scott – three generations. At the time of Zac's disappearance, the eldest Chandler was running the pub, the middle one was managing the fishing business and the youngest – Scott – was a teenager. In the pub last night, Pete told me that he remembered Zac but that he never really knew him. But they'd worked together on the boats for at least six weeks.

I wonder why Pete didn't tell me Zac went fishing with him. There's no way he could've forgotten and he must have known I'd find it interesting.

'What happened next?' I ask.

'No one knows. I usually met Zac on the beach each lunchtime but, the next day, he never showed up. I went to ask Pete where he was but he said Zac hadn't turned up for work the night before.'

'He went missing at night?'

'I guess. I don't know. The last time I saw him was when we got back from the cave.'

Everything feels foggy – like waking up in an unfamiliar bed, where it takes a few seconds to remember who, what, where, when and why. I've always assumed that he disappeared during the daytime. I remember that it was morning when my mother told me Zac was missing – but was it *that* morning, or the day after?

'When did the search begin?' I ask.

Chrissie breathes in heavily and starts chewing the tips of her already bitten-down nails. I guess we have some things in common.

Her words are muffled by her fingers. 'I suppose not until the next day. It's easy to think someone's lost around here when

He turns, letting the bunting drop and sits on the top rung of the ladder, looking down at me. 'What d'yer think? We burn a boat.'

'Why?'

'Tradition. You'll see.'

It's often struck me that tradition can be used to justify anything. If that's enough of a reason to keep doing things, women would still be thrown into lakes to drown as witches. We'd still have slaves. Gay people would still be electroshocked as a cure.

Tradition. It's a stupid word; an even stupider justification.

'You didn't tell me Zac used to work with you on the fishing boats,' I say.

Pete doesn't even blink. 'I thought you knew; thought that's why you were asking me about 'im.'

It's possible that's true. Chrissie seemed to think I knew about Zac being on the boats as well.

'What did he do?' I ask.

A shrug. 'Not much. He was a novice. I only took 'im on as a favour to yer dad. Give 'im something to do for the summer.'

That *does* sound plausible. The last thing my parents would have wanted was Zac getting in their way, either at home or at the cottage. Getting him a summer job would've saved them from having to enrol him in some sort of camp or summer school.

'What did he actually do, though?' I ask. 'I didn't know he was interested in boats or fishing.'

'He'd help pull in the nets, that sort of thing.'

'With you?'

'Yeah.'

'What about Scott? Did he go out with Zac too?'

We both turn to look at the pub, as if expecting Scott to be in the window. There's no sign of him.

'He'd have been a year or so too young then,' Pete says. 'Wasn't as big as he is now. He started on the boats when he was seventeen or eighteen, then took over the business a few years ago. 'Bout time, too. Got better sea legs than I ever had.'

Pete stretches down and picks up the bunting, lifting it over his head and stapling it to the beam above the door. I take that as my cue to disappear, thanking him and then trampling across the road and into the woods. The steep ascent feels tougher each time I make it. I have to stop for breath twice before continuing.

There's no sign of Chloe at the cottage and, with little else to do, I keep on moving, following a route vaguely parallel to the road until I eventually emerge at the spot where I saw Brad and Scott chatting. The caravans are beyond and I follow the chatter of voices until I reach a smouldering fire pit that's been constructed in the wide aisle between trailers. Scorch marks stretch wide on the grass and I notice a series of extinguishers on the ground underneath the caravans. I'm surprised they're allowed to start fires this close to the woods, although Vee did tell me the beach kids get away with doing what they want.

The familiar beach kid faces all seem to be present, some sitting on foldaway deck chairs, others huddled together. When I appear from the woods, they all turn to look at me. I sense an underlying current of unease.

The first person to speak is Mia. 'Is Chloe with you?' she asks. It strikes me that these are the first words she's ever spoken to me. She looks unusually dishevelled: her normally straight dark hair is tangled into the flimsiest of ponytails.

'She went off to the cliffs to paint first thing this morning,' I say. 'I've not seen her in a couple of hours.'

Mia glances to Ebony and then back to me.

'What?' I ask.

'Have you seen Popcorn? He's missing.'

'Not since last night.'

She looks quickly from side to side as if the dog might appear from nowhere. 'He was here after the barbecue. I let him out to have a wee this morning and he didn't come back.'

'I'm sure everything's fine,' Brad says, but he's not convincing anyone. The woods feel vast behind us and beyond the woods are the moors.

There's a crack from behind and I turn to see George, Chloe, Vee and a couple of the other village kids climbing over the gate that leads to the road. Chloe and I exchange a *what-are-you-doing-here?* look, but don't get a chance to say anything before Mia launches herself at one of the village boys.

'You've got him, haven't you?'

The boy pushes her away gently. It's Kev, the sand-kicker from the volleyball game.

'I haven't seen your dog,' Kev says. 'George told us he was missing. We came up here to help look. This was meant to be a peace offering but we can go back to the village if you want?' He glances across to Brad, who shakes his head and puts a hand across Mia's front, separating her from the newcomers.

'They know the woods better than we do,' Brad says. 'They'll be able to help us look for Popcorn.'

And with that, the two groups' Alphas have made a temporary truce.

Mia turns to Chloe: 'Have you seen him?'

'Not since last night.'

'You were playing with him last.'

'But I left the bonfire before you.'

Mia, who must know this is true, bursts into tears. 'He'll be so frightened…'

Brad comforts her on his shoulder and starts dividing us into search teams for specific areas. He doesn't ask if Chloe or I want to be a part of this but I'm not going to ostracise myself by saying no. Besides, I'm quite keen to explore the woods.

George, Chloe, Vee and I all get lumped together and Vee says she'll take us out to the area of woods closest to the cliff line. First, George heads into one of the caravans to change his shoes and Vee says she needs to use the toilet. Brad points her in the direction of his caravan.

Chloe and I stand a little away from the rest of the group, watching the search party unfold. Things are already ramshackle. People are checking phones, pointing in opposite directions and seeming generally unsure of what they're doing. Brad is putting together a party to head towards the road; Kev is leading a group up the slope towards the lightning tree. Meanwhile, Mia is still busy crying on Brad's shoulder.

'I thought you were on the cliffs,' I say quietly to Chloe.

'I was. I went back to the cottage to drop off my stuff and was going to head down to the beach to look for you. That's when George found me and said Popcorn was missing. I hope he's okay.' She pauses. 'What about you? What have you been up to?'

'Finding trouble.'

'A normal day, then?'

'Did you know Zac worked on the fishing boats here? Pete the pub owner was his boss.'

It takes Chloe a few seconds to reply and then all she says is a sullen, 'Really?'

I thought she'd be more interested but all she's doing is watching Brad and Mia. I'm not sure if she's more bothered by Brad or the missing dog.

'Pete didn't tell me about Zac working on the boats when we were in the pub last night,' I say. 'Don't you think that's weird? He acted like he didn't really know him – and yet they worked together every day for six weeks or so.'

'He might've assumed you already knew.'

'Right…'

I want to tell her about Chrissie being Zac's ex-girlfriend and that she's now married to Pete's son. It all feels a bit *too* connected – but then, everything about the village feels the same way.

'Pete told me that business is on its arse,' I say.

'What business?'

'Everything. Fishing. The pub. The whole village. Don't you wonder how they can keep everything going? The pub, the boats – all that. Is fishing *really* that lucrative?'

Chloe turns back to where Brad and his crew are climbing the gate, ready to cross the road and disappear off into the distance. Mia is remaining at the campsite alone, in case Popcorn returns.

'You could say the same about our parents,' Chloe says.

I was about to launch into something else but instantly forget what I was talking about.

'Big house in London,' Chloe adds. 'Cottage in Cornwall, all those holidays. The clothes, the parties, the travel. Didn't you ever wonder where it all came from?'

'Well…'

'Mum's lunches at golf clubs, our school fees. Do you really think it all came from antiques?' Chloe turns, looks me dead in the eye and I know in that instant that I've spent a lifetime underestimating my sister. She's not naïve at all.

'And where did the money come from in the first place?' she says. 'How did Dad start the business? Didn't you wonder what was really going on?'

She hasn't blinked and it's me who has to turn away this time.

'Of course I did,' I reply. 'When I was old enough. When I understood. When I realised that all the other girls at school had dads who were lawyers or bankers.'

'Did you ever ask Mum or Dad about it?'

'I don't think I wanted to know the answer.'

Chloe grips my hand. Squeezes. Rests her head on my shoulder. I can feel her breathing. 'Me either,' she says.

CHAPTER SIXTEEN

The trees become more and more tightly packed the further we move through the woods. Vee says that as long as we keep the sea on one side for the journey out, then we can't get lost. That's all well and good but within minutes, I can neither see nor hear the ocean. Walking is easy at first but we've not gone far before roots begin to sprout from the ground as if nature itself is trying to grab us and suck us down to the depths of hell. Plants and bushes seem to grow on top of and around one another with no plan or pattern, like mangled, soggy spaghetti dropped on the floor.

The four of us spend large amounts of time disentangling ourselves from twigs, or fumbling over hidden brambles. Chloe and George eventually push on ahead. Vee and I stick together, kicking our way through the undergrowth and occasionally stopping to shout out 'Popcorn' – which sounds pretty stupid at volume.

We've only been walking for fifteen minutes or so when the spider webs start to appear. Lower down, the strands of silver are fine and delicate, but higher up the trunks, trees are meshed together by inexplicably large and thick webs.

Vee is in long sleeves again. I wonder if she's somehow immune to the heat. The air is soupy and thick. My clothes are sticking to me and my mouth is dry.

'Horror movie stuff, isn't it?' Vee says, noticing me looking at the webs.

'You can say that again.'

'There's another thirty or forty minutes of this, then it's grass and marshland.'

'We're never going to find this dog,' I say.

'Does Mia really think someone from the village stole it?'

'I think she's just upset.'

Vee kicks out at a vine that has snared itself around her foot. There's a woody snap. 'Can I ask you something?' she says.

'Sure.'

I sense her glancing sideways at me as we continue to walk at the same pace. We barely know each other and yet there was a connection between us the moment I first saw her roll her eyes. I think she feels it, too.

'How do you stay so thin?' she asks. 'You're so… skinny.'

I like the word *skinny*. So many people dance around it, use a different term. Slim. Thin. Slender. Petite. There are all sorts of slightly more polite alternatives. 'Skinny' is one step up from 'anorexic' – and nobody ever dares to call me that.

'Lucky genes, I suppose,' I say.

'Do you diet?'

'Eat like a pig,' I say. 'Chocolate, crisps, pizza. You name it.' I feel bad for lying to Vee about eating but it's a reflex now. I'm too far gone to do anything else.

Vee squidges her middle, pinching the smallest roll of fat. 'I can't seem to get rid of this. I've tried diets, running, these pills that someone at school recommended. Nothing works.'

Vee isn't fat at all, though Mother would think she was. She'd ask how the spare tyre was doing, or 'joke' that she was looking a bit pregnant.

'You look good to me,' I say – and that, at least, isn't a lie.

'I wish I was more like you,' she says.

I want to tell her that she really doesn't, but I can't, so I change the subject instead.

'What's the Burning Boat Festival?' I ask.

Vee doesn't seem to mind the switch. 'It's always the first Sunday in August,' she says. 'It's something about celebrating the time when a bunch of Whitecliff fishermen died in the 1700s. August the first 1750, to be precise. Pirates boarded their ship, stole everything and then set it on fire. They either drowned or burned. Nobody ever saw them again.'

'You celebrate *that*?!'

She laughs. 'Well, commemorate, I suppose. Every year, we float a boat out at dusk and set it on fire. The village will be full. There's food, drink and all that. People come from miles around.'

George and Chloe are out of sight ahead, but only because the bushes and trees are so closely packed. We can still hear the sound of their voices, although not loudly enough to make out the words.

'You're not supposed to wear black,' Vee adds.

'When?'

'On Sunday.'

'Why?'

'Something to do with the fishermen all wearing black when their boat was boarded. I think it was their uniform, or something like that. Anyway, everyone says it's unlucky to wear black to the Burning Boat Festival. It's a village superstition.'

Superstitions are right up there with traditions.

'How do people know not to wear black?' I ask. 'It's not on any of the posters. Surely there's always someone who turns up in black shorts or a black T-shirt by accident?'

Vee kicks out at another low-lying branch. 'I dunno... Everyone just knows. I've never seen anyone in black on Burning Boat day.'

I'm not sure what to say. I don't doubt she's being sincere but the idea that there's some weird festival with unwritten rules seems so bizarre to me. Stranger still that everyone who attends automatically knows the dress code.

'It was always a really big thing when I was a girl,' Vee continues. 'The highlight of the year. Mum would do my hair and my brother and I would have these special festival clothes. They were always really brightly coloured – I've still got a pair of yellow trousers somewhere in my wardrobe. It always felt like we were the centre of everything for that one day. And I still enjoy it. Everyone makes crafts or bakes something to sell to the tourists. It's really fun.'

The idea of so many people converging on such a small place doesn't sound like much fun to me. All that food will be good, though. So many people to watch eating; so much food to salivate over.

'My turn now,' she says. 'What was boarding school like?'

I tell her about the private schools I attended, saying that Chloe and I have always been apart because of the gap in our ages.

'But what was it actually like?' she adds, spotting that I hadn't answered properly.

I'm quiet for a moment, not knowing whether to tell the truth. I like Vee and I want to trust her. That eye-roll. You can tell a lot about a person by the way they roll their eyes and the frequency with which they do it. The world would be a much better place if tyrants were always met with a weary eye-roll. *Really? You want to invade Poland?* It puts people in their place.

'Normal is what's normal for you,' I say. 'To us, boarding school was just… ordinary. It's only later that you realise that most kids see their parents each night and you wonder why yours sent you away.'

Vee doesn't get a chance to respond because we have to wind our way around a giant spider's web. Some of it sticks to her hair and I end up having to separate it out for her. When we finally get past it, I realise that somehow, we've ended up holding hands. Her hand is cool and dry and I'm embarrassed that my palm is clammy and damp. I desperately want to tug my hand away, if only to wipe it dry – but I don't.

'So what was "ordinary" for you, then?' Vee asks.

'Some of it was similar to what you would have experienced at normal school, I suppose. There were the usual divisions – the sporty girls, the smart girls, the would-be models. But some of it was weird – I only found out how weird once I'd left.'

'Weird like what?'

'Girls at every other school play netball. We did fencing and pistol shooting.'

'You *fenced*?'

'I was awful. I was decent with a pistol, though. A good runner, too. There was rowing as well and archery. The school focused on Olympic sports. There were a few ex-students with medals, so they pushed you into it. It was a big deal for their funding.'

Vee says nothing in response at first but she squeezes my hand and we adjust our grip ever so slightly, re-interlocking our fingers.

Eventually, she says: 'My school couldn't afford new goalposts for the football field.'

There's nothing I can say to that, so I remain quiet.

The woods are gradually becoming darker as the overhead branches intertwine more thickly. It's still warm but the light has been replaced by shadow.

'People say the ghost of Deacon the Black stalks these woods,' Vee says, out of the blue.

'Who?'

'He was the captain of the burnt boat.'

I frown. 'If he was *on* the boat that was set on fire, then why would his ghost haunt the woods?'

'Don't ask me.' She pauses. 'Do you believe in ghosts?'

'No.'

'Me neither. It used to scare the crap out of me when I was little. My parents stopped us from running off by saying that Deacon would get us.'

I squeeze her hand this time – and then, as if we're telepathic, we let go at the same time and swap sides, so that my left hand is in her right. Clammy hands need a respite.

'Parents always tell you not to lie,' I say, 'but they're the worst of all for it. Tooth fairies, naughty lists, Santa – you name it.'

'You say that,' Vee says, 'but there was a time when I kept seeing a figure out of the corner of my eye. In the woods, on the cliffs. Never quite out in the open. I always believed it was Deacon the Black.'

I stop, which forces Vee to stop as well. We release hands and turn to look at each other. Vee has caught the sun; a soft pink hue colours her cheeks.

'What's wrong?' she asks.

I think of the figure I've been seeing that is never quite in view. He, she – or it – standing at the edge of the woods on the clifftop and then a little past the treeline by the cottage. It wasn't Deacon the Black, of that I'm sure.

'Do you ever see the figure now?' I ask.

'Course not. It was just something from when I was younger – like the monster under the bed. I grew out of it.'

'Right, I know…'

Vee tilts her head slightly. 'Can I ask you something else?' she says.

'What?'

'Why are you here? I mean, I'm glad you are… It's just…' She stops for a breath, staring past me towards the trees, the nothingness.

I wait. I'm not sure what we're doing together, or why we've been holding hands. It doesn't feel wrong but I don't see how this is going to end well for either of us.

'Your brother went missing,' Vee says. 'And now your parents have died, too. Why come back here? Why not just sell the cottage and forget?'

Vee stretches across and takes my hand again. Her thumb dances across my skin. I should pull away – it's not fair – and yet the part of me that relishes chaos is electrified. If only Mother could see me now… Especially after the kiss I shared with Luke last night. Instead of pulling away, I slip an arm around Vee's waist and her arm slots naturally around my shoulders. We take a couple more steps – and then Vee halts, her fingers gripping the sharp edge of my shoulder.

'What?' I ask.

Vee nods at the tree in front of us. It's thick and wide: a hundred or more years old. Smaller plants and vines are wrapped around its lower half but none of that obscures the damage that's been done to the trunk higher up. At head height, carved deep into the bark, are five characters that I've seen before:

ZS 4 CA.

CHAPTER SEVENTEEN

After a day of hunting through various woods and fields without a result, nobody is in the mood for another barbecue on the beach. Instead, the beach kids have assembled around the fire pit next to the caravans. The sky is a dusky purple and the lightning tree soars high above us like a craning, nosy parent trying to overhear our conversations.

Nobody is saying much and the lack of George's guitar means things must be really bad. Mia has barely stopped crying since the various search parties returned empty-handed. She's curled into a ball on top of a dusty red beanbag, with Chloe at her side. Poor old Popcorn is nowhere to be seen. The village kids, including Vee, have headed back down the hill.

Everyone has settled into small groups, except for me. I'm by myself on one of the other beanbags, trying to catch Chloe's eye. I'm not sure if she's deliberately avoiding me, or if she's busy trying to console Mia. After a while, I give up and lie back, staring up at the darkening sky. The heat from the fire feels wonderfully cosy against my skin – like a cherishing hug from a person who actually cares. I run my fingers across my top, fingering each of my ribs through the fabric and remembering the way Vee called me 'skinny'.

People are passing around more alcohol but I wave the bottles away tonight. There's food, too. Nothing special: mainly burgers and sausages. Someone's even rustled up veggie burgers, which means Chloe can eat. I turn down a couple of offers of food but start to notice people giving me confused stares, silent questions in their eyes. I decide to play along. With practice, it's easy enough to get rid of mangled hunks of meat and crusty bread. Becoming a messy eater so that breadcrumbs tumble anywhere but near a mouth is straightforward. It's like being a talented illusionist performing on a big stage. Never listen to what's being said; never turn to face the way he or she is pointing, or get distracted by loud bangs. Always look for what the *other* hand is doing. If pointed in one direction, check the other.

A magician is only as smart as the audience is stupid – and when someone is as good at not eating as I am, everyone becomes very stupid indeed.

I devour two chicken burgers without swallowing even the tiniest of morsels. The excitement of getting away with it is so overwhelming that there's a chance I might even sleep well tonight.

I'm staring at the sky again when Brad bangs a spoon against a bottle of vodka to get everyone's attention. He's standing on the steps of his caravan wearing shorts and a sports jacket. The jacket is unfastened and his toned, bare chest is on show in the gap. On most people, this would look ridiculous, but somehow it suits him.

'My Lords, Ladies and Gentlemen,' he calls.

A low chortle goes up around the circle.

'It is a sad day' – a nod towards Mia – 'but in these sad times, let us not forget the good. We may not have known her long, but long may we know her: today is the seventeenth anniversary of the birth of our great friend, Chloe Victoria Smart.'

Brad pauses and there's a ripple of applause from around the circle. Even Mia claps, albeit half-heartedly. I don't blame her. I wonder how Brad discovered Chloe's middle name. Whether he asked, or whether she volunteered it. Or whether he looked her up on Facebook.

He has undoubted charisma and a way with words. The sort of privately educated rugger-bugger who'll go far. Mother would have *really* liked him. I wonder who Brad's parents are, what they do. It's not as if I care, not really, but it's hard to switch off from the kind of thing I was brought up with.

Brad continues eulogising my sister for another minute or so and I watch Chloe wilt under the unexpected praise. Then he asks us all to raise our glasses, cans or bottles to toast 'our newest comrade and cohort'. The circle gives three cheers. Chloe stands, bows and thanks everyone for their well wishes. The fact that she's speaking in front of a group of people who were strangers a few days ago makes me feel as if I might cry for the first time in a very, very long time.

As everyone turns back to their own conversations, Chloe ducks and whispers something to Mia. Then she gets up off the beanbag, heading for Brad's caravan. I quickly spin to see if he's heading in the same direction, but he isn't. He's chatting with George and Ebony on the other side of the fire pit. I follow Chloe and realise as I catch her on the bottom step of the caravan that she's simply heading for the toilet.

'Hey,' I say.

She turns, still beaming from the speech. 'Hey.'

'I'm going to head back to the cottage.'

'But it's so much fun up here,' Chloe says.

'You can stay. It's just…' I turn, unable to stop myself glancing over my shoulder. 'Be careful.'

'What do you mean by that?'

I raise my eyebrows and that's all it takes. Chloe knows exactly what I'm getting at.

'You're one to talk,' she shoots back.

'What?'

'You were the one tonguing the lifeguard last night.'

'Yeah, er…'

'And it was only last night you were telling me I could be anything I wanted.'

'I know…' I take a breath. I don't want to be having this conversation. 'I'm not being like our mother,' I say, feeling defensive.

Chloe touches me on the shoulder. 'I wasn't saying that.'

'I'm not telling you to *not* do something, I'm only saying…'

Chloe grins, leans a little closer. 'It's awesome watching you squirm.'

I slap her playfully on the arm. 'Oi! We're supposed to be having a sisterly moment here.'

'We are. But I know, you know, we all know. It's a circle of knowingness.'

I allow myself a grin. 'Do you have your keys?'

Chloe tilts her head once more. 'Now you *are* sounding like Mum. I'll be back later. I'm not going to stay too late.' She stops and the light from the flames flickers across her face, turning her temporarily golden. 'You should stay for a bit.'

'I'm the oldest one here, Chlo.'

'Not by much.'

'By enough.'

I can see in her face that she doesn't understand. For her, we're equals – and that's fine by me. But the eighteen-month gap between me and the oldest beach kid is enough. Small gaps mean big differences at this age.

'I'll see you in the morning,' I say.

She nods and ducks into Brad's caravan. I take a moment to turn and take in the rest of the campsite. Nobody appears to have been watching our conversation. Brad is still laughing around with Ebony and George. I remember the strange exchange I saw him having with Scott. One minute fighting; the next, pally chats in the woods. I'm not sure what to make of him. I feel like I've missed something.

I leave the camp, traipsing onto the road rather than risking the woods – it's too dark for me to be sure of heading through them in the right direction and too real a possibility that I'd find myself lost on the moors, being chased by Deacon the Black, or whatever ridiculous ghost the villagers have invented.

Rather than risk slipping into the verge, I walk in the middle of the road. There's barely any traffic here in the daytime, let alone at night. As I walk, a thought creeps into the back of my mind that I could head straight past our cottage and knock on Luke's door. If I were here alone – if Chloe wasn't a consideration – I probably would.

I'm lost in these thoughts when I get the feeling that something isn't right. At first, I don't quite understand what's happening. There's a gentle hum, a flash of movement – and then I realise a car is heading straight for me.

Everything happens at once. It's so quick that afterwards, I'm left half-wondering whether it happened at all.

I jump out of the way – or I think I do. The next thing I know, I'm in the ditch at the side of the road. The car zips past at such proximity to me that the rush of its wind slashes at my bare leg. The force is such that I wonder if I *have* been hit. I scramble for my phone, using the torch to check for blood. There's nothing on me at all. Not even a graze.

I pull myself to my feet and brush the dust from my clothes, staring along the road after the phantom car, trying to piece together what just happened. It was over and done within seconds.

The engine was so quiet. It must have been one of those new electric cars – the ones that that practically have to run something over before a person realises they're there. But as I rerun the incident in my mind, I realise there is another reason I didn't see it until it was almost too late – and why the driver seemingly didn't spot me.

The headlights were switched off.

Whoever was driving was leaving the village in near silence and darkness.

Whoever it was *really* did not want to be seen.

CHAPTER EIGHTEEN

I have no headache the next morning but take a tramadol and a Seroxat anyway. I don't do this every day, but my confusion over what happened with the car last night makes me feel edgy enough to need them. I like absolutes. If someone is going to drive a car at me, even accidentally, I'd prefer to have a mark to show for it. Yet there's nothing on my legs or arms – not even the tiniest scrape of dislodged skin.

Did it really happen? Did a dark car really come at me, barely making a sound? With no lights on?

I've been seeing shadows in the woods… Have I moved on to imagining entire vehicles?

This is far from the first time I've awoken questioning the very nature of my own reality. Sometimes I wonder if the conversations I've had with people have only been in my head – whether I've dreamed or fantasised entire facets of a relationship. Some mornings, I've even awoken to Mother's voice shouting at me for not being out of bed earlier. For wasting my life. For being ungrateful for what I have. On those mornings, I jump up and then remember she's gone. Father, too. And Zac. It's only Chloe and me left.

I spend a few minutes checking myself for scabs and scrapes, running my fingers over my skin, twisting and turning to look at myself in the mirror. There are no marks. Nothing to explain why I hurled myself into that ditch.

Chloe is already up when I head through to the kitchen. She's sitting on the sofa in her pyjamas, eating some toast, legs curled underneath herself.

'What time did you get in?' I ask.

Chloe is hiding her eyes behind thick-rimmed glasses that she almost never wears. I think they're for reading but I'm not sure.

'After you,' she replies, without looking up.

'How was your evening?'

She bites away a smile. 'I didn't *do* anything, if that's what you're asking.'

'I'm not.'

'Brad walked me back to make sure I was safe and then I went to bed. You were snoring, so—'

'I was *snoring*?'

'Is that so hard to believe?'

I suppose it's not – but it's rare for me to sleep so deeply that I would snore. I usually sleep in fits and starts. Half an hour here, forty minutes there. My stomach's like an alarm clock that has a mind of its own, going off at inopportune times, regardless of when it's been set for. On top of that, I drink so much water through the day that I usually have to take a trip to the toilet two or three times a night.

I change the subject. 'What are your plans for the day?' I ask.

'We've not sorted out much of Mum and Dad's things…'

I grin at her. 'There's time yet.'

'In that case, I'm not sure. Back to the cliffs, I think. Maybe the gallery. I don't know if people are going to the beach again. Hopefully Popcorn's back.'

She munches the final bite of her toast and then stretches her arms high and wide. She washes up her plate and disappears off to have a shower and get dressed. I notice she doesn't ask me what *I* am going to do with myself and feel a tiny bit miffed.

Once I'm by myself in the kitchen, I feel as if the safe behind the painting is calling to me. I lift the picture off the wall and stare at the solid gun-metal front. There's nothing else for it, so I continue on from where I left off, working up through the numbers one at a time, each time getting a beep and then the red dot of denial. Beep-dot. Beep-dot. I'm so entranced by the rhythm of it that it takes me a second or three to realise that there's been a knock on the door. It's probably Alison Wood with her stretched-out face, come back to see how we're doing, or to invite us up to her house once more.

I replace the painting on the wall and cross the floor, unlocking the door and heaving hard until it pops open with a *thwick*.

It's not Alison – it's George, the beach kid. He's in jeans and a loose top, with a baseball cap pulled low – dressed for a day in the woods, not at the beach.

'You after Chloe?' I ask. Then I notice his eyes beneath the shade of his baseball cap: there are red marks around the edges. 'What's wrong?' I add.

'I kinda need to talk to you both,' he says.

'Why?'

Chloe chooses this moment to emerge from her bedroom. I open the front door wider and Chloe stops on the spot as she notices our visitor.

'You were the last to see him,' George says.

Chloe pads along the hallway barefooted, arms behind her back. 'See who?'

'Brad. He, um…' George's Adam's apple bobs up and down. He swallows away the upset before taking a breath. 'Someone attacked Brad last night,' he says. 'He's been rushed to hospital.'

CHAPTER NINETEEN

Chloe is frozen to the spot, her mouth hanging open.

'He… *What?*'

'I've got to get back,' George says. 'I thought you should know. The police are coming to talk to us later. It's all kicking off.'

'What's kicking off?' I ask.

'Everyone thinks one of the village kids attacked him. It was really bad. There was blood everywhere.' George steps away, looking towards the road. 'I've really got to go. Come on up when you're ready. The police will want to talk to you, too. They're not here yet.'

Chloe starts to say something but George has already dashed away.

The front door creaks open wider in a gust of breeze, allowing the warm yellow of the sun to flood across the kitchen floor. The light stops a little short of where Chloe is standing, motionless.

'What happened last night?' I ask.

She blinks and when her eyes reopen, she's looking directly at me. There's fear and confusion in her gaze.

'Nothing,' she says. 'He walked me down the road to make sure I was safe. It was too dark in the woods and there's not a proper path. I didn't want to get lost.'

'He walked you all the way to our door?'

'Right.'

'And then…?'

She shakes her head. 'Nothing. We said goodnight. I said I'd see him tomorrow, something like that. I came inside and locked up. You were snoring.' She takes a couple of steps to the sofa and sits, staring wide-eyed at the floor. I close the door and join her.

'What did you talk about?' I ask.

Chloe doesn't answer at first. She tugs at her hair and then rakes her arms with her nails, scratching an itch that seemingly won't go. The scrapes turn into carved red welts against her tanned skin.

'Things,' she says. 'I don't really remember. Normal things.'

I don't push but the police probably will.

'Did you see anything on the way down?' I ask. 'Anyone? Hear anything?'

She shakes her head slowly. 'The woods are pretty noisy at night,' she says. 'Animals, or whatever. You blank it out after a while. I didn't notice anything in particular… But then, I wasn't looking for anyone or anything.'

I think of the figure I've seen twice, a little out of view each time.

'Have you ever felt… watched?' Chloe asks me, unexpectedly.

Her five words make me shiver to such a degree that she rests a reassuring hand on my arm. It takes me a moment to reply and when I do, I have no idea how my voice remains steady.

'How do you mean?' I ask, although I know precisely what she means.

'With all the woods and everything,' she says. 'There are so many places to hide around the cottage and the village. Sometimes when I'm out, it feels like I'm being watched.'

It's as if a spider is creeping along my back. Everything tingles.

'Have you ever seen anyone spying?' I ask.

She answers an immediate, 'No.'

I want to tell her that I have, or *think* I have – but seeing things is a step too far. Crazy people see things. Crazy people chase shadows.

I say nothing other than that I'm going to get changed. When I return, Chloe's still on the sofa. It doesn't look like she's moved. Her head is bowed, hands kneading her temples. Her hair is damp and straggly, creating wet patches on the back of her top.

I tell her we'll head up to the caravans together. When she stands, she's like a zombie. Her focus is distant and it's hard not to suspect that she's holding something back.

I lock the cottage and we walk into the woods. I'm glad Chloe doesn't suggest using the road instead; I'm not sure I could face walking back past where I encountered the car last night. Neither of us speak for the ten minutes or so it takes us to trample across the uneven ground to our destination. We pass close to the spot where I saw Brad and Scott talking and then emerge by the fire pit between the caravans.

I can hardly believe it was only a few hours ago that we were all sitting around the fire and Brad was wishing Chloe a happy birthday. Now, it feels as if everything has changed.

The camp is quiet. Only George, Mia and one of the other lads – Will, I think – are outside. The three of them are standing conspiratorially next to the ashes of the fire pit. They stop talking as we approach. It's only George who offers us something close to an acknowledging smile.

As we join the circle, Will continues talking to George as if we're not there: '… c'mon, let's go.'

'It's a stupid idea,' George replies.

'So we're just gonna let the village lot mess with us, are we? Someone's stolen Mia's dog and now Brad's had his head kicked in. Who's next? You? Mia? Ebs? We can't stand for it.'

George's gaze flickers to Chloe and then away again. 'The police will be here soon.'

'You said that an hour ago.'

'They *told* me that an hour ago.'

Will's fists ball. He's not a big kid, more one of those mini-me types who charge in with their heads down first and worry about the consequences later. 'Exactly,' he says. 'We're on our own here. We should deal with it ourselves. Some of the others have been talking. We'll go down to the village together and get hold of that Kev kid. See what he knows.'

'You'll make it worse.'

'We won't. We just want to talk. Safety in numbers and all that. It's about time we—'

'No.'

Everyone turns – even me – because it's Chloe who's cut him off.

'What do you think's going to happen if you do that?' Chloe says. Her voice quivers. 'You take a gang of lads down; they'll get a gang of lads together. You know where it'll end.'

There's a moment of silence. I suspect that, deep down, Will knows this is true. He wants a ruck: some sort of vengeance for what happened to Brad.

George speaks next. 'Someone wants us to leave,' he says. 'Perhaps we should go?'

Mia shakes her head. 'I'm not going anywhere until Popcorn's back.'

'I can't leave,' Will says. 'My mum and dad are in Dubai for the next three weeks. There's no way they'd let me loose by myself at the house. Not after last time. They took my keys away.'

'What actually happened to Brad?' I ask.

It's the obvious question but I get the sense that the beach kids haven't quite figured the answer out for themselves yet. George, Will and Mia all turn to look at Chloe.

'All he did was walk me back to the cottage,' she says. 'We said goodnight and that was it.'

George picks up from there. 'He'd been gone a while,' he says. 'I walked out to the road but there was no sign of anyone, so I came back to the fire. Then I thought I'd check the woods. I heard this sort of moaning sound and then I found Brad slumped against a tree. It was dark, so I had to use the light from my phone to see what was up. He wasn't talking. That's when I saw all the blood.'

'Where did you find him?' I ask.

George opens his mouth to answer but then closes it again and instead steps out of the circle and heads to the woods. Everyone follows in silence. It's only a short walk. He leads us to the spot where I saw Scott and Brad talking as if they were old friends. The evidence of Brad's injuries is there for us to see. At head height on the tree there's a sticky sludge of reddy-brown, oozing down to a rust-coloured stain on the grass.

'He was barely breathing when I found him,' George says. 'There was a big gash on the back of his head. He was drifting in and out of consciousness. I had to leave him there while I ran up to the lightning tree to get reception. The call for an ambulance took forever; I was trying to explain to the bloke on the phone where the caravans are but he wasn't getting it. By the time I got back here, I thought Brad was dead. I couldn't get him to wake up. I'd been shouting for people to come and help but I guess everyone was asleep. It took ages for the ambulance to arrive… or it felt like it. Apparently, they'd been tied up with a traffic accident.'

When Mia steps towards the tree, George tugs her back gently. 'Don't. The police are coming,' he says.

As if to put a full-stop on that, the area is suddenly filled with spinning blue lights. There are no sirens but we cross back to the caravans in time to see four police officers climbing out of two cars. We're not the only ones to notice them. More of the beach kids are opening doors and shuffling wearily out of the caravans.

I notice Ebony emerge from her caravan. She has bare feet and is wearing impossibly tiny shorts and a skimpy sleep top.

One of the officers says something to her and she crosses her arms before pointing towards Chloe.

It's no surprise – but that's when they start walking straight for us. Chloe grips my wrist and just for a moment, it's like we're children again. She's six, I'm ten and we're on the drive back home out of Whitecliff, our missing brother absent from the back seat between us.

CHAPTER TWENTY

Sergeant Yardy is one of those blokes who I'm not sure I could describe if he wasn't sitting right in front of me. He's anonymously normal. Square jaw, pale skin and slightly greying hair. I'm here because he's said it's fine for me to sit with Chloe. I'm not sure if this is because she's seventeen, or because he's being nice.

I'd pictured us being taken off to a dark interrogation room with a metal table, two-way mirror and some arsehole banging on the desk, demanding the truth. The actuality is much more normal than that. The officers have separated into pairs to talk to everyone individually. I wonder whether all police work is this informal, or whether it's how it's done here because we're on the edge of a village in the back end of nowhere.

Sergeant Yardy and his near-mute colleague are in a borrowed pair of fold-up canvas chairs, with Chloe and me in a matching set across from them. The officers look so out of place. It's like when the BBC sends a usually serious newsreader to Glastonbury for a jolly and the presenter ends up looking like he's had a breakdown.

Yardy checks Chloe's name, age and address while the other officer makes notes. She tells him about our cottage and fills in what happened to our parents.

'I'd just like to establish what happened last night,' he says, once everything has been noted.

Chloe explains that it was her birthday and that we'd spent the day looking for Mia's missing dog before returning to the campsite for a 'chat and sing-song'. She doesn't mention the alcohol – but it would only take a cursory look in the skip at the edge of the field for the police to gain some idea about that.

Yardy nods along to Chloe's story as the other officer's pen scritches across her notebook.

'So,' he says. 'Were you and Mr Smith in a relationship?'

It sounds strange hearing Brad being referred to in such a formal way. I didn't know his surname before and I don't think that 'Smith' suits him. I would've expected something double-barrelled – or at least incomprehensibly long.

Chloe snaps back her reply too quickly: 'No.'

Yardy glances at me, perhaps wondering if he might have had a different answer if I were elsewhere.

'Really,' Chloe adds. 'We weren't.'

'But he walked you back to your cottage?'

'It was dark and late. He said he didn't want me to go by myself.'

'That's very noble of him. The sort of thing a boyfriend might do.'

'I told you: we're just friends.'

Yardy nods slowly, letting it go – at least for now. 'Do you know if he did have a girlfriend here?'

'You'd have to ask the others.'

The officer looks to me. 'Do *you* know if he had a girlfriend here?'

'I don't really know any of the people here,' I say – which is true enough. I don't tell him of the way I saw Ebony looking at Brad when we were in the caves, though. Nor do I tell him about the conversation I witnessed between Scott and Brad. It's hard to say what's stopping me.

'Did you see or hear anything on the way back to the cottage?' Yardy asks Chloe.

'Animals, things like that, but nothing specific,' Chloe says. 'We walked on the road because it was so dark.'

'But he walked back through the woods?'

'I guess. It is quicker. I didn't fancy it.'

'And do you know anyone who might have had problems with Mr Smith?'

Chloe shuffles nervously, giving it a second or two before she actually replies. 'There was a fight on the beach,' she says.

This literally perks the officer up. He sits up straighter and then angles forward. 'When?'

'The day before yesterday. Wednesday, I think.'

'Who was fighting?'

'Brad and one of the guys from the village.'

'Scott,' I say. 'He works on the fishing boats.'

That gets scribbled on the notepad and then Yardy turns back to Chloe. 'What was the fight about?'

'Nothing, really. I wasn't watching properly. There was a volley-ball game between the kids from the village and the kids up here. There was a bit of shoving and then Scott came running across from the other end of the beach. He picked Brad up by the throat, threw him down and said something like, "What have I told you?"'

'"What have I told you" about what?'

'I don't know. The fight got broken up and that was it.'

Yardy turns to me. 'Were you there?'

'Yes – that's what happened.'

Back to Chloe: 'Do you know of any reason why Scott might have said that?'

Chloe sighs and looks to me quickly before turning back. 'There's this ongoing thing between the two groups. We're sort of caught in the middle. The kids in the village don't like the ones up here and the ones up here don't like those in the village.'

'Why?'

'You'll have to ask them. We only got here a few days ago.'

The officer asks something else about timings – and at that moment, a flicker of something catches my eye on the edge of the woods. A shadow, set back a little behind the caravans. In the time it takes to blink, whatever it is slots in behind a tree. I continue watching, zoning out of the conversation. From the distance, it's hard to tell if the shadow belongs to a person or animal; something or nothing. I force myself not to blink, to focus. A few seconds pass. Perhaps a minute. Chloe and Sergeant Yardy are still talking. I start to convince myself it was only a trick of the light – and that's when the shadow moves again. Whatever it is, the shape is slight and fast. It scoots from one tree to the next and then it's gone again.

'Megan…?'

'Huh?'

Yardy is speaking to me and it's too late to pretend I was listening. 'Sorry,' I say. 'I didn't sleep well.'

'I was asking about the "GO HOME" message that someone wrote on your path.'

'Oh,' I reply.

'Do you know who might've written it?'

'No idea,' I say.

The officer makes a humming sound. 'I need to ask whether you're going to be staying in town for the foreseeable future,' he says.

'I don't know that, either. I think we are. At least until after the weekend.'

The two officers stand, ready to move onto the next interviewee.

'How is Brad?' I ask.

'We're not sure yet,' Yardy replies. 'Stable is the last we heard.'

'When will he be allowed visitors?'

'It's too early to say. I'd usually tell you to keep your phone on but, well…' He tails off and looks to the sky. I know the feeling.

We're on our own.

CHAPTER TWENTY-ONE

It's difficult to know what Chloe and I should do with the rest of day, given everything that's happened. The cottage doesn't feel like much of a safe haven – and I can't face going through any of our parents' things today. It feels too empty a task; too cold.

We stick to the road and head down the hill together, rounding the pub and heading onto the cobbles. Chloe is going to the gallery and I tag along because I have nothing better to do.

Arthur is leaning on his stick behind the counter. As we enter, he pushes himself a little taller and peers over his glasses towards us.

'Thank God you're okay,' he says, presumably meaning Chloe. 'I heard that someone had been hurt up on the hill and I didn't know if perhaps...'

Chloe crosses the gallery to greet him. 'It was one of the boys,' she says. 'He's called Brad. Someone attacked him late last night.'

'Is he okay?'

'"Stable" is all they're telling us. We don't know.'

Arthur lowers himself into his rocking chair in stages: hands on the armrests first, then crouch, lean back and let gravity do its thing.

'There's trouble every summer,' he says. His chair creaks forward and back as he rocks. 'Always. Sometimes it's little things: the odd fight, a few cross words. I think this is the first time anyone's ended up in hospital.' He waves a hand in the vague direction of the rest of the village. 'No one ever does anything. Someone will end up dead one of these days.'

He's only addressing Chloe. It's almost as if he's forgotten I'm there. I get the sense he's been having these grandfatherly interludes with Chloe on a daily basis.

'Someone's already dead,' I say.

His head snaps around to me with surprising speed. It's like he's spring-loaded. 'What? Who?'

'Our brother,' I say.

'Oh… Yes. Indeed.' Arthur relaxes again, bowing his head a little. 'I didn't mean…'

'We know,' Chloe says quickly, flashing me a look to say: *What are you doing?*

'Do you remember him? I ask. 'Our brother.'

'Not really, I'm afraid. Not him specifically. I remember those few days when everyone was worrying.'

'What do you remember?' I press.

'There was a big search. I wasn't much help but lots of people were up on the cliffs, or out in the caves. A couple of coastguard boats came across to help look out at sea. It went on for two or three days and then, well…' He looks up to Chloe and then away again.

'You can say it,' I reply.

He looks quickly at Chloe once more, as if he wants permission and then he continues: 'You have to understand what it's like around here.'

'What is it like?'

'People worry about their livelihoods. Without you kids, without the summers, this place disappears. There's barely enough to go around as it is. Someone going missing' – he points up to the hill – 'or this lad getting hurt? It's bad for business.'

There's silence for a moment.

'That sounds uncaring of me. You lost your brother… I didn't mean it to sound like that,' he adds.

'We know what you meant,' Chloe replies. I sense that she's angry that I'm here, invading their time together – but Arthur seems to be one of the few sane people who live in this village. I want to get as much information from him as I can.

I avoid her stare.

'What was it like when Zac went missing?' I ask.

'Panic,' Arthur says. 'Everyone was so desperate to find him. The idea that he might've been washed out to sea, or caught on the rocks, well... People knew what it would mean. I'm sorry, I know he's your brother, but that's what people were thinking about. They were worried the kids wouldn't come back the next summer. That no one would. Then, when he couldn't be found, everyone feared the worst for their livelihoods. When the tourist season came around the next year, it was like everyone was holding their breaths, waiting to see what would happen.'

'What did happen?'

'Everything was normal. Parents dropped off their kids, people built bonfires on the beach, the shops opened. It was all one big relief.'

I should probably be annoyed but I'm not. It's refreshing to hear an honest take on the situation.

What Arthur's said explains a lot – but I can't get my head around one thing: 'If the village depends so much on the summer visitors,' I say, 'then why is there so much hostility? You said there's trouble every summer.'

Arthur shakes his head, which makes him cough. He begins to stand but Chloe's a step ahead. She disappears into a side room and returns a moment later with a mug of water. He sips at it, calls her a 'dear girl' and then uses the walking stick to push himself up out of his chair anyway. The movements are so creaky that I swear I can hear his joints cricking as he leans on the counter.

'It's for the same reason that people hate the bloke down the road who claims benefits for a dodgy knee but shrug at reports that bankers and businessmen have defrauded millions,' he says. 'It's easier to kick the person in front of you. The village folk see the kids come in once a year with fifty-pound notes and expensive clothes and bags, brand-new surfboards and so on. Things they don't have. It's jealousy. Oldest reason out there.'

His lips crease into a wrinkled sad smile. Everything he's said is an extension of what Vee said on the beach when we first met. I have no reason to think they're both wrong – but it's hard to know how Zac fits into it all. Or whether he does at all. The postcard with 'Z' on the back makes me feel that someone wanted us here for a reason – but, if that's the case, then why hasn't that person come out and said so? The only message we've been delivered since our arrival is the big 'GO HOME' outside our door.

'This might cheer you up,' Arthur says, pointing across to the wall behind us. We both turn to look. Chloe squeals, knocking a stool over and then righting it before skipping across the floor. I follow her to a spot where a pencil drawing of the village has been pinned onto the wall. It's monochrome, not particularly fancy – but it doesn't need to be. The lines are crisp and there's something powerfully imposing about the way the waves have been drawn roaring towards the shoreline.

There's a small card underneath, black type on white, clean and clear:

CHLOE SMART, PENCIL ON PAPER, ORIGINAL, £80

'Ohmygod.' Chloe spins and flits across the gallery so quickly that it's as if she's disappeared and re-materialised in another spot. 'Thank you!' she says to Arthur, who is still leaning on the counter.

'No, thank *you*, my dear. It's a big weekend coming up with the Burning Boat. I need the stock. I'll probably clear half of everything that's here.'

'No one's ever displayed my work before.'

'First of many, I'm sure.'

'Would you be interested in some more? I found a spot on the cliffs where you can see the whole curve of the coast.'

Arthur smiles kindly. 'If the quality is the same.'

Chloe's like a child in a sweetshop with a platinum credit card. She bounces on the spot, ready to rush away. I hate it but I have to crush the moment.

'Can I ask you about the Chandlers?' I say.

The way Arthur's face darkens tells me I'm onto something. His patchy eyebrows dip in the middle. It's as if he's melted slightly in the sun. Everything about him sags.

'What would you like to know?'

I check the doorway, half-expecting Pete or Scott to be there. 'I'm not sure but I think your reaction has said it all.'

That gets the smallest of smiles. 'Whenever there's trouble in the village,' Arthur says, 'no matter who it involves, the Chandlers are always at the centre of it. Always have been, always will be. I've seen four generations of that family and it never changes. There was a time, a few years ago, when it looked like it was all going away. Rumour was that the boats and the pub were out of money. I kept expecting to see boards across the windows – but it never happened. Whitecliff and the Chandlers are stuck with each other.'

'You make it sound like they're a married couple that can no longer stand the sight of one another,' I say.

Arthur laughs, clears his throat and then adds: 'They're trouble, if that's what you're asking. That younger one, especially. His father defends him no matter what.'

I pause on that for a moment and take half a step towards the door before something else strikes me. 'Have you ever seen an expensive-looking car driving round here late at night with its lights off?' I ask.

Chloe spins to look at me, confused by the question but Arthur takes it in his stride. 'I can't imagine we have the same idea of what counts as "late".' He laughs briefly to himself. Then he adds: 'You learn not to ask questions.'

It's oddly sinister.

'Questions about what?'

Arthur doesn't respond. It seems to me like he wants to say something more but is being held back. It might be Chloe's presence stopping him but I think it's more likely to be his sense that the village walls have ears.

'Do you think Zac was asking questions?' I say.

Arthur lowers his glasses and examines me closely. I can feel him probing for motive and reason. He might trust Chloe but he doesn't know me.

'I think I should probably get back to work,' he says eventually, before turning to my sister. 'Could you possibly put the kettle on before you head out? My knees aren't what they used to be.'

CHAPTER TWENTY-TWO

Chloe follows me out of the gallery before launching herself angrily in front of me. 'Why did you keep going on at him?' she says.

'Because no one else is telling us anything. He didn't seem to mind.'

'He was too polite to say that he minded.'

'I don't understand why everyone's so uptight whenever I mention Zac's name.'

Chloe huffs and pushes herself up onto her heels. It's something Mother used to do when she was about to blow a gasket about me leaving clothes or shoes on the floor of my room.

We're not animals, Megan, so why do you insist on living like one? What is wrong with you?

'Because we're outsiders,' Chloe says. 'Don't you get that? Every time you start talking about this, it sounds like we're accusing people in the village of having done something to Zac ten years ago. Didn't you hear what Arthur said? People were worried about his disappearance affecting their jobs, their way of life. They've got past it and now you come along and keep wanting to bring up something they thought was done with.'

'He was our *brother*,' I say.

'I know – but what can we do now?'

'But—'

'It was just a postcard. It doesn't have to mean anything. I told you when you showed it to me: it could be a mistake or a coincidence.'

We stare at one another. I've never felt so distant from my sister. I can hear Mother in her voice. Denying anything that might be inconvenient for her. Is this who she really is?

Chloe must expect something more, because she stands with her hands on her hips, waiting for the kind of smart-arse reply she's seen and heard from me so many times before. I don't give it this time.

'I'll see you later,' she says, when it's clear I have nothing more to add. 'Please don't upset anyone else.'

Our mother's voice. Our mother's words.

'See you later,' I reply.

I turn and head for the hill, not looking back in case Chloe's watching. I can still feel them stinging inside me: Mother's words. She'll never truly be gone.

My stomach growls menacingly. The moment I get into the cottage, I hurl myself at the cupboard. The first peanut butter cookie goes down almost whole and the second doesn't last much longer. I lay the rest on the table in three rows of five. I twist the others so that the logos in the centre are all facing the same way.

I take my time with the other cookies. The calculation on the back of the packet for the number of calories per cookie seems a suspiciously round number but it makes it easy enough to add up. Four hundred calories quickly becomes a thousand. My stomach gurgles. I can feel it straining but it only has itself to blame.

Twelve cookies to go.

I start to get creative, pulling a cookie sandwich in half and using the half to create a triple-decker with another whole one. I eat one cookie after the other until there is nothing but the empty packet left. That gets dumped at the top of the bin, because if Chloe wants to fuss about whether I've eaten today, she can see that I've had her seventeen cookies. Thirty-four hundred beautiful calories in one go.

It's barely a minute later that I start to regret the whole thing. First comes the swirling, surging pain in my stomach and the trembling of my fingers from the sugar rush – and next comes more than that. The loss of control. A betrayal of my own body.

I dig my teeth into the slimmest of gaps underneath the nail of my right thumb, but I can't get any purchase. It's already been bitten down to nothing. I try the next nail and the next. With each nail I can't bite, I can feel the panic rising.

I get to the toilet a second before my gut decides it's had enough of this madness. Everything I've eaten in the past ten minutes launches itself up from the depths of my very soul. It feels as if my entire body is heaving, like I'm turning myself inside out.

After the first two waves hit the bottom of the toilet bowl, I lean in deeper and shove two fingers down my throat. Ripples of revulsion burn through me. I keep going until I'm just dry heaving. I know there's nothing left to come but I keep hitting my trigger point anyway. I want it to hurt. I deserve this.

I've got to almost two thousand on the possible safe combinations when I decide I can't take being in the cottage any longer. Air freshener has cleared away the smell in the bathroom and my clothes are in the wash but I can still sense everything I did. It's as if my sins have been imprinted into the walls. The empty packet of biscuits is right there in the bin, taunting me with its bright red wrapping. I have an urge to burn it.

The air is thick and syrupy outside again, which doesn't help with my stomach. Each day seems to be hotter than the last and, apart from vague notions of thunderstorms, there doesn't seem to be an end in sight. No wonder people come here for the summer.

I walk into the woods, heading towards the caravans, with no particular plan for what to do. I've not quite got to the Scott-

Brad tree when I hear the barking of a dog. It passes me by at first – one more sound to block out – but then I realise what it means.

Mia is sitting by the fire pit, Popcorn yapping at her feet.

'He's back!' I call to her.

She grins up. 'He literally just came back. One minute he was gone and then he was here.'

I find myself a spot on the beanbag next to her. 'Where was he?'

'I don't know. He came back from the woods. Everyone's saying he probably ran off and got lost – but he *never* runs off. He likes to be with people.'

It's against my nature but I ruffle the little dog's stuck-up ears. He responds by licking my wrist.

'I still think it was one of *them*,' Mia spits.

'Someone from the village?'

She doesn't answer directly but asks me to hold onto the dog for a moment and disappears into her caravan. Popcorn sits and watches her go. He seems unaffected by whatever's happened to him in the past day. His dark fur is still glossy – there are no patches of dirt or damage. His ears are pricked tall.

Mia returns a minute or so later with a lead, which she clips to Popcorn's collar. 'There,' she says. 'He can't go anywhere now.'

Popcorn's big brown eyes stare up at her as if to ask why she is betraying him in this way. The poor sod.

The rest of the camp has a different feel about it. There are huddles of people near the lightning tree and a couple of cars I've not seen before parked near the gate.

'What's going on?' I ask.

'Some of the parents are down for the day,' Mia says.

Now that she's said it, I notice a man and a woman standing awkwardly by the lightning tree, arms aloft with their phones. He's in a suit and she's in the type of elaborate flowery dress and hat that Mother would wear to the races. The fact they're in a field makes the whole spectacle somewhat farcical.

'Mad, isn't it?' Mia says.

'I'm not quite sure what to make of it.'

'Me either – and I'm one of them.'

'I can't quite figure out why you're all in caravans and not somewhere more… fancy.'

'There's nowhere else to stay. The nearest hotel is fifteen miles away. There's a B&B over the pub but nowhere near enough space for all of us. It's either stay here in the caravans, camp in tents, or go somewhere that's not Whitecliff.'

'Where are the parents staying?'

Mia swings around to look up to the lightning tree. The man in the suit is striding back and forth, shouting into his phone. His wife is leaning at an angle – I think she has her heel stuck in the dirt.

'When mine come down, it's only for the day. Some stay in the hotel I mentioned for the weekend. Some drop us off and that's it. I don't think George has seen his mum and dad all summer.'

We watch for a minute or so as the man bounds back to the tree, kneeling and yanking at his wife's foot, all the while berating her for getting stuck.

'I told my dad about you,' Mia says.

My stomach is still angry but it's not only that which sets my hackles up.

'What about me?'

'Nothing bad,' she adds quickly. 'I told him you have a cottage here. That your parents died. Chloe said you might be selling it.'

'Oh… Well, I don't know about that.'

'He said to make sure you have his number.'

'Your dad? Why?'

'Because he'd buy the cottage if it's going. It's impossible to get planning permission around here.' She huffs a raspberry with her lips, reciting what she's been told. 'He reckons you can only buy a place when someone dies.' She stops and then quickly adds: 'Sorry, I didn't mean it like that.'

'It's okay,' I reply.

'Anyway. Don't worry about it. I don't know why I said anything.'

'Why would he want to buy it?' I ask.

'I said – because there's nowhere else available.'

'But would he want it as a holiday home?'

'He'd buy it for me.' Mia looks up at me as if this is perfectly normal. As if she's explaining two-plus-two to someone who should already know the answer. As if teenagers frequently have cottages bought for them on a whim.

She strokes Popcorn once more and relaxes back onto the beanbag. The sun is high and warm. There are definitely worse places to sunbathe. I want to do the same, to relax and let my stomach settle, but everything I'm learning about the village feels as if it's going to bring me down.

Both sides seemingly hate each other – and yet the hatred is a mask hiding their own problems. The village kids feel stuck here and are frustrated by the things they can't afford. The beach kids have been abandoned by their parents to their own façade of fun.

Because it is a front. Is it really that enjoyable to be seventeen or eighteen and completely in charge of your own destiny – even if you have a fistful of fifty-pound notes with which to do it? Isn't it better to have someone to cook meals, to wash clothes, to listen to problems?

Perhaps it's not? I'm not sure if I know what's best any longer. Maybe I should call Mia's father and tell him he can have the damned cottage.

And I still don't have much in the way of answers about Zac. Which means I have to go and do the one thing I've been putting off.

CHAPTER TWENTY-THREE

There are two cars parked outside the Wood house, both massive enough to fit an entire family on the back seat. I continue to look through the gap in the front gate – which *can't* be missed – and press the buzzer, waiting for a reply.

Considering both Alison and Dan Wood told me to call by 'any time', they're doing a good job of keeping any potential visitors out of the house. A tall hedge runs parallel to the road and then arcs back to block the view. The wide gate is locked. I've rung the buzzer three times and aside from climbing the gate, I don't really see how I'm going to pay them a visit.

There's a long driveway between the gate and the house and I can't see anything in the way of movement. I press the buzzer for a fourth time, deciding this will be the last try. I'm about to turn and go when there's a static crackle and a woman's voice rattles from the speaker.

'Who is it?'

'Megan Smart. You said I could—'

BEEEEEEP!

Something rumbles and then the gates start to creak open by themselves.

By the time I've got to the front door, Alison Wood is already there. She's wearing gardening knee-pads underneath a floaty skirt and she's carrying hedge pruners with tips so pointy and sharp that I'm surprised they're legal.

'Megan!' She grins – or tries to. Her skin won't move where she wants it to. 'How wonderful to see you. I'm so glad you came.

You caught me unawares, I'm afraid.' She waggles the pruners to make the point. 'How can I help you?'

'Dan – um, your husband – said I could come over to look at some cuttings about Zac. Is he in?'

Alison shakes her head. 'I'm all by myself, honey. I'll see what I can find, though.'

'I think he said he'd leave them out for me.'

She takes me inside, making an elaborate show of wiping her feet on the welcome mat in a way which is definitely meant to encourage me to do the same. That's some top-level passive aggression. Impressive, really – especially since there doesn't appear to be any dirt on her shoes. She could have simply *asked* me to wipe mine.

The front door leads into a massive entrance hall. There's a wide staircase directly ahead and then wings to either side of the house. It's huge and completely out of keeping with the rest of the village houses.

'I'll tell you what,' Alison says. 'You wait here and I'll check Dan's study.' She takes half a dozen steps, then spins. If she could frown, I get the sense she would. 'Sorry, where are my manners? I'll take you through to the lounge.'

She strides back past me and I follow her over the tiles towards a door. She opens it a little, dips her head inside, mutters something I don't catch and then pushes it wider for me to enter.

'Here you go,' she says. 'You wait here and I'll be right back.'

If her abrupt change of direction wasn't odd enough, she then closes the door to the hall as she exits, leaving me shut inside the room.

I look around. The lounge is a decent size, with three sofas arranged into a U-shape. An enormous television is hung on the furthest wall, while the others are lined with framed photographs. With little else to do, I make my way around the room, eyeing the photos. It's all typical stuff: Alison and Dan on a beach somewhere; Alison and Dan on a yacht. There's one of them outside the Colosseum, another of them underneath the Eiffel Tower. There are photos of them in Dubai, Sydney, New York; on Segways outside the White House.

As I make my way around the room, I think of the similar wall of travel photos at my parents' house. It was in their dining room; an attempt to show their guffawing friends what a wonderful life they were leading. Every photo contained Mother and Father – and only them. Each one had been taken somewhere exotic, expensive, or preferably both. My parents struck the same pose time and again in each: arms around one another's shoulders. Weak smiles, squinty eyes and sunburnt skin.

The photographs documented how much they changed physically as the years passed. Father became progressively more overweight. It was as if his waistline ballooned at a rate inversely proportional to the number of words he spoke to his children. The less he acknowledged Chloe and myself, the more he became a lardy heart-attack waiting to happen. While that was going on, Mother was becoming more and more plastic. She must have been twenty to thirty per cent android by the time of the car crash.

Alison knocks and it's as she re-enters the room saying, 'Only me', that I realise how weird she's acting. It's her house!

She's clutching an A4 padded envelope, which she passes across. 'I think everything's in there,' she says. 'Take it with you if you want.'

Before I can reply, there's a solid thump from overhead. I glance up automatically but Alison acts as if nothing's happened.

'Was there anything else I can help you with?' she asks.

'I don't think so.'

She edges back into the hall with an unspoken request for me to follow. I do as I'm *not* told but as soon as I hear our double set of footsteps reverberating on the tiles, I feel as if I'm ten years old again. I stop dead and look around. It's so white in here – and it's not tiles on the floor after all. It's marble, or an expensive fake alternative. The floor, steps and window frames are all made from the same thick, smooth stone.

'Have I been here before?' I ask.

Alison, who's already at the door, turns to look at me as if I've spoken in a foreign language. 'Sorry?'

'It feels like I've been here before,' I say.

'I don't think you have…'

I might not have been. There's plenty that's unfamiliar about the place and I don't know on what occasion I would have been here – but there's something so memorable about the floor and the stairs.

I take a step to the door and there's another thump from upstairs. Louder this time. Alison's smile remains painted on and forced.

'Is someone upstairs?' I ask.

'I'm the only one home.'

It's such a strange thing to lie about – but she is lying. I can see it from the way her mouth is contorted into something that's closer to a grimace than a smile. Mother used to do the same thing when she said she was looking forward to seeing me at Christmas, or when she told Father she loved him. Perhaps that's why we never got on: I could always see right through her.

I remember there are two cars on the drive.

'Do you know when Dan might be back?' I ask.

'I'm not sure,' Alison says. Her mouth screws up even tighter. 'I can give him a message if you want?'

'It's okay. I only wanted to say thank you for the clippings.'

'Of course. I'll make sure I tell him.' Alison glances towards the stairs, then the door. The fact she wants me to leave is clear – which is the very thing that makes me want to stay.

'Is there any chance I could have some water?' I ask. 'It's so hot out today. I was down in the village, so had to walk up the hill to get to you.'

There's a delicious moment in which Alison weighs up my request and it's as if I can read her thoughts. Her inner monologue is screaming for me to get the hell out – and yet she can't say it. The twisted, forced smile appears on her face again as she offers a sweet-sounding, 'Of course.'

I follow her back across the hall, past the lounge and down a short corridor that leads directly into a kitchen. By kitchen, I mean *Masterchef* cathedral of appliances. There's a thick granite counter in the centre, with one of those taps on a hose. Everything else is spotless stainless steel. It's the type of setup Mother would have loved and yet never used. She would have had a panic attack if anyone had got so much as a finger mark on the fridge.

Alison takes a crystal-clear glass from the cupboard and presses it into the water dispenser on the front of the fridge. There's a whoosh and a pop, then she passes the glass to me. In an effort to embed myself a little more, I plop myself on a stool at the counter and take the smallest of sips.

'Thank you,' I say.

'You're welcome,' she replies, maintaining her quite astonishing veneer of friendliness.

'Thank you for the food you brought over the other day as well,' I add. 'Everything's gone down really well.'

'Glad to hear it. Sorry about the mix-up with the meat and everything.'

I take another small sip. We're going to be here all day at this rate. Perhaps sensing this, Alison slides onto one of the other stools. 'Do you mind if I ask you what happened?' she says.

'What do you mean?'

'With your parents. I know what it said in the news – but you never know if that's *quite* right.'

I'll give Alison one thing: she's good. Mother was an expert at this as well. If ever she wanted me out of the room, she'd start

banging on about nails, hair, or some insane diet she was looking at and I'd scarper every time – until I realised what she was
doing, of course. Then I started playing along by talking back to
her about nails, hair, or some insane diet I thought she should
try. That was when she got really nasty.

*You're so vain, Megan. So self-centred. You should think about
your own weight before you talk about that of others.*

What I can't figure out is why Alison invited me here at all.
She badly wants me out of the house, so did I simply arrive at a
bad time?

'They were travelling back from the ballet,' I say, answering
her question. 'They were on the M25; I'm not quite sure where
exactly. It had been raining but the police said visibility was decent. No one's really sure what happened. The police wondered
if an animal had run onto the road, something like that. Dad hit
the central reservation and they ended up spinning back to face
the way they'd come. There were no other vehicles involved and
no traffic cameras on the spot. Nobody seems to know why it
happened.' I pause, just for a moment and then add: 'A bit like
Zac, I suppose. One of those things.'

Alison is listening, despite the fact that she's trying to get rid
of me. She reaches over and touches my knee. Although she was
apparently working in the garden when I arrived, her skin is
smooth and as cold as if she's been sleeping in a freezer.

'Oh, you poor thing,' she says. 'How did you find out?'

'The police came to tell me at uni,' I reply.

That perks her up. 'Where's that, then?'

'Liverpool.'

'Oh.' She's back down again.

'Studying Drama.'

'Oh.'

Her back has slumped so much that I might as well have told
her I was doing a year-long course in pole-dancing. She probably

hoped I was doing Classics at Oxford, or How To Snare A Husband at Cambridge.

Her reaction is still not as over-the-top as Mother's – she dramatically fainted on the kitchen floor when I told her of my plans to apply for Drama at Liverpool. She went down in stages and miraculously came to when she realised I had no intention of helping her up. She told me I'd have to pay my own fees, to which I replied that it was a good job I'd been saving my allowance. Then she told me I'd brought shame on the whole family – which might have had more impact if it hadn't been the third time that week she'd claimed the same thing for various perceived infractions.

'I ended up deferring the rest of the year because there was so much to sort out,' I add. 'I want to make sure Chloe's sorted with her exams and then I might think about going back.'

Alison isn't listening any more. She's been too distracted by the word 'Liverpool', which probably has her believing I live in a heroin-infested hovel somewhere in the darkest depths of The North. I suspect that the word 'Drama' means layabout time-waster to her.

'It's such a tragedy,' she says and I'm momentarily unsure whether she still means the car crash, or if she's talking about my choice of university.

There's another bump from upstairs. It sounds as if somebody's deliberately jumping off a bed onto the floor. Alison winces slightly but makes no further acknowledgement of the noise.

'Such a shame,' she adds. 'Such lovely people.'

The bravado is incredible. In all the weddings, Christmas dos, garden parties and everything else I've been trotted out for, I've never once met Dan or Alison Wood. How can she know my parents were lovely?

I take another sip of water. Alison is starting to become visibly edgy. She smooths her skirt and then begins picking at a pristine fingernail.

'I'm sorry about this,' she says, 'but I do have to get on. I'm on the Burning Boat Festival organising committee and I've got a bit of work to complete on the programmes before Sunday.'

She stands and brushes herself down. She's not wearing the garden knee-pads any more.

'I have to sort out another judge for the model boat competition as well,' she says.

I finally take the hint, pushing myself off the stool. 'The what?'

Alison speaks as she walks, guiding me out of the kitchen and back towards the front of the house. 'Children from the surrounding area make miniature boats out of whatever they want,' she says. 'They get judged. The whole thing is really competitive.'

We're almost at the front door when there's one more thunderous thump from above. This time, it's more like someone has thrown something very heavy onto the floor. Even Alison can't pretend to ignore this one. She angles her head up and mutters, rather unconvincingly, 'Pipes.'

'They're some really loud pipes,' I say.

'I know.' She opens the front door, still smiling and I amble out with the envelope of cuttings in my hand. She doesn't invite me back.

I take my time leaving. When I'm almost at the gate, I stop and turn to look at the upstairs windows. I'm not sure what I'm expecting but the only thing I can see is glare. Alison is still standing at the front door. I give her a small wave, then turn to leave. This time, I don't look back.

CHAPTER TWENTY-FOUR

Considering the low level of culinary expertise I expected, Luke has proven to be a surprisingly decent cook. We're still eating with plastic knives and forks from plastic plates and we're sitting on fold-up garden chairs but the vegetable risotto he's rustled up for Chloe is exceptional.

By exceptional, I mean that *she's* eating it.

It's harder to work the illusionist's magic in someone else's kitchen, especially while being watched more closely by two people but I did come prepared with a pocket full of tissues. For every mouthful I swallow, I'm managing to squirrel two or three away in my pockets. I wore a pair of combat trousers on purpose – Mother's eyes would have been on stalks at my clothing choice. Desperate times call for desperate measures, however.

The argument I had with Chloe earlier has seemingly been forgotten. My suggestion to eat at Luke's cottage was met with a steady, 'Why not?' – which is teenage code for, 'Wonderful idea.'

Luke has clearly made an effort. Most of the kitchen surfaces have been covered with candles. There are so many lit flames, it's like the opening scene of a fire safety movie. We're one clumsy move away from the middle act of a *Casualty* episode.

I ask Luke about his day because he I know he will answer by turning between Chloe and me. I take my moment to bury another tissue of food as he says it was quiet.

'There was no one at the beach,' he adds. 'Not a single person. I ended up going for a walk at lunch. When I got back, the police were waiting for me, asking about that Brad kid. They said he'd been attacked – but that was the first I'd heard of it.'

'I thought news travelled fast around here.'

'Oh, it does – but you have to be in the loop. I am very much *out* of the loop when it comes to this place.'

Luke takes another forkful of food and then asks Chloe if she's enjoying it.

'It's great,' she says. She would have said that even if it wasn't – she's that kind of person – but I get the sense she's telling the truth. I take the opportunity to hide another tissue of food.

'Did they talk to you?' Luke asks, looking at me.

'Who?'

'The police.'

'Of course. They spoke to both of us.'

Luke chews his last mouthful, swallows and then Frisbee-throws his plastic plate towards the sink. There's a moment in which it feels as if time has slowed. There are candles all across the counter top and the plate is spinning towards the biggest. Almost as if he planned it, the plate bounces between two candles and then drops into the empty sink. Crisis averted.

'What did you tell them?' he asks.

'Not much,' I reply. 'We don't know much.'

He nods acceptingly. I've got a small mound of risotto left on my plate but I'm out of pocket space and my stomach is still sore from the cookie incident. I make a big deal of saying I'm full and then place my nearly cleared plate carefully next to Luke's in the sink. I make my excuses and head to the bathroom – only realising after I get there that it's in the same location as the one at our cottage. I didn't ask Luke where to go.

Luke's bathroom is sparse. There's a toothbrush next to the sink, a can of Lynx on the toilet cistern and that's it. I check the cabinet, wondering if there might be any prescription drugs worth stealing but it's empty. I notice mould growing in the ceiling corners above the bath.

I empty the food from my pockets into the toilet and flush. It's not the first time I've got rid of food in this way and I always experience a panicky moment watching the water swirl, wondering if something might get stuck at the bottom. Red meat is particularly bad for this – the damned stuff sinks to the bottom of toilet bowls and stubbornly refuses to be flushed. It's for that reason that I never choose to eat it – and Chloe's veganism comes in handy as an excuse.

When I get back to the living room, Chloe and Luke are talking about Zac – which is pretty much the last thing I expected, given the falling out my sister and I had over him this morning.

'... but I don't even remember ever being here,' Chloe is saying. They both look at me as I re-enter the room. 'Megan remembers a bit more about when Zac disappeared...'

I sink back into my seat. 'Not really,' I say. 'Little bits, that's all.'

As I sit, I realise I've not spoken to Luke properly about his memories of the time. All he said was that he recognised Zac's name.

'Do you remember when he went missing?' I ask.

Luke glances at Chloe and I wonder if they've discussed it without me.

'I only remember being told by people to be careful,' he says. 'None of the adults liked us going out to the caves or up on the cliffs for a while afterwards. I think everyone assumed your brother had been lost at sea.'

'Has anyone else from the village ever been lost at sea? In your lifetime, I mean?'

'I think there may have been someone when I was really young – but that would have been before I can remember. There's not been anything here in recent years, although you do hear about it happening to other people round the coastline.'

There's an awkward pause. It's only Chloe who's still eating and she pulls a face when she realises we're both watching her finish her food.

'Thanks, that was great,' she says, before putting her empty plate down on the floor.

The conversation seems to have run its course. Luke's account is more or less the same as everyone else's. I can't help but wonder how thorough the search for Zac was. I know that Dan Wood said people scoured through the caves and the woods – but all of them seem to have assumed that Zac was washed out by the ocean, so did they really look? What if they were wrong? There's no actual evidence he drowned. No body.

It's Chloe who breaks the silence. 'Did you live here with your mum and dad?' she asks Luke.

There's innocence in her question. We don't come from a background where parents separate or divorce. In our world, they remain married until the bitter end and have affairs on the side instead. Ever since our parents died, I've been wondering whether someone might come forward to reveal they've been seeing either one of them in secret for years and make a claim to some of the inheritance. Money tends to wipe away people's inhibitions when it comes to admitting past sins.

'I lived here with my mum,' Luke says quietly. There's no follow-up and it's obvious enough he doesn't want to talk about it.

'Do you know much about the Chandlers?' I ask, to change the subject.

He looks up, surprised. 'What about them?'

'They seem to be interesting characters.'

I let it hang and Luke eventually cracks a smirk. 'You could say that. They have a lot of power around the village. I reckon

they have everyone's best interests in mind but you should probably be careful around them.'

'That's worryingly cryptic.'

Luke turns from me to Chloe and back again and breaks into
a far wider smile. He suddenly seems like himself again: the laid-
back doped-up hippy. 'Hey,' he says. 'I don't get involved. I just
want to lie around on a beach in the sun all day. It's a small village.
People are always gonna fall out. I just chill. No need to worry.'

It's when he turns to the side that it feels like we already know
each other. It's something to do with the curve of his chin and
the shape of his nose. I'm almost sure I remember him. But when
I was last here at ten years old, he'd have been fourteen or fifteen.
I can't imagine we played together. I wonder whether perhaps he
babysat me while the search for Zac was going on. I want to ask
him – but something stops me. If he knew me back then, surely
he would have mentioned it, like Chrissie did?

Chloe thanks Luke for cooking and says she'll be fine to walk
back on her own. I insist I'll go with her anyway but she practically pushes me back into my seat, telling me not to fuss. Luke
says *he'll* walk her but she's not having any of that, either. In the
end, we don't have much choice other than to let her go.

'I'm fine,' Chloe laughs. 'It's only a short walk.'

'I bet Brad thought the same,' I reply.

Chloe doesn't say anything back but the raised eyebrows tell
me she considers herself old enough to walk a couple of minutes
along a marked path by herself. She leaves, closing the door behind her.

'And then there were two,' Luke says. He gets up and goes
through the cupboards, pulling out a four-pack of cider. 'Want
one?'

'No thanks.'

He cracks a can open and returns to his chair. Without Chloe,
things suddenly feel awkward between us. I have nothing left to

ask him about regarding Zac and the bitchy part of me isn't convinced he's interesting enough for much else.

I know I shouldn't have led him on. I'm not sure why I did, other than that I was thinking about how my dead mother would react. It sounds so terrible in those terms. It sounds like I have a problem.

'I know you don't like me smoking...?' he says, somehow phrasing it as a question.

'You can do what you want. I'm not stopping you.'

He glances towards the drawer with the roll-ups but doesn't shift and takes a sip from his lager can instead.

We sit in silence for another minute or so and it dawns on me that the candles are for my benefit. I wonder if Luke asked Chloe to leave early, or if she thought she was doing me a favour.

'I know this place doesn't look like much,' Luke says suddenly, 'but there is a king-size bed through there.' He nods to the hallway behind me.

It's so cringey, so awful, that I have to try really hard not to laugh in his face. There used to be a me that would have done. There's probably a me who still would – but this village has thrown me off my game.

'Is this your way of seducing me?' I ask, trying to brush the advance off gently.

He shrugs away a nervy laugh.

'I heard that you've had different girlfriends each of the last few summers,' I add.

'Who told you that?'

'Marvin Gaye.'

'Huh?'

'Heard it on the grapevine.'

'Oh...'

I'm not sure he's got it.

He bites his lip and then says: 'That's not quite true.'

'But that means it's *sort of* true…?'

He looks away. I wonder if the candles are something he's used on each of his summer girlfriends. If so, then it doesn't feel so cringey any more. It feels calculating.

'Is that a problem?' he asks, eventually.

'Not that specifically. It's just… You're not my type.'

'Oh.' He stares at me, as if unable to comprehend what I've said. 'What about the other night?'

'It was just a kiss. I'd been drinking.' I push up from the chair. 'I think I should go.'

Luke stands abruptly. There's a moment, the merest second, where I think he's going to try to stop me from leaving. I barely have time to process that, to read the angle of his body, before there's a knock on the door.

We both turn. It's clear he isn't expecting anyone. I get there first, lifting the latch and pulling the door open to reveal Chloe.

'Am I interrupting?' she asks, turning between us.

'No. Are you okay?'

She looks towards the path that leads to our cottage. 'I think you should come and see for yourself.'

CHAPTER TWENTY-FIVE

It's not as bad as it might have been but it is a step up from the message on our path. There's glass in the kitchen sink and half a brick nestling against the wall next to the table.

The hole in the kitchen window is so neat that it's almost as if someone has carved a circle with a glass-cutter. Tendril-like cracks have splintered up through the rest of the glass to the corners of the frame. It will only take a decent gust of wind to make the whole thing implode.

'We were only out for an hour and a half,' Chloe says.

'Only takes a couple of seconds to throw a brick,' I point out.

'Do you think someone was watching the cottage, waiting for us to go out?'

'I don't think so.'

I deny it for her benefit, so that she doesn't get too freaked out – but that's exactly what I think. It's what I've been thinking for days. I've glimpsed someone just out of view three times. It can't simply be a figment of my imagination or the hazy side-effects of the prescription drugs that aren't mine.

'Should we call the police?' Chloe asks.

I take in the scene. 'I doubt we'll get anyone out tonight,' I say. 'It took them long enough to come and talk to everyone about Brad and that was really serious. Besides, we'd have to go up to the lightning tree for phone reception.'

'There might be DNA or fingerprints for them to take.'

This is true but I still don't think a broken window is going to be a high priority for a police force that's based twenty miles or more away. We've been on our own since we arrived and I don't think anything's changed now.

'Did you notice anything missing?' I ask.

Chloe turns to me, confused. This obviously hadn't crossed her mind.

'They could've bricked the window to open it,' I add. 'To burgle us.'

'And lock it back in place afterwards?'

I check it. She's right – the window is still latched but that doesn't mean the culprit didn't let themselves in and out again.

'I'll check our stuff anyway,' she says, heading towards the back of the cottage and the bedrooms.

With Chloe gone, I lift the picture off the wall. I half-expected the safe door to be unlocked, the contents missing – but it's as stubbornly locked as it was earlier.

'My things are still here,' Chloe calls.

I replace the picture and hear Chloe opening another door along the hallway.

'Meg...'

I look round. Chloe is standing in the doorway of the study, holding the door open. 'Did you do this?' she asks.

I go to stand beside her. The lamp, candleholders and photo frames are still smashed in the corner, unmoved after my fit of destruction the other day. It seems so long ago that I can't remember what had made me so angry.

It's not these items to which Chloe is referring.

The three cabinet drawers are hanging open and a hundred Zachariahs are staring up at us. The stack of 'HAVE YOU SEEN?' posters have been strewn across the floor.

'No,' I say.

'So someone broke in?'

I crouch and pick up one of the papers. Our brother's youthful face looks back at me. 'ZACHARIAH SMART' it says, underneath the huge banner.

'I don't know. Perhaps it *was* me...?'

Chloe's hand is on my elbow. We stand together, surveying the mess. I remember stamping on the tea-light holders and knocking the lamp over. I definitely saw the posters in the drawer. Maybe I scattered them across the room?

It's possible. It's not only headaches and dizzy spells that I get, it's also increasingly frequent instances of confusion. It can't be normal to forget the death of parents but I do that frequently. Most mornings I wake up believing Mother has been calling me. I wonder if that figure I keep seeing in the woods is anything at all. I'm so befuddled that there's a moment in which I consider whether *I* might have broken the window. It's only the fact that it happened while Chloe and I were elsewhere that convinces me I couldn't have done it.

Chloe crouches and reaches for the first bundle of posters. 'I'll clean up,' she says.

'No. I'll do it. I want to.' The words come far more firmly than I mean them to. Chloe twists to look at me, searching for a reason for my reaction – but there is nothing I can say to her.

'Okay,' she says simply and then retreats to her room, leaving me alone with a hundred identical clones of our brother.

After shuffling the posters together, I return them to the drawer, then close the door to the study and return to the kitchen. I'm careful to avoid the splinters of glass, sidestepping around the damage to get to the fridge. I find comfort in reading the label of Chloe's chocolate bar. One hundred grams of seventy per cent cocoa solids. She's not started eating it yet. The paper it's wrapped in is pristine. I run a finger across the wrapper, feeling the grooves of the chunks inside. I really want to eat it – but I want the feeling of control more.

I feel better after I've returned the chocolate bar to the fridge. It's a return to self-governance.

There's a dustpan under the sink that doesn't look as if it's ever been used. I sweep the largest shards of glass from the floor, emptying them onto the biscuit packet that had been taunting me from the top of the bin. I repeat the process, swiping the brush around the small nooks and corners of the skirting boards until even the smallest fragments are gone.

I carefully remove the big pieces of glass that have landed in the sink and wash the smaller ones down the drain. Finally, I go digging in the storage room opposite my bedroom. There's a large rectangle of chipboard at the back. I carry that through to the kitchen and rest it against the shattered window. It doesn't fit but it'll do for now.

I knock on Chloe's door. It takes a couple of seconds before she calls, 'Come in.' I enter to find her sitting cross-legged on the floor, phone in hand. She's playing the same game as the other day but when I come in she locks the screen and turns to face me.

'I think we should go,' she says.

'Where?'

'Home.'

It takes me a second to process that. Home for her means the house in London. *Our* house, now. I'm not sure if it'll be home for me.

'Why?' I reply.

'Why would we stay? There's nothing here for us. It's all Mum and Dad's things and it's not like we're going to move here permanently. We don't need to clear it out ourselves to sell it. We could pay someone else to do it. Do you really think we're ever going to return here for holidays?'

'No.'

'So let's go.'

It's hard to argue. Everything she's said is true but once we leave the cottage and return to the city, we'll never be back.

'The postcard,' I say, weakly. 'They sell them in the shop. Someone sent it from here.'

'So what?' Chloe says. 'If someone wanted us to come here, why haven't they said so? We've been here for three days and all we've had are messages telling us to go home and a brick through our window.'

'Don't you think there must be a reason for that?' I say.

Chloe is exasperated. She drops her phone to the bed and sighs loudly, making me feel like the younger sister. 'What reason?'

'If someone wants us to go,' I say, 'if they're trying to frighten us, it's because they're worried we might find something out. We might be close.'

She sighs. 'Find something out about what?' she asks, although I'm certain she knows the answer.

'About Zac.'

Chloe stares at me in the way Mother used to sometimes: like I'm someone, or something, that cannot be understood. Like we're speaking different languages.

I know they can speak English but they choose not to. It's so rude. Such a rude people. Can you believe it, Megan? Can you? So rude.

'Zac's dead, Meg. He died ten years ago.' Chloe breathes in, waiting for a reply I can't give. 'I want to go,' she says.

'I want to stay.'

Chloe presses her lips together and picks up her phone again. 'Well, I guess that's that.'

Saturday

CHAPTER TWENTY-SIX

I've never been a big fan of driving. There's no greater lie than those car adverts that show either impossibly good-looking people or unrealistically happy families in a new vehicle, cruising along empty roads at speed. The reality of driving is either sitting in barely moving traffic on uncomfortably hot or cold days, or having to concentrate intensely on an endless series of twists and turns along narrow lanes with overgrown hedges.

I'm not entirely sure why Mother was so insistent on me learning to drive, though I suspect it was because she wanted someone to ferry her around in later life. Despite my rebellious university choice, I still think that, deep down, she believed I'd end up marrying the son of one of her friends and setting up a *Good Housekeeping* show-home down the road.

The predominant reason I had for buying a car of which Mother did not approve was that she wouldn't have been seen dead in it.

Chloe's head is resting against the passenger window by the time I reach the T-junction on the way out of Whitecliff. She's fast asleep. I follow the signs for the nearest town, although I have to pull over once to check the directions Chloe wrote out.

I generally think of hospitals as large buildings filled with meandering old people, incomprehensible directions and vending machines at every turn – but this is a private hospital, hidden away along a series of country lanes. I almost miss the entrance because, aside from a small sign set back from the road, there's no indication it is anything other than another large house.

There is a small car park and Chloe is still asleep after I've stopped. I wait for a while and then touch her gently on the leg. She jumps awake, bumping her head softly on the window.

'Sorry,' I say.

Her eyelids flutter. 'Are we there?'

'Have been for five minutes, sleepyhead. You slept the whole way. Did you have problems dropping off last night?'

Chloe stretches high and doesn't even attempt to suppress a yawn. She wipes away the tears of tiredness and says, 'Something like that.'

The private hospital makes me think of a dystopian science-fiction lab with its whitewashed walls, high ceilings and unnerving hush. As we're led along a corridor, I half expect some sort of hybrid human-alien to leap out from a side room.

Brad is sitting up when we enter his room. A tin of M&S's finest biscuits is on the table at his side, along with an iPad and a couple of magazines. His head is wrapped in a bandage but he's smiling.

'I didn't know if you'd get my message,' he says. 'Thanks for coming.'

'George came over this morning,' Chloe replies. She settles onto the chair at his side, while I remain standing close to the door. 'How are you?'

'Concussion,' Brad says. 'They say no physical activity for two weeks. I'm not allowed to do anything.'

'Could be worse,' Chloe replies.

He puffs out a long breath. 'Yeah…'

'How's your head?' she asks.

'It was lumpy before, so this has evened it out a bit.' Brad smiles but there's not much sincerity behind it. 'I'm going home later,' he says.

'Back to the beach?'

A short shake of the head. 'My brother's down to pick me up. Mum and Dad are still away but I'm done with that place.'

'Whitecliff?'

'Something's wrong there. Can't you feel it? Under the surface?'

Chloe looks at him blankly – but I know exactly what he means. It's a relief to hear I'm not the only one who thinks it.

Brad looks up at me. 'Can you give us a few minutes?' he asks.

I glance quickly at Chloe, who yields a minuscule nod and I wonder why I even entered the ward at all. I barely know Brad.

'I'll wait outside,' I say and leave, closing the door behind me.

There's a row of three chairs on either side of the corridor outside. I take a spot opposite the only other person in sight: a young man, a little older than me, playing with his phone. He looks up and nods as I sit. He has sandy hair and chiselled looks and it's clear without needing to ask that this is Brad's brother.

'Has he cheered up yet?' he asks me, nodding to the door.

'He doesn't seem too happy about having to sit still for two weeks.'

'Don't think I would either.' He presses a button on his phone and pockets it before looking up. 'How'd you know him?'

'I don't, really. I drove my sister here to see him.'

The unnamed brother shares Brad's slightly lopsided grin. 'The kid always was a lover, not a fighter.'

'I don't think it's much of a fight if someone bashes you in the back of a head with a rock,' I say.

'No…'

I watch his fingers tighten into fists and then loosen again.

'I'm Ully,' he says. 'Short for Ulysses. And, before you say it: yes, I know.'

It's hard not to laugh at that. 'Megan,' I say.

'I don't know how I got "Ulysses" and he ended up with "Brad".'

I laugh at that, too.

'Sorry, but I can't talk to you,' he says.

'Why?'

'Your name's too normal. I only associate with people whose names originate from Greek literature. You're a bit too common for my liking.'

'Megan comes from an ancient Greek poem about watching what you say or getting a boot in the balls.'

'Oh, well in that case…' Ully licks his lips and stretches high, rubbing his neck. 'Are you staying in the caravans with the rest of them?'

'No. My parents have a cottage.'

'Posh. You must have connections.'

'You know the village?'

He uses both hands to do a double point at his chest. 'Former beach kid,' he says. 'We should get T-shirts.'

'When was your last summer there?' I ask.

'Probably six or seven years ago. I went three or four times. One of the lads at school invited me one summer. Mum and Dad didn't object – saved them from having to take me to France with them.'

He must see the intrigue in my face, because he follows up with, 'What?'

'You might have known my brother.'

'Who was he?'

'Zac Smart.'

A line creases into his forehead. 'The lad who went missing?'

I nod and Ully rocks his head back as if not quite able to believe it. 'That was such a long time ago,' he says.

'Ten years.'

'*Really?*' He huffs out a breath. 'Way to make a guy feel old. I guess I was fifteen at the time.'

'So, did you know him?'

'Sort of. We weren't friends – but I saw him on the beach in the evenings. He was off with this girl from the village quite a lot.'

'Chrissie.'

He clicks his fingers. 'Right. Chrissie. Anyway, they did their thing and I hung around with my friends. I remember Zac being around the campfire a couple of times but that's it.'

'Do you remember him going missing?'

'Sort of. It was a weird time. It was my first summer there – my first one completely away from my parents. You know what that's like. It was fun. A blur. Then one day, when we got up, my friend said Zac had gone missing. We went walking through the woods to help with the search but we didn't really know what we were doing or where we were going.' He stops. 'Was he ever found? Or was he, like… dead?' He glances away apologetically.

'No body,' I reply. 'No one knows what happened.'

It takes Ully a few seconds to continue. 'Everything went a bit flat that summer, afterwards. We'd gone to the beach most nights before that but no one was interested in going after Zac disappeared. It was like a balloon had popped. It wasn't fun any longer.' A pause and then: 'Sorry.'

I wait a few moments, not wanting to seem too keen. 'Did you remain in Whitecliff that summer?' I ask.

'There wasn't an option for me to do anything else. My parents were still overseas. The kids who stayed ended up sticking pretty close to the caravans for most of the time afterwards. It didn't feel right to be in the village.'

'But you came back the next year…?'

'Right.'

'Were people still talking about Zac then?'

He winces as he looks away. 'Don't hate me – I know how it sounds – but in all honesty, we'd forgotten him. It's not like there was an anniversary remembrance of him going missing or anything. I didn't know him that well in the first place – I didn't even know he had sisters until I met you just now. We carried on like it never happened.'

'That's fine,' I say. 'I get it. What was it like around the village back then?'

'Awkward,' he replies. 'There were rumours the pubs and shops used to charge the locals one price and us another. That used to annoy people – but, in the end, we were there for the sun, the beach and the girls. There was plenty of all three, so we didn't complain too much about the prices. It was friendly enough other than that.'

As he finishes the sentence, he realises where he is – and why. 'I guess it's not so friendly any more,' he adds, more quietly.

I find myself staring at Brad's hospital door. 'I guess not.'

CHAPTER TWENTY-SEVEN

Chloe and I have only just reached the cobbles of Whitecliff's main street when Scott comes storming across from the docks area.

He's behind us but his shout of, 'You!' makes us both turn. I initially assume it's me he's after – but then I see that he's jabbing a finger towards Chloe. She turns to look behind her, as if expecting someone else to be there. By the time she's spun back, he's already upon us. He stops an arm's length away, his finger level with Chloe's face. His features are twisted and distorted with anger, saliva collecting in the corner of his mouth.

'Did you tell the police I beat up that Brad kid?'

Chloe cranes away from him, taking half a step backwards. 'No.'

'Then why'd they come round asking questions?'

She shuffles closer to me. 'I don't know.' She stumbles over her words. 'I... I just said there was a fight on the beach.'

'Why?'

'Because... there was.'

A vein appears above Scott's eye and starts to throb. The muscles in his upper arms bulge. He doesn't quite seem to know what to do with himself.

'That wasn't anything,' he says.

Chloe holds her hands out, not sure how to reply – so I do it for her.

'It was me who gave the police your name,' I say. 'Not Chloe.'

Scott spins from Chloe to me. 'What?'

'My sister didn't even *know* your name. *I* told them who you were. The officer wrote it very clearly in her notebook. Really neat handwriting. I was impressed.'

Scott starts to tremble. It takes a couple of seconds for him to spit out what he says next: 'You *grass*! You snitching bitch.'

I feel as if everything that's happened since we arrived in the village has been building to this. I lost control with yesterday's binge but I'm back in charge now. It's like those news stories about people who show the most unfathomable degrees of calm while all around them is falling apart. Pilots who know they're crashing and yet speak clearly to passengers and control towers. Civilians caught up in terrorist attacks who lead others to safety. I'm being over-the-top but I don't care: that's how I feel now. As all around me is collapsing, I'm standing tall.

I snort with derision. 'Is that supposed to be an insult?'

Scott raises his finger again, thrusting it towards my face but I slap it away defiantly. It isn't only hunger roaring in my stomach – there's fire there. Scott is caught slightly off-guard by the slap and I take the opportunity to shove him in the chest. He doesn't move – but that isn't why I did it. There's rage in his narrowing eyes. *That* is what I wanted.

'Do you get off on hitting girls?' I say.

'Why are you even in Whitecliff?' he asks.

'Because I want to be. What's it got to do with you?'

'You've been going round the village upsetting everyone, asking about things we've all long forgotten. It's got everything to do with me.'

'It's nice and convenient that you've all forgotten my brother,' I say. 'He walked these streets and played on this beach like everyone else. He worked with *your dad* on the boat. He went out with *your wife* before you did. And all you can say is that you've *forgotten* him? I don't believe you.'

It's all in the open now. I step forward and, miraculously, Scott steps back. He glances sideways and I realise that some of the villagers have come out of their houses and shops. There are at least a dozen locals in the impromptu audience. I see Arthur on the kerb, using his walking stick for support.

I'm too far gone now. I open my arms and turn to face all of them. 'You *all* knew Zac but none of you knows what happened to him. Not one of you!' I turn back to Scott. 'Wouldn't it be convenient if we went away and forgot him, too?'

Nobody says anything. The only reply I receive is a cough from someone out of view. I've crossed a line that can't be un-crossed.

Chloe is tugging on my arm, wanting to go, but I resist her. I lean in towards Scott, lowering my voice so that only he and Chloe can hear.

'I saw you,' I say.

'Saw me what?'

'I saw you and Brad talking near the lightning tree. You know I did – not long before *someone* bashed him in the head.'

Scott stands taller. I catch a glimmer of fear from him that drives me on. 'It all looked very cosy,' I add. 'What was going on with you two?'

He takes the smallest of steps towards me and despite the fact he's a good head taller than me, I don't find it remotely intimidating. There are too many witnesses.

I wouldn't have guessed Scott would be capable of speaking so quietly – but when it next comes, his voice is barely a whisper. 'Did you…?'

'I didn't tell the police, if that's what you're worried about.'

He steps away and lets out a breath. 'You need to mind your own business,' he says.

'My mother used to tell me the same thing.'

Scott starts to say something else but we're both thrown off by a bang from behind. Pete has flung open the pub door and is rushing towards us. He says nothing, but grabs his son's arm and pulls him away. Scott doesn't exactly fight his father but he doesn't allow himself to be dragged away easily, either.

'Stay away from my wife,' he shouts at me, loudly enough for everyone to hear.

There's an audible sigh of relief – or disappointment – from the crowd as he disappears into the pub. I turn to take in the watching villagers properly. There are more people than I thought: probably twenty of them, all on the street for a bit of free entertainment.

'You should go home,' a voice calls over. 'Both of you.'

It's Gwen Arkwright who has spoken. She's outside her shop, leaning on the doorframe. She doesn't wait for a reply before returning inside.

After that, there's a steady stream of shuffling footsteps and closing doors. Someone touches me on the arm. I jump, spinning and ready to lash out – but it's only Arthur. He doesn't flinch but instead smiles kindly.

'Come on,' he says. 'I'll put the kettle on.'

I start to tell him that I don't drink tea but then I realise that I'm shaking. My confidence of minutes ago has deserted me. I want to be by myself. I want to run back to the cottage and smash everything my mother ever bought.

'You're okay now,' Arthur says. 'Let's get you inside.'

CHAPTER TWENTY-EIGHT

The endless twisting and turning from walking across the pebbles is making my knees and ankles ache as if I have chronic arthritis. Perilous stacks of rocks tumble every few steps and I end up sliding sideways several times in an effort to keep my footing.

'We should tarmac this whole beach,' Vee says. She's a few steps ahead but struggling as much as I am – despite her sensible shoes.

'We need a different word for "beach",' I reply. 'I hear *beach*, I think *sand*. Pebbles and rocks are cheating. There's no way this is a beach.'

'What would you prefer?'

'Rocky monstrosity. Then if someone asks whether you want to go sunbathing at the beach, you know what you're getting. If they ask you down to the rocky monstrosity, you can tell them to do one.'

Vee might have laughed but I'm not sure, because I stumble to my knees trying to make it over a crumbling mound of pebbles. I end up using a hand to support myself. When I finally get back into a standing position, Vee is at my side. She's in long sleeves again, with shorts and trainers. I'm glad I didn't put on my sandals this morning because there's no way they'd have survived this journey.

The cliffs tower above us – but they're on the opposite side of the village from our trip to Whitecliff Caves a couple of days ago. Instead of following the beach – the *proper* beach – we've gone the other way, passing the pub and the docks and continuing along the shoreline.

It's not been easy going, with a mix of trees and greenery giving way to sand banks and then this seemingly endless stretch of pebbles. Every step is a crunch-crunch-crunch of rocks grinding together, an ominous drumbeat as we move further and further away from the village.

'Are you sure this is the right way?' I ask.

'If you know a better route to Fisherman's Cave, we can take it?' Vee grins at me.

'All right. It's just hard to believe people actually come out this way.'

'They don't, much. That's why it's not on any of the tourist maps. This is all under water at high tide.'

I turn to look out at the sea in the distance. It doesn't seem like much of a threat – for now.

'Are you sure your brother used to come out to the cave?' Vee asks.

'That's what Chrissie told me.'

'What are you hoping to find?'

'I don't know… Maybe nothing. I think partly I just want to get away from the village after the thing with Scott.'

Vee snorts but there's no malice there. 'It sounds like it was hilarious. No one ever stands up to Scott. I wish I'd seen it.'

'It wasn't hilarious,' I reply. 'He was going off on Chloe and… I don't know.'

Vee takes my hand and steps away so that we're at arm's length from one another. 'It's fine to be protective over a sister. She's the only family you have.'

It's not like Vee is saying something I don't already know – but it feels like a sharp reminder that I'd be alone if it wasn't for Chloe.

I blink away the glimmer of upset and don't think Vee notices. She releases my hand and sets off along the rocks again, wobbling awkwardly from side to side as if on a tightrope. I try to follow her path as closely as possible. As she walks, she lashes out, kicking a stone that clicks and bumps its way into the distance.

'I've had a run-in with the Chandlers,' she says.

'Really?'

'They think they run the village. People never want to say anything bad about them because they employ a bunch of people at the pub and on the boats. If you lose a job with them, or if they turn on you, there's few other places to go for work. I'm a bit different because of the board shop. My dad, my brother and I don't rely on them.'

'What was your run-in about?'

'Nothing really. Scott wanted a discount on some things and I wouldn't give it to him. I think he thought he could bully me into knocking some money off because he's bigger than me. He said he'd go to my dad instead – and then Dad told him there was no discount either.'

Another stone goes sailing off into the distance, courtesy of Vee's shoe. She's getting steadily further ahead, which she realises, stopping for a moment until I'm caught up, before setting off again.

It's another scorcher of a day and I don't know how Vee's managing to tolerate a long-sleeved top. I'm in a vest and shorts and the sweat is pouring from me.

'Gwen Arkwright's another one,' Vee says.

'Another what?'

'She's all chummy with the Chandlers because her daughter's married to Scott. People do what she wants because if she bans you from the shop, the only other option is the supermarket that's way out of town. Not everyone can drive and the buses are all over the place. Gwen's used to getting her own way.'

'You make it sound like the village is run by the mafia,' I say.

Vee puts on a fake – and appalling – Italian accent: 'Do I amuse you?! Huh?' It takes me a second to work out what she's said.

'Isn't that *Goodfellas*?'

'Same deal.'

We stop for a moment, passing a water bottle between us. Vee takes a bite from a cereal bar and then offers it to me. I surprise myself by accepting and having a small bite myself. I feel like I don't want to let her down – as if rejecting the offer of food would be rejecting her.

'Didn't Chloe want to come?' Vee says.

'She's helping at the gallery,' I say. 'Something to do with the Burning Boat Festival.'

'Ah. Good ol' Arthur. He used to buy presents for all the village kids at Christmas. He probably still does – it's just I'm too old to get one now.'

From nowhere, there's a rumbling sound from the cliffs above. We separate as a flurry of soil lands between us. It's followed by a couple of small rocks. We stand apart, both looking up.

'Is this an avalanche?' I ask.

'Not a very big one. They reckon the cliffs are disappearing by a few centimetres every year.'

We wait for a couple more seconds, until we're sure we're not about to get bombarded with more rocks from above, and then we start walking again.

Vee is a few steps ahead once more, still talking over her shoulder. 'Have you heard anything about that Brad kid?' she asks.

'We visited him this morning,' I say. 'He's awake and going home with his older brother. One more victim of Whitecliff.'

I don't know why I say it. It's not a joke and it doesn't get a laugh.

Vee continues as if I'd not spoken. 'Things will probably calm down now,' she says. 'Someone pulled a knife a couple of years back and, as strange as it sounds, it was the best thing that could have happened. Tension had been building all summer but it went away after that. I think both sides realised things had gone too far.'

'I don't think it should take someone being bashed in the head from behind for everything to calm down,' I say.

'I know. I didn't mean that. I'm just saying…'

There's another rumble of rocks and soil from above. We stop to look up. Then I find myself turning to look back towards the village in the distance. There's nothing and nobody behind us, not even a breeze. It's only us.

Vee continues to guide us along the coastline but it's hard to tell how far we've gone because it's such slow and clumsy going over the pebbles. As we round a stretch of cliff that juts out into the sea, I realise the tide isn't as far out as I'd thought. Or, more likely, we've been heading further out towards it. The water is low but the rocks are wet and we've gone from sliding across dry stone to slipping on damp pebbles.

We carry on moving regardless and, as we pass the next kink in the shape of the inlet, I can finally see why Zac and others might have come here.

Whitecliff Caves were open and obvious – accessible relatively easily by either foot or boat. I can imagine tourist boats pulling up to the entrance, dumping out their overpaying clientele for some quick photos and then loading them up again. The opening to Fisherman's Cave is far smaller. There's no gaping mouth in the rock; the entrance is barely the size of two or three regular doors shoved together. And Whitecliff is far enough away from it that the village and its problems seem a distant memory.

There's something close to a natural staircase weathered into the cliff, leading to the entrance. Vee climbs the rocks, stopping at the cave opening to haul me up. Her legs are damp and she smells of the sea. We laugh as we topple backwards into the darkness.

'Spoooooooky!' Vee calls, her voice echoing around the passage before us.

It feels as if we've entered a world of our own.

We use our phones to light the way. The cavern goes back a surprising distance. Unlike the network of Whitecliff Caves, where one cave leads into another, this is more of a tunnel. There are markings on the walls – mainly initials and love hearts. Some are deep grooves in the rock, suggesting the culprit has used a chisel; others are cruder scratches that have barely made an indent.

The sound of dripping water is a constant and there's a literal light at the end of the tunnel. I follow Vee deeper into the cliff, towards the light, until we emerge into a hollowed-out dome of a room. It's not huge – probably the size of an average bedroom. The walls are covered with more initials, hearts and a few games of noughts and crosses. Some of the markings are in chalk, others have been made with blades. There's no need to use our phones in here because there's a vertical tunnel directly above us, spilling the brightness of the day down in a neat circle. It feels like we're at the bottom of a well.

Vee runs her fingers around the walls and then sits on the floor.

'Do you come here often?' I ask.

'That sounds like a chat-up line.'

'Ha! I didn't mean it like that.'

The echoes of our voices entwine, reverberating around the limited space.

'Pretty much never,' Vee replies. 'I've only been here once before and that was a few years ago. I only came then because Dad told me not to. I wanted to see what all the fuss was about.'

'Why'd you come now?'

It's dim away from the main pillar of light and I can't quite see her in the outer gloom. Instead, I can feel Vee's gaze searching for mine.

'Because you asked,' she says.

I slide down the wall opposite her. The shaft of light creates a halo between us. I can only see her shadowy outline.

'We go to the other caves sometimes,' she says. 'Me and some of the others from the village. We have a party the day after everyone leaves. It's like we're getting our beach back.'

I trace my finger around some of the markings on the wall. It's dark in the corners but I use my phone to illuminate the closest one to where I'm sitting:

ZS 4 CA

'Some of the beach kids were saying they come down to Whitecliff for the summer relationships,' I say.

Vee seems to know what I'm really asking. 'Sometimes they do,' she says. 'It happened for me last year…'

It sounds like she wants me to ask for more, so I do. 'Was that a—'

'Xander,' she says, anticipating my question. 'One of the beach kids. Some of the other village lot reckoned I was betraying them by crossing enemy lines.'

'Did you keep in touch with him afterwards?'

'He left an email address but I didn't contact him and he didn't contact me. He didn't come back this year, either. Like I said, sometimes you see the same faces over and over; other times it's a one-time only deal.'

I wait, knowing what she's going to ask next.

'Will you be back?' she says, eventually.

'I don't think so.'

Vee doesn't reply for a while. We sit quietly, listening to the dripping monotony around us. There's a peace to it. And in that moment, I realise that I've stopped thinking about food. Usually, it's always there at the edge of my thoughts – in much the same way that I've seen the person in the woods at the corner of my vision. It's so much a part of my life, that to have gone even a short while without it scratching away at my consciousness makes me shiver.

'Whitecliff is a weird place to grow up,' Vee says, bringing me back into the cave.

'Normal is what's normal for you,' I reply.

She takes a second or two and then says, 'Right. Like you said the other day. I've been thinking about that. It's a good way of putting it. You only realise other people live differently, or think differently, when you get out and meet them.'

'Do you think you'll ever leave Whitecliff?'

Vee doesn't answer and we sit listening to the nothingness. It's the first time in a long time that I can remember feeling comfortable. On a bed with pillows, sheets, a quilt and throws, I can only sleep in bursts; yet here, where it's hard and unforgiving, where there's that tiny needle of pain from the rocks, it feels like I could sleep forever.

I close my eyes, rest my head against the rock and allow myself to drift.

The next thing I know, the dripping sounds significantly louder, having combined into a resounding ensemble. And my shorts are wet.

I jump up, realising Vee is no longer opposite me. Water has seeped into my shoes, drenching my socks.

'Vee?'

'I'm here.'

I follow her voice back along the tunnel to the rocks where we entered. She reaches back towards me and takes my hand. Her skin is damp and slightly wrinkled, as if she's only just climbed out of the bath.

'We have a problem,' she says, quietly.

Or, perhaps she isn't speaking quietly. It's just that I can't hear her over the noise of the water.

The tide has raced in and is now licking the entrance to the cave. The noise is deafening, as if we're completely surrounded. Each wave that crashes sends a slim sheet of water lapping along the tunnel, towards where we had been sitting.

Jumping in isn't an option. Every wave is smashing into the rocks with a thunderous roar. Even the strongest swimmer would be battered back against the cliff face before he or she could get away.

'What do we do?' I ask.

Vee's fingers squeeze mine. 'I guess we wait,' she says.

CHAPTER TWENTY-NINE

It's when the water starts to flow over my trainers that the panic begins to set in. Vee and I have retreated to the room at the end of the tunnel in an attempt to escape the worst of the spray – but it's not going to provide protection against the rising water.

'I didn't mean to fall asleep,' Vee says.

'It's my fault. I wanted to come.'

We are pressed together, mainly because it's the only way of remaining warm. Even though the water is only at our ankles, my entire body is drenched. My hair is sticking to the back of my neck, my vest clinging soddenly to my back. I'm so wet that it feels as if I might never get dry again, as if the water is now a part of me.

Neither of us are speaking, probably because we're both terrified. The speed at which the water is rising is other-worldly. Each wave sends the water cascading along the tunnel, each successive ripple seeming to rise a few millimetres higher than the last.

Vee steps away until she's directly under the vertical shaft above.

'I don't think waiting is going to work,' she says.

The light catches her face and I see that her gingery hair looks black, plastered to her head by the water.

I step closer to her and we both look up towards the light. It's hard to figure out how such a chimney was created. It looks natural, with rocks jutting out from the sides, yet it seems to be a consistent width the entire way up.

'Do you think you can boost me?' Vee asks. 'I might be able to shimmy up.'

I realise instantly that this would mean I'd have no way to follow – nobody to boost me up, too. The chimney's too high to reach by jumping. But there's little time to argue, or plan. Vee lifts a foot and I crouch, cupping my hands underneath it. She counts to three and I propel her up.

It's apparent straight away that this isn't going to work. Vee's hands scrape the entrance to the chimney but she's nowhere near high enough to be able to stretch herself across its width. She jumps down.

'Do you think I can balance on your shoulders?' she asks.

We look at each other and neither of us have to say it. I probably can't support her weight – but she can likely take mine. Without needing to say so, she crouches as if about to leapfrog and I hook my legs around her neck. The moment she begins to stand, it feels as if I'm about to wobble off. She staggers from side to side as I reach up and press my palms into the sides of the shaft, trying to help her balance.

'Can you reach?' she calls, sounding strained.

'Just.'

'Hang on.'

Vee takes a breath and then stands tall. I stretch higher, reaching for some sort of ledge. I manage to dig my fingers into a gap behind a rock. It feels as if my shoulders are going to jump from their sockets, but with one final heave, I lift myself from Vee's shoulders into the chimney.

There's a moment in which it feels like I might fall, but then I press my back against one side of the chute, stretching my legs to push against the other. I'm wedged securely.

Then I breathe.

'Are you okay?' Vee calls.

'I think so.'

I feel like a bizarre strain of caterpillar as I begin to wriggle upwards. The rocks are digging painfully into my back, but it's the only way.

Every movement sends a shower of stones and soil skittering down to the cave below. Gradually, centimetre by centimetre, I edge my way up. I'm terrified of moving too suddenly and dislodging myself, knowing there will be nothing to stop my fall if I do.

Maybe it's because I'm moving so slowly, or maybe it's because I'm conscious of Vee standing below me, anxiously watching my progress, but it takes me a couple of minutes to notice that the chimney is widening the further I climb. It's an illusion that it's the same width the whole way up. I started at the bottom with the soles of my feet pressing flat into the wall, but now I'm having to strain my toes into a pointed position, like a ballet dancer, to keep myself wedged in place.

'Vee?' I call down. 'It's not going to work. I need to drop.'

When she's clear, I edge down, then tuck in my knees. Somehow, I land on my feet with a splosh.

When I straighten myself out, I realise the water is halfway up to my knees – and still rising. The ripples are flooding in faster and stronger and it's becoming harder to stand with each rush of water.

Vee steps towards me until we're directly under the light. The centre of attention: two actresses on stage, illuminated by a spotlight.

She leans in and shouts in my ear – the only way to be heard. 'I'm sorry!'

Even in the light, it's hard to see her properly. I don't know if there are tears in her eyes, or if it's spray from the water.

I tilt her head with my hands and angle in so that I can shout back into her ear. 'Me, too.'

She presses away, glances up and shouts, 'What are we going to do?'

I'm not sure that I hear her, it's more that I read the shape of her lips, knowing she's asking the same thing as me.

I don't know how to reply because, if the water continues to rise, there's only one answer for what we do now.

We drown.

CHAPTER THIRTY

I can't help but wonder if this is what happened to Zac. Maybe he came out to Fisherman's Cave by himself for a bit of peace and, the next thing he knew, the tide was yanking him out to the deepest depths of the ocean.

I think of Chloe, too. The burden of one missing sibling is enough – but how can anyone cope with two? It's not like I told anyone where I was going – and, unless Vee did, nobody is going to know where we are. Chloe will be left alone, wondering forever.

The water is at our knees now. Vee and I are pressed together, swaying with the tide. It's marginally easier to keep our balance with four legs instead of two – but all it'll take is one vicious wave and we'll be sucked out onto the rocks.

'HELP!'

Vee is barely audible over the water but I realise her aim isn't for me to hear her. She's shouting upwards, face tilted towards the light – if someone happens to be walking above, there's a chance they might hear.

I join in until we're both breathless and hoarse from yelling at the rocks. Vee pulls me closer and says something I don't catch. When she steps away, she rolls up her sleeves, showing me why she always wears long-sleeved tops.

There are scars sliced into her wrists. Even in the fading light, I can see the welts. They're sliced along the length of her arms, rather than side to side. The way someone does it if they actually want to do some damage. Vee holds both wrists up into the light until she's sure that I've seen and then rolls her sleeves back down.

She's definitely crying now and I clasp onto her. We hold each other. I wonder how many people she's shown those marks to. Whether her father knows; her brother. Whether they came before or after Xander, last summer.

Vee doesn't need to say why she's shown me, because I already know. If this is it, if we're going to die here, then at least she's told someone. We hold one another and I feel her tapping me on the shoulder.

Except… She *hasn't* touched my shoulder. I can feel both her hands on my back. I pull away, twisting to look up to where a dark rope is swaying back and forth against the daylight from above.

Vee has seen it, too, her eyes wide with surprise.

The water is almost at our waists. We don't need to talk: we act. Vee uses me as a climbing frame, which is fine by me. I lift her up again, my hands under her feet. She grabs for the rope as high up as she can reach, clasping it first time. She swings back and forth for a moment but, within seconds, she's hauling herself up. I hold the end of the rope as taut as I can, hoping it helps. I don't want to try climbing myself until she's out – I don't know what the rope is tied to at the other end and, though it might be able to take both of our weights, it's not something I should risk.

I stare up, watching Vee's shape slowly block more and more of the light until there's only the slimmest of rings around her. It's almost black in the cave. I'm now having to hold onto the rope to keep myself steady as the waves rock me back and forth.

And then, like a miracle, the rope goes slack and light floods onto me once more.

Vee's safe.

I don't hang around. I move my hands as high up the rope as I can reach, then grab tight and pull myself up. It's the type of cord people use for rock-climbing: thin, but frightfully strong. I pull with my arms and shuffle with my knees, heaving myself into the chimney and then bumping back and forth from wall to wall.

My shoulders are on fire, my arms feel like they might drop off, and yet my feet are still in the water. A kaleidoscope of colour fizzes across my vision and I clamp my eyes closed to try to will it away. Vee called me skinny and it was perfect. I don't weigh much and there's not a lot of me to be pushed and pulled around. But pushing and pulling *my own* weight around is another thing entirely. I don't do this sort of thing – climbing, running, jumping – any longer, because I can't.

'Meg?'

My name swoops and swirls down the passage from above. Vee is calling my name but, when I open my mouth to shout back, there's nothing there.

I clamp my knees as tight as I can around the rope and stretch up with my arms. I pull and my shoulder joint grinds into the socket. Pestle into mortar. I tell myself to breathe. To focus. I can control this. It hurts, but so what?

It *always* hurts. It hurts in the mornings and it hurts in the evenings.

'Meg?'

When I open my eyes again, the rainbow has gone and there is only black. I risk a glimpse down and the water is further away than I thought. The light above is closer. My arms still ache but there is a calmness as well.

I use each swing as an opportunity to haul myself a little higher, until slowly, eventually, I feel hands underneath my armpits.

My palms are raw. I find myself on my back, staring up at the blue of the sky dappling through the trees above.

Rocks are digging into my back and when I roll onto my side, I realise I'm on the edge of the cliff. The vent in the ground is open and unmarked: there for anyone to accidentally fall into. A health and safety department somewhere has gone mad.

Vee, who has pulled me out, collapses down next to me and we lie side by side, limbs stretched wide like children making angels in the snow.

She starts to laugh and then I join in. I don't think either of us know what's funny but it feels like we've got one over on fate. We've stared into the abyss and won.

Vee pushes herself up and then reaches down to pull me to my feet. She's soaking: wet hair plastered to her face, the shape of her bra clear through her sodden top.

'I thought—'

I cut her off, not wanting to hear the rest of the sentence. 'I know.'

We both know.

I don't mention the scars she showed me. It feels like a dream. A private moment shared when we thought the worst would happen. Things are different now.

My breath is beginning to return and the warmth of the sun is taking the edge off the chill. Somehow, the ache in my shoulders and arms has already gone. Either that, or I'm so used to ignoring pain that it has blended in with everything else.

I drag the hair from my face and wring it out, as if all is well and I've just got out of the shower.

And then I realise: where is the person who threw us the rope?

'Who rescued us?' I ask.

Vee shakes her head. 'No idea. Nobody was here when I got to the top.'

We follow the rope from the cave exit, along the rocks to where it has been tied around a tree. The knots are tight and expertly tied. Not simply some passing stranger creating elephant ears to tie laces, then. Whoever tied it knew what they were doing.

'It's worn,' Vee says, showing me the places that she means. 'It's probably been here for a while. It might have been left behind by cavers or abseilers.'

'Someone still threw it down,' I say. 'Who?'

The answer to that question feels like everything and nothing. Someone saved us – but the 'saved' is the important part. Part of me doesn't care who it was.

'Shall we go back?' Vee says. 'I could do with a towel.'

I'm about to agree, when a glint of something at my feet catches my eye. Next to the tree, directly underneath the rope, something shiny is on the ground. I crouch and pick it up. It's a thick necklace; the type of chain generally worn by men.

I hold it up for Vee to see. She takes the chain, running her fingers along the smooth links. 'Do you think whoever dropped it was the person who saved us?'

I take the necklace back, passing it from one hand to the other to judge the weight.

'Maybe,' I say, forcing myself not to give too much away. 'Which way?'

Vee turns. I follow her across the craggy rock face towards the trees beyond. I slip the chain into my pocket, hoping Vee doesn't ask about it again.

The truth is that I've seen the necklace before – and I know exactly who it belongs to.

CHAPTER THIRTY-ONE

Vee and I follow the curve of the land back towards Whitecliff, until the steep drop leaves us with no option other than to cut in, away from the cliff edge. There's no path but the trees are spaced far enough apart that it's easy to keep moving.

Neither of us speak much on the journey back. I guess we're both thinking about what might have been. I wonder if I am more upset about my own brush with death, or about what could have happened to Vee. I'm not sure I know the answer.

By the time we emerge into the clearing outside Luke's cottage, our clothes are starting to dry from the heat of the day. I lead the way through the forest until we get to my parents' cottage.

I grab us a pair of towels from inside. Vee rubs her hair down and then passes the towel back to me.

'That was a weird afternoon,' she says.

I shrug at her in bemused confusion. It feels like one of those stories where kids have a big adventure, wake up and assume it was all a dream. Then they find something under a pillow – and that's the final scene or page.

There's a necklace in my pocket, my shorts are damp and my shoes squelch when I walk. So much happened and that's all I have to show for it.

I could leave Vee to return home by herself but somehow it feels as if we have to complete the journey together. I show Vee the route to the road and then we walk down to the village at one another's side.

As we get closer to the bottom of the hill, I notice that the village has changed in the few hours we've been away. Bunting and streamers now criss-cross the main street and the lamp-posts are adorned with flowers and ribbons. Foldaway tables have been stacked flat against the pub, ready to be laid out, and a skip has appeared next to the beer garden. Someone must have had fun getting that down the hill.

'Are you coming down for the festival tomorrow?' Vee asks.

'I'm sure I'll be around,' I say. 'Are you working?'

'Not all day. We'll see how it's going.'

There's an awkward moment, in which neither of us seems to know the best way to say goodbye. A simple 'bye' doesn't seem enough after everything that's happened. We end up doing a weird combination of shaking hands and hugging, almost butting heads in the process.

I watch Vee stride away towards her father's shop and my stomach grumbles angrily, as if sending a warning.

I'm about to head back up the hill when the sound of men's voices catches my attention. They're coming from somewhere around the back of the pub. I edge to the fence and tuck in behind the newly arrived skip.

When I peer around the corner, I see Pete, Scott and – surprisingly – Dan Wood, all standing next to the wooden boat I saw in the dock the other day. It looks flimsy and weak, barely capable of holding a person – and that's when I realise this is the boat they're going to set on fire for the festival.

I can't hear what the three men are talking about but they seem relaxed and amiable. A bit like Scott and Brad were when I saw them together by the campsite.

I move out into the open, not hiding the fact that I'm watching as the men continue to talk. Pete's pointing at the boat and Dan says something which draws a shrug. It's then that Pete notices me on the path. His lips twitch and Dan turns.

'Hi there,' he calls, waving. He's still looking like the distinguished older man from a hair advert. He's in linen slacks, a loose shirt and sandals, like he's about to saunter off for tapas at a late-night Spanish bar. He says something to Pete and Scott, then strolls towards me with his hands in his pockets.

'Just finalising some things for the festival tomorrow,' he says. 'Exciting, isn't it?'

'I guess.'

He grips hold of my shoulder in that fatherly way he has. 'Alison says you dropped over yesterday. What did you think?'

'Of what?'

'The clippings. Did you have a good look through the envelope?'

I only realise he's steered me away from the pub when the path we're on becomes tarmac once more. I hadn't even noticed we were walking.

'It was useful,' I say. 'Thanks. I'll bring them back one evening.'

'No matter,' he replies. 'You should keep them. He was your brother, after all.'

'Are there any more?'

'I don't think so. Certainly not that I kept. Was there something you were hoping for?'

'The reports pretty much stop dead three days after Zac disappeared. Wasn't there any sort of follow-up a week later? Or a month?'

'If there was, then I didn't cut it out.'

We stop at the base of the hill and Dan waves towards a man I don't recognise, calling a cheery, 'Hello!' in his direction.

'Are you coming up?' Dan asks me, nodding at the hill.

I am – but suddenly have the urge to not be at his side.

'Not yet,' I reply. 'I think Chloe's on the beach, I'm going to find her first.'

'Good for you! Make sure you come to the village tomorrow. It'll be very different – the highlight of the year.' He eyes me up and down and I feel terrifyingly exposed. 'There'll be food,' he says.

I stand frozen, unable to reply.

The moment passes and then Dan flashes me another wave – something he seems to do more than a member of the Royal Family – before jamming his hands in his pockets and heading up the slope out of the village.

I watch him go, not sure what to make of his personality. He's charming enough on the surface. I can't quite work out what's drawn him and Alison together. They seem such opposites: Dan calm and friendly, Alison jumpy and fake. I can picture Mother and Alison knocking back a bottle of gin together, comparing diets and surgeons – but it's hard to see where Dan would fit into the picture. Nobody in my family has – or had – the warmth or charisma that he does. Except Chloe, perhaps.

I amble across to the beach. It's empty, aside from a couple of villagers who are fixing a series of flags to poles close to where the volleyball game was a couple of days before. I turn to look up at the road, watching until Dan is out of sight. The tide is in but there's still a large space between the houses that back onto the beach and the stretch of sand that's damp from the water. There's a fluffy foam to the crests of the waves but the sea feels benign, not the rampaging threat it was barely a couple of hours ago.

It's been a long day. The underlying sense of tiredness I always have is beginning to spread. When I yawn, it feels as if I might be able to sleep for more than a twenty-minute burst.

There's no one on the road but I cut into the woods anyway, heading up the slope towards the cottage. I'm only a short distance up the path before I feel like I can't go on any more. I'm sweating but cold at the same time. I have to cling onto a tree trunk for support as one of my oh-so-familiar dizzy spells tears through me. I'm afraid to open my eyes. The world is spiralling out of control.

I wait, staring into the darkness of my eyelids. It's the only thing I can do when my body conspires to betray me.

Time passes. The murk begins to ebb and fade. I open my eyes and can see the ridges in the bark, the shape of the tree. Everything is as it was.

I carry on up the path but haven't gone much further when I hear a crack from behind. I turn but there's no one there. Not that I can see, anyway. I feel watched once more. A sensation that never quite seems to go away.

'Hello?'

There's no reply. It's still light but the sun is starting to dip and the shadows are long. I take a dozen more steps up the trail, until I'm sure there's someone behind me. I spin quickly, ducking to the side at the same time to avoid... Nothing.

There's still nobody there; only a winding dirt path covered with stones, twigs and leaves.

I run this time – or as much as I can when there's such a steep gradient to climb. It feels like I'm trudging through mud; I'm barely doing more than walking a little bit faster than normal pace.

There's another snap from behind me – possibly a twig, possibly my imagination. I don't turn this time. I try to kick my knees higher, move faster, but all I succeed in doing is giving myself a stitch.

Another crack and this time I do spin. There's a rush of movement and I realise too late that someone's bearing over me. There's no time to duck or escape. All I can do is cover my head.

CHAPTER THIRTY-TWO

Luke reels away just as I thought he was about to leap on me.

'Sorry,' he says as I glare up at him. 'I was trying to make you jump.'

I've slipped onto the dirt and am sitting on my backside. Luke offers a hand but I push myself up, furious.

'Make me jump? We're not ten.'

'I know… Sorry. I was heading home and saw you ahead. I thought it would be funny. Are you all right?'

'I was fine until you scared the crap out of me.'

He steps away and sighs dejectedly. 'I saw you resting on that tree. I wondered if…'

'Wondered what? I was tired.'

Luke scratches his head and gives a conciliatory smile. 'I didn't see you at the beach today,' he says.

'That's because I wasn't there.'

'No…' He sighs again and glances up the path, seeming genuinely apologetic. That still doesn't mean I'm ready to let him off the hook.

I continue walking towards the cottage and he falls into step at my side.

'Are you coming to the festival tomorrow?' he says.

'People keep asking me that.'

'Because it's the biggest day of the year! Music, games, food—'

'Stop asking me about food!'

'I wasn't, I—' Luke cuts himself off. I've had enough for one day. 'I heard about this morning with Pete and Scott,' he says, more quietly.

'Everyone will have. It's how things work here.'

'Did you argue because I said you should be careful around them?'

I stop and glare at him. 'Why would it be anything to do with that?'

He shrugs. 'I don't know… It's just… You seem the type to, um…'

'To what?'

Luke takes a step away, realising he's gone too far – but there's no backing down now. 'I didn't mean anything by it,' he says.

'By *what*?'

'It's just… You seem the type of person that if you're told not to do something, you immediately want to do it.'

The fact he's got me spot-on only makes me angrier. I glare daggers at him.

'Don't talk to me again,' I say.

'Meg…'

'It's Meg*an* – and you heard what I said.'

I twist away from him but it's hard to make a showy exit when there's a steep slope. There are no doors to slam, nothing to kick. I huff my way up hill as best I can, grunting a sigh of relief when I get to the top. I head for the cottage, not checking behind me, but knowing Luke will be there, watching on in bemusement.

I grapple with the front door and then rush inside, closing and locking it behind me.

'Chlo? You in?'

No answer.

The board I nailed to the window frame this morning has left the kitchen wallowing in darkness. Even with the door locked and the window boarded, I'm struggling to escape the feeling that someone is watching.

I rush through to my room, unzipping the pockets of my bag until I find the bottle of Seroxat. I'm so desperate that I don't bother with water, dropping it onto my tongue and gulping it down – or trying to. It sticks in my throat, the sour chalkiness coating my windpipe until I force it down further with a series of swallows.

It occurs to me for the first time that I have no way of knowing whether the anti-anxiety pill is truly what the bottle claims it to be. My mother's name isn't on the label and it's clear enough she didn't get much of her stash in any legitimate way. I suspect she threw some money at a doctor she knew – she wasn't the type to go trawling the streets for anything, let alone drugs.

It's often struck me that, regardless of legality, people with money rarely seem to have problems getting what they want. The dorms at my school were always awash with 'miracle' slimming drugs that had never been approved for sale. They were probably the number one currency once we all reached fourteen or fifteen. That and malicious gossip, of course.

Back when I raided Mother's stash, I also found a bottle labelled 'orlistat' and another bottle marked 'sibutramine'. There were more of them than any other pill and it was little surprise to me to find out they were both slimming drugs. I wouldn't have minded quite so much if it wasn't for Mother's insistence that she relied entirely on diet and exercise to keep in shape.

It's simple, Megan. If you want to stop looking like your father in drag, you should stop eating so much.

It's fair enough to say that I took her advice on that one thing.

I pop one of each tablet now and swallow them down. It takes a minute or two but my head finally feels clear enough to think clearly.

'Chlo?'

I head back into the hallway and knock on her door.

'Chloe?'

There's no answer, so I move along the hall and let myself into the study. The pile of shattered ceramics and plastics is still in the corner – but the photo I'm looking for is on the dresser.

It's the only picture I know of that includes the five of us: Chloe, myself, our parents and Zac.

Given everything that's happened, it's strange that it's only now that I'm realising how much I actually miss him.

Zac could always make me smile. Once, he stole Mother's coat from the back of her chair at a wedding reception. He hid it under a table and when he saw that I'd noticed, put a finger to his lips. Mother was furious, stomping around that room for almost an hour until he slipped it back onto her chair without her noticing. Back then, my instinct would've been to tell on him, to side with our parents, but I didn't. It was the way he looked at me. It was like he was saying, 'We're in this together' – and, in that moment, we were. Us against them.

Things could have been so different if he'd left this village with us ten years ago, in the back of our parents' car.

I remove the necklace I found by the rope that saved us and lay it on the dresser. The weight makes me think it's real gold – but it's the star charm that makes it stand out.

When I compare the photo to the necklace, there's no question about it.

It's Zac's.

CHAPTER THIRTY-THREE

Despite my exhaustion of earlier, the moment I go to bed, I'm wide awake again.

Idle minds for idle girls, young lady.

Eventually, I drift in and out of sleep in ten- or fifteen-minute bursts, until it reaches a point where it feels like I might not sleep again. I find myself staring at the ceiling, allowing my mind to drift and create patterns from nothing. My stomach is rumbling, so I go into the kitchen for a glass of water in the hope of calming it. The board is blocking the broken window, leaving the room darker and colder than usual. The water is cool as well and I know it's probably going to wake me up even further. There are sleeping tablets in my mother's bag but I've popped so many pills already this evening that I'm worried one more might be too much.

Back in my bedroom, I open the curtains and stare out to the darkness of the woods. There's nothing there, of course. No one.

I knock gently on Chloe's door and when there's no answer, I open it a crack. She's lying in bed, chest rising and falling in deep, slow breaths. I didn't hear her get back to the cottage until after eleven. She spent almost the entire day doing her own thing. It feels as if I've pushed her away.

In any case, Whitecliff is prising us apart, not least because it's so hard to contact one another. I miss being able to text or instant message when we're apart. After what happened to Brad, it's hard not to worry about her being out by herself – but I suppose

the alternative is worse. Our mother had a contradictory pre-
dilection in that she'd demand to know every facet of our lives,
despite sending us away so that she didn't have to deal with us.

I return to bed but the moment I close my eyes, I can hear the
rustle of the tide echoing along the tunnel of Fisherman's Cave.
The water laps over my feet and Vee is in my ear, shouting that
she's sorry. I picture the marks on her arms and wonder what
happened to make her go that far.

I'm not one to talk, of course. We all have our demons.

The kitchen is cooler than my bedroom. I have another glass
of water in a second attempt to calm my stomach. I also check
the label on Chloe's still-unopened bar of chocolate. If the wrapper was torn, I might have allowed myself a square.

Something snaps outside. Probably a twig, or the wind. The
woods are alive and breathing. After Luke's childish – and successful
– attempt to scare me, I'm wary of reacting to the noises that surround these trees. While I was waiting for Chloe to return, I spent
the evening hearing the endless rustle of leaves, the crack of twigs.
There were times at which it felt like the entire cottage was surrounded by an army of creatures whose primary function was to clump
around noisily. A hoard of stompy-footed teenagers making a point.

I told myself it was only animals going about their business
but what if that's not what the noises are? What if someone is
waiting for me to make the first move?

Before I know what I'm doing, I've wrenched the front door
open and stepped barefooted onto the path where our first 'welcome to Whitecliff' message was left. There are far more little
stones than I thought and I silently ooh-aah across the dried-out
dirt onto the dewy grass. It's like walking on a squishy, damp
carpet. I make my way around to the back of the cottage, until
I'm standing outside my own bedroom window.

'Zac?'

I hiss his name into the darkness, my voice swallowed by the night.

Zac's postcard, Zac's necklace. Zac has been watching us.

'Zac?' I whisper loudly. 'It's me. You can come out.'

I reach into my pocket and pull out his chain, holding it at arm's length for him to see. My heart skips as something rustles off to the side – the sound of someone trying to pass quietly through the woods, but without the grace to pull it off.

There's a crack of wood. A man's voice growls a swear word under his breath. I follow the voice to the corner of the house, pressing myself against the brick until I see something that is unquestionably a man stumble out from between a pair of trees. He catches his foot on a low branch and lashes out angrily, sending another snap echoing through the otherwise silent night. He clearly hasn't heard me – he seems unaware of my presence.

I can only see his back. He's dressed in a jacket, long trousers and heavy boots. It's not summer get-up. This is someone prepared for night-time hikes in the woods.

As soon as he's clear of the trees, he stops at a spot level with the front of the cottage. He digs around in his pockets, muttering under his breath.

I creep closer, my bare feet silent on the ground. Closer and closer, until he's almost within reach. He's real, not my imagination. He's bigger than I thought he would be, especially now he's standing up straight.

It can't be the lack of sleep or the lack of food this time. He's here in front of me.

'Zac?'

I touch his arm and he yelps as he twists and leaps away.

It's not Zac.

It's Pete. He clasps the centre of his chest as he stumbles backwards. A flurry of small stones skid underneath his shoes, making him slip like he's rollerblading. It's only the fact that he stumbles into the wall that saves him from falling over.

He's panting as if he's just finished a marathon, still clutching his chest.

'What are you *doing*?' he yells at me.

A strange calmness has washed across me. 'I live here,' I reply.

He uses a window ledge to push himself up straighter. He's still wheezing, trying to get his breath. 'You scared the hell out of me.'

'I *live* here.'

It's the middle of the night but the moon is white and unimpeded by cloud. I can see Pete as clearly as he can see me. I watch him taking in my bare feet, short-shorts and small vest, clearly wondering why I'm outside in so little clothing.

'Are you okay?' he asks.

'I heard a noise.'

Pete suddenly seems to realise that he's the one who's trespassing. He drops his hand from his chest and ducks his head slightly. 'Right… Yeah, sorry about that.' He pauses, as if waiting for me to tell him it's fine. When I don't reply, he continues stumbling through his words. 'I was looking out for yer. After what happened to that Brad kid and then everything this morning in the village…'

'It was your son I was arguing with.'

'Right, yes.'

He glances both ways as if checking to make sure he isn't being overheard. He has the same expression on his face that I think I have when Chloe walks in on me looking at food labels. That mix of embarrassment and a determination to prove that nothing is amiss.

I continue waiting for the reason why he's sneaking around our cottage. 'It was in front of everyone,' Pete says.

'The argument?' I reply. 'I don't understand what you're saying.'

He holds his hands out as if to say that he can't explain it. Then it's as if he changes his mind. He wasn't looking out for us, after all. 'I often go for walks late at night,' he says. 'Clears the mind and all that.'

'Were you out for a walk, or were you checking on us?'

'I was walking and then I found myself up 'ere. Thought I'd make sure you were okay.'

He squirms like a schoolkid caught in an obvious lie. The dog didn't eat his homework.

'Should probably be getting back,' he says.

I don't say anything, following him around to the front of the cottage, where the door is still open a crack. Pete continues past my car towards the road, before stopping to glance back and see if I'm still behind him. I am – bare feet and all.

'See yer tomorrow, I guess,' he says. 'Burning Boat day. You'll love it.'

'We'll see.'

Pete nods shortly and then turns and keeps going. He doesn't risk looking back this time. I know he can feel my eyes on him. I watch until he's out of sight.

When I get back inside, I lock the front door and wiggle it back and forth, making sure the lock has caught. The wooden flashing underneath is annoyingly higher than it should be and probably needs to be replaced. It might help the door close more easily.

I double-check my handiwork with the board over the window. Once I'm convinced that nobody can break in without making a noise, I hunt through the drawers, shunting aside the mismatched cutlery. Knives, spoons and forks are all jumbled together in a stainless-steel orgy of cross-pollination that would have driven Mother mad.

The sharpest knife is the type that's used to gut fish. It's short and ferociously sharp. The sort of thing that can do some serious damage.

I return to bed and tuck it under my pillow, then close my eyes and listen to the grumbling of my stomach.

Sunday

CHAPTER THIRTY-FOUR

Despite what everyone has said about the Burning Boat Festival, I'm not prepared for the reality of it.

It begins when a steady buzz infects my dazed state of half-sleep, convincing me I'm in Fisherman's Cave surrounded by bees. It's Chloe who brings me back to the present, appearing at the side of my bed, squeezing my hand.

'You were dreaming,' she says.

As I come to, I remember the previous night and touch the handle of the knife under my pillow. I don't withdraw it. Knowing it's there is enough.

The buzz hasn't cleared; the bees are still infecting my thoughts.

'Can you hear that?' I ask.

I fully expect Chloe to say she can't, that it's a figment of my imagination.

'Come and see,' she says. 'You should put some clothes on first. Nothing black.'

I blink away the sleepiness, trying to remember what the time was when I last looked. It's a few minutes before nine o'clock now. I think I might have slept for three full, uninterrupted, hours.

I grab my jogging bottoms, hoody and trainers from under the bed and dress quickly, following Chloe outside. We move past my car to the path along which Pete disappeared into the night.

The noise is getting louder: a hum of chattering voices with an undercurrent of excitement. By the time we reach the end of the path, it's as if I've awoken into another world.

A steady parade of people is making its way along the road, heading towards the hill and the descent into Whitecliff. Cars are parked nose to tail on both sides of the road, each of them half on the verge, creating a gap through the middle.

'What's going on?' I ask.

'The festival,' Chloe replies. She's excited.

There are couples and children walking and chatting together, with the smaller kids in pushchairs or on their fathers' shoulders. People are carrying picnic baskets and coolboxes. Others have blankets tucked under arms or backpacks on their shoulders. Chloe and I become part of the shuffling mass.

By the time we get to the top of the hill with a view of the village and beach below, I'm almost convinced I'm still asleep and this is a dream. One end of the beach has been covered with stalls, each with a different coloured roof. In the village itself, rainbow bunting zig-zags from house to house and the swarm of visitors continues from where we're standing down to every street and side-alley below.

'Wow,' I say.

'Amazing, isn't it?'

We continue down the hill together and the noise continues to increase. At the bottom, we have to weave our way around the crowd that's assembling around the picnic tables outside the pub. The pub doors are already open and there's a sign advertising breakfast.

'They don't even burn the boat until dusk,' Chloe says. 'Imagine how many people will be here by then.'

We stand for a moment, allowing people to pass and I notice that what Vee said is true – no one is wearing black. Not even any of the children. It's a warm morning already, with a hot afternoon predicted for later, so most people wouldn't choose to wear black anyway – but there would always be one person in a rock metal T-shirt.

Not today.

I edge a little closer to Chloe so that she can hear me over the crowd. 'How did you know not to wear black?' I ask.

'Arthur said and so did a couple of the beach kids. Everyone seems to know. Who told you?'

'Vee.'

Chloe's wearing red shorts that I've not seen before, with a yellow top. She fits perfectly into the carnival atmosphere.

There are food trucks parked on the edge of the beach, advertising hot dogs, burgers and ice cream. Even at this time of the morning, there's a queue of adults lining up, with excitable children chasing around. With the cobbled streets, Union Jack bunting and stalls, it's all incredibly traditional. Chuck in a red phone box and some bloke in a top hat and it would be peak Britishness.

Chloe stifles a yawn with her hand and momentarily rests her head on my shoulder.

'You were in late,' I say.

'Yes…' She wipes away the sleepiness from the corners of her eyes and doesn't expand. 'I'm going to check on Arthur,' she says. 'I think I'm going to help him out a bit today. He's going to be busy.' She turns to me. 'Is that okay?'

'If that's what makes you happy.'

She nods but doesn't reply. I suppose there is something a little odd about a seventeen-year-old girl spending her days in a gallery with an old man – but it can't be any unhealthier than the trouble into which I've been getting myself.

Chloe steps away and then turns back. She bites her lip before saying, 'Make sure you eat today.'

There's no time for me to respond because she twists and hurries away through the crowd. I wonder if she would have said it if she hadn't had such a quick escape route.

A shiver flits across me, as if I've been caught in a lie, or snared in a place I shouldn't be. There's a moment in which it feels as if everyone has overheard what Chloe said – all these strangers, shooting me sideways stares.

I hug my arms across my front and duck my head, stepping between a pair of scrambling children onto the main street. The first stall has a pair of tables stacked high with programmes. I vaguely recognise the bored-looking lad standing behind it; I've seen him around. He says the programmes are a pound and I tell him that I don't have any change. He shrugs, checks both ways, and then hands me one anyway. Our little secret. I thank him and then drift away from the worst of the hustle, finding myself a spot in a near-empty side street to sit on someone's front step.

The inside front page of the programme is a schedule for the day. There are lots of little things going on but the main events are the children's miniature boat judging at four, with the boat burning at dusk and fireworks afterwards. There's also a map of stalls offering face-painting, food, drink and the usual list of things.

The rest of the programme is made up of advertisements, some photos from previous years, an appalling poem that rhymes 'Whitecliff' with 'if' over and over and some other odds and ends – none of which add up to being worth the pound it would have cost me. I'm about to toss it into the nearest bin when I spot the list of funders on the inside back page. Near the bottom, under a section marked 'With special thanks to our generous donors', are the names of my parents. I stare at the page, running a finger across the print, not quite able to fathom it.

It's strange to see 'Ian and Anne Smart' in print – not only because they're no longer here but also because I've never thought of them in such terms. I was always expected to call them 'Mother' or 'Father'.

Underneath the donor section is a list of people on the organising committee. The first name listed is Alison Wood.

I head back onto the main street, which feels even busier than it did a couple of minutes before. Up on the hill, a steady stream of people continues to flow down into the village.

A marquee has been erected in front of the pub and it's there that I find Alison rushing around with a clipboard in one hand and a walkie-talkie in the other. She spots me and does the dismissive, hi-bye wave of acknowledging my presence and turning away at the same time. She starts a conversation with someone I don't know and then snaps something into the radio before she realises I'm still hanging around.

'Megan,' she says. 'How lovely to see you here.' She turns to her minion and motions drinking a cup of tea.

'Can I ask you about the programme?' I say.

She reaches for it in my hand: 'You've not found a typo, have you? I told Duncan to check it over properly. It said "Shitecliff" last year.'

I don't bother to ask who Duncan is but show her the inside back page. 'My parents are on here,' I say.

Alison glances at the page, checking I've not invented this. 'So they are,' she says.

'Did they donate money?'

Alison's lips have been plumped full of something that makes her look like she's glued a pair of chipolatas to her face. The attempt she now makes to pout causes them to balloon even further.

'It could be a leftover thing from previous years,' she says. 'Some of the programme is copied and pasted. I've told Duncan about this.' She glances around, searching for the mythical and seemingly maligned 'Duncan'.

'But even that would still mean they've been giving money in recent years…?'

Alison throws both hands up and shakes her head vigorously. 'I've no idea,' she says. 'I'm sorry, Megan, but you must excuse me – there's so much to do!'

She hurries off to the furthest corner of the marquee. She's acted as if I've caught her in a lie – but I have no idea what that lie might be.

What is hard to figure out is why my parents haven't sold the cottage. Mia said her parents would buy it in a heartbeat. There's a shortage of places for sale in the area, so my parents could not only have sold it, but could have done so quickly and for a good chunk of money. In the ten years since Zac disappeared, neither Chloe nor myself have been here, and my parents only ever visited for odd days, never more than a day at a time.

So why sit on something valuable that's largely unused?

A place which apparently holds bad memories because of what happened to Zac. Were they hoping he'd return?

They didn't only keep the cottage – they've been contributing money to the annual festival. They're invested in the village but I have no idea why.

I head out of the marquee, risking a glance towards Alison, who's either *actually* busy, or doing a good impression of looking it for my benefit.

The flow of people has parted near the pub because a police car has appeared. There are the usual sideways glances, as people give when it looks like there might be trouble. Kids are being turned to face the other way by parents who can't get enough of looking themselves.

I'm no different. I make my way through the crowd, feeling tingles that are nothing to do with the warmth of the sun. The police car is empty but I'm certain a pair of officers are going to drag Scott out of the pub any minute.

I'm so focused on the pub doors that I almost miss the officers striding through the crowd from the opposite direction. There's no cliché of someone in handcuffs being strong-armed into the back of the police car as the officer *carefully* ensures the suspect's head isn't whacked on the roof. Everything is calm: two officers walking purposefully with an uncuffed lad in between. It takes me a second or three to recognise him as Kev, the sand-kicking villager with whom Brad had been scuffling on the beach in the first place. Vee told me he lived two doors down from her.

An older man, presumably Kev's father, is walking grim-faced a few steps behind them. The four of them get into the police car.

The crowd parts around the reversing vehicle and then the car makes its way up the hill, engine groaning in its battle against gravity.

Before I can move, Vee is at my side, full of a conspiratorial bright smile. She's dressed up for the day in a bright red and white striped dress, with flat red shoes.

'Did you see that?' she asks.

'What was going on?'

'What do you think? They reckon Kev attacked Brad.'

CHAPTER THIRTY-FIVE

Vee tells me she has to get back to the board shop but that she'll ask for a half-hour off if I want. It's not an offer I'm going to say no to, so I follow her back through the shambling hordes until we reach the shop. The walls are lined with surfboards and paddleboards, with two kayaks hanging from the ceiling. The rest of the space is filled with wetsuits and racks of swimming costumes.

It's busy but not as rammed as the rest of the village and most of the shoppers appear to only be browsing. There are a good three or four mothers telling their sticky-fingered kids to look but not touch.

Vee's father is in a wildly out-of-place Hawaiian shirt with flowery shorts. Combined with his thinning orangey hair, he looks like he's had a midlife crisis and has disappeared off to a tropical island to find himself. Eat, Pray, Love, Get A Grip. There are half-coconuts on the counter and a large punchbowl full of something pink – which is surely asking for trouble. The atmosphere seems friendly, until Vee's dad spies me at her side.

'I'm going to nip away for half an hour,' Vee says, not phrasing it like a question.

Her dad frowns, flashing a quick glance in my direction, but only replies with: 'Thirty minutes – that's it.'

'You're the best,' Vee says and then we leave through the other door, emerging onto the beach.

The sand is covered with blankets and windbreakers: couples staking their claim on their small corner of Britain. We weave our way around the various campsites, walking side by side.

'I don't think your dad likes me,' I say.

There's a pause which is too long before Vee says, 'I'm sure he does.'

We both laugh. The hesitation said it best.

'You make people nervous,' she says. 'You've been asking questions and then you had that argument with Scott in the open. That sort of thing doesn't happen round here.'

'Brad had his head battered in the other night – that's way worse.'

'I know; it's not *me* who's saying this. But people talk. They put the attack on Brad to one side because he isn't one of them. But your argument with Scott is different. Scott's part of the village.'

'It feels like there's some hidden village meeting where everyone gets together and discusses what's been happening on any given day,' I say. 'Everyone knows everyone else's business, unless something happens to an outsider – then nobody knows anything.'

Vee keeps walking, quiet for a moment, until she brushes the back of my hand. 'People don't know *every*thing.'

We traipse around a group of lads who've marked their territory with a row of St George's flag towels and move onto a patch of sand that's not quite as crammed.

'You're very colourful today,' I say.

'This is what people do for the Burning Boat Fest. You can't wear dark colours, or Deacon the Black will come and get you.'

'I guess I didn't realise it was such a big deal.'

We pass the marquee and Alison Wood rushes past us, barking instructions at another woman who is now clutching the clipboard. She either doesn't notice me, or pretends not to.

'Do you know her?' I ask.

'Vaguely. She's around a lot during the summer but I don't see much of her in the winter. Alison something.'

'Wood,' I say.

'That's it.'

I tap my head. 'I've got these weird memories of when I was here as a girl. Like, half-memories. I'm not sure if they're real, or a mix of things I've seen and heard.'

'Like what?'

'Like I thought Alison had a son – Eli or something. I vaguely remember playing with him on the beach. I thought he was about my age. Alison said he was at Cambridge but I was at their house and there's not a single picture of him. Wouldn't you have at least one photo of your son somewhere?'

Vee has slowed a little. She waves to someone I don't know and then makes a 'hmm' sound.

'I do vaguely remember some kid,' she says. 'Years ago. I think he went away to boarding school.'

'But wouldn't he have returned at some point?'

'I don't know. I guess it's one more thing for your list.'

I stop and turn to her. 'My what?'

'Your list of weird things around the village.'

I start to answer but can't get my words out properly. 'I'm not keeping a list,' I manage eventually.

Vee glances over her shoulder and then leans in. 'I'm joking, Meg.' She angles away, smiling kindly. 'It's just, we're all normal people here. We're not super lizards who secretly run the world.'

I resist the urge to correct her to 'Megan'. I feel like I'm under attack.

'Does everyone think I'm crazy?' I ask.

Vee bites her lip – and that says enough. She's exquisitely brutal when it comes to those pregnant pauses. She says so much by saying nothing at all.

'Of course not,' she replies – too late.

'I've not done anything wrong.'

She takes a breath and lowers her voice. 'You've asked everyone about Zac. *Everyone*. If they knew him, if they were around on the day. It's been ten years – most people don't remember what they were doing. But when people say that, you act like they're hiding something. Of course people talk – it's a small village. When one person says the Smart girl has been talking about her brother, it's bound to get around.'

I stare at her, wanting to be angry – but I know she isn't trying to be cruel. Nobody seems to understand. The reason I've been asking questions about Zac is because someone sent me a postcard with his initial on the back. I found *his* necklace by the rope that saved us. I could tell that to Vee, try to make her understand – but I wonder if it's more likely to make her believe I really do have problems.

'I don't like people talking about me,' I say.

'There's not a lot I can do to stop that.' Vee glances both ways quickly, then squeezes my hand for a moment before releasing it. 'Are you okay?' she asks.

'I'll live.'

She nods over my shoulder. 'I think someone's trying to say hello.'

I turn to see Dan Wood making his way towards me, giving what I've decided is the Whitecliff Wave. There's nothing special about it but everyone seems to give it as a precursor to saying hello. Dan's also in bright beachwear. It's like an infestation of madness has taken over the village.

'You made it!' Dan says, as he nears us.

'We're only up the hill,' I reply.

He looks between Vee and me. 'Are you enjoying the day?'

'It's very busy.'

'There'll be music later and all sorts. Make sure you hang around for the main event.'

'What's that?'

'The boat burning, of course!' He chuckles, as if this is the most normal thing in the world. 'Anyway, must be going. People to see and all that. Don't eat too much.'

I stand rigid, wondering if this is a dig. It *sounded* cheery enough, probably the type of send-off he's been giving people all day. *Don't eat too much. Ha ha!* Vee doesn't seem to have registered it as anything other than normal.

'Who's he?' she asks, when he's gone. 'I vaguely recognise him.'

'Alison's husband. They say they were good friends with my parents. They talk as if they were the oldest of mates – but I'd never heard of them until we got here.'

'Put it on the list,' Vee replies, nudging me playfully with her elbow as she does so.

'Don't,' I say.

Vee steps away, examining me crookedly to see if I'm joking. 'I didn't mean—'

'It's fine. Shall we go back?'

Vee stares at me for a moment more, then nods sullenly.

We've not gone far before we get to the Arkwright shop. Gwen walks out at the same time as we're passing. She stops to stare.

I'm not sure of the precise moment when I lose it, or even why. I think it might be when I see the way Gwen glares at me. At *us*. It feels as if she's a foot taller than me, looking down at me with disdain. My mother is the only other person who made me feel so small.

'What are you looking at?' I hiss venomously.

Vee tries to tug me away but I yank my arm back.

Gwen says nothing, which in many ways makes it worse. If she'd called me a name, I'd have a reason to be upset. She folds her arms and simply stares.

This morning, when Chloe told me to get dressed, I did so in a rush, piling on the nearest clothes to hand. I didn't think much over what to wear – but I'm thinking clearly now as I pull the hoody off over my head.

It's a simple thing, the easiest of gestures, and yet the power it holds is vastly out of proportion to the action itself.

I'm wearing a plain black vest underneath.

It shouldn't mean anything, but in the context of this ridiculous village with its ridiculous traditions, it does.

I meet Gwen's eyes and match her silence with my own. It's Vee who does the talking.

'Meg…' she says, gently touching my arm. It's as if she thinks I've done this by mistake.

'Meg*an*,' I reply firmly, shaking her off once more. 'My name is Megan.'

CHAPTER THIRTY-SIX

I spend the afternoon believing I'll spot someone else wearing black. There must be a couple of thousand people who've descended on the beach and village, so surely *one* of them has made a mistake? Or there must be some goth kid, somewhere, refusing to conform.

There isn't, though.

It's as if I've stumbled across a weird cult hidden away on the coast. I could put my hoody back on, of course, or return to the cottage and change – but it already feels too late for that. Besides, there's a big part of me that doesn't want to fall in line with the madness of it all.

A couple of kindly strangers stop me and explain politely that people aren't supposed to wear black today. Someone mentions Deacon the Black and the bad luck I'll be due. I thank them and then continue walking. Considering I told Vee I don't want people to talk about me, I've done a fantastic job of achieving the exact opposite.

It's almost three in the afternoon when I spot Kev and his father walking through the village. There are no signs of the police and I can't believe he's been charged with anything if he's already back out here. My first thought is that I'll ask Vee if she knows – but then I remember the hurt on her face when I shook her off outside Arkwright's.

In six days, I've managed to turn an entire village against me, which, by any measure, is good going.

Y'know, Megan, you can be a real bitch sometimes. I don't know where you get it from.

Perhaps Mother was right all along?

I check in on Chloe at the gallery, almost forgetting my black vest until I realise she's staring at me.

'What are you *doing*?' she asks – and I instantly feel ridiculous. It's hard now to remember what made me so angry. An old woman staring at me? *Really?*

'I'm going back to the cottage to get changed in a bit,' I reply.

Chloe's behind the counter and I watch as she serves a customer effortlessly, taking their money and wrapping a picture in brown paper. Arthur is sitting in a corner near the front of the gallery. I must have walked past him without noticing.

'Have you been busy?' I ask.

Chloe's displeasure at my clothes breaks into a grin. 'Someone bought my drawing!'

'That's terrific.'

'It was a couple. They paid full price and everything. When Arthur told them it was my work, they asked me to sign it.'

'You're a rock star!'

Chloe bites away an embarrassed smirk, which quickly becomes a laugh. 'I pretty much am a rock star.'

'Ha! Do you want to come and get something to eat? There's a curry van over by the beach that has this cauliflower thing. They also have a chickpea option.'

Chloe shakes her head. 'I'll catch up with you later. It's a bit busy at the moment.'

There's a part of me that wants to object but I've been argumentative enough for now.

'You *are* going to change, aren't you?' Chloe says.

'Yes.'

She doesn't seem entirely convinced but then she's distracted by someone approaching the counter asking about prices. Arthur is busy with another potential customer, so I give the Whitecliff Wave and then trudge my way uphill to try a few more safe combinations – and to find the brightest clothes I can.

A cheer goes up from the crowd on the beach as the wooden boat sets off from the docks. The scramble to get a good spot means that many of those with a clear view have been up since the early hours, guarding their land ever since. The sun is setting over the cliffs and the sky is a hazy orange-purple. Red sky at night and all that.

Children are sleeping on parents' laps and plenty of adults are lying on the beach with little view of the ocean. They might jump up when the boat is about to be lit. It's been a long day.

The wooden vessel is being towed by one of the Chandler boats. Scott is steering, cruising along the front of the shore, acknowledging the cheers of the crowd. When he reaches the end, he turns the boat, sending it further out to sea. There's someone else with him on board, someone smaller, but the dimness makes it hard to see who it is.

While that's going on, Pete is standing on a small stage on the beach, doing the emceeing duties. He's telling the crowd a story that is probably to do with Deacon the Black and the infamous boat-boarding and burning – but I'm too far back to hear anything. The only part I catch for sure is when he roars that, 'The Whitecliff boat was pillaged and plundered as the heavens hailed and thundered.'

The crowd cheers once more.

I turn and edge away. Everyone has congregated on the beach, packed in like beans in a tin and there are only a few stragglers left on the main street. I spot a couple of teenagers sneaking away into a dark alley. At least someone's having fun.

The pub has closed for the ceremony and its lights are off. By the time I reach the road, it feels oddly peaceful. There are thousands of people behind me and yet, a short distance away, the village lies untouched.

In the dying sun, the hill back to the cottage suddenly looks steeper than ever. It's almost as if it goes straight up at ninety degrees. I turn the other way instead, rounding the beer garden where I spoke to Chrissie and nearing the start of the rock beach over which Vee and I climbed to reach Fisherman's Cave.

There's a rustle from the trees behind me and, though I want to turn, I force myself not to. If Zac *is* here, if he wanted us to come, then he can reveal himself. I've done enough of the running.

A large cheer goes up from the beach and I change my mind about leaving, heading down to the docks instead.

It's almost dark, but out on the sea, a flaming blob of orange has whooshed to life as the boat catches fire. The reflection stretches long, making it look as if an entire section of the ocean is alight.

It's genuinely impressive.

I stand and watch, certain I can feel a faint warmth across the water. The dark waves ripple gently, sending the reflected flames bobbing towards the shore. I'm lost in the moment when there's a ferocious whoosh from the furthest side of the beach, some-where close to the caves. Moments later there's a boom as the firework explodes, sending a spray of red and blue sparks flashing across the darkening sky to the sounds of more cheers.

The docks feel empty without the rustier of the Chandler Fishing vessels and the wooden boat. There are three smaller sail boats in a separate jetty, along with the second Chandler boat – the one that Scott was working on when we first arrived.

Second and third fireworks shoot into the sky, exploding one after the other, temporarily turning night into day once more. It seems something of a waste to set a boat on fire at dusk if fireworks are then going to be used to light everything up. It does allow me to see that Scott's boat has anchored itself close to the flames.

He's not going to be back for a while…

I'm not sure when the thought occurs to me but, before I know it, I'm already acting. I take a run-up and jump from the dock onto the back of the remaining, unmanned, Chandler boat. A tarpaulin is covering the rear and I drop onto it like a trampoline, spreading the weight across my back and upper arms and landing with an airy thud.

This boat is three or four times the size of the one Scott is currently on. There are long cylinders on either side with nets wound tight around them. I'm not sure what I'm looking for but I enter the cabin at the front. There's a steering wheel and a couple of panels with dials and switches but I ignore those and open the doors built into either side of the panel. These turn out to be cupboards containing a couple of first-aid kits, a pile of blankets and a plastic box containing loose Snickers and Mars bars.

I'm frozen for a moment.

I know the precise contents of the label on the back of a Mars bar. I don't even like them that much – but they're iconic, like Coca-Cola. My stomach rumbles its request and it's all I can do to close the lid and turn away.

I can't spend any more time in the cabin now I know what's there. The only other obvious place to check for anything untoward is underneath the tarp. The lights are still off in the pub and the gate to the beer garden is clamped closed. It feels like I'm being watched – but that's not a new thing. I tell myself there's nobody there.

Pressing myself flat onto the deck, I slither awkwardly under the tarp like an ageing, partially blind snake. It's dark and dank and my bare knees scratch against the deck as I crawl towards the rear of the boat. A rounded bench is built into the stern and there's not much of a gap between that and the stretched tarp. I run a hand along it anyway, tracing the shape until I find a thick padlock clipped into place. There's some sort of chest built into the bench, allowing people to sit on top of it. I can lift the lid a centimetre or so but the lock is hiding whatever lies inside.

I clamber out from under the tarp and leap back onto the dock. If there's one thing that's easy to find in this area of White-cliff, it's large rocks. I rush to the cliffs, following the route that Vee and I took to Fisherman's Cave, until I hit the first part of the pebble beach. The rocky monstrosity. Almost the first stone I come across is the size of my fist.

The fireworks are still blasting into the sky and, though a handful of people are starting to meander up the hill, nobody pays me the slightest amount of attention.

Back at the docks and another splash of light in the sky shows me that Scott is still out close to the burning boat. The flames have dipped as the wood starts to fold in on itself, ready to be swallowed by the water.

I don't hang around.

It's darker still under the tarp, but I know where I'm going this time. I wait for the whoosh of a rocket sizzling into the air and then strike the lock with the rock at the same moment as the firework explodes.

I miss.

The pebble smashes into the plastic, leaving a rounded dent in the lip of the bench and almost crushing my fingers. The clang echoes underneath the tarp: a resounding reminder of my failure to hit something barely a few centimetres in front of me.

There's another whoosh. One second… Two… As the fire-work explodes, I smash the rock into the join where the hoop on top meets the main part of the padlock. I manage two direct hits before the thunder from outside abates. I wait for another sizzle of rocket before adding two more thwacks.

On the final assault, the two pieces of metal fall apart, landing with a clunk at my feet. My arms ache from the weight and strain of wielding the rock and it takes a couple of seconds for the tingles in my fingers to abate.

The lid of the crate has popped open, but there's not a lot of space to lift it without removing the tarp. It feels dangerous and exciting. For all my sins, I've never broken into anywhere before. The combination of destruction and being able to strike back at someone like Scott is an intoxicating mix.

I can't lift the lid high enough to get a proper look inside, so I use the torch on my phone instead, shining the white light into the space under the bench.

It's immediately clear why the crate was locked.

The only guns I know anything about are the pistols we used occasionally at school. They were for sport, with longer scopes and an over-the-top array of safety catches. When it came to fun, much of those shooting classes were up there with getting through airport security. It was hours of safety briefings and explanations of how the scoring worked. In the end, we had a few short minutes of blasting paper targets to pieces.

There are at least half a dozen guns on this boat. These are nothing like the firearms I've shot. These are machine guns, the type of thing stereotyped Russians in eighties action movies shoot at chisel-jawed American heroes. There are long bands of ammunition slung into the corner of the chest, next to a couple of long, thick daggers.

Aside from being locked away, the setup is so casual it's as if the weapons are innocuous life jackets that have been tossed aside ready for next time.

I squeeze an arm into the crate, running a finger along the cool metal of the gun barrel. It's all too real.

It's then I realise there hasn't been a firework for a little while. If the festivities are over, then Scott will be on his way back.

There's no point in pretending to relock the padlock, so I grab both pieces of metal and the stone. After clambering out from under the tarp, I dump the lot over the side, waiting for the satisfying splosh-splosh-splosh as it hits the water.

Then I run.

CHAPTER THIRTY-SEVEN

As I dart around the corner of the beer garden, my heart still thundering from the sight of the weapon haul, I almost run into someone. I stop myself just in time, skidding on the gravel and almost falling into the fence. I call, 'Sorry!' but then realise who it is.

Unless it was Scott, it probably couldn't have been worse.

Gwen Arkwright is standing by herself at the back of the pub, a blanket wrapped tightly around her shoulders. Her bony fingers are protruding from the centre as she forces away a shiver. There's no hope she missed me. Her accusing glare makes it clear enough she suspects I was up to no good away from the crowds.

'I'm looking for a toilet,' I say, the first thing that comes into my head. 'The other ones were occupied.'

She doesn't answer but then she doesn't appear to be speaking to me anyway.

Crowds are filing away as one large shuffling mass, everyone huffing and puffing their way up the hill towards their cars. There's a queue to leave that stretches all the way along the beach. Parents are carrying sleeping children and the temperature has dropped to such an extent that the brightly coloured tops and shorts of earlier have been replaced by jumpers and jackets. I want to find Chloe but the crowd is packed so tightly that walking in the opposite direction isn't an option. I can either head up the hill and wait – or remain where I am and try to spot her.

The lights in the pub suddenly come on, spreading a yellowy glow onto the street. Gwen takes this as an invitation to leave. She flicks me one further wordless glare and then slips along the front between the pub and the crowd, pressing herself through the front door and disappearing.

I continue watching the crowd, hoping for a glimpse of my sister. She's probably finishing up at the gallery but that's on the opposite side of the crowd and I can't see a way of crossing. It's like being on the wrong side of the motorway.

Unsure what else to do, I edge away and head down to the docks once more. A buzz is growing steadily louder as a pair of lights out at sea grow wider and brighter. There are so many shadows at the back of the pub that it's easy enough to slot myself in next to a tree. I press against the trunk, allowing the shadows to swallow me as the motor boat whines its way into the docks. There's a moment in which I'm convinced Scott will climb off the one boat and notice my intrusion onto the other. Everything incriminating I did happened underneath his tarp – but perhaps I've left footprints? Or maybe he has everything laid out in a precise manner and I've disturbed something I didn't notice?

My worries dissipate immediately because Scott doesn't even look at the second boat. He jumps down from the first, hauling a rope over his shoulder. He wraps it around a post a couple of times and ties it in place, all the while muttering something I can't catch over the shuffling crowd.

When he's done, Chrissie appears at the back of the boat. Scott doesn't offer a hand to help her and she ends up stumbling onto the dock, almost falling face-first and only saving herself by clinging on to a post.

Scott strides away and then spins, jabbing that sausage finger towards her. The one I've seen close up. 'What did I tell you?' he rages, voice now clear over the dissipating crowd.

'I know…'

'So why'd you do it again?'

'I'm sorry, I—'

Chrissie doesn't finish her sentence because the back of Scott's hand thrashes across her face. There's a thunderous crack, as if a lion tamer has snapped a whip. It's come as such a surprise – and with such force – that Chrissie reels around in a full circle. Scott's not done there. He reaches to the back of her head, snagging a fistful of hair and pulling her towards him. His lips are moving but he's no longer shouting. Whatever he's saying is measured with terrifying precision. It only lasts a second and then he shoves her away, almost pushing her into the water. Chrissie's on her knees, hair covering her face. Scott doesn't wait for her to get up. He stomps away towards the pub, swinging open the back gate with a creak and disappearing inside.

I haven't moved.

Everything's happened so quickly that it only now occurs to me that I could have intervened. Or tried to.

Chrissie waits until the bang from the pub's back door has finished echoing and then she takes hold of the mooring post again. She pulls herself up and pushes the hair away from her face, brushing the cheek where Scott hit her.

I creep out from my cover, glancing quickly towards the road. The crowd is only a short distance away but has shrunk to only the slowest or drunkest.

'Hey,' I call.

Chrissie looks up, scanning the darkness for the voice. I move further ahead, stepping into the light cast from inside the pub.

'It's Megan,' I say.

'Oh.'

'Are you okay?'

Chrissie moves away from the docks so that we're both outside the gate that leads into the pub garden. She straightens herself, standing taller, clearly not sure how much I witnessed.

'Of course,' she replies, though her voice trembles. 'Did you enjoy the show?'

'I didn't enjoy *that* show.'

It's as if Scott's assault has sucked the warmth from the day. Chrissie's breath appears as mist in the dark and, when she shivers, I do as well.

'I, um…'

'Does that happen often?' I ask. 'Once is enough, but…'

Chrissie folds her arms and takes another breath, sending one more gasp of mist into the night. 'You shouldn't interfere,' she says.

'If he's hitting you—'

'Don't get involved, Megan. Things will never change here.'

'*What* will never change?'

Chrissie takes a step forward so that we're within touching distance. 'You should leave,' she says.

'*You* should leave.'

She pauses for a beat, then sighs a weary, 'You're young.'

'I know there's a bigger world than Whitecliff out there. You don't have to stay here.'

'It's easy for you.'

'You don't know that.'

'I have a baby. I can't just go. You don't know what Scott's like.'

'I have a good idea.'

Chrissie stretches and grips my shoulder hard. I feel her fingers digging against the bony joint. 'You *don't*,' she says.

I fidget and gasp an, 'Ow!' but she doesn't let go.

'You should go,' Chrissie repeats, closer still, almost whispering into my ear. 'Do it tonight. You and your sister. Just leave.'

'People keep telling me that.'

'For a reason, Megan! People get hurt.'

'Like Zac?'

She steps away at the sound of a bang from the pub. Her eyes shoot towards the door and then she's opening the gate. 'I have to go,' she says, not adding anything else before scampering across the beer garden and disappearing through the back door.

I stand and watch for a moment, wondering if she might return. Seconds pass, then a minute. She doesn't, of course.

The crowd has almost disappeared by the time I get back to the road. I'm not sure if everyone has moved quicker than I thought possible, or if more time has passed than I realised. The hum of people and engines is seeping down from the top of the hill and the village itself feels quiet. Like New Year's Day morning, when everyone's sleeping off the night before.

I'm about to head for the gallery when I realise Chloe is standing at the front of the pub talking to Pete. She looks like a child beside his brawny frame, looking up at him with confusion. Other villagers are there as well: Arthur, Vee with her father and some more faces whose names I don't know. There's a frightening moment where, almost as one, they turn to look at me. Dozens of sets of eyes, who seemingly know something I don't.

It's Chloe I talk to. 'Everything all right?' I ask.

Gwen steps out from behind Pete, the blanket still wrapped around her shoulders. She's one broomstick short of a pantomime role. 'That's where I saw her,' she says. 'Sneaking around the back while everyone else was watching the fireworks.'

The villagers turn from Gwen to me, waiting for a riposte.

'I wasn't sneaking around anywhere,' I reply.

'Oh yes you were.'

I shrug, holding both hands up, not sure how to defend myself. 'Shall we go?' I say, talking to Chloe.

'Someone broke into the pub during the burning,' Pete says stonily.

A horrible sinking feeling bursts through the bottom of my stomach and, this time, it has nothing to do with food. 'What?'

'There's almost five thousand pounds missing,' he says. 'The whole day's takings. Someone smashed into the safe.'

CHAPTER THIRTY-EIGHT

Everyone is looking at me. While I was whispering to Chrissie at the back of the pub, they must have been having this impromptu village meeting at the front. Pitchforks and flames at the ready.

'Where were you during the boat burning?' Pete asks.

My mind doesn't work quickly enough. I can hardly say I was smashing open the crate at the back of Scott's boat.

'I, um… I went for a walk.'

It's not only a lie but it *sounds* like a lie. Chloe's reaction is wide-eyed confusion and as she stares at me, I can feel her silent question: *Why are you not telling the truth?*

No one believes me, nor should they.

'Did you see her earlier?' This is from a woman I don't know. I'm not sure I even recognise her face. Someone from the village. 'She was wearing a black top,' she adds.

It was such a stupid thing. A pitiful rebellion against a nothing tradition – but it does look for all the world as if I'm here to disrupt village life. If my choice of clothes wasn't enough, they now think I've stolen their money, too.

'I was on the hill,' I say. 'I watched the boat burning and fireworks from there. It was too crowded on the beach. I couldn't see properly.'

There's a short pause as the villagers look to each other, wondering if it's plausible. Then Gwen smashes my made-up alibi in one simple sentence: 'I was on the hill,' she says. 'And you definitely weren't.'

This would explain why I almost ran into her when I was returning from breaking into Scott's boat.

'I didn't see you there,' I say.

'Don't try that on me,' she says. 'I was there and you weren't.'

There's nothing I can say to that, because she's telling the truth. Even if she wasn't, the villagers would believe her over me. I'm the idiot who's antagonised them with a stupid colour and who's spent the week interrogating anyone who'll give me the time of day.

There's an eerie calm across the path between us. Me on one side, Chloe and a couple of dozen villagers on the other. I'm trying to catch Chloe's eye but she's refusing to look at me. She's staring at the ground instead.

'It's okay,' Pete says, after what seems like an age. 'If that's where she says she was, that's where she was.'

He holds up a hand to interrupt Gwen's, 'But—'

'There were lots of people around,' Pete adds. 'Thousands of strangers. Anyone could have got in. I've been meaning to get double glazing put into those back windows for years. I guess it's a lesson learned. I'll get onto the insurance company tomorrow.'

It's as if he's called a truce. Tossed the football over the top of the trenches on Christmas morning and yelled, 'Come on, lads: who's up for a kickabout?'

Nobody seems quite sure what to say, most of all me. Do I thank him? Would that make me look guiltier?

Pete claps his hands together. 'Okay, I don't know about you lot but I've got some clearing up to do. Best get to it.'

Someone groans but when Pete disappears into the pub, everyone else seems to take it as an invitation to head home. There's an undoubted sense of disappointment. No lynching tonight. Put the pitchforks away.

Chloe waits for me and, when it's just us, speaks before I can. 'I said I'd help Arthur clear up. I'll be back later.'

'You shouldn't walk back to the cottage so late by yourself.'

'I'm a big girl.'

With that, she turns to leave. I watch her, unsure what to say – but then someone calls my name.

Luke is smoking by the corner of the pub. I'd not noticed him before. I realise Chloe has stopped, too. 'I'll walk her back, if you like,' he says, nodding to Chloe. 'I'll be going back that way anyway. I've got to help clean up the beach.'

Chloe's mind is made up and there's little point in arguing. She snaps, 'Fine.' I mutter, 'See you later.' I watch as she disappears into the gallery. I get the sense that Luke wants to ask me something but I can't handle him for now, so turn and head for the hill.

I've only taken a few steps when Vee appears at my side. I wonder if she was waiting for me in the shadows. 'You look like you need some company,' she says, as if to answer my unspoken question.

'I, um…'

'Forget it,' she says, realising I am about to apologise and not making me.

I start to say something more but she squeezes my hand for a fraction of a second and I realise there is no need. Mother would make me grovel for sins either actual or imagined. One apology was never enough. Perhaps the greatest proof of a friendship or relationship is when the word 'sorry' becomes redundant. When it no longer needs to be spoken, because it's already understood.

Vee and I walk slowly up the hill, not saying anything. When we're nearly at the top, we stop and look out to sea. The embers of the boat are barely a smouldering orange. I wonder how many other boats have been burned and sunk to the bottom over the years. Whether it all washes up on shore the next day.

As we're approaching the cottage, I realise that Vee has never been inside. After our run-in at Fisherman's Cave, I brought her a towel while she waited outside. I'm suddenly nervous, unsure what this will mean for me. For us. It's not something I've planned, or even particularly thought about. I'm not even sure if my feelings are real, or if they're a chuntering blend of an empty stomach and a cocktail of Mother's pills.

We both have our scars – hers on her arms, mine with my protruding ribs and joints.

I have to shoulder the door open, as ever. It pops like the lid of a jar and I almost fall inside. Vee is a few steps behind. We've not said a word since we left the village and I wonder if her feelings are as confused as mine.

Vee shuffles around me with an awkward, closed-lip smile. I fight the door back into place and lock it.

When I turn, I bump into Vee's back. She's not moved. I giggle girlishly and nervously. It's not like me.

'Everything all right?' I ask.

She doesn't reply – but she doesn't have to. She hasn't moved because she's staring at what's ahead of us.

There's been no attempt to hide it, nor to sort or count it. A large mound of money is sitting on the kitchen table, some notes screwed and grubby, others pristine and flat.

CHAPTER THIRTY-NINE

I drift across to the table and find myself picking up the notes, making sure they're real. Pete said somewhere around five thousand pounds had been stolen and there must be at least that here. It's mainly ten- and twenty-pound notes. I've never seen so much cash in my life.

'It wasn't me,' I say. 'I came back to change this afternoon and I've been in the village ever since.'

'You weren't on the beach for the boat burning,' Vee says. Fact, not a question.

'No.'

'You weren't on the hill, watching.'

Fact.

I can't look at her but I can't answer either. She already knows. I could tell her about the guns – but how to explain that? I decided to smash open a crate on Scott's boat for no reason. On a hunch.

Chrissie told me that things will never change in the village – that people get hurt – and I'm wondering if that was a warning about who not to trust. 'The village' could mean anyone. *Every*one.

Vee steps to the front door and unbolts it. 'I'll tell Pete,' she says.

'*We* can do it,' I reply. 'We'll bundle it up and go together.'

'I don't want to touch it.' She tugs the door but it needs more than that to open.

'Please wait,' I say, pleading. 'I'll find a bag to put it all in.'

I start digging through the drawers, trying to remember where we put the supermarket carrier bags. I can't think of how I'm going to tell Pete the money materialised in the cottage. It would sound suspicious even if Gwen *hadn't* seen me away from the crowd.

Vee waits by the door. Finally, I find the screwed-up carrier bags in a cupboard next to the bin. I sweep the money from the table into a bag but there's too much, so I have to use a second. I tie the handles to stop anything falling out.

'Please say you believe me,' I say.

Vee looks from me to the bags. 'It *is* a lot of money,' she replies quietly.

I place them back on the table. 'If I knew it was there, do you think I'd have brought you back here? I'd have hidden it away. It doesn't make sense that I stole it and then showed you the evidence.'

'So where were you when the boat was burning?'

She stands, waiting for an answer. I think again about telling her of the guns on the boat – but the knock-on effect is too high.

It's the whole truth or no truth.

The postcard from Zac, the figure I keep seeing in the woods, the fact that I constantly feel watched. In isolation, it's quirkiness; all together, it's madness. If Vee asks *why* I decided to break into that crate on Scott's boat, I have no answer. Instinct? My gut? Curiosity? It's none of those things. There's a pile of smashed items that belonged to my mother in the study because I couldn't help myself. There's a scrapbook of food wrappers in my backpack because I can't bear to throw it out – and because I was insane enough to create it in the first place.

'I wouldn't do this,' I say. Not an answer to *her* question but an answer nonetheless.

Vee won't look at me. 'Okay. Let's just go.'

'I wouldn't do this because I don't need the money,' I say. 'It's only five thousand. It's nothing.'

Vee turns to me now. She's frowning, confused.

'I should've told you,' I say. 'I'm a millionaire. So is my sister. Our parents left everything to us. There's a house in London that doesn't have a mortgage and this cottage. There was a business, which we sold. There's a savings account. All sorts. I never need to work a day in my life if I don't want to. Neither does Chloe. She could drop out of school and go travelling for the next twenty years.'

It feels like a negative, even though most people would consider it a good thing. I haven't lied to Vee about who I am but I also haven't told her the entire truth. I knew the reaction this might have. She's grown up in a place where people live month to month. Where a bad season of weather could put them out of business, or might mean they can't afford the heating bills through the winter. I've never had that sort of life and never will.

'You're rich,' she says. It's so simple, but she sounds stung.

'You must have realised. The beach kids have money...'

It takes her a while to respond. 'I know. I suppose I didn't think.' She stops herself for a moment and then adds: 'With the beach kids, the money isn't theirs, is it? They're spending their parents' money. It feels different.'

'I'm still the same person who walked to the caves with you.'

She stands still, one hand remaining on the door. I can't read her. 'How much money *do* you have?' Vee asks.

I know there's no way I can answer this in a way that will satisfy her. She already feels betrayed.

'Enough,' I say. 'I don't like to talk about it.'

'That's easy to say when you *have* money.'

'I know. I never asked for it. Sometimes I think I don't even want it.'

Vee snorts and yanks on the door once more. 'Do you know how insulting that is? You have money and don't want it, while we have to work hard all the time just to get through to the next year to start all over again.'

'I didn't mean it like that.'

Vee finally gets the door open. I grab the two bags of money and follow her out, ready to head down to the pub.

'I've got to go,' she says. 'Don't worry, your secret's safe with me.'

Monday

CHAPTER FORTY

Clouds have assembled by morning; the dark grey sullenness of the sky reflecting exactly how I feel. It's cool and the day feels harsh. I sit on the sofa in the kitchen, listening to the wind rattle the cottage, waiting for Chloe to get up. When she does, she's already dressed in jeans and a long top. She has her bag with her and places it on the kitchen table.

'I want to go back to London,' she says. It's clear she's been awake for a while. 'We'll sell this cottage. We never have to come here again. Literally everyone wants us to leave – so let's do it.'

'Not everyone,' I reply. 'People like *you*. It's only me they don't like.'

'Someone still wrote "GO HOME" outside our door. They still smashed our window.'

We both turn to look at the board which is sitting in the window frame. It's loose and, although this might be due to my shabby handiwork, I suspect it's how somebody got in to leave the money.

'We'll get someone to fix that,' Chloe says, 'but we don't have to be here. We can leave the keys with an estate agent or someone. Maybe Alison or Dan Wood? They seem friendly enough.'

I want to tell her about Alison's odd reaction to my question about whether our parents helped fund the festival – but I don't. I've been wondering whether it was *my* reaction that was odd. So what if our parents had a standing order to donate money? They owned a cottage here.

I've not moved from the sofa. Chloe takes a couple of steps towards me. 'Shall we go?'

'Don't you wonder *why* people are so keen for us to leave?'

'I don't care.'

'But what if they're hiding something? What if they know what happened to Zac?'

She folds her arms and speaks slowly: 'It's only you who thinks that.'

'Don't you care if someone killed our brother?'

She shakes her head. 'Nobody killed him, Meg. It was ten years ago – and I barely knew him. Think how many times we'd ever met. We were strangers to one another. Nobody thinks he was killed except you. This can be a dangerous place, with the rocks, the cliffs and the tides.'

The last one sticks with me. I wonder if she somehow knows what happened with me and Vee at Fisherman's Cave.

'Someone knows something.' I say the words firmly. I have to believe it.

'Why do you need to know? What are you going to do? The police looked into it and didn't find anything.'

'Everyone *assumes* he drowned. How do we know they investigated properly?'

'How do we know they didn't?! You were ten and it was a decade ago.' Chloe gulps, then adds, 'Ten years.'

It's hard to come up with an answer to that, because we *don't* know whether or not the investigation was thorough. The people I've spoken to have largely said the search fizzled out quickly – but that doesn't necessarily mean the police inquiry didn't continue in a quieter manner.

'What about the postcard?' I say. 'Someone wanted us to come here. Zac, or—'

'Zac's dead, Meg. He died a decade ago. Mum and Dad died. It's only us.'

There's something about the way Chloe says 'Mum and Dad' that I can't get over. Mother would *never* let me get away with speaking so casually – yet things were always more slack for Chloe. Is it because our parents cared less for her? Their interest in children had waned to such a degree that the petty arguments weren't worth having any longer?

Or was it something worse?

Was it that Chloe was the favourite and *I* was the one our mother couldn't stand? Was it that I'm the problem and always have been?

'If someone wanted to get us here by sending that postcard,' Chloe says, 'then who was it? Where are they? We've been here a week. It's not like we're hiding away.'

'I know…'

'So, let's go. Why spend our time here where people hate us, instead of going somewhere they don't?'

She says 'us'; she means 'you'.

I push myself up from the sofa, defeated. I can't argue with anything Chloe's said. I take one step towards my room… and then change my mind.

'One more day,' I say. 'If I haven't found anything by tomorrow morning, we'll go. We can leave as early as you want.'

Chloe stares at me, stony-faced. Whitecliff hasn't been that unkind to her – she's got on well with the beach kids, she likes Arthur, she's sold some of her work. I know she only wants to leave for my benefit. To save *me*.

She crosses to the table and unzips the top pocket of her bag, grabbing her sketchbook. 'I'm going to the cliffs,' she says – and then she leaves to do precisely that.

* * *

Whitecliff's cobbled main street is surprisingly sparse. The stalls, banners and bunting have been removed at a similar speed to that at which they went up. Perhaps there *are* ghosts in this part of the world – ones that really enjoy cleaning.

Vee is sweeping up outside the board shop. She's in long sleeves as ever. Things feel different now I know what's underneath. It's like I get her – and like somebody gets me. Then it was all messed up because of my parents' money. Even after death, I can't escape their shadow.

She looks up as I approach and then her eyes quickly dart back to the ground.

'Hi,' I say.

She mumbles an, 'All right?'

'I was wondering if—'

'I'm busy today. Dad wants me to work, so…'

I wait for a moment, wondering if she's going to finish the sentence. I guess there's no need.

'We're leaving tomorrow,' I say. 'Chloe and I. We're selling the cottage and that'll be the end. I thought you should know.'

The brush has stopped moving but Vee still doesn't look up. 'Okay. Now I know,' she says.

I hover for a few seconds longer but can't think of anything else to add. Vee starts to sweep once more, so I turn and make my way to the beach.

The ocean looks different in this weather. The waves are a dark grey, rippling with menace rather than invitation. Instead of a soft cream, the sand is a mucky brown, more like mud in a field. My trainers sink with every step as I make my way across to Luke at the lifeguard station. There's no sign of the beach kids.

'Quiet day?' I ask.

Luke's in a hoody, baggy cap and tracksuit bottoms. The candlelit seduction attempt at his cottage seems a long time ago.

He's still wearing sunglasses, despite the weather. He looks down at me but I can't see his eyes.

'It happens,' he says. 'It's scorching for a week, then we have a day or two of this before it goes back to hot again.'

I pull my own top tighter and take a spot on the damp sand at the base of his stool. 'It feels like November,' I say. 'It's cold.'

Luke doesn't reply. It feels like the end of everything.

'Does everyone know?' I ask. He doesn't hear me first time and I have to repeat myself, compounding my embarrassment.

'About the money?' he asks.

'Yes.'

'Everyone knows.'

'I didn't steal it,' I say. 'As soon as I saw it last night, I put it into bags and brought it back down to the village. Vee was there. You can ask her.'

'How did someone get it into your cottage?'

'I don't know. One of the windows is broken, so probably that way.' I pause and then add: 'It wasn't me.'

Neither of us speak. I sit and listen to the waves. Even the sound is different without the sun. The ocean feels angrier, like it needs a day or two of throwing a paddy to get it out of its system.

There's movement from the direction of the pub: a few of the beach kids are on their way over. Mia has Popcorn at her side and George is there, too. There might be one or two newcomers. It's not the day for it but they're in jeans and trousers. Probably going for a walk as opposed to anything else.

'You should go,' Luke says.

I wonder if he means now, from the beach, or generally, to leave Whitecliff. I don't reply, pushing myself up. I wipe the sand from my palms and backside before heading off along the beach.

None of the beach kids acknowledge me. With everything else that's happened, I wouldn't be surprised if Mia blames me for kidnapping her dog. Perhaps they think I attacked Brad, too.

I see Chrissie outside the pub but she darts inside in an obvious attempt to evade me.

People are literally running in the opposite direction to avoid having to talk to me. Perhaps even to avoid *looking* at me.

I take the wooded path up to the cottage. It's the easiest journey I've made all week. I'm not sure why I told Chloe we'd stay for another day. She was ahead of me in knowing what everyone would think and how they'd act. I should have left with her this morning.

I'm about to head into the cottage to pack my things when I change my mind again. I follow the same route I did the other night, tracing around the cottage until I'm behind my bedroom window, staring at the woods.

Chloe has been right about a lot of things – but she's especially right about one thing in particular. If somebody did send that postcard to get us here, why not reveal themselves? We've been here for a week and it's not like we've been hiding away.

I wait at the back of the cottage, listening, waiting for my paranoia to catch up with me. I haven't taken any of Mother's pills this morning.

'Hello…?'

My words disappear into the trees. There's no answer, no hint of movement.

I wait a moment and then, not quite sure to whom I'm speaking, add: 'I have to leave. We're going later today. If you're actually out there, now's the time to say.'

My words sound childlike, not like me at all. My voice echoes around the forest and then disappears. It was cold in the village but it's colder here. The ground is covered with dew. The tops of the trees are dripping water onto the ground below.

As I take a step to return to the front of the cottage, something starts to rattle from within the trees. I turn back. There's a snap of a branch and a low rustle. Someone is pushing their way through the undergrowth and then, as if appearing from nowhere, he's in front of me.

It's not Pete this time.

This person is smaller and holds himself in a different way. He's hugging himself not because of the cold but because of embarrassment. He's bundled up in camouflage trousers and a jacket that's too big for him – it seems to be dragging him down.

He takes another step out of the woods. There's only a couple of metres between us.

'Hi,' he says.

I stare closer, squinting, not quite able to take him in.

'Zac…?'

CHAPTER FORTY-ONE

The young man twitches slightly, glancing off to the side as he does. It's as if he's received an electric shock. He shakes his head and then twitches a second time. Some sort of tic.

'Ee-Ee-Ee-Ee…'

I can't work out if he's trying to speak but, whatever's happening, the word is sticking in his throat.

'Ee-Ee-Ee-Ethan,' he manages, eventually. He sighs with relief and stands a tiny bit taller. He's not quite looking at me, more *through* me, as if there's someone standing behind me and he's talking to them.

And suddenly, I know who he is.

'Ethan Wood,' I say. 'Dan and Alison are your parents?'

A nod.

'We played together on the beach ten years ago?'

Another nod.

'Why haven't I met you?'

It takes him almost two minutes to reply. His stutter is beyond anything I've ever seen or heard before. Each attempted syllable is preceded with a gasp and something close to a snort. He eventually tells me that he rarely leaves the house.

I realise that yes and no answers are going to suit us better than a full-on conversation.

'Do you live with your parents?'

This gets a nod.

'I've seen you around,' I say. 'Haven't I? A lot. In the woods, just out of sight.'

He nods and points to me, then to his own chest.

'You wanted me to see you?' I ask.

A nod. I start to ask why he kept running away and then figure he would've been too nervous. Too scared.

'You sent the postcard?' I say, already knowing the answer before he starts to nod.

'You followed Vee and me out to Fisherman's Cave? You saved us.'

A nod.

'Was it your rope?'

A shake this time. It was already there – exactly as Vee had guessed. It probably belonged to a caving club, or some amateurs.

It's an impromptu act but Ethan doesn't flinch when I wrap my arms around his neck and thank him. He doesn't pull away but he doesn't reciprocate, either. He stands with his arms limp at his side. I step away, wondering if I've upset him but the bemused look on his face makes me think it isn't that at all. It's because he's not used to anyone touching him.

'You left the necklace?' I ask.

A nod.

'Did you know it was Zac's?'

He shivers with the nod this time. I wonder how long he's been out this morning. Whether he's been waiting for me all this time.

I unlock the cottage and usher him inside. The kitchen is still dark because of the board in the window and I'm not sure how to get the heating going. I end up lighting the oven and we sit at the table, holding our hands out towards its open door.

Not only does Ethan have a stammer, he has a lazy eye. There are a couple of times in which I realise he's looking at me but when he sees I've noticed, he quickly turns away. One eye always moves slower than the other.

'Your mum said you were at Cambridge,' I say.

He shakes his head. Alison Wood – and probably her husband – are like my parents. It's all about first impressions and keeping up with the neighbours. Chloe and I were sent away to boarding school because we cramped our parents' style and got in the way. Ethan's parents want people to think their son is at Cambridge – but they wouldn't want them to know about his stammer and his lazy eye. That would reflect badly on them.

'What about school?' I ask.

Ethan has moved from his chair to sit on the floor in front of the oven, hugging his knees to his chest. He stares at the floor.

'Did you go to school?'

A nod.

'What about after?'

It takes an age for the story to come out. It was the year after Zac disappeared that Ethan's parents started buying him off with televisions, computers and games consoles. Things to keep him inside during the summer, rather than out. Anything to keep him quiet and away from judging eyes around the village. If anyone asked about him, they'd claim he was at summer camp – or, latterly, at university.

'Why didn't you just leave the house anyway?' I ask.

He buries his face between his knees and starts to make a snuffling sound. At first I think he's sobbing but, when he looks up, I can see his lips moving. He's trying to speak.

'M-m-m-m-m-m-make…. f-f-f-f-f-f-f-fun,' he says, eventually.

'The local kids made fun of you when you went out?'

A shake of the head.

'The beach kids?'

Another shake. He starts to gasp again, eventually managing, 'They said make fun.'

It takes me a few seconds to figure it out and when I do, I have to force myself not to react with horror. Ethan was never *forced* to stay inside. He wasn't under house arrest. He could have left if he wanted to – but his parents had put such fear into him that he didn't *want* to leave. He preferred to live his life with computer games and television, inside, where nobody would judge him or laugh at him. His parents made him believe that the real world would mean people ridiculing him.

With the way he looks and sounds, it's not hard to believe. Ethan certainly took their word for it.

I don't say anything for a while. It's hard to know what words would mean enough. I touch his knee and he doesn't shake me away.

'You're a hero,' I tell him. 'You saved Vee and me and you didn't hang around for thanks. Whatever your parents think, we wouldn't be here if it wasn't for you.'

He stutters nervously, turning to look anywhere that isn't me. I wonder how much contact he's had with other people through the years. My social skills aren't the best but his are zero.

'When did you start getting out and exploring the woods?' I ask.

He shrugs.

'Do you go out to watch what the other kids are getting up to?'

It takes a while – but he nods slowly.

'Not everyone is mean. People would have let you join in.'

He turns away and I realise this is the wrong thing to have said. He might already know this, or he might not. Either way, it feels cruel to suggest that he's wasted the past however many years. He must be about my age, give or take a year or two. That's a lot of summers he's spent alone. It's a miracle he's brave enough to talk to me now.

'Why did you send the postcard?' I ask, knowing I'll have to wait for the reply. It takes a few minutes – but it comes eventually.

Ethan has spent the last ten years wondering if Chloe or my-self would return to Whitecliff. Then he overheard his parents talking about my parents' car crash. He found an article online and, when he saw that his mother was sending a card to commis-erate, he copied the address from that onto a postcard his parents had in a drawer.

'But why?' I ask.

'I thought if I sent the c-c-c-card, you'd come back, so I could tell y-y-you.'

'Tell me what?'

'Zac.'

I press forward, on edge. The hairs on the back of my neck are standing up. 'You know what happened to him?'

Ethan nods.

I feel tingles.

Ethan gasps, his eyes, nose and lips twitching as he tries to get the words out.

'Th-th-that night,' he manages.

'Which night?'

He points to me, then himself. It takes me a couple of sec-onds.

'The night after we played on the beach?'

A nod.

'Van,' he says.

I think about what to say. I don't want to make things harder by asking questions that would require lengthy answers.

'You saw a van?' I ask.

A nod.

'In the village?'

He shakes his head.

I think and then ask, 'At your house?'

A nod. Yes.

'A van was at your house that night?'

Yes.

He takes a big breath and then a series of short ones. I don't interrupt, letting him do his thing. He pulls his coat tighter. He seems so small.

'F-f-f-four,' he says.

'Four vans?'

A shake.

'Four people?'

He points to me and then his own chest. It takes me a second to get it.

'My parents and your parents were in the van?'

A nod.

'What then?'

He uses both hands, as if lifting.

'They picked something up?' I ask.

A nod. 'T-t-t-took... into... h-h-h-house.'

'Your house?'

Yes.

Ethan looks exhausted. He takes a series of long breaths, each of which emits a slight wheeze.

'What did they take into the house?' I ask.

He holds his palms up for me to see, shrugging at the same time.

'You don't know?'

A shake of the head – but he stretches his hands wide and mouths, 'B-b-b-big.'

'Some*thing*?' I ask. 'Or some*one*?'

Another shrug – he doesn't know. He takes a few more deep breaths but, if anything, his distress is getting worse. He points to his neck frantically and I think he's saying that he wants a drink. When I offer him one, he waves a hand and points at my neck instead. I think he's indicating there's something stuck to me at first, but then I understand what he's saying.

'You found Zac's necklace?' I ask.

Yes.

'In your house?'

A shake of the head. He points at the floor.

'On your drive?'

Yes.

'Do you think it was Zac they carried into your house?'

He takes another breath and I realise that I'm holding mine. And then, very slowly, Ethan nods his head.

One final question.

'Do you think he was alive?'

Ethan takes one more wheezing breath and then opens his mouth. He doesn't stammer this time: 'Maybe.'

CHAPTER FORTY-TWO

Ethan leaves soon after our conversation. He seems edgy about being away from his house and all the talking has exhausted him. He's answered some of my questions, important ones, and his very presence has answered others.

He sent the postcard because he wanted to tell me what he'd seen. The problem was that, once he'd brought us here, he didn't know *how* to tell me. He tried leaving the necklace, hoping I'd connect it to Zac. Sooner or later, he knew he'd have to talk to me – but I think it was one of those things he was so nervous about, he kept pushing it away. He didn't know if I'd make fun of him in the way his parents had conditioned him to believe. Talking is genuinely hard for him, made worse by the fact that he doesn't get to speak to many people. A devastating circle.

My own father was never particularly attentive to us children. I don't know if his interest disappeared with Zac, or if it was never there. My mother sent me away because I wasn't what she wanted. She was after a designer poodle to keep in her handbag and instead she got me: some mongrel with its own ideas that she didn't know how to handle. But my life has been nothing compared to poor Ethan's. He's not exactly locked in his house – but what else is there for him to do around this area without his parents' support? He's shy and introverted; he's nervous about talking to anyone – even running away wouldn't have been an option for him. He's an adult but, in many ways he's still a kid.

Despite the answers he's given, I'm still full of questions. My parents can no longer answer them, which means it's only Dan and Alison Wood who can. Perhaps it's no wonder they were so friendly when we first arrived. They were trying to figure out if Chloe and I really were just on holiday, or whether we knew something about whatever happened with that van that night.

I wait for Chloe, thinking it might be best if we go to them together. Then I change my mind because all they'll do is deny all knowledge of anything. Plus, I have no way of revealing what I know without letting them know where the information came from.

I spend a bit more time working unsuccessfully on safe combinations. When it's almost dark, Chloe arrives back at the cottage. She barely says a word as she packs her sketchbook into her bag.

'Can we talk?' I ask.

She's on her way to her room but stops and turns: 'Are we still leaving in the morning?'

I don't answer straight away and she takes that as a 'no'.

'Chlo.'

'What?'

'I met Ethan Wood today. He's the son of Alison and Dan. He's got… problems. They've sort of been hiding him away.'

Chloe comes back to where I'm standing. The wind has caught her cheeks while she's been out; her face is flushed pink.

'I thought he was at Cambridge?'

I shake my head. 'That's what Alison tells people. He's this lonely, sad guy with a bad stutter and a lazy eye. His parents have made him afraid of people. He thinks everyone will make fun of him, so he doesn't talk to anyone other than his parents. I think he was a bit scared of me.'

'What did he say?'

'He saw a van pulling onto his driveway the night Zac disappeared. Our parents and Ethan's parents got out. They carried something large into the house and, the next morning, Ethan found Zac's necklace on the driveway. Ethan sent the postcard to bring us here after finding out what happened to our parents. He thought he might not get another chance to tell us.'

Chloe sits on the sofa close to me and doesn't say anything for at least a minute. She holds her head and massages the area around her temples.

'I want to go,' she says. 'Let's go now. We'll find a hotel somewhere.'

'But we're close.'

'Close to what?'

'Something bad happened here. Something bad is *still* happening here. There's something rotten in this village and I think Zac knew what it was. I think they killed him for it.'

She slams her hands down on the sofa and spins so quickly that I flinch away. '*Who* killed him?'

'I don't know – but Ethan saw our parents carrying something into their house.'

I reach into my pocket and take out the gold chain with the star at the centre. After passing it to Chloe, I grab the family photo from the study and give her that, too.

'It's his,' I say. 'You can see for yourself. Ethan didn't see what they were carrying – but it must have been Zac.'

Chloe compares the chain to the photograph and then hands both back.

'It didn't have to be Zac,' she says. 'Perhaps Mum or Dad was holding onto his chain and dropped it. They could have been carrying anything into the house.'

'Don't you want to know what happened?'

Chloe's hair swishes in front of her face as she turns away but I think I catch a hint of tears in her eyes.

It's then that I realise: she *doesn't* want to know.

When it comes to our missing brother, I've been thinking that the not knowing is the worst thing. If he *is* dead and I know that for sure, it's something from which I can move on. Chloe has been thinking the exact opposite. If the truth is bad enough, it's better to not know. For now, we're tragic young women with a missing brother and dead parents. But if our parents had something to do with what happened to Zac…

'How long have you suspected them?' I ask.

It takes Chloe a long time to answer. When she does, the room feels colder. 'I was six,' she says quietly. 'You were ten. Let's go and forget all this. It doesn't matter.'

'It *does* matter. If someone here had something to do with what happened, we should—'

'We should *what*? What are we going to do? Go and knock on Alison Wood's door and ask her? You can't think she'll just come out with it. Say you figure out what might have happened without her, what then? Are you going to go to the police with some flimsy evidence?' She sighs, throws her hands up. 'It doesn't matter because it's *gone*. We go away, we sell this place and we move on.'

'I can't leave it, Chlo.'

Chloe turns to me, grabs my hands and *squeezes*. 'Please,' she says. '*Please*, let's go. I don't want to be here any more.'

'One more night,' I say, nodding at the wall. 'I want to try getting into that safe. There might be something important in there.'

'Like what?'

'I don't know. I'm up to almost ten thousand.'

There's a moment, just a moment, where Chloe turns and stares at me with the same disdain I used to see on our mother's face. It's something about the angle of her eyebrow. The way it says, '*Really?*' without actually saying it. I know I'm not going to be able to try all of the remaining combinations in an evening – but I can at least hope to get lucky.

'You still think he's alive, don't you?' Chloe says.

I don't reply straight away. 'I don't think that for sure,' I say. 'I don't know.'

'Zac's *dead*,' Chloe says firmly. 'He *died* ten years ago. It doesn't matter what we do here, he's not coming back.'

She stops herself from saying something more, then stands and starts towards the bedroom. Then she turns. She's trembling, barely able to keep herself standing because of the mixture of fury and upset inside her. 'Am I not enough?' she asks.

'What?'

'Am I not enough for you? You don't want to think about a future where it's just us, so you're trying to hunt down someone who's been dead for ten years?'

She sounds so hurt, so *broken*, that I'm momentarily unsure how to respond. We've said so little to each other about our parents' deaths in the three months since it happened. About what it means for us. It's only now that I'm realising she has the same fear I do.

A fear of being alone.

'It's not that at all,' I say. 'It's you and me versus the world.'

I cross to her but she shakes me away, staring up through teary eyes. 'I want to go,' she says. 'Look at what this place is doing to you.' She motions in the vague direction of the bin and even though we're too far away for her to be precise, I know she means the empty packet of biscuits.

We always talk in circles, never quite saying the exact words – but this is as close as Chloe has come to confronting me.

From nowhere, I start to feel tears welling up from my stomach. I can't look at my sister any longer and have to turn away.

'Tomorrow,' I reply. 'I promise. In the morning, we'll leave this dump and never come back. They can have their damned village.'

CHAPTER FORTY-THREE

I get up to ten thousand five hundred on the safe when I lose faith. It's not quite midnight and Chloe has been in bed for more than an hour. I'm not sure if our relationship will recover from this. She'll be back at school in a month or so and I don't know what will happen then.

The unopened bar of chocolate is still in the fridge and I take it out, skimming my fingers over the wrapper and memorising the calories, fat, carbs and sugar from the list on the back. Chloe's wrong about one thing – it isn't *only* this place that's turned me into this.

I return the chocolate to the fridge and have a glass of water, then a second. I rattle the board in the window, making sure it's secure and then walk a dozen laps of the kitchen. I try five more sequential combinations for the safe but all are met with a beep and red light.

If we're leaving in the morning, I should probably pack, so I tiptoe into my room, trying not to make much sound in case I wake Chloe. I know her bag will already be packed with precision. Everything will be folded, with socks in shoes to save space – she'll have followed all the tips people give. My clothes, meanwhile, are still scattered across the floor. There seems little point in tidying them now, so I screw them into my bag, not caring about the fact that I'm mixing clean with dirty. When I try to ram in my shorts from the day of the festival, they won't scrunch up because the Burning Boat programme is still in their pocket.

I uncrease the booklet and turn to its inside back cover, staring at my parents' names once more. I still haven't got a satisfactory explanation as to why they are listed – but now I know Alison Wood might have had something to do with Zac's disappearance, her evasive reaction to my question about the programme is even more curious.

The programme's content is as dull as it was when I first read it. If anything, the poem is worse on second reading. I close the booklet and stare at the cover. There's an image of a boat and the date of the original boat burning underneath: 1 August 1750.

And then I have an idea…

I return to the living room and type 01-08-50 into the push panel.

Beep. Red dot. It's not the code.

I turn away, dejected – and then twist back, thumbing in 1-8-1750. There's a beep, a red dot – and then, almost in slow motion, a green dot. The safe door swings open a couple of centimetres.

I'm so stunned that it takes me a few seconds to move. I gasp a mouthful of air, having apparently forgotten to breathe.

Sitting at the front of the safe is a pile of papers. I know immediately that my mother organised these, because everything is so neat: lined up perfectly and clipped tidily together. She never embraced the digital age, insisting instead on doing everything with pen and paper.

I take the pages to the sofa and look through them. They seem to be accounts, written out in Mother's handwriting on squared paper. She was too much of a Luddite to use Excel and so she's written everything out longhand. I'll give her one thing – she has perfect handwriting.

There are years written at the top of each paper-clipped set and then dates listed down the columns. From what I can understand, it is a chronicle of payments made and received. The first is by far the largest: one hundred thousand pounds, paid by my parents to 'PC' thirteen years ago.

Pete Chandler, the pub owner.

Or perhaps his father – Pete senior? Arthur said it seemed like the Chandlers were going out of business a few years ago. Did my parents bail them out?

I skim the rest of the pages to see if there are any more payments to 'PC', but it doesn't look as if my parents gave any more money after that. Everything else is marked in the 'received' column.

After that initial outlay, it looks as though my parents received intermittent payments every four to six weeks. The amount varies from a little over three thousand pounds all the way up to almost thirty thousand. I add it up roughly in my head and it looks like my parents made more than a million pounds in around four years – up until the date Zac went missing. Each payment is initialled with a neat, crisp 'DW'.

Dan Wood?

After the date when Zac went missing, everything changes. Instead of payments every four to six weeks, they become once every six months. I flick to the most recent payment. It's little surprise that it came in December last year. The last time that my mother came down to, in her words, 'check' on the cottage.

According to the records, 'DW' paid my parents a little under four hundred thousand pounds last year and three hundred thousand pounds the year before.

I consider taking the papers – but, unlike my mother, I'm no Luddite. Instead, I use my phone to photograph every page. As I return the papers to the safe, I realise there's something else in there. Something I missed the first time. Clouded in shadow, pushed right to the back, is a pistol. It's heavy and old-fashioned, but not too far away from the type of gun we used for shooting at school. The safety catch is on and the magazine is full. In one quick movement, it would be primed.

I twist the weapon in my hands, looking for tell-tale signs of use. There's no damage or scorch marks on the barrel and, though I'm no expert, it looks pristine. I doubt it's ever been fired. I feel to the back of the safe and there is a spare magazine, also full.

Could the pistol be legal? Technically, it's stored securely – but I don't know what the law is. I've also never known my parents to have an interest in guns. In fact, I know they weren't interested: when they found out I'd be doing shooting at school as part of Physical Education, my father said, 'Why?' and my mother harrumphed and said she'd 'have a word'.

I return everything to the safe and push it closed. I could alter the code if I wanted to and think about doing so. Then I remove the gun and spare magazine. I pass the weapon from one hand to the other, absorbing its weight. It's no wonder everyone's such a bad shot in action movies – guns are heavy.

Or perhaps I'm just weak.

The weapon is giving me silly thoughts. Silly, dangerous thoughts.

Before I know what I'm doing, I'm back in my room getting dressed. I put the spare magazine in one jacket pocket and the pistol in the other, checking the safety to be sure that I won't accidentally shoot myself. I reluctantly admit that those hours of safety training at school were useful.

I open the front door as quietly as I can – which is still ridiculously loud because of the way it sticks. There's no one outside the cottage this time. No Pete, no Ethan. No anyone. At first, I'm not sure what I'm going to do but I find myself heading through the trees, down to the village. The ground is soft from the day of gloom and the clouds are still hanging around, making the night that little bit darker.

Before I know it, I'm at the back of the pub, heading for the docks and the stash of guns on the boat. I'm going to do what I should have done when I first saw them – head around the coast and bury them somewhere that Scott won't find them. Either that, or dump them in the ocean. People could get hurt in the village. People like Vee.

Except, the Chandler fishing boat isn't in the dock.

At first, I think that it might have been moved to another part of the jetty – but it hasn't. It's gone.

I remember the last late-night expedition I saw Scott taking what seems a lifetime ago, back when we were on the sand for the barbecue with the beach kids. The fishing boat heading out after dark for who knows what reason.

Heading out with guns.

It's madness but I'm too far gone to stop myself now. I *need* to know what's going on in this village, to know why my parents have made so much money over the years. Chloe doesn't want to know but I do.

The cloud helps, making everything darker than usual, allowing me to be confident of not being seen. I head away from the dock and cross the tree line into the woods. I scramble a few metres higher, using my hands and feet to avoid slipping on the damp dirt. I quickly reach the base of a tree that's growing at an angle out of the hill. It's twisted and gnarled up and backwards, searching for sunlight. The crease of its trunk provides a perfect alcove from which I can see the whole of the docks, while remaining shrouded in darkness.

I wait.

It's boring but I daren't risk using my phone in case the light signals to someone that I'm here. I keep myself alert by going over the calories and carbs in certain foods, then calculating how much I might be able to eat in a day, or a week. I can picture Chloe looking at me and then turning to the empty packet in the bin.

Look at what this place is doing to you.

I don't know how long has passed but, at some point, realise I can hear a gentle chuntering in the distance. It slowly becomes louder and then a light appears out on the ocean. It grows and grows. The angle and the darkness make it look like it's floating in the air as opposed to cruising on the water. Aliens coming to save or enslave.

The light is almost at the docks when the shadows around it morph into the outline of a boat. I slink lower onto the ground, the dampness seeping immediately through the seat of my trousers. I experience a dark thrill in knowing there's no chance the people on the boat realise they're being watched. The watchee becomes the watcher.

I wonder if Scott and his crewmates have noticed the missing padlock. It's the only trace of me having been on the boat – could it have been overlooked? Perhaps the guns aren't often removed and the missing lock will only be noticed the next time someone goes to open the crate.

Scott is a lumbering bear of a man. He jumps from the boat onto the dock. The light illuminates his distinctive silhouette as he ties the boat to a post. Then he hurries past the beer garden, around to the front of the pub and out of sight. I can see a couple of other men in the shadows at the front of the boat but they are impossible to identify in the dark.

I wait. Before long, a car appears, reversing towards the dock. It's emitting only the gentlest of engine sounds and its headlights are off. This is the vehicle that almost hit me when I was walking back from the campsite. I guess it must be kept in the garage next to the pub. I watch it reverse until it's as close as it can get to the boat and then it stops. The only light is beaming from the boat, illuminating the boot of the car.

After that, it's a precise, organised operation. Scott gets out of the car. One of the men on the boat picks up a square block that's wrapped with what looks like cling film. It's roughly the width of his shoulders. He passes the parcel from the boat to the second man, who carries it to Scott at the car. Scott loads it into the boot. The production line continues until eight or nine packages have been loaded.

When the job is done, the three men stand on the edge of the docks, talking quietly and sharing a cigarette. They're facing the trees and, though I know I can't be seen, it's hard to push away that inkling of danger. I remain as still as I possibly can.

When the cigarette is finished, the other two men hurry away, rounding the pub and disappearing off into the night. I don't hear any other cars, so can only assume they're locals. Meanwhile, Scott turns off the light from the boat. The sudden flash to darkness leaves me with stars in my eyes. It takes a few seconds to blink them away –

And, by that time, Scott's silhouette has disappeared.

Pets were never a thing in our family but I have seen the hairs literally rise on the back of a dog's neck when it senses danger. The hackles go up; the teeth bare. It's fear in physical form. When the hairs stand up on the back of my neck now, there's a terrifying moment in which it feels as if everything has flipped. While the car was being loaded, I was the one watching with complete anonymity – but now Scott is the one in the shadows. I can feel his eyes scanning the woods, looking for something. Someone?

Me?

I hold my breath, squinting into the dark, feeling trapped and scrutinised. I remember all the other times I felt watched. Can they all be put down to Ethan? Or was there someone else?

Or did I imagine it all?

Time passes. It's probably seconds but it feels like longer. Then Scott steps away from the front of the car. He wasn't scanning the woods at all, he was leaning on the bonnet, probably having a rest.

He dips in and out of the shadows as he walks away from the docks. Then I hear the squeak of the gate that leads into the beer garden. A few seconds pass. I can't see a thing but I hear the sound of a door opening and closing and I'm as sure as I'm going to be that he's inside the pub.

I wonder if he's done for the night, or if he's taking a break before driving the car up and out of the village. I count to one hundred and he doesn't emerge. Two hundred and it's still quiet.

As I push myself up into a standing position, my stomach lurches dangerously, my back clicks and my knees crunch. The noise of it is so loud that I freeze, convinced the pub lights will come on.

They don't.

I count to fifty and, when nobody appears, I slide my way down the bank, treading quietly across the gravel to Scott's car. It's almost new, some sort of hybrid.

I carry on past the car to the boat, leaping carefully from the docks onto the stern. The tarp hasn't been pulled over the benches this time and it doesn't take me long to find that a new padlock has been fitted onto the bench seat which contains the guns. I stare at it for a couple of seconds, heart pounding. A new padlock doesn't necessarily mean anyone's realised *for sure* that the boat was broken into – but the whole village knows I crept away during the burning of the boat. It wouldn't take a genius to put two and two together.

Scott probably knows.

It would make too much noise to bash the new lock to smithereens, so I clamber off the boat and walk towards the car. I'm almost past it, ready to head up to the cottage and wake Chloe. We're done.

But then I stop.

It's almost as if the car is beckoning me. I couldn't tell from a distance what was being put in the boot but the secret is within touching distance, cocooned in the back. I picture Scott standing at the front of the car once the other men had left. Was there a *plip* of indicator lights to show he'd locked it? Did I hear a clunk of central locks being engaged?

When I ease the handle on the driver's side door, there's a quiet *thunk* and it pops open. The light turns on inside, momentarily blinding me. I'm convinced an alarm will go off – but it doesn't. I can hardly believe he's left the car unlocked. Perhaps it's a mistake, perhaps it's a trap, or perhaps people simply don't lock their cars in Whitecliff.

The boot won't open, so I return to the front and scan the dashboard and central panel, looking for any sort of button that might open it. There are logos for heaters, one to open the bonnet, another for the lumbar support. Nothing obviously related to the boot. I crouch and check the side of the driver's seat, then under the seat and then, finally, I find a catch hidden underneath the steering wheel. I have to pull a lever and there's a solid click from behind.

At the rear of the car, the boot has hinged open. It feels big… Important… As if what's inside is the key to understanding everything. I have a second to compose myself and then wedge my fingers under the hood.

Which is when someone grabs my shoulder.

CHAPTER FORTY-FOUR

'Go!'

I spin. Chrissie is so close that I can't believe she got so near without me realising. She releases my shoulder and flashes a quick glance towards the pub.

'You've *got* to go,' she hisses.

I make my decision, turning back to the boot, opening the lid wide and looking inside. The contents of the square blocks are hard to see for sure under all the layers of cling film, but I press down on it until I can see the shapes within: doughier parcels of powder.

'Go!'

I twist back to Chrissie and slam the boot. Too loudly.

'Is he selling drugs?' I say.

Chrissie's eyes are wide with fear. 'Who?'

'Scott.'

She shakes her head quickly. 'Not him. Just go. Please. Go now.'

Chrissie takes a half-step away. She's in a dressing gown and slippers and starts to shiver.

'I saw him bringing this in on the boat,' I say.

She shakes her head. 'Not him,' she says. 'Not *only* him.'

'Who?'

There's no time to answer because, at that moment, there's a bang of a door from the pub. I don't hang around, racing past the car and skidding across the gravel in front of the wooded area where I was hiding. If Scott is behind me, there's not much I can do now. I cut up and into the woods, calves aching with the steep climb as I use the tree trunks to pull myself up and away from the village.

My heart is thundering from what I've seen and from the exertion of the climb but the adrenalin is flooding so quickly that I'm at the cottage before I realise it. The damned front door sticks and I make so much noise opening it that I'm certain it will bring Chloe out into the hallway, wondering what all the racket is.

When I finally get inside and lock the door, it's almost a surprise to find that Chloe isn't waiting for me. I rush along the corridor to wake her – and then stop myself, realising I don't know what I'm doing.

Should we run?

Is Scott coming?

There's a chance he has no idea I was at his car. When I ran for it, I didn't stop to look behind me. Did he see me? Chrissie did – but that's not the same thing.

Things are beginning to fall into place. Scott's main business is, on the surface, Chandler Fishing – but he takes late-night expeditions to import what I assume to be drugs.

I'm not sure how the rest slots together but my parents must have been involved in some way. It would explain how my father's small antiques business was so lucrative.

There's the 'DW' in Mother's ledger, too. Dan Wood.

Is everyone in on it?

It feels like I have a puzzle where all – or *almost* all – the pieces are in front of me and yet I can't quite see the full picture. Some bastard's hidden a couple of the key pieces.

I start towards Chloe's room and then stop myself once more. The weight of the gun in my pocket is heavy – in all senses of the word.

And then another thought arrives and it feels as if my entire world has turned upside down.

When our parents sent us away to boarding school, what if it was to protect us?

I've spent all these years resenting them, *hating* them and feeling unwanted. But perhaps boarding school wasn't to get us out of the way – perhaps it was to keep us safe. Perhaps whatever happened to Zac was something they didn't want to happen to us, too. Perhaps my mother's cruel words were intended to push me away, so that I wouldn't be drawn into the world into which she and my father had fallen, wilfully or otherwise.

Could this be true?

The idea is so staggering, so life-changing, that it's as if my legs don't work any longer. I find myself on the sofa, clasping my knees to my chest.

It takes me a while to force myself up. I pace the kitchen on slow, sluggish legs and then head into my bedroom. The adrenalin has gone and it's such a long time since I had a proper meal that I'm not sure I have any reserves of energy left.

The idea of my parents protecting us could be nonsense. Perhaps they genuinely didn't want us around; perhaps my mother *was* simply cruel. Perhaps I'm giving them a lot more credit than they deserve.

I stand at the window, staring into the darkness of the woods and then I sit on the bed. I want to wake Chloe and go – but it feels as if my whole life depends on the answer to one question.

Did our parents send us away to school to keep us safe, or did they do it because they didn't want us around?

The very core of who I am rests on the answer to that.

But how can I know their motivations if I don't also know what happened to Zac?

I put the pistol under my pillow and lie down, staring at the ceiling. It's almost three in the morning and I'm still in my clothes. I know I won't sleep but my thoughts at least feel clearer in the bedroom. I stare into the shadows and let my mind drift. There's an answer in there somewhere... I'm sure I could see it, if only I weren't so exhausted.

Somebody is banging around, as usual. It's impossible to sleep properly in a dorm room – there's always someone for whom shutting up is an existential problem. Even when I am asleep, it's as if I'm always on edge, never far away from being awake.

Bang-bang-bang-bang!

I go to put the pillow over my head to block out the noise – except there's something heavy under the pillow. Something that shouldn't be there...

I'm back in the cottage and it's still night. The dream of being back at school was so vivid, so close, that it feels like a physical pain to realise I'm somewhere else. It's as if I've been snatched from one place and dropped into another.

Bang-bang-bang-bang!

The noise is coming from my window. I stagger across, throwing the curtains aside. The view would normally be of the shadows of the trees swaying in the night breeze – but what I see now is so shocking that I stumble backwards, almost falling back onto the bed.

Ethan has pressed his face against the glass. His eyes are wide, the whites almost glowing. When he sees me, he steps back a pace, motioning frantically with his arms. He's struggling to say something but I can't hear him through the glass.

The window sticks almost as badly as the front door but I slam the frame with the palm of my hand until it pops open with a *thunk* of flaky paint.

'Get out!' he says, no stutter.

There's a moment in which I wonder if he's real, if this is another dream. It's only when he grabs my arm and stumbles with another, 'G-g-g-get out!' that my mind clicks into gear.

'Why?'

He nods towards the front of the cottage: 'They're coming.'

I start to ask, 'Who?' but then the letter box clangs like someone ringing a bell in a silent church. The noise booms through the cottage inexplicably loudly and, when I turn back to Ethan, he's already running for the woods.

I grab the pistol from under my pillow, shoving it into my pocket as I move into the hall. A quick glance towards the kitchen is enough to know we're in trouble. The mat is on fire, with a trail of flames licking from the letter box down to the floor.

Oh, no.

I hurtle towards Chloe's room, throwing the door open and skidding across the floor as I shout her name. There's only one problem: she's not in her bed.

CHAPTER FORTY-FIVE

Chloe isn't in any of the other rooms. She's not in the cottage at all. I check my phone, despite knowing there is no reception.

The kitchen fire has already grown. Thick, dark smoke is spiralling up to the ceiling and starting to spill towards the back of the cottage. Towards me. It won't be long before the fire hits the wooden beams and everything starts to implode.

The back door is locked and in the panic of feeling the heat from the fire, I can't remember where I left the key. I check Chloe's room one more time, hoping she's somehow materialised. Her bag is there – but she isn't.

I rush into my room. Smoke is starting to coat the ceiling and I slam the door, knowing it won't do much to stall the inevitable.

There's nothing else for it. I push the window open as far as it will go – and then launch myself head-first outside. In my mind, I perform some sort of gallant, graceful forward roll. The reality is more likely closer to a seal flopping around on dry land – but the result is still the same. I'm out.

I hurry to the front of the cottage. The fire has gripped the whole of the door. The flames crackle and snarl, consuming everything in their path, snaking up towards the roof. If Ethan hadn't knocked on my window, I'd have been done for.

That's twice he's saved my life.

There's no sign of him anywhere around, nor of anyone else. I call Chloe's name but there's no reply. There's still no reception

on my phone, either. I head to my car — then realise my key is
still inside the cottage.

There's that momentary panic that everyone gets when they
think they've lost their phone, or something else important. That
sinking, sickening pain in the stomach. I haven't simply left behind my car keys, I've lost my sister.

I try to think of where she could be — and the only answer I
can come up with is that she's visiting Arthur for some reason. I
thought for a while that she might have a thing with Brad — but
he's gone home and it was hard to keep track of her after that.

I avoid the road, assuming that whoever set fire to the house is
more likely to be there than in the woods. The trail feels steeper
than ever — but I'm reckless, slipping and sliding but letting gravity do its thing. I feel like one of those people who chase cheese
down a near vertical slope every year.

It feels like seconds before I'm at the bottom, gasping and
fumbling my way to the area at the back of the pub.

Scott's car has gone — but Chloe is more important. I run
along the cobbles of the main street, my knees screaming their
disapproval. Arthur's house is attached to the gallery. I jump up
the wooden steps and bang on his door.

Whitecliff is the type of place where sound carries. My knocking booms along the cobbled streets. I half-expect barking dogs
and lights to be turned on but nothing happens.

I wait and press an ear to the door, then knock again. This
time I can hear a shuffling, combined with what I quickly realise
is the *thump-scrape* of someone crossing a floor with a walking
stick. The door creaks open and Arthur's tired, wrinkled eyes
squint into the darkness. When he sees me, he straightens himself, looking with such resigned conviction that it's as if he knew
this early morning wake-up call would arrive sooner or later.

Enough people warned me, after all.

'Chloe,' he says.

'Is she here?'

'I've not seen her. Is she—?'

'She's gone.'

We both turn as one to look up at the hill. An orange glow is starting to seep through the trees. When I turn back to Arthur, there's fear in his eyes.

'Do you know where she might be?' I ask.

He shakes his head and then tells me something I don't need to be told: 'Find her and go.'

The clouds are starting to clear, allowing the moon to douse the village in white light. The streets are empty. There's nobody on the beach, no one at the docks. The only other place I can think of that Chloe might be is the beach kids' camp site.

The trail up to the cottage feels particularly hard this time. My calves, knees and thighs burn but I keep moving. As I near the cottage, the warmth of the fire increases. When I emerge from the woods, I see that the entire cottage is burning.

I can't carry on through the woods. The path that would take me to the caravans comes too close to the fire, so it's the road or nothing. Before I can dash along the track, a voice calls my name. At first I think I'm imagining it, conjuring the word from the crackle and pop of the fire.

But then it comes again: 'Megan!'

When I turn, Luke is at the edge of the trail that leads to his cottage. He hurries across, mouth agape.

'What happened?' he asks, turning to the fire.

'Chloe's gone,' I say, not answering him properly. 'Have you seen her?'

He blinks from me to the flames. 'I… Well…'

I can't tell what he's thinking.

There's a huge crackle and we both step back as one of the front beams of the cottage collapses in on itself. Sparks fly up and fizz in the air.

I grab Luke's arm. The fire doesn't matter for now. '*Chloe!*' I shout over the noise of the flames. 'Have you seen her?'

He points towards the track that leads to the road. 'A few hours ago, when I was coming back up from the village.'

'After dark?'

He nods, which means that Chloe must have left her room at some point after initially going to bed. At some point after I found the gun in the safe and went down to the village. Perhaps I woke her up with that sticky front door? She could have trailed out to look for me, or perhaps just to get some air.

'Where was she going?' I ask.

'I don't know. Away from the village. She had this book thing under her arm. The one she draws in.'

I turn and start to hurry away but Luke is quickly at my side. 'Where are we going?' he asks.

'The cliffs. She'll have gone there to draw. She didn't want to be in the cottage with me.'

Luke doesn't question this. He doesn't say anything – he keeps pace as I cross the road and pass into the woods on the other side.

The journey to the cliffs is a lot harder than when Chloe and I made it on our first day in Whitecliff. The loose rocks and tangled roots are hidden and I find myself stumbling every few paces across the uneven ground. Eventually, Luke and I burst out onto the rocks on top of the cliffs. The grass ahead is blackened by darkness.

Luke lets me lead and I stumble across the rocks until I reach the spot at which Chloe sat to draw the village below. I was so certain Chloe would be here – but she isn't. Nobody is here. The ocean rumbles beneath us, crashing onto the rocks at the base of the cliff. Whitecliff itself is blanketed in darkness. High above the village, masked by the trees, the orange blaze of our cottage burns bright.

I call Chloe's name but there's no answer. Luke drifts away and I turn to see him on the edge of the cliff, peeping over the edge. He calls her name, too – and then he gestures frantically to me.

There's a moment where it feels like I'm sinking. Chloe has fallen and I'll never see her again. I'm alone.

Luke shouts something that's lost to the waves and the wind. He motions me over towards him again, calling something but I still don't catch what he says. Then I'm next to him and it feels like the world is rushing. Luke's too close to the edge and so am I. He's peering over the edge. I'm terrified to look. I'm going to see Chloe. Her coat will have snagged on a rock and she'll be lost to the waves and the rocks.

I force myself to look.

But I can't see anything other than the cresting white surf against the black sea.

I turn back to Luke but he's a step closer than I'd realised. I reel back slightly and, as I do, I see him in profile for the merest of moments. It might be the angle of his face or it might be the light but, in that instant, I know who he is. I know *what* he is.

He moves so quickly that I have no time to react. In a flash, he presses his hands into my shoulders and pushes me off the cliff.

CHAPTER FORTY-SIX

Chloe

George rolls over and reaches across his bed for me.

'So that's it,' he says, not phrasing it like a question.

'We're leaving in the morning,' I reply.

'It *is* the morning,' he replies.

'When the sun comes up.'

He props himself up onto an elbow and looks at me so intensely that it feels like he can see my soul. I find myself wondering whether Mum would have approved of him. Megan thinks she would only give her blessing to boyfriends with money and privilege. I suppose George has both of those – but his goal is to write and play music. He won't end up working in the city like his father.

'This has been fun,' he says.

'I don't think I like sneaking around.'

That gets a half-laugh, half-smile. 'That's where you and I differ.'

He rolls onto his back and I do the same. The bed in his caravan is soft and uncomfortable. I can't understand how he spends a whole summer here.

'Are you going to tell your sister about us?' he asks.

I think for a moment. 'Maybe when we've gone. *She* thought I liked Brad.'

'The ol' switcheroo.'

I swing my legs off the bed and sit up, bumping my head once again on the ceiling above. I'm never spending another evening in a caravan. *Any* caravan.

George doesn't seem to notice. 'So… this is it,' he says, again.

I fumble for my clothes on the floor and start to get dressed. 'You've got my number and I've got yours,' I say. 'When we get back to the real world, we can message, or whatever.'

'Right.'

He doesn't sound convinced and in all honesty, I'm not either. Whitecliff doesn't feel like the real world. *This* doesn't feel like the real world.

When I'm dressed, George drops down from the bed and puts his arms around my shoulders. I clamp mine around his back and we stay in the moment, holding each other for a few seconds.

'I'll see you soon,' he says.

'Of course,' I reply, knowing that we're both lying. That this is the end.

I let myself out of George's caravan. I know I probably won't tell Megan about all this. I'll let her carry on believing I was with Arthur or out on the cliffs all the times I said I was. Sometimes I *was* where I was supposed to be; other times I was here, with George. Megan thought I was interested in Brad – but she never asked. In reality, Brad was infatuated with Ebony and I only spent time with him because I was trying to find out if George had a girlfriend.

I have the feeling that once we leave Whitecliff, neither Megan nor I will spend much time talking about what we've seen and done in this place.

Megan has her secrets, too.

The route to the cottage through the woods is one I could almost take with my eyes closed. Something's different about it tonight, though. There's an orange haze in the distance. As I get closer, the air prickles my skin.

Fire.

My walk becomes a jog and then a run. By the time I'm almost back, I realise that our cottage is on fire. The beams are starting to crack and sparks are sizzling. I have to retreat and trace a route around the trees to get to the front of the cottage – where I find Megan's car unmoved on the path.

No.

As another beam crashes and collapses inside the cottage, it feels as if the same is happening to me. I'm convinced Megan's inside but there's no way of getting in through the front. I rush round the side to her bedroom window – and it's wide open. I breathe again. That *must* mean she got out. My relief only lasts for a moment, because my next realisation is that she'll be looking for me.

I try Luke's cottage first, partly to warn him – but also to ask if he's seen Megan. I hammer on his front door but there's no answer. Either he's out, or he's such a heavy sleeper that I don't have time to wait for him to wake up.

I can still feel the heat of the flames on my back as I slip and slide my way down the wooded trail to the village. I turn my ankle a couple of times in my haste to get to the bottom. The cobbles are equally unforgiving when I reach the streets but my heart jumps a beat when I realise there's only one light on in the entire village.

Arthur's.

Megan must have come here to look for me. She'll be waiting inside.

I knock and hear the soft *thump-scrape* of Arthur's walking stick. He must be close to the door because it only takes a couple of seconds for it to swing open. He stares down at me in bewildered wonderment.

'Chloe,' he says.

'Is Megan here?'

He blinks and I know immediately that she isn't.

'She was looking for you,' he says. 'You're safe: thank God.'

A strange sense of relief and concern hits me at once. Megan definitely got out of the fire – but now she's off searching for me somewhere and it's my fault.

'The cottage is on fire,' I say. 'Can you call the fire brigade on the landline in the gallery? I can't get any reception.'

He leans awkwardly to the side. 'Of course,' he says.

'Did you see where Megan went?'

Arthur points towards the pub and the road. 'I think she went back up the hill.'

I turn, wondering what to do. If she went up the hill, then where is she? There was no answer at Luke's; she wasn't at the cottage – but perhaps she was on the road to the caravans while I was in the woods? Perhaps we passed each other without knowing. She might be with George or the other beach kids right now, asking if anyone's seen me.

I offer a quick, 'Thank you,' to Arthur, then run.

The slope of the road is unrelenting but it's easier in the dark than the trail through the woods. There are no cars, so I run up the middle of the road. Our cottage continues to burn through the trees in the corner of my eye.

I'm out of breath by the time I get to the track that leads to the cottage. I figure I'll check there in case Megan is waiting for me in the clearing at the front – but before I can turn, someone shouts my name.

Luke is crossing the road towards me. He's out of breath, too.

'Chloe!' he calls. It's hard to tell if he's relieved or surprised to see me.

'Have you seen Megan?' I ask.

He's puffing and, despite the situation, we exchange a knowing look of exhaustion. Getting around Whitecliff really takes it out of a person.

'She's in the village,' he says.

'I was just there.'

'At the pub,' he says. 'I think she went to call the fire brigade. Everyone's been really worried about you.'

He smiles with such relief that it's crushing. I feel myself deflate. I saw the look in my sister's eyes when I let her know that *I* knew what had been going on with the food since we got here. It's harder for her to hide when it's only us in a place so small. At the house, there are more rooms, more bins, more space in the fridge, freezer or cupboards. She has a problem and we play this game where I pretend not to know and she acts as if everything is fine. In that moment earlier this evening, I know that I hurt her. If that's not bad enough, I then snuck away without saying anything.

I can't say sorry enough.

Luke takes a couple of steps back down towards the village. Up-down-up-down. On and on we go.

'You coming?' he asks.

I take a breath and hurry to his side. I have no idea how or why the cottage caught fire – but if Megan's safe, then everything's going to be all right.

CHAPTER FORTY-SEVEN

Chloe

Luke takes me around the back of the pub, squeaking open the gate and leading me through the beer garden to the back door. It's already unlocked but he holds it open for me. We end up in a cold, concrete room filled with crates of drinks and metal barrels. Luke knows where he's going, passing through another door and along a short hallway. He holds the door open for me again and we emerge into the bar.

The lights are on dimly and the blinds are down, leaving everything in a dark yellow murk. I step forward, looking for Megan and there's a solid clunk from behind. When I turn to look, Luke is slipping a second bolt into place. He's locked the door.

A shiver flits through me. He stands in front of the door, blocking any way out. His smile has gone, replaced by a stony-faced inevitability.

I turn to face the rest of the room and see that Pete is sitting in one of the alcoves. His son, Scott, is standing next to him. They're both looking at me. Off to the side, in another alcove, are two more people I recognise: Dan and Alison Wood. They're in dark, thick clothes, as if they've been out for a midnight hike.

'Where's Megan?' I ask.

I turn from one pair to the next and then twist to look at Luke. He hasn't moved from the door.

Dan ignores me, staring at Luke over my shoulder. Something about him has changed; the smiley friendliness has been replaced with a harder edge. 'That's exactly what we've been wondering,' he says. 'Where *is* the other one?'

Luke steps forward, gripping my upper arm and urging me on. He grabs one of the chairs and places it in the middle of the two booths.

'Sit,' he tells me.

I resist. 'Where's Megan?' I ask again but he doesn't answer. There's steel in his gaze. There's little point in trying to run.

I sit.

He pulls my arms behind me and then uses a pair of cable ties to attach my wrists together behind the chair.

'Does that hurt?' he asks.

'No.'

He wriggles my wrists, making sure they're tight enough to keep me secure and then steps away.

'*Well?*' Dan repeats.

Luke steps behind me, out of view. I can sense him turning between the two parties. The Chandlers on my left; the Woods on my right.

'She's dead,' he says.

It's hard to describe the silence in the moment after he says it. It's like there's no air left in the room, as if those two words have created a vacuum. I try to breathe but it gets stuck and I find myself choking. Nobody moves to help. My tongue feels too big for my mouth. I'm coughing and it's only Luke's hand on the back of the chair that stops me from tipping over and falling onto my face.

'Dead?' I manage.

I'm not even sure I've said it out loud until Dan replies.

'She had to keep causing trouble,' he says. 'Day after day: new questions, new people. Why couldn't you both just go? Nobody wanted this.'

I stutter, unsure what to say. Unsure whether I should speak at all.

'We left that message for you,' Dan says, nodding at Luke. 'Told you to go home. Smashed a window. Beat your friend's brains in. Nothing seemed to make a difference. What is *wrong* with you?' He stops for a beat and shakes his head. He's speaking as if we've done something hurtful. As if we've hurt him.

'And then tonight,' he continues. 'Sneaking around Scott's car. What was she *thinking*?'

I have no idea what he's talking about, so keep my mouth shut. Speaking is only going to make things worse.

Dan turns across the pub, pointing a finger in Scott's direction. 'Can Chrissie keep her mouth shut?'

'She told me, didn't she?'

'You'd better keep her on a tight leash.'

Scott pushes himself away from the booth and takes a step towards Dan. 'You talk about my wife one more time and I'll drag *you* out of here on a leash.'

Pete slaps the table with his hand and everyone goes quiet. 'What have I told you?' he says, talking to his son.

Scott glares across the room but takes a couple of steps back, suitably chastened.

There's a silence in which it feels like everyone is looking at everyone else. Nobody seems to know what to do.

'I don't understand,' I say.

Dan sighs and turns to me. 'No… Well, it's all a bit late now, I'm afraid. Your sister *did* understand and she's gone the same way as your brother. It's only you left.'

I fight for breath. 'What *about* my brother?'

Dan suddenly seems to realise that I don't know much of anything and he turns away from me. Nobody is looking at me now. It's as if I'm not in the room. Alison breaks the silence this time. She looks so strange in hiking gear, the dark colours offset against her plastic face. She reminds me of Mum – except Mum would never have been seen dead in those clothes.

'Look,' she says, 'what's the story? Can we at least get that straight? We can't have both of these two going missing. People will notice. They'll ask questions.'

'Wasn't my idea,' Pete says. 'But it is what it is, so let's say nuffink. People will think they set the cottage on fire and ran off. There are no bodies inside. Nobody else knows nuffink. We'll go with that. We woke up and the cottage was on fire and the girls were gone. End of.'

Alison turns to Luke behind me: 'How did they even get out of the cottage?'

'No idea. I assumed they were inside.'

She examines him for a moment more. It looks like she's trying to frown but her stretched skin is having none of it. She turns back to the Chandlers. 'What if the police ask questions?' she asks.

'What if they do?' Pete replies. 'Say you were sleeping. The older one's a known thief – the whole village saw her lying. What are the police going to do?'

The adults all turn to each other and I can feel their minds working to come up with something better.

Luke speaks next. He's chillingly close behind me. 'What about this one?'

Everyone looks at me and I can't stop myself from shivering. The silence seems to last forever – but there's a certain inevitability when Pete next speaks. He nods beyond me, to Luke.

'Go with your brother and take her out to sea before it gets light. Get some bricks. Don't want her washing up on the beach.'

It's strange but it takes me a second to realise he means me. He doesn't want *me* washing up on the beach.

'Please don't,' I say. 'Please.'

No one seems willing to meet my eyes. I'm wondering when Luke's brother is going to arrive but as Scott steps towards me, I suddenly realise.

'You're… *brothers?*'

Nobody answers but I already know it's true. Megan was spending some of her time, perhaps a *lot* of her time, with Luke and yet never once realised he was a brother to the very person with whom she'd been arguing in public.

Before I know what's happening, Luke jams something into my mouth, pushing it so far into my throat that I gag and end up snorting through my nose. It's a rag, or a cloth. Perhaps a bar towel. Scott is the bigger of the brothers by a long way and, as I struggle to breathe, he lifts me up from the chair with barely a grunt. I'm suddenly over his shoulder. Luke unlocks the back door.

I try to squirm, kick and thrash but Scott squeezes. His arm is so tight around my middle that it becomes impossible to breathe.

They're taking me to the boat.

I can barely breathe, let alone scream and every time I move, Scott squeezes a bit tighter. I'm trying to think. Megan's dead. Zac's dead. Mum and Dad are dead. It's only me left – but this is the end.

The gate creaks open. Scott turns towards the docks. I have seconds left before I'll be on the boat and it will be too late. But what can I do?

There's no hope, no chance. I start to see stars. They swarm the edge of my vision, swimming and merging.

And then there's an ear-splitting bang.

CHAPTER FORTY-EIGHT

Megan

Luke's hands push hard and, as I stumble over the cliff, a rush of air surges from beneath me. I feel a strange calmness and even have time to wonder if it's better for a person to know when it's the end.

When I hit the rocks below, will I die instantly? Will it hurt? I close my eyes, deciding that's the last conscious thing I'll do.

There's a thump as my back slams into the rocks.

I should be in pain. The waves should be thrashing me into the cliff. I should be getting tugged underwater, struggling for my life.

But I'm not.

I open my eyes.

I can see the sky above. The clouds have cleared enough that there is the gentlest twinkling of stars. Death is such a strange thing. People say it's a part of life, or that it's all part of God's plan. Others believe in reincarnation and karma. Nobody knows what death is: that's the truth.

And I'm not dead.

When I wriggle into a sitting position, I feel rocks crumbling beneath me and I realise that, somehow, I've landed on a small, jutting-out platform. The dark cliff is directly behind me and the water is rampaging below. Miraculously, I'm alive.

There's a bewildering clarity to my thoughts. If I'd been pushed off the cliff half a metre to either side, I'd be gone. But, sometimes, fate is what it is.

I'm still part-way down the cliff. I can't jump down and there's no obvious route back up. It's too dark.

I roll towards the cliff, wedging myself tight against the rock, so that if Luke peers over the edge he won't be able to see me. There's the slightest scraping of rocks as I move but that's covered by the roar of the water below. I wait but Luke doesn't call after me. If he's bothered to check, he thinks I'm gone.

I catch my breath and count to a hundred. It feels like I've done all this before. He *must* have gone by now.

Luke is a Chandler.

I'm not sure how I missed it, other than that he looks nothing like his brother, Scott. It's only from the side, at one precise angle, that they look similar. I hadn't asked him about his family, because after I found out that his mother died, it felt off-limits. All he said was that his mother left him the cottage – which is probably true. I wonder why Vee didn't tell me – but she probably assumed I knew who he was. I never asked – and that was my mistake.

I let him kiss me. I kissed him back. I felt sorry for him. I even asked him about the Chandlers when Chloe and I went to his place for dinner. He did well not to laugh.

I have to get away from this cliff. I have to find Chloe.

The platform is relatively stable, although I don't fancy the edges too much. There's not a lot of space – perhaps enough for me to lie down if I tuck my knees in. There's little room for movement or error.

I risk a peep over the edge, in case there's some miraculous route down. There was the rope that was left near Fisherman's Cave that rescued me and Vee – but it's too much to ask that there's a rope lying here. There really is no safe way down. The rocks are protruding from the sea and even if I somehow missed them when I dropped, the ocean would hammer me back into the wall.

As the song goes, the only way is up.

From what I can tell, I've not fallen as far as I thought. The top of the cliff is just a few metres above. It felt like I was falling for ages – but must have been a couple of seconds at most.

I look carefully at the cliff face. The rock is smooth in parts but there are divots that I could use to propel myself up. One wrong handhold would send me careering down to the ocean – but I've already spat in death's face once tonight. Bring it on.

Or, I *would* bring it on – if I could see anything further away than directly in front of my face. It would be one thing to free-climb the cliff in the daylight, another entirely to try it when it's too dark to see the next handhold. Dangerous, either way.

As I'm trying to figure out what to do, there's a ruffling from above. I quickly shuffle back to the rock, pressing myself against it, assuming Luke is back to double-check I'm gone.

There's another sound and then the silhouette of a head appears over the ridge above. I hold my breath, squeezing myself as tight against the cliff as I can. The head disappears for a moment and then reappears. This time, a light beams down towards me.

'M-M-M-Megan?'

'Ethan?'

He doesn't say anything – but then, speaking isn't really his thing. I'll take a mute guardian angel. Without needing to say anything, he angles his light so that I can see the crinkles in the rock above my head. I've never climbed in my life – let alone up a rock face without ropes – but confidence is an amazing thing. I feel as if I could do anything.

The distance is probably two or three times my height – not far. Handhold by handhold, deep breath by deep breath, I haul myself up. My problem isn't only the dizzy spells and creaking innards, it's the lack of strength. Usually, doing anything physical, my bony joints and protruding ribs *hurt*.

Not tonight, though. Not now. I'm still here and, fate or not, that means something.

The light remains steady until I near the top, when it suddenly disappears. There's a second or two in which my panic starts to return but then I feel a hand under each of my armpits. There's a grunt from above and before I know what's happened, I'm lying on my back again, staring at the stars.

Ethan appears over me and stretches down, offering a hand to pull me up. He's far stronger than he looks. Like that picked-on kid wearing glasses in the YouTube video, where some would-be mugger tries to bully him and ends up trying to find his teeth in the gutter.

I try to hug him but he shakes me off, uncomfortable with the contact.

'You saved me,' I say. 'Again.'

Ethan shrugs modestly.

'Where did you come from?' I ask.

His twitchy gaze flickers to the woods. 'Followed,' he says.

There's no time or point in pressing him now. I've got to find Chloe before Luke does.

'Have you seen Chloe?' I ask.

Ethan shakes his head.

'Luke?'

He points back the way we came, then sets off over the rocks as if this is his natural terrain. My whole body seems to be creaking. I've no chance of keeping up as he dances across the uneven surface like a video game character.

Ethan waits for me at the trees and then we push on through. I'm out of breath by the time we get to the road. On the other side, through the trees, the cottage fire looks like it's starting to burn itself out. I was worried about the whole of the woods going up but perhaps the dew saved it.

I've almost taken the turn to head towards the caravans when I notice the faintest glimmer of light creeping out from the windows of the pub, far down in the village. My instincts haven't been good recently – but this time, somehow, I know this is where Chloe is.

I set off down the hill at once. It feels like my legs are moving faster than my body. Leaning back does little to help but I somehow keep my balance and end up racing on towards the back of the pub. When I stop in the shadows, I turn and look for Ethan – but he's disappeared somewhere. If he has any sense, he's coming down the hill at a sensible pace.

I'm about to move to the front of the pub when there's a bang from the back doors. The gate creaks and then Scott and Luke emerge together. They're heading for the docks and Scott has something slung over his shoulder like a sack of grain.

No, not some*thing*. Some*one*.

CHAPTER FORTY-NINE

Even though I'm the one who's fired the shot into the air, I still jump as the gun goes off. There's a moment in which I wonder where the bullet will come down. It has to land somewhere.

The moon is clear now, the clouds gone, ready to signal another blue-skied scorcher of a day.

Chloe has something crammed into her mouth and her eyes are wide with terror. I step into the open, the pistol in front of me, aiming for Luke.

The two brothers turn together. I can no longer see Chloe's face.

'Put her down,' I say.

They seem to be frozen to the spot, stunned that I'm here. I send another shot over their heads and it wakes them from their stupor. Scott does as he's told, lowering Chloe to the ground.

'Untie her,' I say.

Luke and Scott look at each other. It's as if I'm speaking another language. I take two steps forward and send a third shot booming into the night – this one thundering deliberately into the boat. The splintering of wood spurs Luke into action. He drops to Chloe's side and pulls the cloth from her mouth. She gasps, close to hyperventilating as he reaches into his pocket and digs out a penknife. There's a fraction of a second in which I can't see his hands. He reaches behind her and I tense – but then a pair of cable ties drop to the ground and Chloe pulls her freed arms in front of her.

My arms are aching. It's all I can do to keep the gun level.

'Are you okay?' I call.

Chloe rolls onto her back. She seems dazed and confused, rotating until she's crawling away from the Chandler brothers.

'Chlo?'

She manages a 'Yes,' as she continues to pull herself towards me.

'It's all of them,' she says. 'Dan, Alison, Pete. They're inside.'

I should be nervous, panicking – but I'm used to being in control of myself. I'm not sure I can explain it. Somehow, I'm holding it together.

'Throw the knife away,' I say.

Luke has it in his hands – but he must know there's no way he could get to me before I'd shoot. With a flick of his wrist, the knife sails off towards the boats.

'Inside,' I add.

Luke and Scott exchange the briefest of glances. I know they're wondering if one or both of them should rush me. The weight of the pistol has lowered my arms but I lift it again. They don't know how tired I am. How heavy the weapon feels. They can try to overpower me if they want – but I'll definitely get one shot off. Perhaps two.

It seems that neither of them fancy their chances. With little other option, they file towards the gate of the beer garden.

'Wait,' I call – and they do, hands raised.

I risk the briefest of sideways glances to Chloe. She's on her feet, but staggering around like a baby giraffe, weak-legged.

'Are you all right?' I whisper.

'Yes.'

'Run,' I say. 'Get to the lightning tree and call the police. Tell them everything you know.'

'I don't know much!'

'You know enough. Luke and Scott Chandler tried to abduct you. That's enough to get them here. Dial 999.'

'I could try Arthur's.'

'No. I don't trust anyone in this village.'

Chloe takes a step away. I sense her behind me but I can't see her. I'm still focusing on Luke and Scott. They've twisted a little to look at each other and I'm certain Scott's saying something, though I can't make out what. There are faint, but all-too familiar, green and pink stars speckling the edge of my vision. Too much action and trauma, not enough food.

'What about you?' Chloe asks.

There's a moment in which I want to grab her and hold her. Tell her everything's going to be all right.

'I'm going to find out what happened to our brother.'

'Don't,' Chloe says. 'Let's go.'

I flash another quick glance to her.

'I don't want to be alone,' Chloe says.

I take another, slightly longer, look towards the road. I have no idea where Ethan's gone but I hope he's somewhere in the woods, listening.

'Trust me,' I reply. 'We've not been alone since we got here.'

CHAPTER FIFTY

Pete is on his way out of the rear of the pub as I shepherd Scott and Luke back towards it. I assume he heard the gunshots. It makes little difference: I'm the only one of us with a gun.

The three of them file back into the main area of the bar and I usher them into a single booth. Dan and Alison Wood are sitting in another, agog at what's unfolding in front of them. I put as much distance between us as I can, taking a stool close to the bar. There are five people and if they rush me together, they'll definitely get to me before I can fire off enough shots to stop them all. They know I'll be able to fire at least once, though – which is enough to keep them on the back foot.

Luke can't keep his mouth closed. It's hanging open like that of a dopey goldfish.

'If you're going to push someone off a cliff,' I tell him, 'you should probably take a better look over the edge afterwards. Check you've done the job properly.'

I hold the gun in my lap, if only to rest my arm.

'Somebody's going to tell me what happened to Zac,' I say.

The five of them look at each other but it's Dan who opens his mouth first. 'I think there's been some sort of misund—'

The bullet blasts into the wall above his head, sending a shower of plaster onto the head of a shrieking Alison. I take great pleasure from seeing the crumbling flakes peppering her hair and her stretched, plastic face.

There are four bullets left in the magazine. I wonder if any of the people here know enough about guns to have figured that out.

'My mother kept records,' I say, nodding to Pete. 'I know that years ago, she paid you a hundred thousand pounds and I know she's been receiving money ever since. Now tell me what happened to my brother. The next shot won't miss.'

Dan clears his throat. There's a dusting of plaster in his hair, too. Not so 'Just For Men' any longer.

Pete holds up both hands, showing me his empty palms.

'Zac worked on the boat with me,' he says. 'We'd go out once or twice a week to pick up some... goods.'

'Drugs,' I say. 'You pick up drugs.'

He blinks. 'We were ambushed. This was ten years ago. The other side had guns. We were naïve, cocky. Didn't know what we were doing properly.' He turns to Dan. 'It wasn't me. None of it was my idea.'

Dan can't stop himself. 'Give it a rest, Pete. For the love of God. I never heard you objecting.'

'*Shush*,' I tell them.

They stop arguing and turn to me. Luke makes the gentlest of movements away from the booth but I raise the gun a fraction and he relaxes back. More stars flutter across my vision and I blink. A long blink.

I turn to Dan. He's hazy, as if I'm viewing him through rippled glass.

'Zac,' I say, with another blink.

'They shot him,' Pete says, matter-of-factly. 'I know you won't believe me but I didn't want any of this. It weren't my fault. I liked him.'

I lower the gun a little. My shoulder is raging from the climb up the cliffs and now the weight of the gun. My adrenalin is ebbing away.

'What happened?' I ask.

'The ambush. We thought we were going out for a pick-up. We intercept trawlers on their way to Liverpool, France, Ireland or wherever. The police can stop them at the ports but nobody bothers them at sea. We head out and grab the goods that go over the side. We bring the goods back and pass them on to his guys.' He nods at Dan.

'They're not *my* guys. I—'

I don't need to raise the gun this time. I flash a warning look at Dan and he goes quiet.

'It's different now,' Pete says. I understand immediately what he means: Scott has his own guns. 'This was in the early days,' he adds. 'We had a smaller boat and they boarded it. They were ready for us; they had guns. Zac was there and he...'

'He what?'

'He got shot. There was nothing we could do. He was trying to be a hero. He thought he was doing the right thing. We had to bring his body back to shore and then...'

Pete nods to Dan. I already know the next bit. Then Dan, Alison and my parents loaded my brother's body into a van and took him to the house – where Ethan saw them from his window.

'Why was Zac there?' I ask.

Pete huffs a long breath and looks to the floor. 'Your mum and dad insisted,' he says. 'Zac was enjoying being out on the boats in the day. He'd found out we were doing night-time jobs and didn't want to miss out, even though he didn't know what we were doing. I told him no but your parents...'

So I have my answer. Zac complained he wasn't allowed to do something, so my parents told Pete to let him do it, to shut him up. It's the story of our lives: shut up and go away.

'What happened to Zac's body?'

There's a short silence. Alison looks at her husband but his lips are firmly clamped.

'It was your mother's idea,' she says, suddenly. 'All of it. It's not like we could say he'd been shot at sea. She thought we should just say nothing. Claim we'd not seen him. Let everyone else take the story on.'

I can easily believe that's what happened. My parents simply stepped back and allowed the myth of Zac's disappearance to grow, until it was forgotten. He was trapped in the caves, lost at sea, sold to Eastern European paedos. The more stories, the better. Anything that wasn't the truth.

'Look,' Alison says. 'You and your sister can take your parents' cut. We can carry on as before. It's probably better now it's out in the open. Nothing has to change.'

'Someone burnt our cottage down thinking we were inside,' I say. 'I think that's the *definition* of something changing.'

They probably don't mean to – but everyone looks at Luke when I mention the cottage. I wonder quite how much of the campaign against us he's been responsible for, while simultaneously trying to get me into bed. It was almost certainly him who planted the 'stolen' money in our kitchen, knowing it would turn the village against me. I was supposed to be watching the boat burning anyway – but I helped them out by sneaking around the pub. It was probably him that left the 'GO HOME' message, too. Someone else must've broken our window because it happened while we were at dinner with Luke – but that left Luke with an alibi, meaning I'd never question him.

And then, when we still didn't leave, Luke was the one to carry out more drastic measures, too.

'You can still stop this,' Alison tells me.

'Do you really think I care about my parents' money? Look at me.' I hold my arms wide. 'Do you think I have any interest in what they left?'

That's enough to give them their answer.

'How were my parents involved?' I ask Pete.

Pete turns to Dan and Alison and the pair of them shrink into the booth.

It's Alison who replies in the end. 'This whole thing only happened because they put up the money. Pete didn't have it, we didn't have it – but they did. Everything since then has been them recouping their investment.'

'Did you kill them?' I ask Dan.

It takes him a second but it feels longer. An age. 'Kill who?' he replies.

'My parents.'

Even through my speckled vision, I see his eyes widen. I know the answer before he says anything. He has no idea what I'm talking about.

'Why would you think that?' he says.

I suppose that, deep down, I liked the idea of a conspiracy. That the car crash was something more than an accident. That my parents had enemies in high places and it was that which led to their downfall.

It's apt, I suppose. They died in the way they lived – away from their children, leaving questions and mysteries in their wake. I suppose this is the most I'm ever going to know. There was no conspiracy when it came to my parents' deaths. People die in cars. It happens all the time – and it happened to them.

Good.

There's a moment in which it feels like nobody knows what to do. My plan – if it can be called that – begins and ends with this.

'What now?' Dan asks. He leans forward, interlocking his fingers as if about to deliver a sermon. 'You're the one in charge.'

The truth is that I have no idea – but I realise they've still not answered one thing.

'Where's Zac?' I ask. 'Where's his body?'

Dan and Alison exchange another brief glance and in that moment, stars dance across my vision. I can see only pink and green. My stomach screams in the way it so rarely does.

'Your kitchen,' Dan says, though I can barely hear him.

I'm confused and disorientated – my kitchen? And then I realise what he means: Zac's body.

'By the front door,' Dan continues. 'I think that, in some strange way, your parents wanted to keep him close. It wasn't my idea but the kitchen was the only place we could get the stones up. We dug down and—'

Somehow, from nowhere, Luke is upon me. The shape of his body materialises through the cloud of stars. I twist and fire the gun but it's already too late. The bullet slams into something hard but I know I've missed. The force of the shot ricochets through my shoulder. I reel and twist backwards as Luke's fist thunders into my cheek. Everything starts to whirl. New spinning stars join the ones already there and I'm trying to pull the trigger on a gun I'm no longer holding. Something else crashes into the other side of my face and then I'm on my back, Luke straddled across me. I try to push back against him but my legs are pinned. I think there are two of them on me now but can't tell for sure. It's all one tangled mess of limbs and pain.

Luke's thumbs press into my throat and I gag, fighting for a breath that isn't there. I'm coughing, retching, but there's no air and no hope. My eyes slip closed – and this time there's no Ethan to save me.

CHAPTER FIFTY-ONE

Air floods into my lungs in one breathy gush. I'm coughing and the all-too-familiar sense of impending nausea explodes through me. If there's one thing I know about, it's being sick.

I'm on my side, not sure what's happening. The black is slowly fading, replaced by blue stars that spin and warp.

Luke's weight has disappeared. I roll into a sitting position, gasping and fighting to breathe.

The stars aren't stars at all. A spinning blue light is outside, casting light around the lounge. I hear the sound of running feet but can't see anything other than the swirling blue swarming across the room. It feels as if I'm alone.

And then, all of a sudden, I'm not.

'Meg…?'

'Chlo?'

Hands are on my back and then Chloe's chin slots into the crook of my neck. She squeezes too hard, which sets me coughing once more and then she frees me again.

'You're okay,' she says.

I blink. The stars have gone. Everyone's gone. It's only me and her. Her blonde hair is across her face and there's a smudge of dirt on her chin.

'Are you okay?' I ask.

'*Me*? I'm fine.'

She helps me up. I lean on the bar, still coughing. There's someone else in the room – I flinch when I realise they're close beside me.

'You're safe now,' a woman's voice says.

I just about take in the police uniform. Everything's still spiralling and blurring. Only Chloe is clear. She's holding my hand: I hadn't realised.

'They knew,' I say.

'Who?' Chloe replies.

'Our parents. It was their idea. They knew everything. They knew Zac was dead and let us think he wasn't.'

Chloe squeezes my hand. 'I'm here,' she says. 'You've still got me.'

CHAPTER FIFTY-TWO

If red sky in the morning really does mean sailor's warning, then I would not recommend anyone taking a boat out of Whitecliff harbour today. The orangey-red of the sun stretches from the horizon to the furthest reaches of the sky, with such dazzling depth that it looks as if the very heavens are on fire.

Chloe didn't make it as far as the lightning tree, because dear old Arthur had already called the police after seeing the cottage on fire. She was on her way up to the campsite when she met the police on their way down to the village – and then she brought them to the pub.

The officer said I should wait inside the pub for the ambulance, but the air is crisper and cleaner on the front step. Chloe and I sit together, watching the sun come up, knowing we're being watched ourselves.

The pub has been taped off by the police, while the beach is being used as a staging point for every nosy bastard in the region. Beach kids and villagers alike have united around one single goal – trying to find out what the hell is going on. Meanwhile, specialist officers are on their way to the burning embers of our cottage, preparing to check underneath the kitchen floor. Preparing to find Zac's remains – assuming Dan was telling the truth. No wonder the front door never closed properly.

Chloe has asked what happened and I'm explaining as much as I remember. She sits solemnly, not interrupting.

'Our whole lives have been paid for by this,' Chloe says quietly, when I'm done.

'I know.'

'Our school fees, clothes, Christmas presents… Everything. They chose money over our brother.'

We rest our heads together and say nothing, listening to the waves and the chatter of the onlookers.

The three Chandlers, along with Alison and Dan Wood, are on their way to a police station somewhere. That's the problem with trying to make a run for it from somewhere like Whitecliff: there aren't many places to go.

'Where were you last night?' I ask.

'George's caravan. We've been seeing each other a little bit.'

'I thought you liked Brad?'

'I thought if I could talk to Brad, then George would want to talk to me.'

I snort. Despite everything, it's hard not to. Teenage relationships are funny things.

'Brad was dealing,' Chloe says.

'Dealing what?'

'Coke, I think. He was buying from Scott. I only found out at the hospital. It's why Brad didn't make a bigger deal of the attack: he wanted to go home and lie low, forget it all.'

I suppose that explains the meeting I saw between Scott and Brad close to the caravans.

'I should've told you,' Chloe adds.

'There's a lot *I* should have told you.'

We're quiet for a moment and then Chloe lifts her head. She nods towards the village. 'Do you think they knew?' she asks.

'About what?'

'Zac. Everything.'

It takes me a little while to reply. My throat hurts; my eyes hurt. Even thinking feels sluggish. 'Maybe,' I say. 'Perhaps some of them. More likely, people turned a blind eye. I expect they didn't want to know.'

Chloe sighs acceptingly.

I'm not sure I can blame people for choosing to look the other way. If a person's entire way of life is at stake, keeping quiet is the easy option, I suppose.

'What did you mean before?' Chloe says. 'When you said we hadn't been alone since we got here.'

'Ethan Wood,' I reply. 'He saved me three times.'

Chloe doesn't seem to know what to say at first. She's never met him. 'What do you think will happen to him?' she asks.

I scan the beach, the village and then the trees, wondering if he's still watching. The police will be raiding his house sometime soon. Proceeds of crime and all that. Our lives will change – and so will Ethan's.

'I don't know,' I reply. 'There's Chrissie, too.'

'She told Scott about you,' Chloe says, suddenly sounding urgent. 'Something about you sneaking around Scott's car. I didn't understand.'

I bow my head. Everything hurts but my neck is particularly sore. 'It's not her fault,' I say.

Chloe is quiet. Perhaps she agrees, perhaps she doesn't.

'Do you see the madness of this place?' I say. 'The burning boat; the story about the pirates; Deacon the Black in the woods. It sounds ridiculous – but we're here because Zac was *literally* killed by pirates.'

'People,' Chloe replies. 'He was killed by *people*.'

My back is beginning to hurt even more. I guess falling off a cliff will do that to a person.

There's a silence for a moment and then Chloe speaks. 'Do you think Luke took Popcorn?'

I blink. I'd forgotten about the dog. 'Who knows?' I reply. There are bigger questions but it's little surprise Chloe is concerned about the one creature that actually loved her without conditions.

I creak my way up until I'm standing – and that's when Vee appears on the cobbles.

Chloe touches my arm and pulls me close.

'What?' I say.

'You should stop being angry at her,' Chloe says.

'Vee?'

'Mum. She's gone and she's not coming back.' Chloe pauses for a moment and then adds softly: 'Will you talk to someone when we get home? You're allowed to ask for help.'

I bite my lip. From nowhere, a lump has filled my throat. She doesn't need to say anything else. We both know what she's talking about.

I have a problem.

I don't reply – I *can't* – but Chloe seems to understand.

She squeezes my arm, then lets go, before smiling weakly and nodding to where Vee is weaving between a couple of onlookers. The lone officer guarding the scene waves her backwards – but he has little choice other than to relent as I stumble across to the tape. I ask if I can have a minute and he shuffles aside, leaving Vee on one side of the tape, me on the other.

'Are you okay?' she asks.

'Someone tried to burn down the cottage while I was sleeping and I got shoved off a cliff. Then someone tried to strangle me. Other than that, I'm not too bad.'

Vee's brow crinkles and I can feel her wondering if I'm joking. She's barefooted, wearing bobbly cotton shorts with a long-sleeved T-shirt and a jacket over the top. It looks like she's come straight from bed.

'A simple "yes" would've done,' she says.

I grin and she returns it.

'What are you doing later?' she asks.

'Police statements, I would imagine.'

'Sounds like fun.'

'Not so much.'

She nods. 'What about after that?'

I turn and look to Chloe, who's still on the step. She smiles at us and gives a little wave. The Whitecliff wave. It's infectious. For the first time in a *really* long time, it feels as if I know what I want.

'I think we're going to go out for something to eat,' I say. 'Something small for now.'

I want to believe I mean what I'm saying, but it's not as simple as that. Old habits.

Vee bites away a smile and I know she gets it.

'Can I come?' she asks.

'Definitely.'

NOTE FROM
THE AUTHOR

The character of Megan has been in my head for quite a while. She wasn't necessarily fully formed, as she is here, it was more the attitude, suspicion and resentment, combined with complete loyalty to the one person for whom she actually cares.

I read quite a lot of first-hand accounts from people who suffer from similar things to which Megan does here and it was always the self-awareness that struck me. The people who know they're ill and yet can't do anything to stop it. The internal monologue of knowing what's a bad decision and yet doing it anyway.

When it comes to writing fiction, the advice is always clear – to write what you know – but I've never been quite sure about all that. There's an assumption that 'what you know' is correct, and not a load of old nonsense. I also think it shows a lack of adventure and, especially beyond a first book, makes it all too easy to end up writing the same story over and over, albeit with a few character names changed.

There was a fine line to walk in acknowledging Megan's condition and yet allowing her to be able to get through the story in the way she does. I really hope I've done at least some justice to her.

If anyone wants to email me, I'm at kerrywilkinson@live.com – or tweet me at @kerrywk

For anyone wondering, Whitecliff is fictional but based upon an amalgamation of any number of similar villages that pepper Britain's coast. They're generally a lot friendlier than portrayed here!

Thanks to Claire and Gabbie for making the story better. I've said it before – but it's astonishing how seemingly small lines here and there can make an immeasurable improvement.

As ever, reviews are enormously appreciated. There's nothing better in helping to spread the word to other potential readers.

Thanks for reading. More soon.

Kerry